In the
SHADOW
of the
KING

BOOK ONE IN THE UNVEILED SERIES

In the
SHADOW
of the
KING

MELISSA ROSENBERGER

Carpenter's Son Publishing

In the Shadow of the King

Published by Carpenter's Son Publishing, Franklin, Tennessee

Published in association with Larry Carpenter of Christian Book Services, LLC
www.christianbookservices.com

Cover and Interior Design by Suzanne Lawing

Edited by Christy Distler

Printed in the United States of America

978-1-949572-16-2

All thanks to the Lord who planted this story in my heart and provided for its completion long before I had faith to write a word. He is truly good. I dedicate this book to my family and friends—your joyful encouragement has fueled my soul.

CHARACTERS

In Nazareth
Hannah, age 8½
"Abba," Hannah's father, Yosef (Joseph)
"Emmi," Hannah's mother, Miryam (Mary)
Hannah's Siblings:
> Yeshua (Jesus), age 12
> Ya'akov (James), age ~7
> Yosi (Joses or Joseph), age 6
> Shim'on (Simon), age 5
> Y'hudah (Judas or Jude), age 2
> Shlomit (Salome), infant

Elan, Hannah's best friend and foster of the family, age 8
Cleopas, Hannah's uncle, brother of Yosef
Miryam, Hannah's aunt, wife of Cleopas
Villagers: Itamar (the hazzan); Uri (Itamar's grandson); Silas (the blacksmith); Tobias (neighbor and potter); and Tobias's wife, Rachel

In Sepphoris
Aunt Lilit, Hannah's distant maternal cousin
Uzziah, Lilit's husband
Rivkah, Lilit's daughter
Gal, Uzziah's older brother/Lilit's brother-in-law
Raziela (or Raz), Gal's wife
Hakon, Gal's son
Keturah, Hakon's wife
Olmer, Gal's son
Tabitha, widow of Gal's deceased son
Theokritos, Raziela's cousin
Iakovos, Gal's steward
Myrinne, Iakovos's wife, servant of Gal's household

PART 1

NAZARETH

Late Summer of the Hebrew Year 3765 (~CE 5)

CHAPTER 1

I squirmed and sat as tall as I could, trying to get Emmi's attention without success. She stared right past me. Even without looking over my shoulder, I knew who held my mother's interest—Yeshua. Who else?

A turn toward the grunts and shouts coming from a friendly wrestling contest several paces behind me confirmed that Yeshua lounged among the male spectators. Half the village had gathered on the ridge this evening, not for the impressive views of the valley below, but hoping to catch a westerly breeze. But the air refused to budge. Fanning the collar of my tunic back and forth, I studied my older brother as he shouted encouragements and then threw his head back in laughter at the younger boys' antics.

Yeshua's face wasn't striking. And lately he seemed gangly, as if his body didn't grow fast enough to appease his limbs. I couldn't find a single feature to merit Emmi's endless admiration. Even strangers remarked that I was the prettiest girl they'd ever seen. Why didn't Emmi stare at me?

The women's boasting interrupted my thoughts.

"My son's spoken three words already," said the blacksmith's wife. "He's so intelligent."

"My Honi nearly pulled over an entire rack of pots the

other day." Apparently our neighbor Rachel, the potter's wife, wasn't to be outdone. "He doesn't know his own strength."

I looked at the lumps of drooling baby fat under discussion. One was absorbed with a study of his toes while the other ate dirt. Surely these women weren't serious. A groan escaped my lips, drawing the attention of my two-year-old brother, Y'hudah. I crossed my eyes and was rewarded by his giggling.

My focus returned to Emmi, willing her to look my way. She still wore the frayed linen scarf she had donned this morning to keep her hair off her face while we brought the last olives and figs into the storehouse. But one wavy strand of hair had escaped its confines and trailed over her left shoulder. She wound it around and around her finger—a habit that usually meant her mind was elsewhere. The youngest of my six siblings, Shlomit, wriggled on a cloth spread out beside her.

"They grow up so fast, don't they?" Rachel asked of no one in particular.

Several women murmured their assent.

"How old is your eldest, Miryam?" the blacksmith's wife asked with a raised eyebrow. "Why, Yeshua must be almost eleven years of age by now."

Emmi lowered her head, but her tone was polite when she corrected the woman. "He'll be twelve soon."

"*Twelve?* I didn't know you and Yosef were married long enough to have a son so old." The faint smirk that accompanied her words undermined her show of surprise.

Rachel frowned, but Emmi graciously smiled. I chewed on the side of my thumb and stared at the blacksmith's wife. I didn't like that woman.

"Hannah."

I looked over at her. Finally. Emmi had noticed me.

She tilted her head as if expecting an answer from me, but

I just stared. "You're too old to be sucking on your finger. Take your thumb out of your mouth, please." I whipped my hand behind my back. She laughed and held my gaze warmly. Joy blossomed inside me. When her eyes flitted from me back to Yeshua, it withered.

"Hannah." Elan slid to a stop on his knees beside me, grinning from ear to ear. "Hannah, come sit with the boys. Your father's telling stories about Egypt."

"Emmi, can I?" I asked, but Elan and I were up and trotting away before she could answer. "What story is Abba telling? The one about Cleopatra?"

"Mmm." Elan glanced down, his mouth twisted to the side.

"Abba said they wrapped her up special when she died so her flesh wouldn't rot. I wonder if she's still beautiful after forty years in the tomb."

Elan opened his mouth to speak.

"Someday, I'll be a queen."

He shrugged. "If that's what you want."

"And I'll hire you as my shepherd." I went a few more steps, then turned to see why Elan had stopped walking. "Why are you pouting?"

"I'm not."

"Yes, you are." I put my hands on my hips. It wasn't like him to object to my ideas. Ever since he'd been orphaned and Yeshua had brought him home to live with us, Elan had been my best friend. Some villagers even mistook us for twins because we were inseparable—though he had just turned eight and I was half a year older.

"You said you *wanted* to be a shepherd like your father was."

"I do."

"Well then, you will be *my* shepherd." I folded my arms across my chest.

Elan dug the ground with the toe of his sandal, releasing a tiny plume of dust. Curls of ash-brown hair obscured his hazel eyes so I could only stare at the freckles sprinkled across his nose and cheeks.

"If you're the queen, then who will be your king?"

"King?" I took a moment to consider the possibility before deciding against it. "Who said anything about a king? I'll rule alone."

"Oh."

My answer seemed to satisfy him, and we continued toward the ring of seated men. Yeshua slid over to make room for me, patting the ground beside him. I sat next to Abba instead, leaving Elan to fill the vacancy between me and Yeshua.

Abba ignored the shuffling at his side as he stroked the wiry black beard that crept high up his cheeks nearly joining his unruly eyebrows. "It's true, I tell you," he said to his listeners. "The whole city of Alexandria is practically afloat. It's surrounded by sea to the north, a lake to the south, and a massive black river to the east."

I scowled at Elan. This sounded like a lesson on mapmaking, not the story of royal intrigue I had come to hear.

"I don't believe you, Yosef." The blacksmith, Silas, crossed his arms over his barrel-shaped chest, making their girth even more menacing. "I've never been anywhere with so much water."

"You've never been anywhere at all," Uncle Cleopas said, winking at me. The other men laughed. Silas didn't look amused.

I tugged on my father's sleeve. "Abba."

"Hmm?"

"When I grow up, I'm going to live in a palace."

"Oh?" He turned and bopped me on the nose with his

rough finger.

"And I'll let you build it for me."

He chuckled. "Is that so? Well, it will be my honor, your majesty." With an arm wrapped around my shoulders, he pulled me close. He hadn't yet washed away the sweat and dust from working the fields earlier, and I wrinkled my nose in protest, earning an even tighter hug. Despite the heat, I was content to lean against his chest and admire the brilliant display of oranges and pinks painted across the sky above Mount Carmel in the distance.

"Look at those colors." Uncle Cleopas followed the direction of my gaze. "It's like a residue of Eliyahu's fire remains in the sky from the day the prophets of Ba'al were killed." My uncle seemed wistful as he studied the sunset. If it had been in his power, he'd no doubt enjoy calling down some fire of his own—not to impress evil prophets, but to roast the Romans he loathed so much. "Can you picture the look on their faces when they saw that fire?"

Most of the men smiled or shook their heads.

"Yes, it was just as Eliyahu declared." Yeshua gave his own nod of confidence. "That day, everyone knew the God of Avraham, Yitz'chak, and Ya'akov was Lord in Isra'el."[1]

My uncle stared at my brother while others shifted uneasily. I couldn't help glaring at Yeshua. Why did he always need to show off?

Itamar, the village hazzan, must have been waiting for the opportunity to speak, because he sprang to his feet with a speed that astonished me given his age.

"Oh, no," I muttered. The hazzan was caretaker of our synagogue and Torah scrolls, and in a village our size—six or seven hundred people at most—probably the closest thing to a rabbi we'd ever get. So I tried to listen to him, but he was so boring.

I pinched Elan's arm and, when he looked at me, feigned a yawn. He pursed his lips and looked back to the hazzan. I rolled my eyes. If I'd wanted to sit next to someone virtuous, I would've sat next to Yeshua.

The dark weathered skin on Itamar's bald head receded in the growing twilight. I focused on his wispy white beard as he recounted some ancient battle from the Torah. He appeared old enough to have witnessed the event personally, but Elan insisted the hazzan was only in his sixth decade of life.

A bat swooped overhead, drawing my gaze to its erratic path of flight through the darkening sky.

Itamar cleared his throat loudly then waited for everyone's attention before delivering what I hoped was his lesson—the hazzan always ended with a lesson.

"It does not matter which enemy has sought to conquer our land," he said, pointing his finger heavenward. "Egypt. Assyria. Babylon. Persia."

I looked up at Abba in alarm. How many foes did we have?

"Greece . . . and now Rome." Itamar strutted along the ranks of seated men as if he were general of a conquering army himself, then stopped in front of Yeshua. "Though many foes seek our defeat, we remain. Always remember, this is a sign of the Lord's favor upon us."

As the townsmen pondered this, I leaned against Abba's shoulder. "Maybe it'd be better to be less favored by the Lord and have fewer invaders." My comment broke the reverent silence.

Abba clamped his hand over my mouth.

As the hazzan clutched his chest, Uncle Cleopas exploded with laughter. "Tobias," he called out to our neighbor, the potter, "perhaps this is a good time for a song. We have much to celebrate, enemies or no enemies. The wheat is threshed, the grapes turned to wine. Let's praise Adonai for the abundant harvest that will carry us through the coming shemittah year."

A chorus of amens rang out, and the mood turned festive again.

Tobias fiddled with the strings of his lyre, grinning. With his long-lashed brown eyes and jumbled teeth, he reminded me of a camel. "Here's one you may know."

My uncle laughed and slapped him on the back. Tobias played well but only knew a handful of songs.

Hearing the notes, the women brought the little ones to join us. Tobias's wife, Rachel, settled at his side, and he plowed into a rousing tune.

Elan grabbed my sleeve and pulled me to my feet. As the last light waned, we ran and danced with the other children.

"Quiet!" Silas suddenly instructed and flapped his massive arms. "*Quiet.*"

Tobias tamped down the strings with his palm and the singing tapered off. Like everyone else, I looked around in confusion. Then we all heard it.

Hoofbeats.

No one in Nazareth owned a horse. No visiting relatives owned a horse. Horses only brought trouble.

Abba acted first, rushing forward to get a glimpse of the riders. Yeshua followed him while Uncle Cleopas herded children toward their parents. Anxious mothers snatched up babies and ran. The hazzan huddled next to Tobias and Rachel. I searched the whirling crowd for Emmi and found her waving at me. As the sound of hooves pounding earth intensified, I sprinted to her side.

"Mind your brother!" Before I realized what was happening, Emmi'd left me alone with Y'hudah.

Mind my brother? Who will mind me?

"Yeshua, come back!" she hollered, chasing after him as she clutched my baby sister.

I crouched, shielding Y'hudah as people fled in all directions. Emmi grabbed Yeshua's tunic and pulled him to a stop. She stood behind him, one protective arm across his chest and the other balancing Shlomit on her hip. I longed to be inside my mother's embrace, too, but couldn't move. The horses' strides shook the ground beneath me.

"Hannah, *run!*" Elan shouted from behind me.

It was too late. The horsemen crested the hill.

CHAPTER 2

Three riders charged past Abba. A cloud of dust swirled around them, lending a sinister backdrop to their grim faces. I didn't know who they were but, thankfully, they didn't wear the uniform of Roman soldiers.

Fear changed to hostility on the faces around me. My ears detected a name whispered among the stragglers on the hill—Alvon, the tax collector.

Two men as big as our blacksmith dismounted, thrusting their reins to the closest villagers. Alvon, the third rider, remained mounted. His skin was so pale it was almost translucent, and his frame matched that of a large child. I doubted he'd ever known a day of physical labor in his life. But somehow his sickly form was more menacing than that of the brutes swaggering in front of us.

"Where is Tobias?" Alvon's strident words pierced the silence. "Where is he?" When he turned my direction, I cringed.

The tax collector's question garnered defiant stares. Eventually, Silas tipped his head in Tobias's direction. The hazzan attempted to block Tobias, but the potter gently pushed the older man aside and stepped forward.

The tax collector rode closer to him. "Your time is up. I

want to be paid—now."

"I told you, Alvon, I'll give you the money." The lyre still clutched in one hand, he held up the other—to ward off or soothe the man, I wasn't sure. "I have a new batch of pots that are ready to be sold and—"

The two thugs snickered. "You mean you *used* to have a batch of pots," one said. "We've already paid a visit to your house. And when you weren't there . . . well, let's just say I was a bit disappointed. I might have accidentally broken a thing or two." Both cackled.

Tobias's already-big eyes protruded in his red face. "How do you expect I'll pay you if you've destroyed my—"

"Enough." Alvon commanded. "Be thankful you lost only clay, not your life. Next time you won't be so fortunate. With a word in the right ear, I could have you *crucified* for treason."

The earlier flush drained from Tobias's cheeks. I didn't know what crucified meant, but it couldn't be good.

"Treason?" Rachel cried. "What are you talking about? My husband is a good man. He's done nothing wrong."

Alvon's lip turned up in a sneer, and his horse sidestepped impatiently. He addressed the crowd. "Good men don't aid rebels."

Several villagers cast accusing stares at Tobias, and the few who had stood in solidarity with him a moment ago now took a step or two backward.

I hugged my little brother tighter. Y'hudah watched in wonder as the tax collector's horse snorted and tossed its black mane.

"Listen," Tobias said. "I don't know what you're talking about."

At a flick of the tax collector's reins, the two henchmen lunged forward. One pulled the lyre from Tobias's hand and stamped on it while the other punched him. A sickening crack—wood or bone breaking, I didn't know—sent a tingle down my spine. Rachel screamed and her son Honi wailed in her arms. I bit my own trembling lip to keep from crying.

Emmi rushed to console Rachel, and free of her restraining arm, Yeshua sprinted forward.

Alvon's horse spooked at my brother's approach. The beast leapt sideways, kicking its hind leg out and sending my brother soaring backward. Yeshua grunted as his body smacked the ground.

"Watch it, man!" Abba shouted, running to shield Yeshua from the stamping hooves. "What's wrong with you?"

Alvon adjusted his seat in the saddle as he gained control of the horse but didn't deign to glance my father's way before addressing Tobias again. "Either you pay me now or I tell Herod it wasn't just your cousin who revolted against him."

"We don't want trouble here," Abba said. "Tell me what Tobias owes, and I'll pay it."

Now that money was being offered, Alvon assessed Abba with a cold stare. Abba stood in front of Yeshua with his shoulders back, fists clenched at his sides. I was both proud of him and terrified that he'd be trampled underfoot.

No one breathed as we awaited the outcome.

"Bring me the money within the hour. And don't think you get credit for playing the hero. I'll be back next month for the regular collection. No excuses." Alvon turned his attention toward the hazzan. "Old man, open the synagogue. We'll lodge there tonight." He jerked the horse's bit to send it galloping back toward the village.

His lackeys mounted up and followed.

"Uri? Where's my grandson?" the hazzan called. "Uri, there you are. Come on, boy. Hurry." The two of them scurried in the direction of the synagogue.

I sensed a presence behind me and looked back. Elan. Sniffling, I wiped my face with my sleeve. He soothed Y'hudah while I stood on shaky legs.

Emmi ran to where Yeshua still sat on the ground. He winced when she examined his thigh but managed a smile. "Don't worry. I'm fine. No broken bones."

"What were you thinking?" She fiercely hugged him.

Tobias hesitantly approached Abba, still trying to stop the blood trickling from his nose. Even with his hand in front of his face, his nose was obviously bent at an unnatural angle.

"Thank you, Yosef. I'll pay you back," he muttered. "That man's a liar. What he said before about rebelling . . . I didn't—"

Abba held up a hand. "We'll talk later. Just get your family home."

As our neighbors left, Uncle Cleopas and Silas moved toward Abba. "That was a foolish thing to do at the start of a Sabbath year," Silas said. "There's no way the potter will earn enough to pay you back before you have to forgive the debt at the end of the year. You should've left well enough alone. Tobias and his kin are nothing but trouble."

Abba rubbed his forehead but kept quiet.

Uncle Cleopas clasped Abba's shoulder. "You could use the prosbul law. Turn the debt over to the courts for the year, make it public. Then take it back once the shemittah year passes. I'm sure Tobias would want to pay you back given more time."

Abba looked at Yeshua and smiled. "I'm not going to fret over money. We'll get by, right, son? The Lord always provides what we need."

"Hmpf." The blacksmith shook his head and walked away.

***

Hours had passed since we brought our bedding to the roof to sleep under the stars. But despite my exhaustion, sleep eluded me. I flopped about like a fish thrown onto shore, trying to find a comfortable position.

What if Alvon came after Abba next? What if we couldn't pay our own taxes? Abba snored loudly in the house below, which only added to my frustrated wakefulness. Shouldn't he be awake with worry too?

The swish of a straw mat announced it was being dragged toward me. I squeezed my eyes shut, feigning sleep, fearful of a reproach from one of my brothers for keeping him awake. When no admonishment came forth, I risked peeking.

Yeshua stretched out on his back next to me, one hand supporting his head, and admired the moon.

"Does your leg still hurt?" I whispered.

"It will heal."

"What were you thinking? Why didn't you just stay where you were?"

"When I saw how they treated Tobias . . . it wasn't right."

"Oh." I gave this some thought. "Are we poor?"

"We have enough."

Mama's cooking pot was dented and the boys always needed new sandals. It didn't seem like we had enough to waste money on the potter.

"We're not as rich as Cleopatra was."

"No." He smiled.

"And Abba has taxes to pay too."

"Don't worry. You heard Abba. The Lord will provide what we need."

"Or maybe the Lord already did—and now Abba's giving it away."

Yeshua turned onto his side to face me. "Remember how

Abba took Elan in, when he was orphaned?"

What did that have to do with anything? Reluctantly, I nodded.

"What if Abba had said no? What if he had closed the door on Elan because he worried about having enough food for the rest of us?"

"But Elan didn't come empty-handed," I pointed out. "He had his father's flock."

"Still, those animals need to eat. That's even more mouths to feed." Yeshua rested his head back on his mat and stared at the sky. "Abba didn't take him in to gain something. He knows it is right to bless others. The Torah says when we give generously, the Lord will bless our work and everything we put our hand to."[2]

I squeezed my lips together in annoyance. Lately, Yeshua had a habit of doling out wise sayings and quoting Torah at any and every opportunity. Who did he think he was anyway? Wise King Shlomo? And what if the Lord *didn't* bless us? Then I remembered my other question. "What does *crucified* mean?"

Yeshua closed his eyes.

I lifted myself up on my elbow to look at him. Hadn't he heard me?

"It's also written that he who hangs is under a curse of God."[3]

I exhaled heavily and lay flat again. Why didn't he ever just say what he meant?

"It's a fatal punishment the Romans use."

"Oh." The chorus of chirping bugs didn't waver and the air was still warm, but I rubbed my arms to ward off a chill. "We're not cursed. Right? That won't happen to us, will it?"

He took my hand in his and squeezed it. "You don't have to

be afraid of anything."

His touch comforted me, but I wasn't entirely assured. I pulled my hand back to brush at imaginary dust on my mat. It was easier to tell someone not to be afraid than to not be afraid.

"That one is named Kesil," he said.

I didn't respond but followed the direction his finger pointed to one of the brighter lights above. The cloudless night heavens loomed vast above us. For a moment I had the odd sensation that I might come untethered from the earth and float into their starry depths.

"That star is Kimah, and there is Ash Ayish. Before man was created, Elohim prepared these lights to be a sign pointing to His purposes. Do you remember that the Lord told Avraham to count the stars if he could, and that is how numerous his offspring would be?[4] I wonder if he was able to count them all."

"I could." Proud to show off my knowledge of numbers, I lifted a finger in the air. "One, two, three—"

"Shhh," he whispered, sounding amused. "Don't wake the others."

"Five, six," I continued more quietly.

He nodded.

I didn't reach twenty before drifting to sleep at his side.

CHAPTER 3

"The old she-goat escaped again," Elan announced as he entered the work shed.

Abba tossed his chisel on the table with a clatter. "Again? That creature is impossible. I don't know what other type of pen to build. She's broken out of every one."

"Maybe she's bored." I uncrossed my legs to stretch, letting the drop spindle I'd been using to twist wool into yarn rest on my lap. After an hour of such tedious work, my fingers ached. I would have escaped, too, if I could have gotten away with it.

Since the beginning of the shemittah year, I'd been nothing but disappointed. The hazzan had explained the fields must lie fallow every seventh year, giving the land a release from work. I had assumed we'd live a life of leisure this year, relaxing and playing games. Emmi had quickly ended that notion. Apparently, just the fields rested. Girls still had chores to do.

"You checked the potter's roof?" Abba asked. "You know the goat's fond of thatch."

Elan nodded. "I can't find her anywhere."

"What about the garden?" I asked.

Elan folded his arms across his chest and looked insulted.

Abba smiled. "Why don't you ask Yeshua to help you find her? You can take the rest of the flock out too."

"I can take the flock by myself. I'm old enough now."

I chimed in, "I'm still half a year older."

"Half years don't count."

Abba massaged his temples. "Just in case you need an extra hand, I'd like Yeshua to go with you."

"Abba, can I go? Please?" I clasped my hands to my chest and tried to look endearing.

He held my gaze. "All right . . . but listen to Yeshua. I don't need another silly goat roaming the hills by herself."

I jumped up and planted a kiss on his cheek, then ran out of the shed before he could change his mind.

***

I trailed behind the flock of goats and sheep, kicking a rock along. This wasn't fun at all. Had I known Elan and Yeshua would ignore me the whole time, I would've stayed at home.

Ahead, Elan groaned. I looked up to see a sheep scampering away from him.

"How come you're so much better at catching them than I am?" he asked Yeshua.

"Watch." Yeshua pointed at the sheep. "When a sheep's head is down, it sees all directions, so it can watch for predators while it grazes. But when its head is up, it has a blind spot. If you sneak up behind it, you can grab it before it knows you're there. Try again."

I pushed past Yeshua. "I'll show you. Watch me." I tiptoed forward, but whenever I got within two cubits of a sheep, it scuttled away with agitated cries.

Yeshua grinned. "Sheep also have a good memory."

Elan doubled over with laughter.

I tried to frown in annoyance but only managed a lopsided grin, thinking back to the day I had lunged onto a ewe, hoping to ride it like a horse. It did seem like the older sheep had kept their distance from me ever since.

Yeshua studied the gray bank of clouds in the distance. "Let's go a little farther."

A few minutes later, Elan cried out, "Look, there she is."

The shameless old goat lifted her head from chewing and rejoined the herd as if she'd been waiting for us to catch up.

Yeshua picked up a young lamb and set it in the right direction as he turned the flock for home. Elan and I slapped our thighs and clapped our hands behind the flock, moving the animals forward. We walked at a steady clip for nearly an hour. The sky darkened, and the herd scampered along faster, eager for the safety of their pen.

A gust of wind slapped hair into my eyes and lifted the hem of my cloak. Thunder rumbled in the distance. The approaching mass of clouds would certainly overtake us before we reached shelter.

I stopped for a moment to lift my arms and inhale the crisp, tangy air as the grass around me swirled and danced, buffeted by the wind. The energy of the coming storm enthralled me.

"Hannah, come on!" The urgency in Elan's tone made me open my eyes. The hair on his head hovered in the air like a crown.

Before I could speak, a metallic taste filled my mouth. Lightening ripped through the sky, trailed by booming thunder. The sheep's ears bounced up and down in their frenzied trot toward Yeshua.

"There was a tree back there!" I shouted. When no one answered, I glanced over my shoulder. Yeshua had vanished.

I whipped my head from side to side. Yeshua emerged out of nowhere back onto the hillside and flailed his arms in circles as if hoping to take flight. I stared at him dumbfounded, but Elan seemed to catch his meaning and jogged toward the edge as even the sheep followed Yeshua's retreating form over the precipice.

I looked back again. The gnarled olive tree's branches beckoned me into their shelter, but being alone scared me worse than any storm. So I flipped onto my stomach and half slid down the rocky hillside after the boys, feet first.

Yeshua must have discovered a hidden opening in the rock below, because I only saw Elan. The sky opened up and water pommeled the ground, the first drops leaving tiny craters in the dry earth around me. The goats apparently decided being wet was worse than their aversion to the dark space. They bounded frighteningly close to my head in their hurry to reach the cave.

I clung to an outcropping of rock and squeezed my eyes closed. Elan grabbed my ankle and guided my trembling leg to a sturdy foothold, and I scrambled farther down. We hurried into the cave's opening.

Inside, Yeshua pressed against the back of the low, broad grotto. He held two doelings in his arms above the press of shuffling hooves. Rain now poured down over the ledge above, curtaining off the cave's entrance like an impromptu waterfall. As I turned to Elan, the sky exploded with blinding light and a violent crack. I yelped, and Elan cringed. We stared at each other with enormous eyes before giggling nervously.

After a quarter of an hour, the rumbling quieted. The rain continued but lighter now, bringing a sense of loss. If only the storm would carry me with it so I could always feel so alive. The she-goat nuzzled my sandal, and I sighed. Our adventure had ended.

We climbed back up the muddy slope with less grace than the flock, slipping and grasping for purchase on the wet rocks.

When I reached the safety of the ridge top, Elan caught my eye and pointed to the olive tree, scorched black and smoldering.

The hair on my arms stood on end. Had we sheltered under it, the lightning strike could have killed us! "How did you know that cave was there?" I called back to Yeshua who counted the sheep.

He shrugged. "I didn't."

"Look." I pointed to the tree.

He looked impressed by the damage, and paused to send a prayer of thanks heavenward.

"Elan," I whispered, "do you think Yeshua could be . . . cursed?"

A puff of air escaped his lips. "What? No."

"Shhh. Haven't you noticed bad things happen around him? First the horse kicked him, now this."

He angled his head to search the sky as he considered the evidence. "I'd say that makes him blessed. He's always rescued from real injury."

I exhaled. "Maybe."

But I wasn't convinced.

**

I practiced drawing letters, watching satisfying rows of dirt pile up as I pulled my stick through the damp soil. When I reached ה, my head popped up. I took in the buildings around me. If I turned the letter in reverse, it could represent the stable to my left connected to our house in front of me with Abba's work shed standing alone to the right. Pleased with my observation, I started a new row of backward-facing letters.

"Blossom, shouldn't you be helping inside?"

I looked up but Abba had already returned to sharpening the blade of his planer. Besides, I recognized from the tone of his voice that the question could only have one answer. Tossing my stick into the fire pit, I dragged my feet to the door.

Because the house had been built deep into the side of the hill, I had to step down from the entrance into the sunken main room. It was already dim inside, with only meager light entering from square windows built high into the back wall where it emerged from the earth, and the one smaller window facing the clearing in front.

"Emmi, when are we going to eat?" Shim'on whined from his perch in our sleeping loft that spanned the left side of the room. I ducked under the loft and flopped onto my parents' bed where Shlomit slept. I pulled one of her feet free of its wrappings and rubbed my chin back and forth over her soft heel.

"In a while. Yeshua hasn't returned yet." Emmi waved a knife my direction before returning to chopping scallions at the long table across the room. "And leave the baby alone. She just got to sleep."

"If we have to wait for Yeshua, it may be hours before we eat." My brother Ya'akov looked grim as he hacked at some wood carving, flicking the shavings into the small square hearth in the back corner of the house. "He's *praying*."

Shim'on moaned like he was mortally wounded and dangled his head over the edge above me. "But why did Y'hudah get to eat already?"

"Y'hudah is two years old," Emmi said. "You're five. Don't you want to be treated like a big boy? Little boys have to take naps like the baby. And little boys don't get to go to school like you do now."

Shim'on looked uncertain about this reasoning. The hazzan's lessons must not have been as enticing as Emmi's cooking.

"Why does Yeshua pray so much?" Ya'akov asked Emmi.

Normally, I found Ya'akov's endless questions tiresome, but now I listened for the answer because I was curious too. What could someone who never got in trouble find to pray about for so long? Besides, hadn't he already prayed after the storm this afternoon?

"He prays because he loves the Lord." She didn't look up from her work. "He wants to honor him with his time."

"I love the Lord," Ya'akov said.

"I know you do. Yeshua is just . . . well, he's special."

"The other day I heard him praying out loud," I said.

"Hannah." Emmi glanced at me. "You weren't spying again, were you?"

"I wasn't. Yeshua was in the garden, and I heard him blessing the plants."

The rhythmic crunching ceased as Emmi held the knife still. I had her attention now.

"He was talking to the trees, declaring they'd make lots of fruit." I lowered my voice. "There's something wrong with him, isn't there?"

She resumed chopping, faster than before, and tossed the scallions into her cooking pot. "There's nothing wrong with being optimistic. Perhaps you should try it yourself."

I crossed my arms. There was something odd about Yeshua. For one thing, he never complained. And he always told the truth. That couldn't be normal.

"Hannah." Emmi tapped the rim of the pot with a wooden spoon to get my attention. "Get the bowls, please."

I ambled to the shelf by the hearth. So intent on sulking, I didn't bother to acknowledge Yeshua's entrance. He crossed the room and placed a quick kiss on the side of Emmi's head. She kept stirring but looked over her shoulder and smiled at him.

I rolled my eyes at their display of mutual adoration and banged the bowls on the table.

Yeshua removed his mantle, and as he tossed it onto a hook by the door, Emmi suddenly put her hands on her hips, the forgotten spoon dripping on the floor. "What happened to your tunic?"

Had Yeshua finally misbehaved? Sure enough, a swath of cloth had been neatly torn from the entire hem of his garment. It was one of Abba's old tunics, but had still been in good condition—until now.

"What happened?" Ya'akov and Shim'on asked nearly in unison. Shim'on slid down the ladder from the loft and looked hopeful of a forthcoming tale of bandits or wild beasts, whereas Ya'akov seemed disturbed. Probably because he stood next in line to receive Yeshua's outgrown clothes.

"If it was too long, I could have hemmed it for you," Emmi said.

"I needed the cloth for something," Yeshua answered.

My hand halted in midair, all pretense of setting the table discarded as I awaited the scolding to come.

My mother's face displayed a range of emotions. Annoyance, puzzlement, and then, to my consternation, understanding. She simply said, "Oh."

"That's it?" I blurted out. "Aren't you going to punish him?"

"Hannah, you'd do well to mind your own actions," she warned with her usual calm restored. "If you're finished with the table, go fetch Yosi and Elan."

I opened my mouth to protest, but Emmi raised her eyebrows. And just like that, Yeshua was absolved while I was back under my mother's scrutiny. I stomped across the room. Shim'on blocked my path, and I stomped on his foot as I stepped around him.

"Emmi," he cried.

"*Hannah.*"

I pulled the door closed behind me with a bang and heard Shlomit's muffled wail.

It wasn't fair that I always got scolded. After passing the animal pen, I climbed the hill overhanging our roof, balancing carefully on one of the lower walls of the terraced garden. If only the stones were a road that would take me far away. My ankles brushed the weeds that had sprung up amid Emmi's dill since the new year started and she no longer tended the garden. Pretending the stalks were loyal subjects lining up to pay homage to me, their queen, I paraded regally along the wall until I spotted my brother Yosi under a tree farther up the hill.

He turned his head, exposing Elan's hiding spot. "She's *coming.*"

Elan squatted, hunched over, hiding his hands from view.

"Are you two spying on me? What do you have?" I demanded. "Let me see it."

Yosi grinned, his fleshy gum exposed where two front teeth had recently fallen out.

Elan must have held a snake or an especially large insect to garner such secrecy. Bees launched into flight as I trampled through a patch of rue in my hurry to climb the hill.

"Wait. I'm not ready," Elan said.

"You better not throw anything at me or I'll tell Abba," I shouted, torn between the terror of touching a bug and my eagerness to see what he held.

"Close your eyes," Elan said.

"No." I'd nearly reached them.

Elan tilted his head to the side, and Yosi shrugged as if to say, *What else do you expect?*

"Fine. Here you are." Elan swung his arm from behind his back.

I shielded myself with upraised hands, then froze when I saw what he offered.

Elan smiled. "Do you like it?"

Like it? I was mesmerized. Gingerly I reached out to touch the gift. "Is it . . . for me?"

"I guess I could give it to Yosi if you don't want it," he teased.

Yosi snorted.

It was a doll. I turned it over in my hands, admiring the carving under her dress. Her head and body were made from a block of olive wood, with a piece of rope passed through a hole to give her movable arms with knots for hands. A turban wrapped her faceless head, and tufts of wool protruded out from under it. The turban and dress material looked familiar.

"Oh." The word sounded like an echo of Emmi's earlier understanding. The fabric missing from Yeshua's tunic.

"She's beautiful." I cradled the doll in my arms. "Thank you, Elan."

Yosi clasped his hands in front of him and fluttered his eyelids. "Oh, thaaank you, Elan," he mimicked in a high-pitched voice.

I punched his shoulder.

"Ow."

"But why did you make it?" I asked.

Elan shrugged, but I could tell he was pleased with himself. "I wanted to give you a gift. But Yeshua had the idea for the doll. He thought you might want one. We've been working on it for weeks."

"I see." No wonder Elan and Yeshua had been conspiring so much lately.

And it was true that I'd wanted a doll. Two weeks ago at the village spring, the other girls mocked me because I didn't have any toys. On the way home, I had prayed and asked the Lord for a doll too. But I hadn't told anyone, not even Elan. And I certainly hadn't told Yeshua.

Guilt about my earlier anger towards Yeshua tainted my surprise. It seemed no matter how right I felt in resenting him, he always proved himself innocent of wrongdoing. Sometimes I even resented him all over again for making me feel ashamed about misjudging him. But now I was simply grateful.

"What are you going to call it?" Yosi asked. "Elana?"

This time Elan punched him for me. Yosi rubbed his arm and snickered.

I studied the doll again. "I'm not sure."

I also wasn't sure what to make of Yeshua answering my prayer. My parents seemed to think Yeshua was exceptional. I was beginning to believe he was at least not normal.

That idea produced a peculiar mix of admiration and envy, but I decided to enjoy the doll and think about that later.

CHAPTER 4

Shabbat was glorious. The sky was a rich blue without a cloud in sight, and the almond trees blossomed, signaling the approach of drier, warmer days. This break in the rains was a tantalizing gift, the kind of day meant for running free. But on this one day of the week that we were absolved of chores, we were trapped at the synagogue.

I sat on the front stairs, growing impatient with the adults' discussions as the sun marched relentlessly across the sky. My younger brothers fidgeted and paced like young foals eyeing a green pasture from behind the stable door. Ever since we'd found the cave on the outskirts of town, it had become our favorite place to play—and every passing moment here was one less we'd have to enjoy.

I circled around Emmi, hoping she'd excuse herself so we could leave. She gave me a stern look and kept chatting. This would require a different approach. Weaving my way through the group of men, I sidled up to Abba and tugged on his cloak.

He absently patted my back but didn't look away from the two debating villagers. "But it is written, 'to obey is better than sacrifice.'"[5]

"But that does not absolve one from making the sacrifice. That in and of itself would be an act of disobedience."

Murmurs came from the other onlookers, and all eyes turned to the hazzan to clarify this conundrum.

Itamar cleared his throat and looked at Yeshua. My brother stood by, neither assenting nor objecting to either side of the argument. The silence grew uncomfortable as the men awaited the hazzan's wisdom.

"There is merit to both interpretations." Itamar shifted from foot to foot and combed his fingers through his beard. At last he lifted his head. "To be sure, this is a most important question. Before I give the answer, I'll allow one of our students to try his hand at it first." He glanced at my brother. "Yeshua?"

Yeshua nodded. "Thank you. I'll shine what light on it I can."

The hazzan leaned back and patted his belly, a slight smile replacing the earlier frown on his lips as if relieved to pass responsibility onto someone more capable. The man treated my brother like some great authority. Admittedly, Yeshua had an uncanny ability to recall writings from the law and the prophets. But why would the hazzan defer to an apprentice carpenter?

I'd had enough. "Abba," I whispered. "Abba, I'm hungry."

He noticed me for the first time. "Hmm? Yes, Hannah, we're going home shortly. Go play with the others."

Defeated, I marched over to my brothers who enacted the battle scene we'd learned about earlier in the reading. Their play distracted me, and I even cheered when Elan mock-impaled Ya'akov with a stick and a dramatic death scene ensued. My parents and Yeshua approached us. At last.

"And who are you brave warriors defeating?" Abba asked.

"The kings of Midian," Yosi said.

"Very good. And what did you learn today from the story of Gid'on's victory over Zevach and Tzalmuna?"[6]

Ya'akov blurted an answer out first. "It was wrong to worship Ba'al."

"Yes, that's true," Abba said.

Shim'on crouched on all fours. "It's fine to drink water like a dog." He made slurping sounds as he lapped up water from an imaginary stream like Gid'on's warriors had in the reading. Yosi put his hand on Shim'on's hip and pushed him over. Shim'on let out a crooning bark from the ground, and we all laughed.

But I had the best answer for Abba. "Adonai let the enemy oppress the people because they were fools and didn't follow His commandments."

Yeshua tilted his head and studied me. "It's true there comes a time for judgment. But when Isra'el cried out to the Lord for help, Adonai was merciful and compassionate. He appointed Gid'on to save them out of the enemy's hand." He smiled. "Adonai is slow to anger and rich in grace."[7]

Abba placed his arm around Yeshua's shoulder. "You speak the truth. We can all be thankful for God's mercy."

Heat surged up my cheeks. I wasn't feeling very thankful at the moment. And Yeshua didn't impress me with his fancy words. When Elan ran forward to walk home next to Yeshua, my annoyance built into a seething jealousy.

Abba placed his palm on the top of my head.

"What's that sour look on your face? Aren't you glad we're going home?"

I nodded, and he lightly pinched my cheek.

But I still felt angry. Why did Yeshua correct my answer and not my dimwit brothers' answers? I scowled at his retreating figure as Elan skipped back to my side.

He must have sensed the danger of my mood because he extended his stick in offering. "Here, Hannah. You can be

Gid'on next time."

"I don't want to play your silly games."

"Do you want to go to the cave later?" He looked to Abba. "Can we?"

"Certainly. I may even come with you," Abba said.

I crossed my arms. "I'm not going."

Elan's face crumpled. "But, Hannah—"

"Why don't you ask Yeshua to go with you?" I snapped at him.

Elan stepped backward.

Abba gave him a reassuring smile. "You go on with Emmi and the other boys. Hannah and I will catch up in a few minutes." Once Elan did as instructed, Abba squatted in front of me, blocking the path. "What has made my little blossom wilt today?"

I pouted.

Abba started to laugh but quickly composed himself. "It's not like you to be so irritable. Do you want to talk about it?" When I dared a glance at him, his expression was kind.

I dragged my foot back and forth through the dirt. "I guess it's just that . . . sometimes I wish Yeshua weren't my brother."

Abba's eyes widened in surprise, but he didn't correct me. I looked him straight in the eye, defiantly standing by my statement. He chose to let silence draw more out of me, and soon I cracked under his patient stare.

"It's not fair. He knows so much. And everyone likes him. And he never gets in trouble. Even Elan likes him better than me. How will people ever notice me if I'm always standing in Yeshua's shadow?"

"Your brother is special, it's true. He's not like anyone else." He paused to stare at the sky as he did whenever he carefully pondered an answer. I waited, tense with anticipation.

"Shabbat shalom," Rachel and Tobias said as they passed us on the path.

"Shabbat shalom." Abba stood and tipped his head in reply. Then we began walking again. Whatever he had been about to say, he kept to himself. "Sometimes it takes time to understand what the Lord has planned and purposed for each of our lives," he finally said. "That's part of the beauty and mystery of Adonai, that His ways and thoughts are higher than ours. Our privilege is to spend a lifetime striving after His deeper truths."

I frowned, not grasping what this had to do with my gripe.

"It's true Yeshua is special. I can't explain everything. But I do know that when the Lord made your brother, He chose me to raise him. And . . . He chose you to be his sister. So I guess that makes us special in our own way." Abba stopped walking and stooped to take my hands in his. "You can look at it like you're in a shadow compared to Yeshua being in the light. But I choose to think that the light poured on him makes those of us around him shine brighter too."

I furrowed my brow to show my skepticism.

He chuckled. "Oh, blossom. I promise . . . you'll never be invisible to me." His beard tickled my nose as he embraced me and planted a kiss on my forehead. "Now, I have a special announcement to make when we get home, but only to people who are smiling."

I squealed and twisted out of his arms, skipping ahead to tell the others.

***

Abba gathered us in front of the fire pit to hear his news. Even Emmi seemed excited.

"Who knows what the next month is?" Abba asked.

Ya'akov's hand shot into the air, pulling his entire body to his feet. "I do. Nissan."

"And what happens in the month of Nissan?"

"Pesach!" we all shouted.

Everyone knew that answer—the Passover and the Feast of Unleavened Bread. With great anticipation we counted the days leading up to the Lord's appointed times, happy for the break in our usual routine.

Abba and Emmi exchanged a smile. At first I thought it was because we'd answered correctly. But then Abba stood behind Yeshua and placed his hands on my brother's shoulders.

"This will be a special Pesach. Yeshua will be presented as a grown man at the temple for the first time."

"Will he have to pay taxes now?" Ya'akov asked.

"No, not until he is twenty years of age," Abba answered. "But he'll be able to read in the synagogue. And his word will be binding."

Yeshua sat taller and his face beamed at Abba. I gouged my fingernail into my thigh. It was just like I said. Yeshua got all the attention.

"And . . ." Abba glanced my way with a twinkle in his eye. "This year the whole family will go to Jerusalem."

Celebration erupted. I sprang to my feet, jumping and shouting with the boys. Even baby Shlomit clapped her hands.

My first journey to Jerusalem! Well, the first one I'd be old enough to remember. Last year, only Yeshua and Ya'akov had gone with Abba. When they'd returned, Ya'akov had tortured me with unbelievable accounts. I had pretended indifference—what else could an older sister do?—but inside, I had burned with desire to see the temple for myself. Now, at last, I would visit the city of the Great King.

Not even Yeshua's presentation at the temple could spoil my joy.

CHAPTER 5

The morning of our departure, I could scarcely sit still to break our fast. When I envisioned the temple, it seemed like an otherworldly place, although we'd make the journey in a little more than a week's time. Abba explained there was a shorter trade route that coursed directly south through the hills of Samaria, but we'd avoid the towns of the *goyim* and travel southeast along a flatter route that followed the course of the river Jordan. That would give us time to prepare our hearts to visit the temple, he said, but mine was ready right now.

We made a last stop at the spring where Emmi had each of us pass her our waterskins to be filled before leaving the village.

"Are there lions in the wilderness surrounding Jerusalem?" Ya'akov asked Abba.

Y'hudah's eyes grew wide and he swallowed. "Li-ons?"

Emmi quickly intervened. "No, Y'hudah. No lions."

The toddler looked around, clearly unconvinced.

"Can I walk with the men, Abba? Please?" I pleaded. I wanted to be one of the first to arrive and couldn't risk being hindered by women and babies.

"All right," Yosi said before Abba could answer. "But if she can't keep up and gets eaten by lions, it's not our fault."

"Li-ons," Y'hudah cried, his worst suspicions confirmed.

Emmi shot Yosi her that's-all-we-care-to-hear-out-of-you look while Yeshua picked up Y'hudah to comfort him.

Abba smiled and lowered himself to my height. "Just remember, if you get tired, you can sit to the side of the road and watch for Emmi to come by. And Yosi, you'll mind your sister," he added as an afterthought.

When Abba turned away from me to help Emmi, I triumphantly waggled my tongue at my brothers.

Yosi pointed at me and whined, "*Emmi.*"

"It's decided, Yosi. Not another word," Emmi said, misunderstanding his objection.

Waterskins full, we set off, my steps even jauntier for my latest victory over my brothers. The winding path offered no challenge except the occasional loose stone, and we made good time descending the thousand feet into the flat open expanse below.

My hope of making a quick march across the Jezreel Valley, however, was soon dashed. Mountains that appeared touchable from the elevated vantage point of our ridge at home now remained elusive. I judged our progress by turning around every few minutes to watch our village shrink. Soon the pale mudbrick and fieldstone homes appeared indistinguishable from the lichen clinging to the hillside.

By late afternoon, I lagged behind Yosi, who I suspected deliberately hastened his stride. Ya'akov was even farther ahead with the hazzan and his grandson Uri. And I was thirsty. The spring of Harod was miles away yet, in the foothills of Mount Gilboa. The caravan of women behind me had full skins, but turning back meant admitting defeat to the boys. So I ran and flailed my arms in a desperate attempt to gain ground. Would this valley never end?

My sandal caught on a rock, propelling me forward. A strong pull on my cloak from behind kept me from falling, and I turned after regaining my balance.

Yeshua, who hadn't missed a step, pointed to a grove of trees in the distance. "We'll stop there to rest."

"I'm not tired," I lied.

"Would you like to climb on my back to get a better view?"

I was torn. I didn't want to risk ridicule from the other boys, but the leather strap of my sandal had been chafing my little toe for the last hour. Up ahead, Ya'akov and Uri wove back and forth, crossing paths—playing some game, no doubt. No one seemed to be paying attention to me.

Yeshua put his waterskin over my neck. I giggled when it nearly came down to my knees, then helped myself to some deep gulps. He helped me scramble up his back, and soon my head bobbed rhythmically with his steps.

My eyelids grew heavy. Snug against his warmth, I rested. Sometimes—not often, but sometimes—I was glad to have Yeshua as my brother.

***

As we passed between Mount Tabor on our left and Mount Gilboa on our right, the temperature dropped. The wind buffeted then disappeared as if it played tag with us. The city of Beth Shan—or Scythopolis as the gentiles called it—loomed before us like a sentry guarding the exit through the ring of mountains circling the valley behind us. Uncle Cleopas said Beth Shan's citizens had hearts so full of corruption and decay that they were as black as the basalt blocks on which the city was built. He might have exaggerated, but it relieved me to know we'd camp our second night outside this lair of sin.

Ya'akov cleared his throat. "King Saul and his army were defeated near here. Right, Uri?"

The hazzan's grandson looked startled that someone had acknowledged him. "Maybe," he whispered.

"Maybe? You don't know?" My heart leapt. I'd been desperate to get a closer look at the Torah scrolls. This might be my chance. "Why don't you open the scrolls? That way we'll be certain."

Uri's eyes widened. "I . . . I don't have the scrolls."

I didn't bother hiding my disappointment. "Why not? You're the hazzan's grandson, aren't you? Why didn't you bring them?"

"I'm sorry." Uri flushed almost as scarlet as his frizzy hair, as if he had forgotten to bring his clothes, not the writings. He sent a desperate glance to Ya'akov.

"It doesn't matter. Yeshua will know." Ya'akov scanned ahead of us. "Yeshua!"

Yeshua and Yosi joined us, and Ya'akov pelted Yeshua with questions about history. Yeshua was smart but too concerned with truth to be a good storyteller. I was glad when Yosi interrupted him.

"I know what happened to Saul, here." Yosi plunged an imaginary weapon through his belly and stuck his tongue out the side of this mouth. "His guts covered the battlefield. They sliced his head off and threw his body on a wall. And so much blood shot out his neck hole, it looked like a fountain."

"Eww. I bet his neck crunched when they sawed through it." Elan touched his own protectively.

Yosi's eyes shone with excitement and he nodded. "I'm sure you can still see blood stains on the wall."

Uri grew pale and swayed like he might faint.

I looked around, expecting to see a corpse dangling before

my eyes at any moment. Who had told Yosi this grisly tale? Probably Uncle Cleopas.

Yeshua placed a steadying hand on Uri's shoulder. "It may not have happened exactly like that," he said with a pointed look at Yosi, "but yes, Saul's body hanged on a wall. But in the old ruins of Beth Shan, not on the walls of the modern city you see now."

Maybe so, but we all walked faster to put more distance between us and the scene of such violence.

***

That night I dreamt of disembodied heads floating through the air. I awoke with a start, but the details of the nightmare faded before the lingering terror it had produced. Hearing Abba's voice among the men gathered at the fire, I crawled closer to be near him. A pang of guilt plagued my conscience as Emmi's admonishment not to spy replayed in my mind. Then again, I reasoned, she had also said I shouldn't interrupt my elders when they spoke. So actually, I wasn't spying. I was being polite.

"I tell you, it's not right that someone in another part of the world decides who should rule over Judea," Uncle Cleopas said, meeting each man's gaze. The remaining charred wood on the fire popped, and sparks erupted outward as if emphasizing his point. I groaned inwardly. Another boring talk of politics.

The hazzan grunted. "When my father was alive, men held their heads high. We ruled ourselves. All I can say is I'm glad he's not here to witness our shame."

Men settled onto their packs, anticipating the usual rant that followed Itamar's expression "all I can say is . . ."

As always, he didn't disappoint. "Now we're forced to obey

laws issued by some heathen emperor who's never set foot in Judea. Our own leaders are corrupt. Wicked men practice blatant immorality, and no one objects . . . and there's no regard for proper lineage in the priesthood. Since when did the size of a man's purse outweigh the Lord's anointing?" Itamar waggled his finger menacingly. "We're violating holy statutes, and mark my words, we'll pay for it. The day we let Pompey ride into Jerusalem was the day we surrendered life as we know it. If I'd been a man at the time—"

"But you weren't," Silas said.

Itamar ignored the blacksmith's interruption. "It's no wonder we're suffering now. We get what we deserve if we allow these despicable goyim to rule us."

"You're right." Tobias nodded. "That's why we need to fight back."

Silas snorted.

Tobias looked at him. "What?"

"Haven't you caused enough harm?"

He sat up straighter. "What's that supposed to mean?"

"You talk and talk without thinking of the consequences. You got your cousin so stirred up with your speeches, he joined the rebels in Sepphoris. But did you risk your neck to fight?" The blacksmith shook his head. "You'd rather complain than act."

"Rachel was about to give birth to our first child. She begged me not to go. Otherwise, I would have," Tobias said. "Besides, they weren't rebels. They were heroes, keeping what's ours from Herod's vile offspring."

Silas scowled. "Call them whatever you want. They died like fools when the Romans retaliated."

Tobias squared his shoulders, and the others exchanged nervous glances. I chomped on the side of my thumb, waiting for trouble.

"My cousin wasn't a fool. I won't let you speak that way about the dead."

"I'll speak any way I want,"—the blacksmith had raised his voice—"and I say—"

"Shhh," Uncle Cleopas said. "Do you want to get us all killed? Who knows who's listening?"

The men glanced around, and I plastered myself to the ground.

"I say it's better to live a life of subjection than no life at all." Silas spoke with quiet intensity. "I'm sure the two thousand men crucified with your cousin would agree with me on that point."

Tobias threw a pebble at the fire but didn't reply.

"Wait." Silas leaned forward. "That's why you didn't have the money when the tax collector came, isn't it?"

Tobias's jutted his chin forward defiantly, but it quivered and he broke eye contact with Silas first.

"You're still sending money to your cousin's widow, trying to assuage your guilt, aren't you?" Silas sat back and crossed his beefy arms over his belly. "I knew it."

Tobias's eyes flitted to Abba's face then back to the ground. "I'll pay back the money. I swear."

Abba shook his head. "It's not good to swear oaths."

For a few moments, the only sound was the crackling fire. I had come here to feel better, but thinking about that tax collector again only upset me more. Now I'd never get to sleep.

"I remember when we only paid the temple tax," Itamar said softly. "Now there's water taxes, city taxes, road taxes, home taxes . . . next, they'll tax the air we breathe."

Uncle Cleopas stood to stamp out a stray ember. "I hate to relay more bad news, but I heard they're raising the tax on meat and salt again in Sepphoris. And that poll tax is sure to be the end of some souls. The Romans keep sending new bureaucrats, and every one squeezes what they can from us before they're assigned somewhere else. How much longer do they think we can go on like this?"

Tobias nodded. "We have to do something. It's the tax collectors who should be thrown in jail, not men trying to earn an honest living."

Abba's forehead creased. "Silas is right. We must respect the authority of the Romans if we want to live a peaceful life."

"For now," Uncle Cleopas murmured.

Abba held his gaze for a moment before looking away.

"Don't misunderstand, Yosef," Silas said. "I respect the Romans . . . but I don't trust them. You're a braver man than I am, bringing such a young family to Jerusalem. These days you never know if you'll live to return home again."

The blacksmith's words sent chills through my body. I dug my fingers into the dirt to make sure the very ground beneath me wouldn't disappear. Silas couldn't be right, could he? Besides, I knew Abba would always keep me safe. But what if something happened to Abba?

"Silas is right," Itamar said. "I thought I'd seen the worst acts imaginable with that Idumean 'king' Herod. But I was wrong." His hard mask dissolved and his voice wavered. "What did Herod's dear boy Archelaus do when he got power? Did he put things right or appease the people after his father's violence?"

I'd never witnessed the hazzan so emotional. I held my breath, awaiting the answer.

"No, the son surpassed his father's madness." Itamar bit his lower lip and took a deep breath before continuing. "I don't believe for a second that he sent that army into the crowds gathered for Pesach to maintain peace. He knew exactly what would happen when armed men met a mass of disgruntled people. It's like throwing a lit torch into a barn full of hay." Itamar stared at the men's somber faces. "Anyone could have seen where that would end." His voice cracked on the last words and tears poured down his cheeks. "Why couldn't I? Why couldn't I save my boy? They struck him down right in front of me . . ."

The men sat frighteningly still.

I sniffled. Poor Uri. I didn't know what had become of his father. No wonder he was always so timid.

The hazzan wiped his tears down into his beard. "The people had just come to worship, to remember . . . never expecting to be murdered at the temple of all places." He thrashed his head from side to side as if he could dislodge the memory. "The Lord took many innocents in His wrath that day."

Abba squeezed the hazzan's shoulder. "It was a terrible day. But I don't believe it was the Lord's will for innocents to die. This was an act of men. The Lord's will is that we follow His commands so it goes well with us." He looked at the others. "Is it Adonai's fault that men have forsaken their covenant obligations? That they've embraced evil and shunned His blessings?"

Itamar made a throaty noise and launched a glob of phlegm onto the fire, releasing a tiny sizzle. Whether he spat out of necessity or to demonstrate his disagreement with Abba, I couldn't say.

"At least the emperor removed Archelaus from power." Uncle Cleopas broke the tension. "We'll just have to see what the future holds with this new fellow. Who knows? Maybe it will be better to have an appointed governor in Judea rather than the son of a madman." He tossed a nervous glance over his shoulder as if Archelaus could be lurking in the shadows even now.

I hugged myself tighter.

"What do we even know about this prefect?" another man asked. "Coponius? Is that his name? I don't remember getting consulted about his appointment."

Some derisive chuckles rounded the fire.

"We know he's Roman," Silas said. "What more needs to be said?"

The men entertained their own thoughts for a moment.

"We must pray that Adonai is merciful," Tobias declared. "May He send His deliverer soon."

"Perhaps our hope is closer at hand than most would suspect." Uncle Cleopas threw another cryptic look Abba's way.

Abba acknowledged him with the smallest nod of his head.

Long after the fire died out, I heard the men turning fitfully, still searching for sleep. It comforted me little to think grown men were kept awake by fear too. No wonder Emmi told me not to spy.

CHAPTER 6

We slogged our way south through silt-covered roads—lasting evidence of a winter flood. I shuffled along with my head down, despairing we'd never make it to Jerusalem.

"Look," Elan said.

My spirits rose when I saw the explosion of greenery along the banks of the river Jordan. We stopped under a towering sycamore tree where unknown travelers before us had piled a ring of stones beneath its canopy of dark leaves. Women set up a hearth on top of the stones, taking turns preparing their family's evening meal.

The fare on the road was tasteless and bland at this point, and I ate with little enthusiasm. Emmi rocked baby Shlomit, coaxing her to rest. Y'hudah had already fallen asleep at Emmi's feet in what appeared to be an impossibly uncomfortable position with his knees bent under, arms askew, and face planted on the edge of a woven mat.

"How much longer until we get there?" I asked.

"Not long now," Emmi answered. "We're near Jericho."

I gasped, standing. "Jericho? Why didn't you say so before?"

"Shhh," she whispered. "Where are you going?"

There was no time to answer. I jogged over to Elan, then after some huddled conferring with my brothers, we set our well-rehearsed plan in motion. Our neighbor Rachel fixed a suspicious eye on us the third time we paraded in a circle around the cook site, but she quickly returned to consoling her fussy son.

Round and round we marched, with other children joining our ranks on each pass. I glanced over my shoulder and saw my own grin mirrored on Elan's face. When we approached the cooking hearth for the seventh time, my excitement almost tripped me.

I took a deep breath and offered up my best imitation of a trumpet blast. Elan and Shim'on let out a whooping war cry behind me. The subtlety of our reenactment may have been lost on some of the other children, but they joined in with frightening screams and shouts of their own. Well, frightening to the sleeping Y'hudah and the other startled infants, whose wails joined our bellows as if on cue. We couldn't have planned it better—victory was ours!

Sadly, victory was short lived. A half dozen irritated mothers descended upon us like angry geese honking protests.

"If you have that much strength left, go wash the dishes," one woman scolded.

"Have you cleaned your teeth already, Shim'on?" Emmi asked.

"I left my stick at home." Shim'on didn't bother to conceal his pleasure about the oversight.

"You haven't cleaned your teeth since we left home?" Emmi sprang into action, locating the chalky powder she'd need to polish his teeth. "Don't worry. Go fetch a twig or piece of reed and we'll make do."

I stared at her, dumbfounded. Shouldn't our victims be showering us with loot, not concerned with tooth decay? This certainly wasn't how the story of Jericho ended when the hazzan had read it to us at the synagogue.

"Go on now, all of you. Go find your father. But make sure you stay close together," Emmi said, leaving us to imagine the consequences if we didn't.

We trudged along the course of the river as we hunted for Abba among the hundreds of pilgrims milling about the camp. Yeshua stood by himself on the bank, staring at the water. He was so strange.

"Yeshua, have you seen Abba?" Elan called.

He turned and waved. As we walked toward him, he let out a satisfied sound of discovery and stooped to the ground.

I tried to see what he'd picked up, but he promptly hurled the object. It seemed to bounce across the top of the water.

"Hey, what was that? How'd you do that?" Ya'akov ran up behind me with Elan in tow.

"I'll show you. Look for a smooth, flat stone . . . like this." Yeshua held one out.

We ambled about like chickens, scratching at the earth until each of us had an acceptable rock. Yeshua demonstrated how to throw, and soon we were all competing to see who could skip a stone the most times across the river's surface. After Yeshua, Elan had the most success. Once he mastered the wrist flick, he helped me with my throw.

"Here's my bunch." Abba walked toward us. "What are you doing?"

"Watch, Abba," Ya'akov cried, managing three skips with his throw.

Abba looked intrigued and set his pack down. "Let me give it a try." He inspected the water, then popped a finger in his mouth and held it in the air. He wound his arm around and around in a circle. Finally, he hurled his stone and it immediately sank with a loud kerplunk.

We all howled with laughter.

"That was terrible," Shim'on declared.

"Didn't you teach Yeshua how to do it?" Ya'akov asked.

Abba shook his head. "No, not me."

I cast an accusing stare at Yeshua. "Then how'd you learn how to do it?"

Yeshua shrugged. Elan nodded, but this hardly seemed like a satisfactory answer to me. I let Yeshua know it with my doubtful expression.

A baby's wail disturbed the tranquility of the setting, and we started back toward the cooking fire. I turned to where the infant writhed on the ground while two women pulled a pile of sticks back and forth above its head, seemingly oblivious to its deafening shrieks.

"Give them back. You saw me put them down," one woman cried, kicking at the other in an attempt to pull the kindling free of her grasp.

"I did not. I found them. Go get your own, you—"

Both women froze as Yeshua strode past them. They appeared stunned. I looked at my brother, who didn't even slow down. Stopping, I put my hands on my hips, astonished at their absurd expressions.

One of the women released the sticks and picked up the infant. He stopped crying. The other woman placed the sticks on the ground by the mother's feet like an offering and wandered off without another word.

I waited for Elan and Ya'akov to catch up. "Did you see that?"

"What?" Elan asked.

"Those women. They stopped fighting."

Ya'akov shrugged. "So?"

"*So?* Don't you think that's weird?"

"I think *you're* weird if you want people to fight," Ya'akov said and elbowed Elan.

"No. They stopped fighting when Yeshua walked by."

They both just stared at me.

"Oh, never mind." Boys could be so dim.

But I knew it wasn't the first time Yeshua had provoked an unusual reaction in someone. Once, when Yeshua worked in the shed at home, a stranger walking by had stopped and fallen to his knees. Yeshua set his chisel down and smiled magnanimously, as if he were holding court there amid the wood shavings.

On this trip alone, I'd noticed others who seemed nervous or even hostile for no apparent reason when Yeshua came near. Sometimes people looked pleased, as if they'd recovered something they hadn't realized they'd misplaced.

I didn't care what Ya'akov thought. Yeshua was the strange one, not me.

***

Despite the uphill climb, our strength built as we approached our destination the following day. Abba said we'd sleep tonight in the city called the paragon of beauty, the joy of the whole earth—Jerusalem. Children jumped and circled about their parents as we hiked, giddy with the excitement of seeing the adults so animated.

As the afternoon shadows lengthened, Rachel produced a tambourine from her bag and slapped it against her thigh as she marched. As if on command, other instruments emerged. Anticipation swelled with the growing volume of music until at last we crested the Mount of Olives.

The view across the Kidron Valley mesmerized me. The city covered the mountain before and slightly below us as if the Lord Himself had draped a cherished necklace upon the hill for safekeeping. Even with the sun setting behind the temple, the radiance of its gold was stunning. I craned my neck upward, half expecting angels to descend in greeting. Truly, this must have been the home of the Lord.

My forward steps hesitated when I caught sight of the Roman soldiers crossing the colonnades between the temple and their fortress to the north. Thousands of the brutes had to be living inside the massive compound there. But I reassured myself Abba wouldn't have brought us here if he thought we were in danger—no matter what Silas said.

Words of praise leapt back and forth through the crowd of pilgrims, and singing erupted around me. Abba and Uncle Cleopas danced and shouted with my brothers. A fine sheen of sweat covered their flushed cheeks, and their faces seemed to glow from within as they worshiped.

Yeshua caught me around the waist and spun me around, and I couldn't help but laugh. Now I understood why the psalmist had rejoiced at the gates of Zion.

CHAPTER 7

I hopped in place, unable to contain my excitement, and surveyed the campsite as the last preparations were being made for Pesach. We'd have a great view of the temple from here when the time came to eat the Passover meal. My mouth watered just anticipating the roasted lamb.

"Please don't wander away today," Emmi said. "Hannah, are you listening?"

I nodded absently.

"There are hundreds of thousands of people in this city during the feast. We all have to stick close. I don't want anyone getting lost."

"I'll watch Hannah," Elan said. His offer evoked a dramatic display of gagging from Yosi and a groan from Ya'akov. Shim'on did a combination of both—he was at the annoying stage of mimicking everything his older brothers did.

"Thank you, dear." Emmi ruffled Elan's hair. She made one last assessment of us, looking resigned like a general heading to battle with lackluster troops. "Well, if everyone's ready, let's go."

An eternity seemed to pass by the time we crossed the valley. Then we had to wait for Abba to wash in the enormous *mikveh* pool. Normally I'd be entertained watching all the people, but I was anxious to reach the temple. After yesterday's climb, my thighs ached by the time we hiked up the steep road to the temple. But I refused to rest.

"Hannah, wait there, please," Emmi called from behind me.

I stopped on the broad stairs built against the southern wall of the temple and tapped my toes impatiently. Why were adults so slow?

Yosi pointed to the two openings in the wall at the top of the stairs. "Why's everybody going through one side, not the other?" he asked.

"We'll enter on the right too," Yeshua said. "When we leave the temple, we'll come out through the other door. Only people who are grieving enter and exit in the opposite direction. That way everyone knows who mourns and can offer a word of comfort in passing."

Abba caught up to us, and at last we ascended the stairs to the Huldah gate. To my surprise there were even more stairs to climb inside a wide tunnel once we were through the archway. I felt both hesitant and eager to reach the top. After all the walking it took to get here from Nazareth, what if I was disappointed?

Stepping up into the sunlight and grandeur of the court of the gentiles, I gasped. How could such magnificence come from the hands of men?

"Please stay close," Emmi reminded us.

Now I understood the warning. Never had I seen so many bodies packed in one place. I dutifully nodded while my eyes flew back and forth, unsure of where to land first. I didn't want to miss anything. Counting the rows of immense columns lining the perimeter, I strained to make out a familiar word among the dozens of languages spoken around us.

"Everyone ready? The money changers are this way." Abba

veered off to the right.

"What do they change the money into?" I asked.

Ya'akov laughed at me, and I shoved him.

"Hannah," Emmi scolded.

Abba just smiled. "Sometimes when I work in Sepphoris, I get paid in foreign coins. But only shekels can be used to make offerings, so I need a half-shekel to give my temple tax."

A dense crowd packed around the money changers' tables. I couldn't see a clear queue, but by some unspoken arrangement, we shuffled forward every minute or so.

Elan stared off to his left, wearing a forlorn expression. I followed the direction of his gaze but saw nothing to account for his sullen face.

"What's that ring for over there?" I asked, pointing.

"Hmm?" Abba kept his eye on a man who maneuvered to get ahead of him.

"That's where the Pesach lambs will be tied for the sacrifice," Yeshua answered.

"Oh."

I poked my finger into Elan's shoulder. "Is that what's wrong? The lambs?" Elan was too softhearted when it came to animals. "You don't have to be sad. None of yours were pure enough to be a *korban.*"

"I know. That's why I'm sad. I have nothing to offer Adonai from my father's flock."

Yeshua seemed strangely pleased with this answer, as if Elan had just spelled a word right or did his sums correctly. It made no sense to me. I decided to ignore them and studied the strange dress of the woman behind us.

A sharp voice rose above the din at the next table. "That's not fair!" shouted a stick of a man.

No sooner were the words past his lips than a temple guard

sprang into action, thrusting his hand out to snare the customer by the collar. My thumb reflexively found my mouth as I watched in fascinated horror.

"But I gave you eight denarii," the man croaked to the man at the table, ignoring the guard trying to strangle him.

"I assure you, our exchange rates are no different from the other tables."

"But last year—"

"*Next!*"

The guard shoved the poor wretch into the people amassed behind him with enough force that they swayed and nearly toppled to the ground themselves before propelling him back onto his feet. What kind of place was this where people were thrown about like sacks of flour?

"Hannah, let's go." Ya'akov yanked my arm.

I followed. "Coming, coming."

The inner courts of the temple perched on a platform, rising like a majestic island above the sea of tile paving the outer court where we now stood. The others waited for us outside the *soreg*, a stone wall ten handspans in height that surrounded the entire platform.

I craned my neck upward to take in the height of the building that housed the Holy of Holies. Suddenly, my belly fluttered with nerves. At least Elan had *wanted* to bring a gift. I hadn't even thought to bring an offering. Hopefully, the Lord wouldn't be disappointed.

"Look." Yosi indicated signs carved on pillars near the opening in the wall.

I recognized Hebrew letters, but not the other two types written underneath. "What's it say?"

"'Gentiles do not enter under penalty of death,'" Abba read.

"What happens if a gentile passes the soreg who can't read?

Will he get struck down?" Ya'akov asked.

Abba considered his answer.

"What if he just sticks one toe through the opening? Will his toe fall off?" Yosi asked, tossing a sideways glance at Elan.

Elan bounced up and down. "What if *all* his toes cross over the line, and he loses them, but the man thinks he's safe, but then he tips forward and falls across by mistake?" He giggled.

"Boys," Abba reprimanded.

There were no further comments.

I stared at the opening in the wall as my brothers crossed it one by one and ascended the stairs into the women's court. This was what I'd waited for, wasn't it?

But now the idea of being so close to the Holy One's glory set my knees to wobbling. Even priests fell dead before him. I couldn't go farther than the women's court because I was a girl, but even that seemed dangerously close. What if wind blew the veil covering the Holy of Holies aside, and we were all exposed to God's wrath?

"Hannah. Come up." Yeshua stood at the top of the stairs and beckoned me.

I held my breath and stepped across the threshold, expecting a blast of fire or hail at any moment. I didn't exhale until I'd climbed the steps and entered the women's court with my limbs intact.

***

After the morning sacrifices, we crossed the outer plaza to exit the temple courts. A man with his hand held over his head squinted in our direction. I moved closer to Abba's side.

"Yosef? It *is* you." The stranger bounded forward and whacked Abba's back.

Caught off guard, Abba stared at the heavyset man for a

second before recognition animated his features. "David. My goodness, how long has it been?"

Abba and the man embraced with more back slapping.

"Too long, my friend. Where's your wife? I hear you've been blessed with another daughter . . . Shlomit, I believe?"

The surprised look on Abba's face appeared to amuse the man. "What? Just because you're far from your relatives in Bethlehem, doesn't mean you've escaped their web of gossip."

Abba grinned. Then some shadow of remembrance dimmed their reunion and both men exchanged their smiles for somber expressions. Abba gripped the man's forearm and looked at him with concern. "How is it there these days?"

The man sighed. "We're getting on the best we can. It's probably a blessing that you've settled in Nazareth. Our home has never been the same since . . ." He glanced around for the first time, aware of the small crowd of children soaking in his words.

Abba nodded at the man's unspoken question, indicating we were his.

Since what? Adults had an annoying habit of not finishing sentences.

"David, where have you been?" A shrill voice cut the tension. "I've been looking all over for you. You know I don't like it when you go off without telling me." A giant woman with a beak-like nose swooped down on us.

"And you'll never guess how much they're charging for . . . Oh." She stopped short as if slapped by an invisible hand when she saw us all staring at her.

I tittered until I saw her obvious distress.

"Oh," she repeated, staring at Abba. Tears brimmed on her lashes.

She inspected each of the boys' faces, searching for something. When she didn't find it, her eyes scanned the crowd behind us and then stopped. I stood on tiptoe and saw Emmi and Yeshua approaching in conversation, Shlomit asleep in Yeshua's arms and Y'hudah straddling Emmi's hip.

"Mariamne," David murmured, but she was deaf to his call. The odd woman fixed her eyes on Yeshua and held her hand against her lips like she clasped an imaginary handkerchief and drew in its remembered fragrance.

Then Yeshua noticed her. He stepped forward and transferred Shlomit's limp form into Abba's arms. As if that were all the invitation she needed, Mariamne threw herself at Yeshua and clung to him, weeping.

My jaw fell open in disbelief. What was she doing? What was *he* doing? Men simply did not touch strange women in public, yet my brother returned her embrace. I looked at Elan and Ya'akov, who shared the same stupefied look. Who were these people?

Others around us took note of the spectacle. Whispers were accompanied by fingers pointed in our direction. My mother sniffled, and I watched a tear roll off her cheek and stain her cloak. Emmi must have been mortified at Yeshua's indecent behavior. I surely was.

David came up behind Mariamne and tugged on her shoulders. "Come, my dear, let's get you somewhere to rest, away from the crowds."

The woman nodded and released Yeshua but continued to hold his gaze. Yeshua squeezed her hands in his, and her mouth rose in a hint of a smile.

"It was good to see you, Yosef. And your beautiful family," David said. He tipped his head at Emmi and led Mariamne away without further goodbyes. None of us moved.

"Who are they? And why was Yeshua touching her?" I

asked with disgust.

"Abba? Why was that lady so upset?" Ya'akov's tone held more concern.

Abba crouched to our level. "She's sad because her little boy was slain when he was very young." He paused to take a deep breath. "Had he lived, he would be the same age as Yeshua."

"Why?" Elan asked. "Why would someone kill a child?"

Abba looked at Yeshua, who wore a pained expression. He put his arm around Yeshua's shoulders and pulled him against his side.

I felt more confused. Why was Abba hugging Yeshua? My brother had been born in Bethlehem, but my parents left the town when Yeshua was still an infant. Certainly he wouldn't remember the couple's dead son.

Abba's free hand opened and closed into a fist, and he stared at us as if weighing the decision to speak. "All the boys Yeshua's age were killed in one of King Herod's last murderous acts. He hoped to stop a threat to his power. But the plans of evil men never prevail against the plans of the Lord."

This was the second time in a week that Abba had spoken of evil men doing terrible things. Were there so many of them roaming about? The tremendous joy I had felt on arrival to the temple was now tainted with sorrow and fear.

Ahead of us, I spotted Mariamne's headdress. The couple made their way to the gate and exited the doors in the direction opposite the flow of the crowd.

CHAPTER 8

Before dawn, rustling at the opening of our tent woke me. I froze, my eyes still closed. Could it be one of those evil men?

Abba snored softly above the sighs and moans of my siblings. I squinted through half-closed eyes so the trespasser wouldn't know I'd awakened.

Yeshua stood with the tent flap lifted. When he looked back over his shoulder, our eyes met. He gave me a crooked smile, then was gone. I didn't think much of it. He usually went off by himself to pray before we broke our fast.

I fell back asleep and dreamt I had climbed high in a mulberry tree where I ate my fill of juicy black fruit, unconcerned about the purple stains they left on my dress. There were enough to eat that I'd never have to worry about going down to the ground again. Then something poked my leg. A woodpecker. I tried to kick it off, but it just pecked, pecked, pecked . . .

"Hannah. Get up, would you?"

"Huh?" I managed to say.

Ya'akov kicked my leg with his big toe. "Come on," he whined. "Abba says I have to pack the bedrolls."

I felt more tired now than the first time I had woken up. Dragging the back of my hand across my face, I rubbed my eyes. The roof of the tent quaked ominously as someone on the outside started pulling pegs from the ground. Ya'akov lifted the corner of my mat in desperation and tried to heave me off.

"All right. I'm getting up."

The next hour was spent in the organized chaos of packing up a family with seven children, eight if you included Elan. Finally, everyone was more or less ready, and we set off. At the top of the Mount of Olives, I glanced back one last time before the city was lost from sight. In that moment I realized Yeshua was missing.

My parents chatted with other adults, and the boys were busy with a shoving match. No one noticed Yeshua's absence. Fear and giddiness mixed inside me. How intoxicating to hold such a secret.

The cool of morning yielded to the hot midday sun. The farther we traveled into barren wilderness, the more anxious I grew—less concerned for my brother's safety than for my own when Emmi learned I had known he left camp and didn't say anything. Really, it was his fault for getting lost. He should be punished, not me. Anticipating my brother's fall from perfection made me feel better.

The shadows stretched across the rocks around us, which changed from a blinding tan to a reddish hue as the afternoon progressed. We'd descended nearly to the valley where we'd set up camp for the night when Y'hudah became especially fidgety, wanting to be carried one minute and walk the next. He kicked Abba's chest and attempted to lunge off Abba's shoulders.

Abba finally lowered him to the path. "Maybe you'd like to walk with Yeshua for the last bit, Y'hudah. Hmm? Want to walk with Yeshua?" He turned to me with pleading eyes. "Where is Yeshua?"

Dread gripped me and I squatted, making a show of adjusting my sandal strap.

Abba stepped to the side of the road and leaned against the rock face, scanning the passing travelers. After a few moments, Emmi rounded the bend looking weary, pulling Shim'on by the hand and carrying baby Shlomit.

"Ah, there's your mother. Miryam!" Abba waved with one hand while using the other to keep Y'hudah from climbing his leg. "Where's Yeshua?"

Emmi opened her mouth to answer, then her brow creased in worry. "I'm not sure where he is."

I felt a twinge of panic, yet I couldn't tear myself away from the scene about to unfold.

"He must be back with Ya'akov and Elan," she said. "Hannah, run back and tell the others we're waiting for them."

"Me?" I croaked.

"Yes, you. Go on." She pointed back up the road behind us.

"Why are you standing there like a startled goat?" Abba asked. "Your mother told you to fetch your brothers."

My eyes darted back and forth. Maybe I could say Yeshua had been mauled by an animal. No, they'd want to collect his bones. Maybe I could say he went to relieve himself and accidentally fell off a cliff. Yes, that sounded better. I opened my mouth to convey this tragic news when Ya'akov and Elan approached deep in discussion.

"Ya'akov!" Emmi called.

My brother's head jerked up and his lips made a comical circle.

Emmi let out one of her exasperated sighs. "Where is Yeshua?"

He shrugged.

"I'm not sure," Elan responded. "He hasn't been with us all day."

"No one has seen him?" Emmi's voice rose. She looked moments away from yelling or crying—and neither boded well for me.

Perhaps this wasn't a good time for the cliff story. It sure wasn't a good time for the truth. I stared at my feet.

"Oh, Yosef. We have to go back."

My head popped up. Back? She wanted to climb all the way back up to Jerusalem?

"Can't we keep going?" I asked Abba. "I'm sure Yeshua knows the way home."

Emmi whipped her head around and fixed me with a crazed stare. "Hannah, would you want us to leave you behind? Your brother is probably frightened and alone." A look of even greater alarm clouded her features. "No, not alone. He's surrounded by strangers. From strange places. Without any food." She broke into tears.

"There, there, Miryam." Abba tenderly placed his arm around her shoulders and drew her close. "He's a resourceful boy. I'm sure he's fine." But over her head, he scrunched his eyebrows together in silent warning to keep any more unwanted suggestions to myself. "We'll get to camp and ask around. He probably got ahead of us and is eating with Cleopas and Miryam at this very moment."

Emmi relented but looked far from relieved.

***

We spent hours searching in vain among the hundreds of pilgrims gathered at the evening campsite. The sun set on a new day. And, thanks to Yeshua, no one got to eat while Emmi interrogated every relative, friend, and neighbor she could find.

As my appetite grew, my guilt gave way to annoyance.

I hoped Yeshua was happy that he'd put us through such torment.

***

We broke camp at sunrise. Abba suggested leaving the baby with Aunt Miryam, but my mother refused to let another child out of her sight. So we all trudged our way back to Jerusalem, arriving shortly before evening. Abba set out on his own to inquire about Yeshua while Emmi prayed. When Abba returned after nightfall, he was alone. I fell asleep listening to my mother's whimpers.

The next morning we resumed the hunt for Yeshua. After hours of combing streets and alleyways, we made our way back to the temple.

Then Ya'akov let out a shout. "There he is! Under the colonnade . . . speaking with the old men."

Abba followed Ya'akov's pointing finger and blanched when he took in the scene. Yeshua wasn't part of the crowd listening to the Torah teachers—the Torah teachers were part of the crowd listening to Yeshua. My brother appeared at ease, holding class amid his gray-haired pupils.

I hid and peaked around my father's legs. Should I deny having seen Yeshua leave the tent? Emmi would never believe my word over Yeshua's. So I decided to place all blame on my brother for not returning on time.

Yeshua glanced up and saw us. I gulped. He held my eyes with an unreadable expression as he finished making his teaching point, then excused himself and walked over to us, calm as could be.

All the emotional turmoil Emmi had carried for the last three days spilled into one dramatic question: "Son, why did you do this to us?"

"But you didn't have to worry for me," Yeshua said and touched her forearm. "You know I have to attend to my Father's business."[8]

Abba's eyes bulged. Emmi was speechless.

I waited for the yelling to come. This time he'd definitely be punished. What business of Abba's could Yeshua possibly have here? He didn't even have any tools with him.

Abba just blinked, staring at Yeshua as if meeting him for the first time. Then, to my utter disbelief, he bowed his head to my brother, accepting Yeshua's absurd claim.

I almost protested, before remembering my part in this misadventure. So I kept quiet. But as a matter of principle, I moped the whole way back to Nazareth for the perceived injustice.

CHAPTER 9

Elan split off from the pack of boys walking to the synagogue and jogged to where we stood by the spring. "Let me help you, please," he said, lifting the weight of the full waterskin Emmi struggled to secure across the donkey's back.

"Thank you, Elan. Now hurry up. You don't want Itamar to scold you for arriving late to your lessons."

Adoration glowed in his answering smile. After all the years living with us, Elan still eagerly sought to please my parents. Once I had told him that he didn't have to try so hard, that we'd accepted him as part of the family. He had shrugged and replied, "I know. I just like to show them how grateful I am."

He cleared his throat. "I said goodbye to you, Hannah. Aren't you going to say it to me?"

"You're only going to be gone a couple of hours."

Elan didn't move.

"Fine. Goodbye, Elan." I elongated each syllable.

His face lit up despite my mocking tone and he trotted off.

Emmi smiled and stroked my cheek with the back of her fingers. "It seems you have an admirer. The first of many, I would guess."

I made a face, but inside, her words pleased me.

Shlomit had been making a pile of pebbles on the ground.

Emmi picked her up and placed her on the donkey, keeping a hand on my sister's back. "What's wrong, Hannah? You've been sulking ever since we left Jerusalem."

I rounded up Y'hudah, who was having a one-sided conversation with a beetle he'd found. Taking his hand in mine, I gathered courage to ask her my question as we started walking.

"Emmi?"

"Hmm?" She sounded distracted.

"Why do people act strange around Yeshua? And what was he doing at the temple? Why do grown men listen to him speak?"

She slowed her walk and seemed to consider her response. "Your brother is special."

I grunted. "I know. You and Abba say that all the time. But *why* is he special?"

She stopped altogether and studied the ground. The donkey pranced in place a few steps before standing still. "Hannah, you know every living creature has a mother and a father. Both are needed to make a baby." She glanced at me sideways and blushed.

My eyes grew big. Of course I knew about mating and birthing. But what would prompt her to discuss that now or here of all places?

"I'm Yeshua's mother and . . ." She hesitated. Emmi still held a protective arm around Shlomit, but she pulled me in front of her with the other. She stared at me, eyes shining, a strange glow lighting her features.

My gut flipped and flopped like a fish thrown from water.

"A wonderful thing happened. I don't fully understand it. I can't explain it. But it happened and I know it to be true." Her words tumbled out faster and faster, and I could tell she was excited. She giggled and smoothed her skirt.

At last, I thought, she's revealing the truth.

"What? What happened?" I asked, smiling with her.

"The Spirit of the Lord fathered Yeshua." Emmi looked elated now that she'd released the words.

I was dumbstruck. Still wearing a silly smile, I blinked several times as my mind screamed a thousand questions. What? *The* Lord? Did she mean what I thought she meant? Chills rippled through my body, and my hair stood on end.

"A messenger of the Lord appeared to me and told me in advance," she said. "Then, just as the angel declared it, it came to be."

I laughed nervously, hoping she'd share the joke.

She beamed at me, nodding her head.

The smile melted off my face as I realized she spoke in earnest. How could this be? Everybody had a mother and a father . . . didn't they?

A small persistent thought niggled. What if she was making this up? No. I'd never known my mother to tell a lie. Maybe she believed this story but she was confused . . . or even worse—deluded. I didn't want to entertain the idea, but how could a woman have a baby without a man?

She stared at me with an expectant grin.

Suddenly, I thought of Abba. "So Abba's not my father? The Lord is?"

She roared with laughter until she had to wipe a tear from her eye. "No, Hannah. Abba's your father."

"Oh." I didn't know if I felt more relieved or disappointed. So Yeshua *was* special.

She tousled my hair in amusement. "There can only be One who is righteous, the *Tzaddik*, and he is Yeshua. Isn't it wonderful? Our family has truly been blessed." She lifted Shlomit down off the donkey and pulled Y'hudah and me in for a big hug.

Her exuberance was contagious. Shlomit squealed happily and Y'hudah clapped his hands. When the donkey brayed and tossed its head up and down as if in agreement, Emmi laughed again and shoved it playfully. Even I smiled, despite my confusion, to see her so joyous.

She started for home with jaunty steps, humming a tune to herself. She seemed satisfied that my question had been answered. And it had been.

But now I had a dozen more.

***

Emmi rushed to greet Abba and Yeshua when they returned from building in Sepphoris. She pulled Abba aside, and they huddled in conversation. Yeshua lifted his eyebrows in silent question, but I was suddenly too bashful to look him in the eye.

After washing the dust from the road, Abba gathered the boys outside—I figured to share the story with them—while Emmi and I prepared the meal. She noticed we had left the water outside in the earlier commotion, and I volunteered to retrieve it, hoping to find Elan and compare Abba's and Emmi's accounts of this revelation.

The only person in view was Yeshua. I fumbled with the waterskins while peering at Yeshua around the edge of my head covering, watching him clean Abba's tools and return them to the work shed. He hardly radiated the splendor or loveliness one would expect from a heavenly creature.

Aunt Lilit, one of Emmi's cousins from Sepphoris, once told us a Greek tale about a half-human, half-god hero. It had been amusing, but we mocked people who could believe such fantasies. Now I wondered, had the Greeks been wrong in identifying the hero, but right in the possibility of a man who is also divine? But the heroes in their stories had strength or gifts or at the least physical beauty. Yeshua lacked all those.

Suddenly, the subject of my scrutiny returned my stare. "What thoughts are you wrestling with today, Hannah?"

I shook my head quickly. "I don't have any thoughts."

He smiled. "Why don't you let me help you?"

A jolt of excitement shook me. Was he going to provide an explanation for my musings? Would he unmask his special power?

He reached for the waterskins at my feet and carried them to the house.

I was being silly. He couldn't know my thoughts—he was just my brother.

***

The conversation at the table that night had an awkward formality. After the blessing, Abba regarded Yeshua with blatant delight, as if at last, hopes and reality were uniting. Ya'akov's hands trembled so much he had to put down his spoon to keep from dropping his lentils. Yosi and Shim'on exchanged furtive glances. Only Elan ate with relish, seemingly oblivious to the tense atmosphere.

I watched Yeshua. When had he found out about all of this? Had he believed our parents when they told him about the angel? Or had he always known? But, as a baby, how could he have known anything?

Emmi nudged me, and I took the bread from her without interrupting my pondering. Shouldn't he be taller? If he was the Lord's son, why were his hands rough with calluses? He should have had armies working for him. And, more importantly, why did I have to spend hours grinding grain for bread if he could just ask the Lord to create it for us?

I remembered what he had said in Jerusalem the day we found him at the temple. He must have gone to his Father's house to do an errand for the Lord. A terrible thought occurred to me. What if Adonai decided to visit Yeshua here at our house? We would all fall down dead and never know what happened!

Across the table, Yeshua cleared his throat.

Oh no, maybe he *did* know what I was thinking. I watched him eat. He didn't seem to be listening in, but maybe he was just being polite. Finally, I couldn't stand my own ignorance.

"Can you hear my thoughts?"

Yeshua grinned. "Only if you're thinking, *Yeshua would like some of the bread and is probably wondering when I'll pass it to him.*"

Shim'on snorted and everyone seemed to relax as the mood lightened.

Then Yeshua grew serious and said, not unkindly, "I listen for my Father's voice and what my Father reveals to me for His purpose."

Confused, I turned to Abba, but he seemed to be reflecting on Yeshua's words too. Yeshua's answer reassured me a bit, but I would've felt better if he had just said no. Until I got a definitive answer, I resolved not to think any mean thoughts just in case.

"Yeah, Hannah, are you going to hoard the bread for yourself?" Yosi asked.

Y'hudah twittered beside him.

I made a face at Yosi and hurled a piece of bread at him. So much for that resolution.

CHAPTER 10

The next morning, Elan and I sat under the shade of the lightning-scarred olive tree near the cave below. He rested his elbows on bent knees, scanning the landscape. I reclined and watched the clouds glide past.

"Abba told you the same story?" I asked.

He smiled. "It's wonderful, isn't it?"

"Why do you think they waited so long to tell us?"

"Maybe they were waiting for the right moment, for us to be old enough to understand," he said.

I nodded at this possibility—unwilling to admit that I still couldn't understand it.

"Or," he added, "maybe they didn't tell us so if anyone questioned us, we wouldn't give away any secrets."

I turned my head. "Like the Romans?"

Elan shrugged. "Anybody, I guess."

"I think Uncle Cleopas must know. Probably some of the other adults too. Why else would they act odd around Yeshua? But wouldn't you think everyone would know about such a miracle if it had happened by now? Why keep it secret?"

Elan uprooted a thick stalk of grass and pulled it over and over through clenched teeth. I could tell he was already thinking of other things. He didn't seem to worry himself about things too deep to comprehend.

After a minute, I realized I'd been holding my breath, a habit I did frequently of late. When had I become so stingy with air? I took a deep breath and exhaled fully, for a moment letting go of the need to figure everything out, the constant striving for answers.

Elan's contentment with life must have been contagious, because I felt an ease in his company that usually escaped me. I once told him my dreams for the future. That someday I hoped to be so wealthy that I would never have to fear the tax collector's knock. When I had asked him what his dreams were, he said he didn't have any—he knew he would be a shepherd like his father before him. But he hadn't been bitter or resentful when he said it, just accepting. I had gotten annoyed and accused him of having no determination. He had just laughed and said he was determined to be the best shepherd he could be.

I allowed the quiet to seep in and kneaded the dirt beneath my fingers. A strand of a spider's web interrupted a leaf's journey to the ground. The leaf fluttered in the gentle breeze above us, appearing to dance in midair.

"Look." Elan pointed as he whispered. "Do you see the fawn?"

I didn't, though he indicated the hill right in front of me. But Elan had a sharp eye for spotting creatures. He'd spotted mice and snakes—even a jackal once—that went unnoticed by others. So I believed the fawn must be there if he said he saw it.

I concentrated on the brown patch of hillside. And, sure enough, there was the slight movement of a leg, then, in a matter of seconds, I could make out four, then six mountain gazelle. Once I saw them, it baffled me that I'd missed them before.

Elan smiled proudly at my side as if he had conjured the herd for my entertainment.

I smiled back, touched by his sweetness. And for a few moments, it felt as if we had been invited into a special world of our own.

The fawn leaned onto its hind legs to stretch back under its belly for a morsel of grass, almost as if it curtsied. Then its head came back up and a tiny pink tongue darted out twice. Elan and I laughed.

And then it occurred to me. Maybe that's how it had to be with Yeshua. Maybe if I first believed what Emmi and Abba told us, then I would see how it all made sense. After all, I trusted my parents as much as I trusted Elan's eyesight, didn't I?

I determined to believe their story, or at least let my questions go for now. Serenity embraced my soul like a comforting blanket, and I tried to soak in every detail of the moment and my surroundings to firmly hold this peace in place.

Suddenly, all the gazelle craned their necks upward. Before I could wonder what had startled them, Yosi and Shim'on ran through the grass behind us.

"*Shhh*," I hissed.

But the gazelle had leapt forth with a burst of speed, summiting the hill and disappearing from sight.

Catching my scowl, Yosi tossed up his hands in surrender. "*Now* what'd we do wrong?"

***

"Emmi?"

"Mmm?"

"When will Yeshua be king?" I asked.

We were alone in the house except for Shlomit, who napped next to us on the bed.

Emmi paused from combing my hair then resumed teasing through the tangled ends. "I don't know exactly. But I know his time will come."

"How do you know?"

"The Lord's word always comes to pass at the proper time." She pulled harder with the comb, causing my head to bob with each tug. "Adonai's messenger said the Lord will give Yeshua our forefather David's throne. We just need to be patient."

I hunched forward over my crossed legs and rested my chin on my knuckles, exhaling loudly through my nose. Patience wasn't my strongest trait.

"Hold still. I'm almost done."

"Does he want to be king?"

"Of course. Yeshua wants to fulfill the Lord's plans for his life."

"But why can't he just make it happen now if he wants to, if it'll happen someday anyway?"

"You remember the story in the Torah about Yosef, don't you? He dreamt he would rule over his eleven brothers and even told them about it. But just because the dream was true, didn't mean it would happen immediately." She smoothed my hair with her hand. "If he had ruled over them sooner, he might not have been in Pharaoh's household at the right time to save his family and to save the whole land from famine. The Lord had a bigger plan in mind from the beginning."

I mulled this over. To my way of reasoning, the sooner Yeshua started his reign, the sooner I would become a member of the royal family. I couldn't wait to dress in fine silks and gold jewelry. "But how will Yeshua know it's time?"

"When Abba wants you to do something, he tells you, doesn't he? And you listen and obey. We just need to trust that the Lord will tell your brother, and trust that Yeshua will listen."

I twisted my mouth sideways. This wasn't a satisfying answer. I hoped Yeshua was a better listener than I was, or we might miss the whole thing.

CHAPTER 11

As I ground flour in the clearing in front of the house, I covertly observed Yeshua for signs of greatness. Weeks had passed since Emmi had told me to be patient, and nothing had happened. I had thought while Yeshua and Abba were in Jerusalem for the fall feasts, he'd be crowned king. But he returned the same as he'd been before. I was beginning to think his strange birth story meant nothing more than a righteous, boring life for my brother.

Yeshua chiseled square ends on an immense beam of wood hanging over either side of Abba's workbench. A few arm lengths away from me, Abba and Ya'akov worked the lathe to make a new handle for a hoe. Ya'akov quickly pulled a wound rope that spun the wood as Abba scraped shavings from it.

Noting the pause in the chinking noise, Abba looked up. "That will make a fine lintel, son," he called to Yeshua. "Certainly better than the rotten one he has now. You can take it to Silas's house today and we'll put it up in the morning. Here, let me help you."

Abba came around the opposite side of the workbench from Yeshua, and together they lifted the beam off the table and carried it to the far side of the shed. Perhaps Yeshua just pretended he needed Abba's help to make Abba feel better?

Shimshon, the Nazirite, had killed a thousand Philistines with the jawbone of an ass and brought down an entire building with his strength. And he had been born of two human parents. Shouldn't Yeshua at least be able to lift one beam of wood if he were the son of God?

"Psst." Ya'akov tilted his head toward the village.

I nodded in understanding. The blacksmith's workshop was a fascination to us—the smoky gloom, the clanging hammer, the hiss of water turned to steam on contact with the glowing metal. Silas himself was an impressive man. When he worked his forge, he was downright terrifying. It thrilled us to watch him.

Ya'akov and I milled about in front of Abba.

"What is this fine pair up to now?" he asked.

"We were thinking that Yeshua could use our help to take the lintel to the blacksmith's."

"I'm not sure how we'll fit the harness on both of you, but if you want to take the donkey's place, I don't see any reason why you shouldn't."

Ya'akov frowned. "No, Abba. In case the lintel becomes unhitched from the donkey. We would be there to help Yeshua hook it back up."

"Oh, I see, I see." Abba's face was serious, but his eyes twinkled mischievously. "Have you finished your chores?"

"Yes." We grinned, sensing his approval.

"Then ask your mother if there's anything she needs you to do while you're in the village."

I groaned. Only Emmi could take an exciting adventure like visiting the blacksmith and make it into an errand. And, sure enough, she soon had us weighed down with all kinds of jars and parcels and instructions for elaborate exchanges to be made at neighboring homes along the way.

At last I smelled the acrid fumes signaling we were close to the forge. But instead of the usual ringing of a hammer, I heard the clash of fiery words.

"But I'm here now, and I have the money."

Recognizing Vana's voice before seeing the old widow, I unconsciously stood straighter as I always did in her presence—not to mock her, but in fear that one day my spine would also twist in upon itself like hers had. The poor woman could hardly raise her head for the hump on her back, and her fingers bent at awkward angles. But she managed to pinch a coin and waved it in front of the blacksmith's face.

"You took too long to pay," he said. "Someone made a better offer for the tongs. If you make up the difference, then maybe we can arrange something. Otherwise, be gone."

"But that's not fair," she whined.

"What is it, Vana?" Yeshua halted the donkey and fixed his attention on the widow.

Silas glared at him. "This doesn't concern you. Just take the lintel over to the house and unhitch it. I'll settle with your father later."

"Oh, Yeshua," Vana said. "Thank the Lord you're here. Silas told me he'd repair my tongs for one dinar. Now he's threatening to sell them to someone else unless I come up with more money."

Yeshua faced the man. "Is this true? Did you have such an agreement?"

The blacksmith appeared unconcerned. "She said she'd be back within a week. It's been more than three. I did the work, and she never showed up. I have to make a living, you know."

"I had to buy a *seah* of flour," she said. "I can't glean with the other women or grind anymore with my back as it is. But I have the money now." She presented the coin again.

Yeshua looked back and forth between them. "Silas, I've decided that you must honor your original agreement."

"You've decided?" Silas grunted in derision. "Others may welcome your opinion, but you don't impress me. Leave the lintel and go home."

Yeshua stepped in front of Vana, putting himself between the two. "It is written, 'Speak up for those who cannot speak for themselves, for the rights of all who are destitute. Speak up and judge fairly; defend the rights of the poor and needy.'"[9]

"What about preventing men from becoming destitute when customers don't pay?" Silas quipped. "Is that written anywhere? Besides, you can hear that she has no problem speaking for herself. They can probably hear her screeching all the way in Damascus."

Yeshua regarded the blacksmith with detachment that only made Silas's words angrier.

"I'll only say it once more. If you don't want trouble, you'd best do as I say and be on your way."

Ya'akov and I exchanged astonished looks. Silas had done it now. Didn't he know who he'd angered? Yeshua was probably just being merciful by starting with a proverb.

I stepped back, expecting him to call a plague from the sky or, at the very least, give the man leprosy.

Silas took a menacing step forward, smacking the head of the hammer over and over in his palm. Yeshua calmly held his ground. My brother was lean and strong from toiling on building projects, but Silas had a height advantage of about three hand spans, not to mention the sizable girth of his forearms and meaty fists. If Yeshua had any anointing, now was definitely the time to use it.

Instead, Yeshua lashed out with his tongue. "You wicked man. Your crooked speech reveals you for a fool.[10] And my father does not do business with fools."

Yeshua's raised voice shocked me. Shock became fear when Yeshua turned his back on the irate blacksmith. Ya'akov hastily jumped back as Yeshua led the donkey in a wide birth, steering it and the lintel back in the direction we had come from. From his demeanor, you would have assumed Yeshua was out for a casual stroll.

Vana smiled and seemed to stand taller despite her deformity.

"Wait!" In a softer voice, Silas said, "She can have the tongs. Just leave the lintel."

Yeshua stopped but didn't turn around. "For the price originally agreed upon."

"Yes, yes. You're putting me in a bad place with my other customer, I'll have you know. This is costing me money as well as my reputation."

Yeshua looked over his shoulder to appraise the man.

Silas shifted uncertainly, then dropped his hammer.

Vana put the dinar into his outstretched hand, and he entered the workshop.

Once Silas was gone, Vana clasped her hands to her chest. Her eyes sparkled. "Oh, bless you, Yeshua."

"Please, come break bread with us soon," my brother said as he unhooked the wood. "You're always welcome."

"Oh, I will. Thank you, thank you." Vana bobbed up and down.

That was it? It was all over with no fiery wrath or plagues?

Silas returned and glowered when he noticed me staring at him.

I bolted for home without looking back. As far as I was concerned, if Yeshua didn't have any supernatural powers, then it was every child for herself from now on.

PART 2

NAZARETH

Summer of the Year 3769 (CE 9)

CHAPTER 12

Aunt Lilit should be pleased, I thought, admiring the strands of blue wool in the pot of hyacinth flower dye I stirred over the embers of a fire. The sound of footsteps approaching the clearing interrupted my musings.

"There's my boy." Uncle Cleopas jogged toward Yeshua in the shed and pounded his back. "You know we're all supporting you. Just give us the word."

"Oh, Cleopas. Leave him in peace," Aunt Miryam said, lagging behind.

"What? I'm just proud. My nephew is on his way to great things, isn't that right?"

Yeshua smiled indulgently. "Right now, I'm on my way to fix the gate the goats have chewed through."

"Go on, dear," Aunt Miryam said with a smile.

"Uncle Cleopas?"

He looked to me. "Yes, Hannah?"

"We're going to Sepphoris in the morning. Aunt Lilit says my sewing's good enough to help with her daughter's wedding garments."

"Your Aunt Lilit approves of something made in Nazareth? Now that *is* something."

"Cleopas," my aunt warned.

"Why wouldn't she?" I asked.

"He just means that you should be proud of your embroidery." Aunt Miryam put an arm around my shoulders and gave me a squeeze. "Out of all the beautiful items she could purchase in Sepphoris, she wants your work."

I smiled. "I can't wait to visit the market."

"Just be careful while you're there." Uncle Cleopas frowned and stepped forward to take the pot off of the fire for me. "Sepphoris isn't an isolated village like Nazareth. It's the capital for the whole region of the Galil. And all that commerce attracts unsavory types."

"You mean lepers?" I wrinkled my nose.

"Actually, I was referring to the powerful people like your aunt's husband. Their thinking is all backward. They're proud that they're more knowledgeable about worldly affairs than the rest of us. As if being like gentiles were a good thing. We're supposed to be a people set apart for the Lord. We can't let Greek and Roman influences destroy our society."

Aunt Lilit wasn't really my aunt but rather my mother's second or third cousin. But this was the first I'd heard of any gentile leanings. "I don't understand. Is Aunt Lilit still a Jew?"

Uncle Cleopas scowled. "I'll tell you what she is. A—"

My aunt coughed, and Uncle Cleopas closed his mouth before finishing.

"Yes, she's Hebrew," Aunt Miryam said. "But she's married into a Sadducee family. They don't believe the same things we do."

"They don't believe the Torah?" I whispered, aghast.

"No, no, they do. They just interpret things differently. They don't believe in angels, spirits, the resurrection to come, that sort of thing."

"Oh." I wondered what Lilit thought of Emmi's visit from

the angel. Maybe that was why my family wasn't often invited to Lilit's house.

"Cleopas." Abba emerged from the house and greeted my aunt as she passed him to go inside. "What brings you here? We weren't expecting you."

My uncle nodded at the pottery he carried. "I came to see Tobias." He tilted his head toward me. "I promised your aunt I'd replace her wash bowl. Your cousin says it flew off the table of its own accord."

I smiled at the expression of disbelief he wore.

"Speaking of Tobias," my uncle said, "did he ever repay his debt to you?"

Abba shook his head.

The smile disappeared from my face. Ever since the tax collector's men had beaten Tobias, I made sure to hide indoors when they came to the village. My fear for Abba's safety only seemed to increase with each of Alvon's visits.

Uncle Cleopas slapped his thigh. "I knew I should have just taken the bowl as payment for money owed," he said.

"That's all in the past. Besides, he's been a good neighbor to us for years."

"Abba, is that tax collector coming back again soon?" I asked. "Do you have enough to pay him?"

"Blossom, I've told you we have nothing to fear from Alvon."

"Tobias mentioned there's more trouble brewing in the north." My uncle's statement came out more like a question, and he searched Abba's face as if fishing for confirmation.

Abba looked grim. "Tobias will stay out of it if he knows what's good for him. And you will too."

"We've been financing others' wars for decades. We can't tolerate these exorbitant taxes and censuses forever. Men are bound to take action. I certainly don't agree with those who coerce their neighbors to take action by force—burning up houses and punishing people for obeying the rule of the land. But I understand the frustration that drives the rebels to do what they do."

"The rebels?" I asked.

Abba frowned. "Hannah, shouldn't you go lay out those threads in the sun so they're dry for tomorrow?"

"But . . ."

He lifted an eyebrow. Uncle Cleopas winked at me as I climbed to the roof.

I had turned twelve years of age and still wasn't old enough to stay for the interesting conversations.

***

Abba left us for his work site when we reached the main intersection in Sepphoris. Emmi allowed us a few minutes to stroll through the marketplace where goods had been brought from the two nearby highways.

Hours wouldn't be sufficient to explore the countless treasures spilling forth from every shop. New fragrances emerged from each alcove along the way. I sniffed cloves, pepper, cedar, and other spices I couldn't even name. Musical notes trilled past our ears as potential buyers played delicate instruments carved of sandalwood. Even Emmi couldn't resist stopping at a stall to run her hand over the smooth ivory utensils on display.

The bustle of life in Sepphoris enthralled me. Despite my uncle's dire warnings, I saw nothing frightening here. Sometimes I thought he exaggerated his warnings to tear at our complacency, like ripping a scab off to keep a wound fresh, lest we grow comfortable and forget our people's struggle for independence. But, if anything, I felt important mingling with the citizens of such a grand city. How fortunate they were to live here.

"Hannah, come on," Shim'on called. "I've seen snails move faster than you."

"I'd walk faster, but I didn't want to be seen with you," I retorted without taking my eyes from the strands of glass beads glistening in the sunlight.

As we entered the older section of town, the part unscathed during the revolt, it became difficult to know where one home ended and another began. After a series of climbs and turns through the maze of pale stone, we encountered a building I recognized—the synagogue.

Emmi kept her eyes down and adjusted her veil as we crossed the small plaza out front where a group of men argued about the weather. From the synagogue, my brother and I counted doors until we arrived at my aunt's home.

We scarcely knocked before the door swung open. Aunt Lilit lunged forward, taking us all into an embrace at once. Despite her petite frame, she managed to set us off balance with her enthusiasm. "Shim'on, you have grown so tall, I hardly recognized you. Miryam, are these some of your dried pomegranates? How wonderful, we'll have them tonight for a treat. Oh, Hannah, wait until you see the cloth I have for you to embroider. It's a rich yellow. But what am I thinking? Come in, come in."

I'd tried to hold my breath for as long as she spoke, but found myself gasping halfway through the assault of words. Lilit probably surpassed Emmi's age by nearly a decade judging from the silver streaks in the hair framing her face, but she brimmed with youthful energy. She buzzed from one person to the next, asking questions and snatching our responses like a bee collecting pollen. Her malachite earrings captivated me, swinging like counterweights as she flitted about.

She ushered us into an inner courtyard decorated with colorful plaster designs. A girl not much older than I brought us a basin of water to wash, and I stared at her, uncertain how to address a servant. The girl paid me no mind and set to work cleaning my brother's feet. Shim'on laughed and squirmed—he was the most ticklish boy I knew.

Once clean, we entered a workroom off to the right. Tied bundles of herbs draped the ceiling and filled my nostrils with an earthy, pleasant scent.

Aunt Lilit's daughter Rivkah looked up from the loom.

"Aunt Miryam, thank goodness you've come. I need you to break the tie over the color for my bridal slippers."

Emmi stepped forward and hugged Rivkah. "You'll make a lovely bride no matter what color they are. Do you think your bridegroom will arrive soon?"

"I hope so."

"I suspect within the month," Aunt Lilit said. "I've received a few hints so we won't be caught unaware. I know it ruins the surprise of not knowing the exact day or time. But as often as my husband travels, well . . . it wouldn't do for the bridegroom to arrive and no one be here to greet him."

"They've already finished building the addition to his father's house so it could be any day," Rivkah said, her cheeks flushed with anticipation.

Emmi beamed. "That's wonderful. We better get to work, then."

Aunt Lilit instructed the servant to bring refreshments while Rivkah unfolded stacks of material from a shelf, draping the fabric over the loom to display possibilities for several gowns. Without asking permission, I stepped closer to fondle the fine cotton and linen.

"Is this made from flax?" I asked Lilit with reverence. Flax plants were delicate and required special skill to grow. Their threads snapped easily, too, making weaving difficult. Linen this fine was reserved primarily for priests' garments and the wealthy. I'd never felt anything like it.

"Of course. What else? When you marry into an influential family like that of your Uncle Uzziah, there are certain standards that must be met. Uzziah may have less than his older brother Gal, but he's still one of the richest men in Sepphoris. Possibly the whole province."

I knew it was wrong to covet. Abba had certainly ingrained this command in us. Yet I couldn't help but wonder how the delicate fabric would feel against my skin, what it might be like to wear items like earrings just for ornamentation, not practicality. As my aunt kept up a steady stream of chatter about family lineages, I lifted the bottom edge of the linen and wrapped it over my arm to admire the effect.

Aunt Lilit sighed dramatically. "I can hardly believe my youngest child will be married. How quickly they grow up. Hannah, you really should be engaged by now yourself." She eyed me like I was a prized ox, then looked to Emmi. "What prospects do you have for her?"

I pulled my arm free from the cloth as if it had scalded me.

Aunt Lilit let out a melodious laugh. "It's never too soon to plan these things, you know. You want your parents to arrange the best possible match for you. Don't you want a prosperous husband like mine? I'll wager you could get one with your beauty. Not that you couldn't use some touching up, of course."

Shim'on scrunched up his nose.

Emmi looked flummoxed as if the reality of this impending responsibility had just dawned on her.

I couldn't imagine leaving Abba's house for any man. Then again, the blow of separation would be lessened if I could marry into such luxury. "Emmi, do we know any princes?"

"Goodness, Hannah," Emmi scolded.

Aunt Lilit laughed again. "Oh, she's delightful. As a matter of fact, there may be a new prince available soon."

The servant girl returned with a tray full of dried fruits, almonds, and honeyed walnuts, interrupting whatever gossip Aunt Lilit had been about to divulge. Our earlier gift of a few dried pomegranates seemed paltry in comparison to this afternoon snack. I observed Emmi to see if she showed any signs of embarrassment, but if she felt any slight, her demeanor didn't betray it.

As soon as the girl left, I blurted out, "Well? Who's the new prince?"

"*He* may be a *she*. Time will tell."

Aunt Lilit had our full attention now. Even Emmi, who never gossiped, remained suspiciously quiet as if hoping for further elaboration.

My aunt leaned toward us. "I have it from reasonable sources that Phasaelis is with child. So perhaps there will be a prince soon enough."

Shim'on looked up from surveying the tray, and with a mouth full of nuts asked, "Who's Phasaelis?"

"Who's Phasaelis?" My aunt turned a dismayed face to Emmi. "What are you teaching these children?"

"Phasaelis is the daughter of King Aretas, ruler over the kingdom of Nabatea," Emmi calmly answered my brother. "She's also Herod Antipas's wife."

Shim'on shrugged with indifference and shoveled more food into his mouth.

"She's a real princess?" I asked. "Have you met her, Aunt Lilit?"

"Yes, she's rather sullen and brooding. She always looks like she's plotting some dark deed. But what do you expect from a heathen raised in Petra where they live among the dead."

"Does Antipas love her?" I asked.

"Love her?" My aunt looked confused. "When you're the tetrarch, you don't marry for love. You marry for political reasons."

I blinked at her.

Aunt Lilit directed another incredulous look at Emmi before turning back to me. "By the time King Herod died, he'd left several wills. His sister and his sons fought with each other over which will was valid and who should get which territory. Finally Emperor Augustus settled the matter."

I nodded. Sibling squabbles I understood.

"The emperor divided the land between the three brothers. Archelaus became ethnarch of Judea and Samaria, and Philip the tetrarch over the northeastern lands. Antipas received the Galil and Perea, but as part of the agreement, he had to marry Phasaelis."

"Why didn't he want to? Is she ugly?" Shim'on asked, curling one side of his lip up.

"Actually, her face isn't the fairest, but she has an ample bosom. And my goodness, some of the garments she wears are indecent. Am I right, Rivkah? Just the other day she wore—"

My brother's eyes were enormous as he listened rapt with attention.

Emmi coughed.

"Oh." My aunt cleared her throat. "I mean, besides the obvious, Phasaelis is attractive to Herod for other reasons. Her father's kingdom, Nabatea, lies next to the land Antipas rules in Perea southeast of here. Nabatea is all that stands between Rome's holdings here in our land and its greatest threat."

"The rebels?" I popped a fig in my mouth.

"Rebels? No, dear. I think we've seen the last of anyone rash enough to revolt again."

I turned to Emmi in surprise.

She shot me a warning look, so I kept quiet and chewed.

"Parthia, dear. It's a powerful empire to the east, and Rome's greatest threat. Miryam, I know Nazareth is as far away from anywhere as you can get. But it's your duty to educate them."

Emmi inhaled deeply, and Rivkah gave her a sympathetic smile as Aunt Lilit rambled on.

"By marrying Antipas to King Aretas's daughter, Rome has ensured that Nabatea will be friendly. So it's like having a neutral neighbor living between your house and your enemy's house."

"Yeshua says we're supposed to love our enemies," Shim'on said.

"Mmm. Your brother is full of sayings, isn't he." I couldn't tell if my aunt thought this was a good thing or not.

I turned to Emmi. "Abba won't make me marry someone I don't know, will he? For political reasons?"

"No. And who knows? You may already know your future husband."

I frowned.

Emmi smiled. "Why don't you let Rivkah pick which threads she'd like you to use? Shim'on, perhaps you can find your uncle to see if you can make yourself useful. Your father will be here before you know it, and I'm sure he'll want to get back to Nazareth right away."

"We're not staying overnight?" I didn't hide my annoyance. It was really Emmi who was in a hurry to return home. My sister had been weaned long ago, but Emmi still missed Shlomit's physical presence if they were apart more than a few hours.

"You'll just have to come for another visit, now, won't you?" Aunt Lilit pulled some of the fabric off the loom and handed it to Emmi. Other pieces she folded before replacing them on the shelf. As she stared at the finest piece of linen still hanging on the loom, I held my breath, awaiting its fate. I watched with remorse as it joined the pile on the shelf. "Once you finish the garments for the wedding, of course," she added.

I was beginning to see that a good match might prove advantageous. This Phasaelis might have been traded like livestock, but at least she was wealthy and could afford the richest of wardrobes. I doubted she ever worried about harvests or taxes. And I was sure she got to visit her aunt for as long as she wanted.

CHAPTER 13

"Hannah, I've asked you once already," Emmi said with arms crossed. "Don't make me ask again."

I sighed and put down my embroidery. I hated churning milk. It was so boring.

Outside, someone had already set up the wooden frame in the clearing. I dragged my feet over to the pen and stared into the darkness. I'd had the strength to lift the filled goatskin and tie it to the frame myself for years, but I preferred not to if I could find someone else to do it.

"Yosi, bring me the goatskin."

Yosi sneered at me. "Get it yourself. I'm busy."

I lingered by the gate.

"Wait a minute and I'll help you," Elan called out without looking up from milking a goat.

There'd been a subtle change in our relationship. In the past, whenever he hadn't been shepherding the flock, Elan seemed to have been shepherding me. I had taken his constant presence for granted. Lately, he didn't seek me out the way he used to. And when we were together, our conversations were awkward. I missed the easy flow we had shared before. Something was wrong, and I was determined to root it out.

Elan tied off a full skin and thrust it toward me without

making eye contact. I made a big show of struggling to lift it. "Maybe you could carry it for me?" I asked as sweetly as possible.

Elan raised his eyebrow at the demure tone of my voice but exited the pen. He hoisted up the bag, making quick work of lashing the leather strings to the top of the frame.

I stepped closer so I stood directly across from him. Elan looked nervous, like he might startle and flee at any moment. As I planned how to begin my interrogation, I smiled to reassure him. Elan lowered his head but not before his cheeks colored. I pushed the skin toward him and he pushed it back until soon we had established a good rhythm between us. Now we were getting somewhere.

"Elan."

"Hmm."

"I've wanted to ask you something. Is there—?"

"Hey, Elan," Yosi called out from inside the pen. "Are you a girl?"

"No."

"Then why are you doing girls' work?" Yosi wheedled.

Normally, Elan would have countered Yosi with a quick retort of his own. But today he huffed back into the pen, swinging the gate closed with a bang. The sheep bleated noisily and crowded into the corner. I scowled at Yosi, and he disappeared back inside.

***

Two days later was a particularly hot ninth day of Av—a somber anniversary day already, made worse by the oppressive humidity. We sat as a family in the shade of a tree near the ridge above our garden. Sticky and cranky from our day of fasting, my brothers and I fidgeted and covertly threw pebbles at one another to relieve our frustration. Yeshua alone sat quietly as Abba recounted, for what seemed the thousandth time, the events leading to the destruction of Shlomo's temple on this date, and our people's exile.

"Then the long siege ended. The walls of Jerusalem were breached. The Babylonian army stormed the temple and—"

"Were there elephants?" Y'hudah interjected.

Caught off guard mid-recitation, Abba stared blankly. "Elephants? What do you mean?"

"You know . . . the big animals with the long noses you told us about."

Abba ran his hand through his hair, and Emmi hid a smile.

Warming to this new theme, Ya'akov chimed in. "It would take an army of elephants to pull down the temple we have now, right, Abba?"

"Don't be foolish," I chided. "No one could pull down the stones of the temple now."

"Hannah, don't call your brother foolish," Emmi said halfheartedly.

Pulling off my headdress, I leaned forward to twist my hair onto the top of my head, exposing my neck to the air. I glanced at Elan who usually could be called upon to support my opinions, but when our eyes met, he promptly flushed pink and swallowed. I raised an eyebrow in silent question, but it only seemed to fluster him more. I wished I knew what I'd done to upset him.

"So remember what the prophet Z'kharyah said." Abba had regained his composure, and thankfully we'd reached the conclusion of the discourse. "We fast on this day. But the Lord doesn't want us to only fast outwardly. We should fast inwardly also. And we do that by . . . " He looked from face to face.

"Not thinking evil of one another, but showing mercy and compassion and lifting up the widow and orphan, the stranger and those in need,"[11] we responded in chorus.

"Er, right." Abba seemed startled and impressed that we gave the correct response, as if he didn't ask the same question every year on this day. Taking advantage of his pause, I interjected a question of my own. "Emmi, can Shlomit and I put our mats on the roof tonight with the boys? It's so hot inside."

Emmi gave Abba one of her conspiratorial parental looks as if they'd had some previous discussion about this very topic.

"She can have my spot," Elan said. "Abba, I think I should sleep outside with the animals. It'll make it easier for me to keep watch on them during the night."

Yosi bent toward Shim'on. "What does he think they will do, build a ladder and climb out of the pen?" The two doubled over with fits of laughter. Elan squirmed uncomfortably.

"That sounds like a wise plan, Elan," Yeshua said. "I'll help you clear a place in the loft above the pen after we break our fast. Come walk with me and we'll talk it over."

The other boys followed them, probably in case Abba decided to resume his teaching. Emmi jumped up to catch Shlomit, who lurched unsteadily in their wake down the steep hill.

"Abba?" I said.

"Hmm?"

"Why doesn't Elan like me anymore?"

"Oh, Hannah." He reached forward to cup my cheek in his hand briefly. "Of course he likes you. It's just, well . . . you and Elan aren't children anymore. My blossom, you're turning into a beautiful woman."

He held my eyes, and realization dawned. I could feel my cheeks flush and my heart pounded. As it was, I hadn't come to terms with the recent changes in my body, let alone the social implications of becoming a woman too.

"Ugh. Elan and I are practically siblings."

Emmi returned and took a seat by my side. She brushed a strand of hair from my face, tucking it behind my ear. "Elan is part of our family. But he isn't your brother." She held my gaze meaningfully. "Now that you're older, there are certain behaviors that must be put aside. I'm sure Elan is just thinking of your reputation, as he should. Your future husband will have certain expectations—"

"Ahh. Is that what this is all about? Abba, I don't have to get married, do I? I want to stay here with you."

He chuckled, but the firm line of Emmi's mouth indicated she wouldn't be as indulgent.

CHAPTER 14

Fall harvest kept everyone too busy to dwell on marriage propositions. Then the rains set in, making the earth soft enough for plowing, and we focused on sowing the winter seeds. As the coldest temperatures arrived, Yeshua and I passed a week in Sepphoris as guests of Aunt Lilit and her husband Uzziah. Yeshua built new shelves for a merchant while I embroidered veils for my aunt, who pestered me incessantly about marriage prospects. By the end of the week, I didn't think it would be possible for her to dole out any more wisdom on matchmaking, but I was wrong. Even as we departed for Nazareth, Aunt Lilit insisted my parents must decide on my future spouse soon. She wouldn't let us leave until I assured her I'd bring it to Emmi's remembrance again.

Yeshua pulled his mantle over his head as the cold mist increased to a drizzle. Without speaking we both picked up our pace. My thoughts returned to my aunt's words. Who *would* I marry? Would he be kind like Abba? Would he be wealthy like Uncle Uzziah?

The idea of a husband left me uncertain. Nazareth held a dearth of potential mates—except for Elan, of course. But that would be like marrying a brother. Well, as Emmi pointed out, that wasn't entirely true. Just the other day, Elan had uncovered a bee's nest in a rotting tree and brought me a piece of the honey-laden comb before bringing the remainder to Emmi for rationing. My real brothers didn't seek me out to give me gifts.

But could I be satisfied being wife to a shepherd? Elan had no options for earning a living other than raising his animals, so I'd never enjoy the luxury of fine linen and jewels as his wife. Still, he was a friend and well loved by my family. I could do worse. And I wouldn't have to leave Abba. My heart warmed to the idea as we trudged along. I had to admit, I had missed Elan this past week.

I collided with the back of the donkey when Yeshua stopped short in front of me. "What is it?" I asked, somewhat annoyed. He stared off at the horizon so his face was hidden from me.

"What are you doing?"

"We need to stop somewhere before going home."

"Where? There's nothing here."

"Follow me." He veered off the road onto a narrow path, one I didn't recognize. This confused me even more, but I'd come to expect eccentric behavior from my brother. Even so, with each step closer to nowhere, I became more irritated and more convinced we followed an animal trail. Then my nose detected an unmistakable putrid odor.

I had been wrong. No creature would willingly follow this path. Such a stench could only come from one place—the *burseki*. "No. You can't seriously be leading me to the tannery?"

I'd seen men salt the still-warm hides of butchered sheep but had never visited the location where the skins were taken. By law a *bursi*'s business couldn't be within fifty cubits of town. The urine and dung of pigeons, dogs, and who knows what other beasts made his whole place unclean. So the bursi brought a cart to the village edge to collect the skins and return the finished leather for a fee. Even when he came near the town, most steered clear because of the smell lingering on his clothing. And if we got any closer to the vile burseki, we'd smell just as awful.

"The daylight is short as it is," I said. "We can't afford to lose time retracing our steps."

Yeshua kept walking.

"But now we'll have to bathe before Shabbat, and I'll have to rush and . . . Yeshua, are you even listening?"

"You'll have time to do all you need to do. The bursi has need of us now."

I puzzled over this statement. Why would we help a tanner? I couldn't help but make a face before wrapping my cloak around my mouth and nose.

We passed an open structure with vats containing untold horrors. Short of not breathing, there was no avoiding the unbearable stench. My eyes teared, and I gagged. "This is disgusting. How can anyone live here?"

Yeshua tossed a measured look over his shoulder, and I held my tongue.

Several yards up the hill stood a forlorn stone structure. It was no wonder the track to get here seemed so narrow. No one but the bursi and his immediate family would willingly visit such a dreadful place.

Yeshua called out a greeting. The feeble reply from within the house was cut short by coughing. Yeshua let himself in the door and disappeared into the dark interior. I reluctantly followed, hoping to escape the smell outside.

The shutters on the windows were closed and covered with skins to keep out the cold. The large single room was dank and reeked of full piss pots. Or perhaps reeked of the unwashed tanner who occupied a cot in the corner. I held the door open behind me, unsure of which way to go, in or out, horrified and repulsed by either option.

Yeshua struck a flint stone to light the wick of an oil lamp. The light flickered over the tanner, who lay in a tangled mass of cloth as if he'd battled and lost to the triumphant blankets that now pinned him in place. His glassy eyes feebly looked my way.

I still held the cloak in front of my face, but couldn't bring myself, even out of politeness, to lower my hand.

"Hannah, fetch the food and water from our bags," Yeshua instructed.

Aunt Lilit had sent us home with choice sweet breads to enjoy. I almost objected, but the look in Yeshua's eyes didn't invite discussion. After stomping back to the donkey, I buried my face against its neck, speaking soothing words—less for its comfort than for mine. I hoped to inhale its familiar smell, but the stink of urine still assailed me. So I breathed as shallowly as possible as I set about untying the parcels and waterskin from its back.

From the cloth containing the three loaves of bread, I removed one. But as I rewrapped the other two, the sunken cheeks on the tanner came to mind. After a moment's deliberation, I wrapped all three loaves again and took the whole bundle into the house.

"Come over here," Yeshua beckoned.

A change had taken place during the minutes I'd been away. The tanner sat up in bed. His eyes sparkled. The blankets had been folded back into submission across his lap. Even the air smelled more tolerable. Yeshua must have emptied the man's chamber pots outside the back door.

I crossed the room and presented the food to Yeshua, carefully avoiding the bursi's gaze.

"Thank you, my child," the tanner croaked. "How kind you are."

"You're welcome," I mumbled, ashamed at my earlier reservations in coming.

If Yeshua remembered them, he made no indication as he busied himself starting a fire in the hearth. He refilled two other lamps with oil and placed them within reach of the tanner's bed.

I considered taking a seat on a stool under the window but noticed the dust upon it and remained standing.

"My daughter is with child." The tanner supplied the explanation as if in answer to an unspoken question.

I looked at him.

"I'm on my own until after the birth," he said. "That's why my wife is gone. Otherwise she'd be here."

I nodded, having suspected he lived alone. Tanners' work was so vile that the law allowed their wives to divorce without cause. I wouldn't blame the woman if she never returned. Who would willingly come to such a place? Well, except for Yeshua.

"I have only one daughter left alive," the bursi added. I didn't know if it was the company or the warmth that had suddenly animated him. Now he chatted away as if we were here for a social visit. "I hope she'll have a son. I never did. I don't know who will take over for me now that I'm . . . if I should . . ."

Yeshua stopped what he was doing and placed his hand on the tanner's shoulder. "No need to worry about that," Yeshua stated. For some reason, it sounded like a promise, not just the requisite reassurance one normally offered the infirm.

It certainly seemed to put the bursi's mind at ease. He patted my brother's hand. "Thank you, Yeshua."

"Eat now. I'll come back after Shabbat to check on you."

The man coughed several times before nodding. "And

thank you, Hannah. Give my greetings to your mother and father."

I managed a weak smile but was disconcerted that the man knew my name. It had never occurred to me to learn his.

Yeshua and I headed toward Nazareth, following a path leading from the back of the tanner's home. We more than made up for our lost time because this route was more direct. Fortunately, unlike my other brothers might have, Yeshua didn't gloat that he had been right and I had been wrong.

I watched as he led the donkey up the rocky ascent to the village. He was so familiar to me, yet such a mystery. Whenever I questioned Emmi about Yeshua's lack of greatness to date, she said the same thing: "Be patient. His time will come." The bursi looked improved after our visit, but certainly not healed. When would Yeshua finally perform as a great prophet should?

Questions abounded. What had the great prophets been like when they were his age? When had they realized the Lord's anointing on them to heal the sick and throw armies into confusion? Had they practiced first or just discovered the power one day?

I conjured a young Eliyahu commanding chickens to be blind and goats to rise from the dead before working his way up to miracles on men. When I chuckled, Yeshua glanced over his shoulder at me, a questioning smile on his lips. I shook my head in dismissal.

But why would the son of our great Lord be willing to empty another man's piss pots? And why out of all the people in all the places in the world would the Lord choose my parents to raise His son? It didn't make sense. True, Yeshua carried himself with great assurance for a young man. Not proud, but with an unshakable confidence that he conveyed whether reciting the Torah or performing menial tasks. But somehow I couldn't reconcile my brother the carpenter with the idea of my brother the future king and commander of Isra'el's army.

We visited the mikveh to cleanse before going home. The spring water was frigid, and I submersed myself as quickly as possible, then wrapped my cloak back over my tunic and wrung out my hair. I wrapped my veil over my head and around my throat, feeling fresh and clean and invigorated despite the dampness and chill. Leaning against the donkey for warmth, I waited for my brother to bathe and smiled to myself. Helping the tanner had left me strangely satisfied.

When Yeshua rejoined me, I directed my smile at him. His whole face lit up as if he were surprised and happy. A bittersweet twinge gripped me. Was it so rare that I showed him affection?

I stepped toward him. He placed his arm around my shoulders and gave me a squeeze as we set off in companionable silence. I was glad Yeshua had thought to visit the tanner and that I had contributed, if only in small part, to cheering the man. Maybe Abba was right after all; Yeshua's light made us all shine a little brighter.

I was so content thinking on these things that at first I was confused to see Emmi pacing in the clearing despite the rain that had resumed in earnest. She twisted her hands together, and her brow was furrowed. The moment our eyes met, the peace I'd just managed to grasp was stripped away.

CHAPTER 15

"What are you doing outside?" I asked.

Emmi lunged for Yeshua and grabbed his forearms. "There's been sickness in the village."

I didn't think much of her words. Thoughts of getting warm and dry distracted me. Then I heard the great wracking coughs coming from within the house. My eyes grew wide, and I turned an accusing stare on Emmi.

"Abba is ill." She confirmed my worst fear. "Y'hudah also."

"I knew we shouldn't have visited the tanner's house." I twisted free from under Yeshua's arm and shoved him away. "We brought illness upon our home."

Emmi kept her eyes on Yeshua. "Of course not. Your father and Y'hudah have been sick two days now." Fear shook her voice.

I turned a hopeful face to my brother expecting him to reassure her as I'd seen him do for the tanner earlier.

But Yeshua's countenance was etched with concern. "Tell Abba I'll be in shortly."

"Where are you going?" I asked. "You can't leave. Aren't you going to see Abba?"

"I'm going to pray."

"Pray?" I demanded. "If you're the son of Elohim, can't you

do something *yourself*?"

"Hannah," Emmi scolded, but she couldn't hide the same question in her own eyes.

Yeshua looked grave as he left the clearing, climbing up the hill to the garden.

Hurrying inside, I directed my anger at Emmi. "You should have sent for us."

***

Over the next day, Y'hudah improved. Abba got worse. He struggled longer and harder to catch his breath between wracking, dry coughs that left him wincing and holding his chest. Then during the night, Abba's fever raged. We all lay awake listening to him wheeze, seemingly drowning on air. By the dim light of dawn, Abba's skin had a bluish tinge.

"Abba?" I shook his shoulder, but he didn't respond.

"Let's let him sleep." Emmi crossed the room and sat at the table, setting down the untouched cup of elderberry tea she'd prepared for him.

By midmorning, we heard Abba stirring. Emmi pushed back the blanket hanging from the loft above that served as a curtain dividing off a sick room for him. We all glanced up expectantly as she scanned the room. Her gaze rested on me for a moment, and my stomach fell.

Grim resignation lurked behind her feeble attempt at a smile. "Yeshua. Come, Abba asks for you."

He rose smoothly from the floor and bent to kiss Emmi's cheek before ducking under the blanket. I listened to their soft conversation, detecting only the occasional clear word.

I moved toward Emmi. "What's happening? Why does Abba want to speak to Yeshua? When do I get to see him?"

"Be quiet, Hannah," Ya'akov hissed. "Can't you just behave

for *once*?"

"I'm allowed to speak if I want to."

Shlomit moved closer to Emmi, hugging her around the waist, and began to cry.

"Hannah, *please*," Yosi admonished.

"Oh, I understand. I'm not allowed to talk, but Shlomit is allowed to howl like a wolf?"

At a gentle touch on my forearm, I glanced to my left. Shim'on gave a small shake of his head. I wasn't sure whether he disapproved of my words or the futility of the situation.

"Fine." I sat on the floor with a thump.

No one spoke as we stared at the makeshift curtain. I had a fluttering sensation in my chest, like my ribs trapped a sparrow that tried frantically to escape. Never had I been so terrified. How had I lived all these years and never appreciated the frailty and uncertainty of life?

After a few seconds, the murmuring behind the curtain stopped.

"Abba?" I called, leaping to my feet. "Abba!" I darted forward and reached for the edge of the blanket.

Yeshua stepped out from behind it at the same time, and my hand rested awkwardly on his chest. He covered my hand with his, the rough calluses scratching the back of my hand as he gently squeezed it. It felt like he gripped my heart, not my hand. In that instant, I knew Abba was gone.

Shock altered my perceptions over the next few moments, giving me a heightened awareness of every detail in my surroundings. I saw the fine dark stains of sap on Yeshua's fingers that remained from the branches he'd fed to the fire earlier. I heard the impatient clucking of the chickens outside, waiting to be fed. I smelled the sour perspiration on Ya'akov's body as he brushed past me to pull back the curtain and kneel by the cot, taking Abba's limp hand in his smaller trembling one.

My eyes drifted across Abba's eerily still chest, up to the head of the bed where his face was already rendered strangely unfamiliar in death. His jaw fell slack, his mouth open in a way I'd never seen before, even when he had slept. Panic welled inside my chest. I couldn't accept the devastation evidenced before me. I chose anger instead, a comfortable fallback.

I clutched the cloth of Yeshua's tunic. "What did you say to him? Why didn't you do something?"

Yeshua released my hand.

"Hannah, come here," soothed Emmi as she came up behind me to place her hands on my shoulders.

"No. I want to know what Abba said to Yeshua. Why did you spend so much time with him? What did you have to say that was so important the rest of us couldn't say our goodbyes?"

"Hannah, that's enough." Emmi whispered reflexively rather than with real conviction.

Yeshua didn't speak, but the sympathy in his eyes incited more accusations.

"Ya'akov should have been with Abba last, to receive his blessing!" I shouted. "He's Abba's eldest son. He's Abba's *real* son."

Yeshua walked past me.

Ya'akov looked up from Abba's side to glower at me out of loyalty to Yeshua. But I caught the flicker of uncertainty that belied his disappointment.

Emmi's grip on my shoulders tightened, and she gave me a shake. "We're all hurting. Don't make things worse. Go outside until you can control yourself."

I wanted to scream at someone, but no one met my defiant stare. With a huff, I spun around and pushed past Emmi. The door slammed shut behind me.

At the sound of the bang, Elan looked up from milking a goat, an unspoken question in his eyes.

My face contorted into an ugly grimace and tears flooded my eyes. I ran to the pen, my body wracked by heaving sobs. He leaned over the fence with the milk-filled skin still in one hand and reached forward to pull me into an awkward embrace above the post between us. The rough wool of his mantle rubbed against my teeth and lips as my head bounced on his shoulder with each sob. He patted my back and murmured soothing nonsense words into my ear.

I half laughed as I cried. He used the same voice with me that he used to calm frightened animals. But it sounded so comforting that I didn't care.

My tears subsided, and I heard footsteps behind me. Elan let his arm drop to his side and stepped back. When I turned, my eyes met Yeshua's. The tears started again in earnest. "I'm sorry."

"I know. It's already forgotten." He put his arms around me and held me.

CHAPTER 16

In the days following Abba's death, such emptiness filled my soul that I wondered if it would consume me and I'd cease to exist, disappearing from the inside out. Villagers flooded our home demanding responses to their useless utterances of sympathy. I listened to their wailing with detached curiosity. How did they have the energy to produce such a response? Even the idea of forming words seemed tiresome.

The first night after the psalms were sung, after the burial procession ended and the mourners departed, we found ourselves alone. The reality of living out our remaining days without Abba confronted us. We were as quiet as the dead themselves as we prepared and ate our meal, taking refuge in habit to tether us to this world. Once we finished cleaning up, we sat around the hearth, each entertaining our personal grief. Abba had filled the winter evenings with stories. Now there was only a mocking silence.

I stood to step outside and Shlomit whimpered. Yeshua opened his arms and she lunged into his lap, burying her face in the crook of his neck. He rocked her gently. I looked down at my sister with envy as she abandoned her pain in his embrace. For a second, I contemplated wiggling in beside her or putting her on my lap so that both of us could sit on his.

Yeshua looked up at me with compassion and reached to take my hand, but I turned away. I wasn't a child anymore.

After pulling a cloak from the peg by the door, I wrapped it over my shoulders and walked outside. Rationally, I knew we all missed Abba, but my grief seemed unique. I slouched to the ground against the stable wall and wrapped my arms around my knees. Maybe if I could make myself as small as possible, the hurt inside would shrink as well.

***

Late one evening a few weeks later, I overheard Yeshua humming a tune as he settled the flock for the night. I marched over to the gate of the pen and saw that a smile touched his lips.

"What are you doing?"

He looked up. "Hmm? I'm finishing—"

"No, the humming. How can you be humming?"

He studied me as I fumed at him but offered no explanation.

"How can you be joyful at a time like this? How?" I shook my head in disgust.

"Hannah, I can be sad because I miss Abba and still rejoice. I take comfort from the Lord's word. 'Those who walk uprightly enter into peace; they find rest as they lie in death.'[12] We can hope in the glory to come. We'll see Abba again."

My only response was to stomp away. Obviously, he hadn't loved Abba as much as I had if he was so easily comforted by trite words. I entered the house.

Emmi looked up and then refocused her attention on knitting a cap for Shim'on. I didn't know how my little brother could have been so careless as to lose his old one. We couldn't afford to lose anything now that Abba was gone.

"When will the tax collector come again?" I asked.

"What?" Her hands paused. "Oh . . . We have another month yet, I suppose."

"Do we have the coin we'll need?"

Her gaze returned to mine. "I'm sure we will by then, yes."

"So we don't have it now?"

"Hannah, what's gotten into you? I've already told you not to worry. Yeshua and Ya'akov have plenty of building work. The Lord will meet our needs. We just need to trust."

I snorted.

She lowered the needles onto her lap in silent warning not to be impertinent.

"I'm just tired of hearing about the Lord's word," I said. "I'd like to see the Lord's action for once."

Y'hudah's mouth opened in surprise. Elan put an arm around Shlomit as if trying to physically shield her from such blasphemy. Their reaction only made me angrier.

"How could you say such a thing?" Emmi asked.

"Well, it's true," I said. "You told us the Lord said Yeshua would rule. That hasn't happened. So how can we be sure we'll have enough to pay Alvon?"

Shlomit stared at Emmi. "The Lord's word is true, isn't it?"

"Of course," she said, keeping her eyes fixed on me. "The Lord's word always achieves its purpose."

"Tell us, Emmi." Y'hudah moved toward her. "Tell us about the angel again."

She smiled. Then she lifted her gaze upward and wore the same dreamy expression she always did when she started recalling the story. Everyone else inadvertently followed the direction of her eyes, just like they always did, as if the angel stood there now.

I huffed. They acted like strangers who hadn't heard the story a hundred times by now.

"Wait," Y'hudah said.

I breathed a sigh of relief. Maybe we'd be spared the retelling after all.

"You forgot to say it was a crisp evening. You should start over—"

"Stop. Just *stop!*" I shouted. "If I have to hear this nonsense one more time . . ." I clenched my teeth and let out a throaty scream, unable to convey just what I'd do. Whirling around, I stormed out of the house.

We'd just marked the start of a new month, so only a sliver of moon illuminated the sky. In my fury I scrambled uphill through the garden before my eyes could adjust to the dark. Below me the door open and shut. I started running with no regard for the unseen rocks that banged and bruised my toes, wanting only to escape.

"Hannah, wait!" Elan called. "You'll hurt yourself." The heavy breathing from behind proved he'd nearly caught up to me. He grabbed my arm, but I whipped it out of his grasp as I spun around.

"Let me go," I growled.

"Fine. At least take the lamp. I don't want you to fall."

His concern dampened my wrath, and I lowered my arm. My actions were irrational, but I didn't care. We faced each other, chests heaving from the climb, like opponents gauging our next strike.

I broke the silence first. "I can't go back there."

"You don't have to. Let's walk for a bit."

Even with the lamp, we had to concentrate on our footing as we made our way along the ridge. Without speaking, I knew our destination—the cave. Elan climbed down the slope first, holding the meager flame high so I could make my way down. By the time we reached the entrance, much of my fury had dissipated.

"Shlomit isn't five years of age yet. Will she even remember him in a few years' time?"

"We'll just have to remind her of all the wonderful things we learned from him."

"I still had so many things I wanted to say to Abba." I sniffed and squeezed my lips into a flat line and sat on the ground. Elan joined me but remained quiet.

"He'll never see me married or hold my children or tell me again how much he loves me." I covered my mouth with my hand and took a shaky breath. What I didn't say was that Abba promised I would never be invisible to him. Who would see me now? Who would comfort me and make me laugh and tell me I was special?

Elan kept his head bowed. "I'm sorry." The sincerity of those two words meant more to me than all the elaborate tributes spoken in the last month.

I pondered this for a moment before sharing a bigger concern. "What are we going to do without him? How are we going to have enough to eat? How will we survive?"

"I don't know. But Yeshua said not to be troubled, that—"

"Yeshua, Yeshua, Yeshua," I said, raising my voice. Elan blinked at me and said nothing, so I filled the awkward silence.

"Of course Yeshua says don't be troubled. He's old enough to support himself. Why should he care if the rest of us suffer?"

Elan's expression hardened. "He cares very much. He'd never leave us to fend for ourselves. And he's grieving just like the rest of us."

I crossed my arms. "Like the rest of us? Abba wasn't even his father. Yours either. No wonder you two don't understand."

Elan pursed his lips. The light of the flame flickered across his angry features, casting frightening shadows on the stone ledges behind him. "Hannah, I *know* you don't mean that."

"How do you know what I mean? Don't tell me what I can and can't say. I have to listen to Yeshua because he's my brother. But I don't owe you anything."

"No. You're right, you don't." He put the lamp on the ground between us and stood. "I'll leave you alone."

"Elan . . . wait."

He stopped and turned around, his eyes searching my face.

I knew him well enough to know what he sought—some assurance that there could be peace between us again. I didn't want him to go, but I wasn't ready to apologize. I averted my eyes. "I can't get up the slope by myself and carry the lamp at the same time."

He laughed without humor.

I didn't have to see his expression to know it was filled with pain. But I hurt so much myself, I didn't know how to make things right.

CHAPTER 17

Aunt Lilit's invitation for me to stay in Sepphoris came as a welcome relief, perhaps more welcome to Emmi than me. She was at a loss over what to do for me and weary of fighting my hostility every day. Even I was at a loss over what to do for myself.

My aunt immediately put me to the task of sewing garments for her new grandson, Rivkah's child. Unlike the practical coarse sheaths I was accustomed to weaving for my brothers, I was able to be creative with the clothing I made for her. Soon I took pleasure in watching individual stitches form complex geometric patterns on the precious linens and silks that only someone of Uncle Uzziah's riches could afford. And, surprisingly, my mood improved away from the barrage of constant memories at home. The pain hadn't left. But instead of violently exploding outward, it became a contained, if still festering, wound.

My adept handiwork had gained popularity within Aunt Lilit's circle of companions, leading to commissioned projects. Pity might have motivated the offers in part, but the quality of my embroidery deserved compensation. After only a few months, I had several coins to show for my efforts.

As my aunt and I set off to deliver my latest completed

project, I realized that I could be content here—if not for suffering remorse over my words with Elan. My family would tolerate me no matter what, but it worried me that I hadn't set things right with him before leaving Nazareth.

"Hannah, what has you so downcast?" Aunt Lilit asked. "I thought you were looking forward to visiting my brother-in-law's home."

I smile politely, readjusting the bundle of fabric I carried to our appointment with my Uncle Uzziah's niece by marriage. "I am. I'm eager to see how Keturah likes the headdress I've made for her."

"You're not still pining over that little shepherd friend you left in Nazareth, are you? You'll make new friends here. Now it's time to think about your future."

I looked at her out of the corner of my eye as we left the paved streets of Sepphoris and headed onto a dirt road.

"I told your parents for years, it's never soon enough to secure a good engagement. But they just wouldn't heed my advice. Don't get me wrong, your father was a kind man . . . but a bit indulgent letting you think you could stay at home forever. Don't pout. The time has come to be married, like it or not. So . . . isn't it better to make the best possible match while you still can?"

"I suppose."

"Your mother is struggling as it is with so many little ones. It will be years before your youngest brothers can earn their keep and she can marry Shlomit off. It's going to be hard enough for her to keep food on the table. You don't want to burden your family when you don't have to, do you?" She paused for a breath, but not for my answer. "Of course not. Fortunately, we're not too late to salvage the situation. Why, with your stunning looks, you could have any man you set your heart on—if we act quickly."

I nodded and smoothed my veil, unsure if I should be offended or complimented. It had never occurred to me that I burdened my family, but I had to admit my aunt might be right. In a few years, my brothers would be bringing home wives of their own. Maybe they had all been thinking it was time I left but they just didn't have the heart to say it so soon after Abba's death.

"Ah, here we are," she said.

Even having heard a description of the manor from my aunt, the scale of the property astounded me. The enormous main house, a three-winged stone structure with a wall enclosing the fourth side to create an immense central courtyard, hugged the slope of the hill below us. As we approached, Aunt Lilit pointed out the stables, vineyard, and threshing floor as well as outbuildings for field laborers and tenets. My Uncle Uzziah's wealth apparently paled in comparison to that of his older brother Gal. The manor was like an entire village unto itself.

"Lilit. It's always a pleasure to have you visit," said the man who greeted us, looming over us in height and looking anything but pleased by her presence. To say he was thin was an understatement. The skin on his face was pulled so taut, I imagined if someone flicked his cheek it would resound like a drum.

"Thank you, Iakovos," Aunt Lilit said. "How is your wife, Myrinne? Please send her along with refreshments."

The man tipped his head, but I noted he didn't lower his eyes in deference as a servant should to someone of a higher station. It left me feeling like *we* were the hired help, not invited guests.

Iakovos escorted us through the courtyard into a grand

hall located in the wing of rooms to our left. I was glad to see Keturah hadn't already arrived to greet us. It gave me a few minutes to admire my surroundings. Diamonds of red and green paint adorned the plaster walls and swirls of mosaic tiles underfoot. An enormous triclinium carved of oak occupied the center of the room with padded benches surrounding it. Against the wall, two carved stone pedestals displayed iridescent glass bottles containing unknown liquids.

"My husband's brother is quite prestigious as you can see," Aunt Lilit murmured. "Gal's one of the wealthiest merchants in the Galil and holds a council position in Sepphoris."

I stepped forward and stroked one of the carved table legs. Abba would have loved to work on a piece like this. "He must have dozens of children to need a table this big."

She laughed. "No. This is the room where Gal hosts banquets and conducts business. It even serves as a courtroom once a month. You can't know how troublesome it can be to have dozens of men under your employ. There are endless disputes. It's so hard to find good help." She turned. "Ah. Keturah, dear."

My customer entered. Her chestnut hair was intricately braided into a pile high on her head, and her eyes were rimmed with kohl. The woody fragrance of her perfume enveloped me before she approached. She was perhaps only a few years older than I, but her elegance made me feel like a child . . . and a poor one at that.

"You look as lovely as ever," my aunt said. "Sit down, sit down. You'll be even lovelier in a few minutes once you put on this headdress Hannah has made for you."

Keturah looked skeptical, so I hurriedly unpacked the wrapping and smoothed it out on the table before her. I'd sewn tiny glass beads into the design where the material would frame her face. It was so luxurious, I felt both pleased with the results and sad to give it away.

"Yes, this will do. It will have to. We're going to the palace next week," Keturah said as she gave a cursory inspection of the seams.

It wasn't the praise I'd anticipated, but she must have many such garments. Hoping for more enthusiasm, I produced the rest of the fabric. "I've also brought samples of cloth we could use for a matching dress. Beautiful, aren't they?"

"Mmm," she grunted.

Now she was just being rude. Before I could voice a curt reply, the door swung open and my words dissolved. There stood the most captivating man I'd ever seen.

Individually his features were hard and angular, but they came together in a pleasing way. His nose was long and straight and flared back up at the bottom almost like an anchor. His high cheekbones were set off by a shortly cropped beard below, as black as raven's feathers. As I stared at it now, his full lips curled up into a rakish smile.

"Olmer. What a surprise." My aunt clasped her hands to her chest, looking strangely satisfied.

"Aunt Lilit," he replied while blatantly appraising me.

I tried to be coy and rearranged the cloth on the table.

"Hannah, this is one of Gal's sons. Olmer, may I introduce my niece? Hannah's visiting from Nazareth."

My heart sank as my cheeks grew hot. Why did she have to tell him where I came from?

I risked a glance his direction.

He grinned, perhaps sensing my embarrassment, but politely bowed his head with his hand across his middle. "I have travelled far and wide acquiring riches. Oh, the time I would have saved had I but known of the treasures of Nazareth, right at my doorstep."

I couldn't detect mockery in his tone, but his eyes gleamed mischievously.

"Olmer," Keturah said, shaking her head with a smile. "You're incorrigible. You'd better not let Raziela hear you. You know what a fit your mother has when you flirt."

Flirt? Is that what he was doing?

"Don't worry, Keturah. I haven't forgotten your beauty. I'm able to admire many beauties at once. But sadly, I can't enjoy your presence much longer. My brother, your husband, awaits you outside."

She smirked at him as she strutted past, my hard work carelessly tossed aside.

Olmer followed my gaze and picked up the headdress. "What exquisite craftsmanship. Is this your work?"

I nodded, bashful for the first time in my life. Say something. Say *anything*.

"I'd like to possess something so lovingly rendered," he said. "Perhaps we could meet again to design something together?" He added a dramatic bow to my aunt. "With your permission, of course."

"Hannah is quite in demand these days. Does your grueling schedule afford the time needed to craft such an intricate pattern?" she asked.

"Yes, I'll be home until Shavuot. That's plenty of time to arrange something to both of our liking, don't you think?"

She nodded demurely. I got the impression I was the only one thinking about sewing.

He addressed me again. "Perhaps Lilit will bring you to dine with us during your stay in Sepphoris? It seems we don't have the natural beauty of Nazareth, but I hope you'll find something to your liking in our humble city."

Aunt Lilit smiled at me. "Oh, she just adores *all* that the city has to offer. Am I right, Hannah?"

Heat rose to my cheeks again and my wit abandoned me, aghast at my aunt's forward reply.

Olmer smirked and tipped his head before leaving the room.

As soon as he was out of hearing, we both collapsed in childish giggles. "Well, that went even better than I could have hoped," she said.

"Aunt Lilit. You're not playing matchmaker, are you?"

"Of course I am. And now that he's seen you, he's interested."

Her scheming scandalized me—but I felt alive and exhilarated for the first time in months. It was refreshing to be seen and admired for me, not because I was a grieving daughter or Yeshua's sister.

***

I decided to return to Nazareth the day before Shabbat. While proud to present my earnings to Emmi, I was more eager to make amends with Elan. I couldn't wait to share my experiences with him.

My aunt's servant left me at the top of our garden, and I skipped down the hill and around the side of the pen. I searched the gloom for Elan. Only animal eyes returned my stare. The door to our house opened and my heart soared.

"Hannah. You're home," Ya'akov said with a smile.

"Where's Elan?"

"I'm well, thank you. And how are you?"

I laughed. "Sorry. It's just that I was hoping to see Elan."

"He's not here."

"Oh . . . well, I'll wash and see him at dinner."

"Not unless you can fly."

"What's that supposed to mean?" I folded my arms over my chest, hating when someone knew something I didn't.

"He's in Jerusalem with Yeshua."

"Jerusalem? But Pesach has passed and Shavuot's still weeks away." I put my hands on my hips. "How dare they just leave Emmi like that to go traveling? We should all be doing our best to help out. You don't see me frolicking about. I've been earning for the family. I can't believe he's acting so selfish."

"Don't worry. You still hold the honor," Ya'akov quipped. "When did you become such a nag? Elan's come of age. Yeshua thought it important to present him at the temple."

"Oh." I'd been so consumed with my own interests I had forgotten this significant event in Elan's life.

"'Oh' she says." Ya'akov shook his head and pushed past me into the stalls.

***

After spending days running to the door at every sound outside, I was rewarded by Yeshua's return.

"Where's Elan?" I asked as he lifted a blanket off the donkey's back.

Yeshua smiled and walked forward, placing a hand on my shoulder. "How are you? You've been in my thoughts lately. I've been praying for you."

I stared over his shoulder to avoid his caring scrutiny. "I was hoping to speak with Elan before I return to Sepphoris in the morning. Did he stop off at Vana's home?"

"No. He's not coming back to Nazareth." Yeshua turned and led the donkey into the pen. "He is putting his flock together, his father's inheritance."

"I see." It felt like a rock sat in my gut. Of course, I had known this day would come. When Elan's father Heletz had died, Abba, Tobias, and the hazzan rounded up the shepherd's flock. No one in the village had owned adequate pastureland or possessed the time needed to shepherd so great a number of beasts. The flock had been divided up among friends and relatives in nearby villages and contracts agreed upon so that when he came of age, Elan could recoup an equivalent number of livestock or their monetary value.

I followed Yeshua into the stable. "Shouldn't you have stayed with him? To help?"

"He's a man now, Hannah. And he's certainly capable of assessing an animal's soundness."

I swallowed the lump in my throat. "Once he has a flock of his own, will he be away all the time?"

"That depends." Yeshua stopped filling the manger and looked up with one eyebrow raised.

I wasn't willing to find out on what it depended, so I let it go. But my heart was troubled, knowing Elan was free to leave us now. To leave me.

"Maybe it's for the best. That he's gone." I folded my arms. "That's one less mouth to feed."

"You don't mean that. Are you still anxious about us starving?" He chuckled.

"It's not funny."

When he saw my scowl he stopped smiling, but the amusement wasn't fully extinguished from his eyes. "Hannah, I'll take care of you. Trust me."

"Trust you? Why should I?" I demanded with more vehemence than I'd intended.

His face grew serious.

"How will Emmi pay taxes?" I asked. "How will she keep us fed and clothed? It will be years before Shlomit is married and Y'hudah is old enough to support himself. At least you're a man. I'm just . . . just a burden to her."

"You are not burdening anyone. And you don't have to worry about lack. The Lord will provide all that we need. He always has, and He always will."

My thumb flew to my mouth of its own accord and I nibbled on it furiously. If only it were that simple.

He brushed his hands on his thighs to shake off some bits of straw, then stepped toward me. "Is this about Abba?"

I resented the concern in his eyes. I didn't want his pity or to be treated like a child. When he reached his arms out to embrace me, I turned my back on him.

He put a hand on my shoulder. "I know your heart is broken. I understand the hurt. But this time of grieving will pass. The Lord is gracious, and He will restore you. He longs to give you days of rejoicing again. Trust Him. Trust me."

I wrenched my shoulder free of his touch and shook my head in disgust. How dare he speak of rejoicing? He didn't understand at all.

"Hannah," he called, but I tramped back to the house without a backward glance.

CHAPTER 18

"This gown better be worth the wait," Keturah said as she followed my aunt to her bedroom.

"It will exceed your expectations, I'm sure." Aunt Lilit discreetly winked at me. "Why don't you get the pieces you've made so far, Hannah. Keturah can try them for fit."

I bobbed my head and crossed the courtyard to retrieve the sewing. The dress represented more than my craftsmanship. All of Aunt Lilit's matchmaking efforts were tied up in the delicate strings of beads stitched around the cuffs and hem. Hopefully Keturah would be so enamored with my work that she'd commend me to her mother-in-law, Olmer's mother, Raziela. "Who wouldn't want to acquire a daughter-in-law with such skill?" Lilit had assured me earlier.

I smiled at my aunt's confidence, but didn't share it. Emmi had left Shlomit here this morning before leaving with my brothers for the market. My aunt had wanted to take Emmi aside to discuss her plans for Olmer and me, but I dissuaded her, reasoning we should have an assurance from his family first that they were even interested in a match. But my caution was also rooted in my own ambivalence in even wanting that assurance from them.

Entering the workroom, I sensed trouble in the drama

unfolding before me. Shlomit's jaw jutted out, her hands balled into fists at her side. She appeared ready to strike Tabitha, Olmer's other sister-in-law.

"Shlomit!" I shouted.

She jerked her head my direction, and I saw fire in her eyes. What could have provoked such fury from a little girl? She spun back to Tabitha and pointed at me. "Hannah knows. She'll tell you."

Tabitha crossed her arms and smiled at me, affecting the perfect blend of amusement and skepticism.

"She'll tell you what?" Keturah asked.

Her question startled me. I hadn't realized she'd followed me.

"About the angel and Emmi," Shlomit said. "Tell them."

I froze as if a viper had crossed my path. Silently, I pleaded with Shlomit to leave the room, to leave the city. To do *anything* besides bringing up such talk.

"An angel?" Keturah laughed.

"Yes. Can you imagine? This child has been regaling me with a fanciful account of a heavenly messenger."

"Oh, I must hear this. Did the angel knock on the door or fly through a window?" Keturah winked at Tabitha who smirked in reply.

"Tell them, Hannah," Shlomit insisted. "An angel talked to Emmi. And to Abba. It said Abba shouldn't be afraid to marry Emmi."

Keturah's look changed from amusement to genuine interest as she detected potential gossip. "Dear child, why would your father be afraid to marry your mother?"

Tabitha wrapped her arm around Shlomit's shoulders, and I prayed for my sister to be struck mute.

Shlomit looked disconcerted by her now-rapt audience

and played right into their trap.

"'Cause of Yeshua," she said, holding up her hands by way of explanation.

Keturah inhaled so strongly, I feared she'd suck the very breath from my body.

A thousand alarms sounded in my head. *"Pah."*

Everyone looked at me. It was a pathetic imitation of a laugh, so I slapped my knee for added credibility. "You have such an imagination! How could Yeshua have anything to do with Emmi and Abba's marriage? He wasn't there. He wasn't even born." I yanked Shlomit from the embrace of still-speechless Tabitha. "Now come on, or I'll tell Emmi you've been fibbing again."

Shlomit's cheeks turned the color of beet juice. Her lower lip trembled. "It's *true*. The angel was real," she whimpered.

"Yes, yes I'm sure it was," I agreed while rolling my eyes dramatically for Keturah's benefit. My fingers dug into my sister's arm. "Next you'll be telling your tale about Persian kings visiting us in the night bringing treasures from kingdoms to the east . . ."

The outraged betrayal on her face gave way to tears, but thankfully, Shlomit stopped talking.

"Yes, Shlomit, tell us about the royal visitors," Tabitha said, looking to Keturah for encouragement.

Shlomit stomped on my foot and fled the room.

I bit my lower lip. She had to learn that some stories just weren't meant to be shared outside our family. I hated to be cruel, but causing a few tears today could prevent her from suffering real harm in the future.

Keturah twisted her mouth in puzzlement as if her mind had been tickled by a feathery wisp of past conversation. Could Aunt Lilit have told them the story at some time?

Before Keturah could recall anything damaging, I spoke up. "Is that what you'll wear for the banquet tonight?" I asked her with mock concern. Fashion usually outweighed all other concerns in Keturah's mind.

"Hmm?" Her eyes focused on me again. "No, you're right. We'd better get home before the council members arrive. Come on, Tabitha, help me carry my packages."

When we returned to the courtyard, I was taken aback to see Elan standing there consoling Shlomit. I hadn't known he was in the city. "What is it? Why are you crying?" he asked her.

Shlomit just clung to his legs, refusing to speak. Elan looked up at me and his puzzled expression transformed into something more intimate. His eyes shone with warmth as he smiled.

I grinned back. I hadn't realized how much I'd missed him.

"I left your mother and brothers in the market because I couldn't wait to come see you," he gushed. "Wait until you see my flock. One of the sheep has had a new kid, and it's just perfect."

Keturah cleared her throat, and I held back my initial response. "A new kid? That's what you're excited about?" I asked. "Really, Elan, you're so unrefined."

He looked perplexed by my sudden change in demeanor.

The women snickered at the derisive remark, the response I'd intended. But I wasn't prepared for the dejection on Elan's features. He set his hand on Shlomit's head as if to shield her.

She glared at me and wiped her nose on her sleeve.

"Come along, Hannah," he said. "Your family's waiting and I believe we have much to discuss."

"He's not one of your brothers, is he?" Keturah asked me. She circled around Elan and Shlomit, appraising him as if he were a slave at auction. She must have found him lacking because she sniffed in distaste. "How dare he think you'd go out in public with a man who's not your relative."

Her words surprised me. It had never occurred to me to think of Elan as a man despite his recent journey to the temple and new business affairs. He'd been a constant part of my surroundings, as unchanging as the moon or sunshine, so I rarely took the time to consider him. But now I saw him with clarity. He'd grown in height over the past few months, and I detected a faint shadow of hair above his lip. I raised my gaze higher and saw the anger burning in his eyes and abandoned my inspection.

"Are you coming or not?" he asked.

"Hannah, you're not going to let your family's shepherd speak to you like that, are you?" Keturah asked.

I swallowed, unsure of my decision. In my defense, I was still flummoxed by this new appreciation of Elan. If only Keturah and Tabitha had left before he arrived. I looked back and forth between Elan and Keturah, then cleared my throat. "Run along, Elan, and fetch one of my brothers." I tried to apologize with my eyes and hoped he'd understand.

Elan let out an angry laugh and shook his head. "Yes, mistress." He made a show of bowing before spinning on his heel and marching out the entrance with Shlomit in tow.

"That's more like it," Keturah said. "If you're ever going to run a household properly, you'd best get used to demonstrating your authority over the servants."

I stared at the closed door, wondering if it was too late to call him back.

"Come, help us with our things." Tabitha lightly touched my shoulder.

I nodded. What was done was done. If Elan really cared, he would understand. I just wanted to make a good impression, a good match so I wouldn't have to worry about the future anymore. Was that so wrong?

I let pride coddle me and justify my wretched behavior toward him until I almost believed once again that I was the victim here.

CHAPTER 19

Elan had already taken the flock into the hills by the time I returned to Nazareth.

Yeshua and Ya'akov didn't mention hearing of the incident at my aunt's house, but their silent disapproval annoyed me more than open criticism would have. I was glad when they left the village to help Uncle Cleopas make repairs to his roof. Now only my youngest siblings remained to pester me. And pester me they did. After I snapped at Shlomit for the third time in an hour, Emmi sent me to the garden to gather herbs.

I wandered well past it while I ruminated. When I looked up, I saw the pile of stones marking the drop to the cave just up ahead. I hesitated and considered returning but realized that had been my true destination all along.

Inside, my eyes needed a moment to adjust to the light. I found the natural ledge in the stone where each of us had stored trinkets over the years. Yosi had left a fragment of a pot that he had found on a trip back from Jerusalem, Shim'on the remains of a warbler's nest. I picked up my own treasure and unwound the rough strip of cloth protecting my doll.

It'd been almost a year since I'd held it. Nostalgia washed over me as if I was being reunited with a dear friend. I squeezed it to my chest, then chided myself. I was grown now and couldn't hold on to childish things. My childhood had died when Abba did.

Aunt Lilit was right. It was time that I became engaged. Eventually, I'd find myself married to some other poor villager anyway. Didn't I deserve to be safe and secure, to own beautiful things like Keturah and Tabitha? I might as well try for the best possible match. What kind of future would I have if I put all my hopes in a mere shepherd? Besides, if Elan really cared for me, he would have returned by now.

Just thinking about him angered me. I was sure he meant to shame me with his absence. Well, he was more immature than I thought if he couldn't discern when words were spoken in jest. Clutching the doll in my fist, I stepped to the mouth of the cave. I'd show Elan. I'd show them all.

I hurled the doll skyward, watching it arc and then fall from sight somewhere on the hill far beneath me. Before it even hit the ground, I regretted being so rash and searched for footholds on the steep drop-off so I could retrieve it.

What was I doing? I didn't want to leave home. I loved my family. Maybe Yeshua was right. Maybe we *could* manage. And if I gave it time, things might get better. He was working and Ya'akov was almost a man himself. I could help Emmi by earning with my sewing too. I just had to trust that things would get better.

I looked up to judge my progress toward the landing site of my doll and froze. From this vantage point, I could see men on horseback approaching the village.

No, it couldn't be time for them to come again. Oh, please don't let them be coming for Emmi.

I changed direction and clawed my way back up the slope, unconcerned about the pain from scraping and banging my legs. Once on the ridge top, I sprinted for home. Before I reached the village, my chest burned from the effort, and I paused to take a few labored breaths. Hearing a crash and a woman's scream, I hitched up my skirts and ran again, envisioning the worst.

I came to the garden and half slid down the hill, jumping off the terraced wall at the bottom. Rounding the stable, my eyes found the clearing in front of our home deserted. Then came another yell and a child's wail. The riders were at Tobias's home.

I passed Abba's workshop and creeped along the wall of the neighbor's house, watching in horror as two men threw Tobias's limp body across the back of a horse. My hand clamped over my mouth. Then I saw that he breathed yet. He wasn't dead but beaten unconscious.

His son Honi bawled, clinging to his sister's legs. She seemed oblivious to him and stared ahead, stunned. I risked peeking farther around the corner to see what held her attention.

Rachel knelt, grasping the tax collector's feet. "No. Alvon, please," she begged. "You can't put him in debtor's prison. I can't raise the money to free him. Give us more time." I'd never seen anyone humiliate themselves so.

Alvon's pale features showed no empathy or any emotion at all. He looked at his companions and lifted his chin. One of the other men tore her off and threw her aside.

She crawled back. "Pl-e-ease," she sobbed, clutching her hands in front of her. "Don't put him in prison."

Alvon cocked his head to the side. "Who said we were sending him to prison?" he asked serenely.

"W-what?" Rachel exhaled and stopped crying. "You're not?"

"He should be so fortunate. I'm turning him over to the authorities for treason. The reward money is paltry, but it's more than I'd get from you."

"No!" she cried. "He's never done anything wrong. *You can't.* You can't. They'll kill him."

Alvon put a foot in the stirrup and swung himself up onto his horse. "He should have thought about that before wasting his tax money aiding rebels."

Emmi touched my arm, and I startled in terror before realizing who it was. "Hannah, get inside the house," she whispered fiercely.

I stared, uncomprehending.

"Get inside." She repeated in a more soothing tone. "I'll stay here. You go home and watch your sister. Go on, it's all right."

"No, it's *not*. It's not all right." I burst into tears.

"Shhh." She hugged me tightly, and I felt her own legs trembling against mine. I clung to her, but she freed herself. "Go on, I'll be there soon."

The other men mounted up, and they all rode off with Tobias's head bouncing perilously close to the trotting hooves.

"You're the traitor, do you hear me? Traitor. Traitor!" Rachel screeched as she ran after them, waving her arms like a possessed woman.

Emmi rushed to Rachel's children and bent down to inspect them, then embraced them both. The girl still stood rigid with a vacant look in her eyes. It could just as easily have been me and Shlomit standing there. What if we were next?

I couldn't let that happen. My presence in the household only added to Emmi's burden. We were in danger even if Yeshua denied it. It had been absurd to let myself believe even for a moment that his promises were true. That everything would be well.

He hadn't saved Abba. Why would I think he would save us?

CHAPTER 20

"Don't worry, dear," Aunt Lilit said as we neared the manor of her brother-in-law Gal. "I told you . . . I have everything well in hand. I managed to marry your Uncle Uzziah, didn't I? Trust me, I know what's best for you."

I felt nervous now that we were actually here. "But how do I know we'll be compatible? Olmer and I have hardly spoken three sentences to each other since we met."

"So? Many marriages are arranged on less. You'll have your whole lives to talk."

She was right. But still, I had hoped to know my future husband a bit better even if we didn't share a genuine caring. Like Elan and I shared—or *had* shared. "What if Olmer rejects me?"

"He's ready to take a wife. Who could he find lovelier than you? He just needs the opportunity to declare himself, you'll see. As soon as I get you two alone—"

"Alone?"

"You don't need to look so stricken. I'll just scoot out and return within moments. That way, if he doesn't declare himself, I can make a few carefully placed innuendos about improper appearances. Then he'll be obliged to make the match."

"But you just said he would declare himself!"

"Really, Hannah. You're getting tiresome. Wipe that frown off your face or you'll ruin the whole thing. Who cares how it happens, if we get what we want?"

Was this what I wanted? I'd be taken care of forever. Emmi wouldn't have to worry about me again. Of course this was what I wanted. Besides, what other choice did I have?

Lilit pushed me forward through the open courtyard doors.

***

My aunt and I reclined at the grand table with Keturah, Tabitha, and Olmer. It wasn't an ordinary occurrence for Olmer to be spending time with women in the middle of the day, and I took encouragement from that. But my nerves made it difficult to follow the conversation. I plastered a smile on my lips and concentrated on not perspiring. Then Keturah excused herself, and only Tabitha remained to hinder our plans.

"Tabitha, dear, do you think you could bring me some wine?" Aunt Lilit batted her eyelashes at Tabitha. "My throat is scratchy from the dust on the road. And maybe some dates?"

Tabitha wrinkled her brow, perhaps discerning an underlying motive in the request, but dutifully left to comply with my aunt's wishes.

"I think I'll just take care of some necessities before she returns," my aunt then announced, wasting no time with subtleties. She stood and left the room, pulling the immense doors firmly shut behind her.

Suddenly, Olmer and I were alone. He raised an eyebrow as he considered the closed doors. Did he suspect the plan? My mouth was so dry, I couldn't speak even if I had something intelligent to say. His awareness of our predicament and choice to stay excited me. I also felt affronted that he didn't respect me enough to be appalled and remedy the situation.

I sprang to my feet and paced the sizable length of the room, wiping damp palms on my thighs and counting the seconds since my aunt's departure. It had been long enough.

"You know, my mother is not going to be happy about this," he stated as if commenting on an undercooked meal or unexpected rain shower.

I stared at him, unsure how to answer.

"You're not going to act shy now, are you? Do you really expect me to play the fool?" He grinned, but not with any lightheartedness.

"So . . . so you don't mind?" I stammered, hoping for reassurance if not a confession of love.

"Do you really think you could've orchestrated this if I hadn't wanted it to happen? Do you think a girl from Nazareth could outsmart me? I will never be outmaneuvered by you, Hannah. As long as you understand that, I believe we'll get along quite well."

I didn't like the tone the conversation had taken. Maybe my aunt and I had erred in thinking he found me appealing. Where was she?

He took a gulp from his cup and banged it down with more force than necessary. The bench scraped across the tiles as he stood, reminding me of our significant size difference.

A bead of sweat trickled down the small of my back, and I swallowed convulsively.

"You see, my father hopes for a betrothal between myself and a young woman living south of Jericho," he explained. "But the only thing attractive about her is the share of her father's balsam production we'd acquire. Not to say that its value doesn't compensate for her distasteful appearance. However, I have no desire to move south and have my throat slit in the middle of the night by a looting Nabatean."

He crossed the room to where I stood, and I fought the urge to take a step backward.

"Fortunately, my mother has been sabotaging my father's negotiations. Unfortunately, she has another candidate in mind. Her desire is for me to marry someone from her home-town of Miletus, one of her cousin's daughters. She's already recommended that I build a house there, ostensibly to better oversee shipping of our wares to Athens and Rome. We all know she dreams of returning there herself one day."

I bobbed my head like an idiot, so nervous I couldn't follow his words at this point.

"This doesn't bother me as much as the fact that the young lady in question is young . . . very young. Five years of age to be exact. I have certain needs that I fear won't wait another decade to be satisfied." He stepped forward so all I saw was his broad chest. "You could help me with those needs," he whispered, his breath caressed my forehead.

Do something, my mind yelled. *Do anything.* But I was paralyzed, torn between fear and excitement.

"Your aunt's plan was for us to get caught in an indelicate situation, was it not?" He tipped my chin up and bent his face down to mine.

My eyes shifted back and forth, uncertain where to land. I'd never studied someone's face from so close a distance. I should push him away. Or scream. But I couldn't move.

Footsteps approached the door—footsteps too numerous to be just my aunt. But his trance over me didn't break until I registered the terrifyingly familiar voices. No, it couldn't be.

I began backing away. His arms shot out, reaching behind me and pulling me against him. A queer satisfaction filled his eyes. I panicked as the doors opened with me caught in his embrace.

Iakovos, the household steward, stepped into the room and abruptly stopped. Disapproval registered on his features. He quickly composed himself and attempted to back out the doors. But Elan and Ya'akov pushed forward behind him, stepping into the room. What were they doing here?

My brother's words halted mid-sentence and his mouth opened. Elan let out a bestial grunt and clenched his fists at his side. I untangled myself and realized with sickening dread that he intended to fight Olmer. The steward must have realized it too. He blocked the attempt as soon as Elan darted forward.

Olmer just laughed. "Look. Here comes our dear Aunt Lilit. I'm glad you weren't delayed any longer, Aunt. You'd miss this demonstration of brotherly indignation."

Lilit entered the doorway holding on to the post, alarm clear on her face. Then she looked apologetically in my direction.

"I thought it rude not to invite your brothers to visit the manor," Olmer explained to me. "So I asked Iakovos to fetch them. I hope you both had a good journey?"

Olmer's polite tone in the midst of such a scandalous scene seemed to baffle Ya'akov. He nodded.

Elan stared at me with narrowed eyes. "I'm not her brother."

"Ah," Olmer said, "then you'll excuse us. I'm sure her brother and Aunt Lilit would like to join me for a word with my parents at this . . . indelicate juncture." Olmer's fist covered a fake cough, but his smirk was plain to see.

My brother swung his head back and forth between my guilty face and Elan's apoplectic one.

"Iakovos, escort Hannah to the ladies' quarters," Olmer said. "It wouldn't be seemly to leave her unchaperoned with this . . ." He left us to finish the end of his sentence and marched past Elan, leaving Ya'akov and Aunt Lilit to follow in his wake.

Elan stood taller and glared at Olmer's departing figure.

"Elan," I pleaded, but no words followed.

He shook his head and marched out the door without a backward glance.

"Come along, miss," the steward said.

CHAPTER 21

Aunt Lilit insisted on accompanying us home to speak with Emmi. She sent me pitying shakes of her head when I managed to meet her eye. As anxious as I was to hear the details of what transpired with Olmer's parents, I kept silent, appreciating belatedly the severity of my imprudence. Thankfully, neither Olmer nor I were betrothed to another or we could've been stoned for adultery if found in such an indelicate position. Glancing at Ya'akov, I got the impression my brother might still like to stone me.

I wondered where Elan had gone—probably the cave, if I knew him. I winced just recalling the expression on his face. But I couldn't think about him right now. There was enough to worry about.

When we entered the house, Yosi and Shim'on were absent. They'd hear the story soon enough, though. Emmi smiled warmly, clearly surprised and happy to see Lilit. But seeing our faces caused Emmi's smile to falter.

I looked away. It sickened me to think about the news we brought. I wished we didn't have to say anything at all.

Yeshua stood from the table where Y'hudah and Shlomit sat. He pinned me with a stare that devastated me. My heart pounded in my chest, and I felt like I couldn't get enough air.

He knew.

"Excuse me. I need to refresh myself," I whispered and fled outside to buy a few more minutes before facing the consequences of my actions.

I braced myself against the side of Abba's work shed, fearing I would vomit. I heaved a couple of times but was disappointed that I was a failure even at getting sick. After smoothing down my tunic, I took a deep breath and returned inside.

All conversation stopped.

Ya'akov turned to Emmi. "He should be killed for putting his hands on her."

"Ya'akov," Yeshua said with quiet authority.

"Then he has to marry her." Ya'akov paced, lips pursed in rage.

"The way this happened may not have been ideal," Aunt Lilit piped up, "but let's forget about Hannah's youthful lapse of judgment for a moment."

I opened my mouth to object, but she held up her hand.

"The important thing is Uzziah's family is respected and very wealthy," she said. "Olmer isn't Gal's eldest son, but still, Hannah will never want for any comfort. And her children will have a generous inheritance."

Yeshua ignored Lilit and focused on me. "The marriage contract hasn't been written yet. One rash decision need not lead to more rash actions."

"Your brother's right, Hannah," Emmi said. "Lilit assures us word of your . . . indiscretion has not traveled outside the family. Your honor remains intact." She raised the inflection on the last words, her eyes pleading for confirmation from me, but I remained stone-faced. "There are many things to be considered—many people to be considered—before anything is decided."

My eyes darted back and forth between Emmi and Yeshua. I knew they both thought of Elan. I could hardly admit to myself, let alone to them, that Elan had already distanced himself from me and even if he had still cared for me, after what he witnessed today, he wouldn't want me. No one would. Olmer was my only hope now.

I attacked to cover my despair. "Is it so hard to believe that a wealthy, important man desires me?"

"No, of course not. That's not what I meant," Emmi said. "They're so *different* from us. They're Sadducees." Emmi turned apologetically to Lilit.

Aunt Lilit dismissed the comment with a wave. She looked at the young children absorbing this drama with wide eyes. "Perhaps I'll just take the children outside for some . . . something." She grabbed Y'hudah and Shlomit by the hands and half dragged them toward the door. "Ya'akov, are you coming?"

Ya'akov faced Emmi. But she stared at the ground, tapping her foot—a clear sign she tried to rein in her anger. Yeshua placed his hand on Ya'akov's shoulder and nodded. Ya'akov glared at me once more before stomping after the children.

"If I don't marry Olmer, what man will have me? Sooner or later the story will come out and then I will be alone or . . . worse."

"No, there are other possibilities," Yeshua said with an unwavering gaze. "There's another suitor who is worthy of, and deserves, your consideration. Please, think of Elan."

I felt desperate and trapped, cornered by my own actions, and lashed out like a wounded animal. "Hmpf," I snorted. "Of course you'd side with him over me."

Yeshua sat heavily upon the bench and rested his head in his hands. He closed his eyes and inhaled slowly before answering. "I'm not judging between the two of you."

"Then why do you care so much about Elan? *I'm* your sister," I shrieked. "Why don't you ever think about *me*?"

"My every thought is about you, Hannah. Please trust me. I want what's best for you."

"I'm tired of hearing about how you know what's best. Oh, I'm sorry. I forgot that you claim to know the will of the Lord. Maybe because in all the years we've shared a home, I've missed seeing the seas part for you and the bushes igniting as you walk by."

Emmi gasped. "Hannah."

"Well, it's true. He's nothing but a lowly carpenter with no wife or children of his own to mind. And now he's envious because I'm making a family for myself." I felt the heft and sharpness of the words I hurled from my lips as if I spat daggers through the air. Each word struck him, the first bringing a shocked expression, then the barrage that followed seemingly pelting his cheeks and throat with crimson splotches. He stood from the table, but his silent composure only stoked my anger.

"Maybe you should be more concerned about your own romantic prospects than mine," I went on. "Oh, I forgot. You're not interested in getting married. And why is that? Because you think you're so much better than the rest of us? Or is it because you'll never find anyone who thinks you're as special as Emmi does?"

Yeshua placed a restraining hand on Emmi's arm before she could slap me for speaking the ugly words. One look at the set of his jaw and I felt the sickening exhilaration of having gone too far, having uttered the unthinkable.

"Emmi. Emmi, I didn't mean it." I offered my apology tentatively, my hands in front of me, shielding myself from her response.

"I'm not the one you should apologize to." She squeezed her lips together into a grim line and didn't look at me again as she busied herself with the evening meal preparation.

I stood still as tense minutes passed, uncertain how to proceed.

"I expect Olmer's family will visit tomorrow," Yeshua finally remarked in a flat voice. "We'd best ready ourselves."

I nodded, knowing Yeshua would abide by my decision. The day didn't go as hoped, but in the end my future was settled. I'd be the wife of a wealthy merchant. It was a hollow victory.

I turned and walked out the door, nearly kicking the rooster, which darted away with a squawk and an indignant flutter of wings. My feet headed for the rocky path along the ridge. Then my stomach lurched, and I stopped mid-stride, realizing my first instinct was still to seek Elan for comfort. The cave was no longer a welcoming haven for me.

I changed direction and walked blindly into the fields below.

CHAPTER 22

The morning before my engagement celebration, I sat in the clearing, grinding flour to bake braided challah bread for the occasion. Thinking of braids, I let go of the wooden handle protruding from the top circular stone quern and gingerly touched my hair. Aunt Lilit had braided and twisted it high on my head after the fashion of Keturah and the other society women of Sepphoris.

"A new hairstyle won't make you any more beautiful."

I turned, preparing a retort, but the look on Yeshua's face caused my scowl to fall away. Genuine caring filled his eyes. I lowered my head to avoid the warm intensity of his gaze and self-consciously touched my hair again.

"You couldn't be more beautiful to me, Hannah."

Just when my lips turned up at this kindhearted comment, Shim'on walked up behind him. "If you ask me, there's room for improvement."

"Oh, you." I cried out, picking up a pebble to launch at his head.

He laughed while expertly dodging the stone and hurried into the house.

When I turned back, Yeshua still stared at me. I resumed grinding. Though ashamed of the words that came from my mouth last night, I couldn't think of others that would make things right between us. He studied the flour gathering in fine piles around the base of the stones and seemed content to stand there all day waiting for me to speak.

"You know, I never . . . Nothing ever happened between Olmer and me," I said.

"I know."

I risked glancing at him, unsure if he meant he knew by divine inspiration or if Aunt Lilit had already clarified this with him.

"I know because I know you, Hannah."

I suddenly choked up for some reason and focused on turning the stone in front of me. He placed his hand in between my shoulder blades, and the warmth of it seemed to travel to my heart. "I know who you are, and you're a good daughter."

I nodded, determined not to cry.

He lifted his hand from my back and extended both his arms, welcoming me into his embrace, tempting me with love.

I shook my head and attempted a weak smile as I sniffed. If I stood and went into his arms, I might come apart. I might think about Abba and how disappointed he'd be in my actions. I might think about the pain in Elan's eyes when he saw me at the manor. I might realize I'd made a terrible mistake. So I swayed back and forth over the mill, putting all my effort into keeping the stone spinning. The only thing holding me together was my determination not to think about the decisions I'd made.

Yeshua watched me, appraising the emotions that crossed my face. He lowered his arms to his side. For an instant I saw the hurt in his eyes caused by my rejection, but he quickly recovered. "I'll let you finish your work so you can get ready." He smiled. "We don't want you to be late for your own engagement."

***

A lamb had been butchered and roasted for the meal. I wondered if Elan had helped with this, as it was usually his responsibility to select the animal. The hazzan had arrived to act as both witness and scribe. I wasn't sure how much Itamar knew of the circumstances dictating the promptness of this gathering, but whatever he knew was kept to himself. He smiled and shared stories of his own engagement night to his wife, now long departed. No one paid him much attention.

The knock at the door came shortly after sundown. Yeshua looked to me one last time to see if he should open the door. If I asked him to, he'd send Olmer away and cancel the whole ceremony. I nodded, indicating I wished to proceed.

Yeshua's face was expressionless as he admitted Olmer, his father Gal, and their steward into our home. They maneuvered into the tightly packed room, and I felt ashamed that my life must appear small and shabby to these men.

After some stilted conversation, the men sat to negotiate the *ketubah*, our wedding contract. Once everyone drank the ritual first cup of wine, the mood lightened and I began to hope the evening might end well after all. I listened as pledges were made, binding the families together. As Yeshua and Gal drank the second cup of wine with Olmer and me, Abba came to mind. I glanced at Emmi. She must be missing him too.

Olmer discussed the details of preparing our living quarters at his parent's home. I bit the inside of my cheek to keep from crying. This would be my last year living with my family. I thought I'd be glad to escape the constant reminders of Abba in my surroundings. Now it saddened me to leave the place where so many objects kept the memory of him alive. I blushed furiously when I realized they were discussing my keeping pure until the wedding night, but no one seemed to notice. Finally, after much back and forth, everything was arranged.

Olmer and I alone would share the third cup of wine, which sealed the engagement contract. I met his gaze fully for the first time and wondered who this assured man sitting in front of me was. Was he the charming man I had first met or the determined one who so easily frightened me? Olmer's answering smile appeared genuine. Perhaps I'd exaggerated my earlier misgivings at the manor. Would he keep tradition and not drink wine again until we shared the fourth cup together on our wedding day? We drank, and celebratory cries went up from those around the table.

Shim'on, Yosi and Y'hudah hurried outside, and I heard the blasting of shofars a moment later. I even grinned when Olmer tipped his head toward me and winked.

Only hours later did I remember the neighbors probably weren't the only ones to hear the blast from the ram horns. The sound would have carried across the fields and hillside to one sitting alone in the dark, tending his flock.

***

Well-wishers from the village trickled in during the next hour, surprised but happy at the news of the hasty match. We gathered by the fire, and the women shared recollections of their own weddings.

Uncle Cleopas, Aunt Miryam, and my cousin Shim'on arrived well into the night. Determined to be cheerful, I rushed forward to embrace them. "Oh, are these early wedding presents?" I asked jokingly, lunging for the large bundle on the back of the donkey.

"Oh, Hannah, my love, no," my aunt objected.

A cold fist grabbed my heart as I lifted the edge of the rough cloth. The pale stone vessel underneath was an ossuary meant to house my father's bones. Could it really be a year since Abba's burial? How could that be when the pain was so raw?

"Hannah, we were already on our way here, did you forget? We didn't find out about your happy news until we reached the village. I'm sorry." Aunt Miryam squeezed my hand as her forehead creased with concern.

"It's all right," I stammered.

"Your father's bones will be surrounded from the earth of Jerusalem," my uncle explained. "It's carved of limestone from the Mount of Olives."

I nodded more times than necessary. "Abba would be pleased."

Uncle Cleopas placed his hand on my shoulder, the weight of it so like Abba's hand that my eyes grew moist.

"Your father would be proud of you, Hannah. His blossom has turned into a beautiful flower."

"Thank you." I forced a smile and stood on the tips of my toes to kiss his woolly cheek before making a hasty departure.

***

Dozens of people milled about the clearing in front of our home now, and wine flowed freely. I felt Elan's absence keenly and found my eyes scanning the hills for a sign of his fire. Seeing no one paid attention, I slipped away.

With each step along the ridge, I grew more determined to confront Elan, to put our arguments behind us, to have his blessing for my future. As I searched for the path descending toward the cave, the crunch of gravel behind me alerted me to his presence. I whirled around, but was disappointed to see Ya'akov, not Elan.

"Really?" he asked with exasperation. "Did you think Elan would wait here to congratulate you? You're promised to another now. You're not free to roam the hills meeting other men."

I stomped recklessly down the hillside to the cave entrance. It was, of course, empty.

Ya'akov followed me, but his tone was sympathetic now. "You can't expect to have it both ways. He'll need time to accept this after the way you rejected him."

My eyes widened. "The way I rejected him? You don't know what you're talking about. He rejected *me*." I kicked a stone, sending it careening downhill. "He hasn't been home for months. And he's never shown any indication that he cares for me more than he cares for his dumb herd."

"Real caring is respecting you, not cornering you alone in a room and jeopardizing your honor."

I flinched. "You're just too young to know anything about what really goes on between a man and a woman."

"I'm not too young to know Elan was planning on asking Yeshua's permission to marry you."

The weight of this revelation caused my knees to buckle. I sat heavily on the ground and stared into the dark void before me.

"The reason Elan went away wasn't to snub you," he said. "You've been harping about tax collectors and starvation for the last year. The poor man just wanted to put your mind at ease. He put the flock together as a means to provide for you." Ya'akov shook his head. "If he's been distant in any way, it's out of a sense of propriety. Honestly, Hannah, for all your boasts about worldly wisdom, you don't seem to know very much."

I fell silent, both relieved I'd misinterpreted Elan's actions and devastated at the same time.

Ya'akov observed me with a mixture of annoyance and compassion. At last he sighed. He reached a hand out and lightly brushed my chin. "I'm sure he's happy for you. Well, maybe not now. But he will be. We all are. You'll have a wonderful life as Olmer's wife."

Despite his best intentions, the words rang false even to my own ears. But there was nothing to be done now except continue on, so I determined to smile.

He squatted beside me and took my hand, squeezing it gently. After a minute he stood.

"Don't be long," he said and climbed back up the hill.

I focused on the dark hillside below me, remembering the childhood toy that I had so recklessly thrown away from this very spot. Oddly, it was the loss of the doll that finally caused me to weep.

PART 3

SEPPHORIS

Summer of the Year 3787 (CE 27)

CHAPTER 23

Someone had removed the oil lamp, so the windowless cellar room became dark as a tomb when I shut the door. It didn't matter. After making this monthly trek for fourteen years, a staggering half of my life, I could read every indentation of stone beneath my bare feet like familiar words—*you've failed again*. Failed to conceive a child, failed to please my husband.

I entered the mikveh's water with determined steps, accepting its cool embrace, and ducked beneath the surface. Suspended in that womb-like state, I held my breath, waiting for some sense of renewal, a fresh chance for happiness. But as the waters of the bath washed me ritually clean, they further diluted my hope.

My head broke the surface, but I lingered a moment listening to the trickling of rainwater brought from a rooftop cistern far overhead. Despite the vastness of the manor, time alone was a treasured commodity. I thought back to the first year of my marriage to Olmer, how determined I'd been, as if by sheer force of will I could dictate my future. Olmer had been freed of his family's business obligations to stay home with me. Everyone had expected that I would be with child imminently. I certainly had. Olmer had shrugged off my disappointment each month and cheered me with his ribald joking about trying harder next time. But only shame had grown inside me.

Eventually, the time had come for Olmer to resume traveling, child or not. That's when I first began the waiting. I'd wait for chickens to lay eggs, wait for bread to bake, wait for the sun to set so I could mentally mark a day passed and another one beginning. Each day became an obstacle to endure while I anticipated Olmer's next arrival and another chance for a child and happiness. And around every corner stood my mother-in-law Raziela, staring at me as if I were a cow who didn't give milk, and wishing, no doubt, that she could butcher me and cut her losses.

Thinking of my mother-in-law provided the impetus to pull myself up the steps on the other side of the stone bath.

I bent and twisted my hair to my side, waiting to hear the splatter of water drops cease before dressing blindly. The sounds of the bustling household above me intruded the moment I opened the door to the cellar hall. I covered my head and reluctantly emerged into the light.

"Hannah, over here," Tabitha called as she exited the storeroom. Her smile faltered ever so slightly, and I saw the flash of pity in her eyes when she realized where I'd been. But she quickly hid it. "Help me with these, would you?"

She piled jars of olive oil into my arms, and I traipsed up the stairs behind her. As we stepped into the courtyard, my mother-in-law burst through the entrance doors. I flinched and considered ducking back into the shadows of the stairwell behind me.

"Hannah? Tabitha?" Raziela cried. "Ah, there you are."

Too late. She covered the ground between us with confidant strides, then opened her mouth to speak, but snapped it closed into a thoughtful pucker as her eyes darted to and fro, taking in the servants nearby. The expression reminded me of a fish, but I didn't dare laugh.

"Come with me," Raziela commanded, propelling Tabitha forward by the elbow. I followed alongside, mentally reviewing past events for some perceived transgression we had committed that might have caused her agitation. When I caught the hint of pleasure in my mother-in-law's eyes, I knew we were safe from reproach—for the moment. She must have had gossip to share.

The meaning of Raziela's name, "secret of God," fit her well. It wasn't out of affection that I shortened her name to simply "Raz," or "secret" over the years. She still impressed me with her ability to sniff out any whiff of scandal. Not purely for sport, but for the assurance of knowing she could defame someone's character in the event she needed to defend her own.

We piled through the doors to the main salon and closed them to prying eyes.

My other sister-in-law Keturah looked up from cutting fresh wicks for the dozen lamps spread before her on the table. She sat forward, eyes shining. "What is it? News?"

"Herod's wife is *gone*," Raziela pronounced, looking expectantly from face to face.

We blinked at her.

"What do you mean, gone?" I asked with furrowed brow. "She went to Machaerus weeks ago when Herod sailed for Rome, didn't she?"

Keturah leaned forward onto her elbows. "People are saying Herod seeks an audience with the emperor for one reason alone—to obtain permission to divorce Phasaelis. Can you believe it? No wonder she's hiding in the desert fortress." She giggled.

Tabitha shook her head. "I'd go into seclusion too. The palace gossip here has been fierce. But I still don't see why Herod would favor another. Isn't Phasaelis a good wife?"

"A woman is only as good as the number of sons she gives her husband." Raz's eyes glimmered with spite, and I felt the sting of the words like a slap in the face.

Keturah also remained uncharacteristically quiet. She'd given her husband Hakon four beautiful daughters, but I knew she still yearned for a son. Only Tabitha had managed to produce three healthy boys, guaranteeing her a secure place in the family even as a widow.

Raziela crossed her arms and turned to the others. "Listen, do I have to explain everything to you? She's left Machaerus. She's gone. Her party rode out of the fortress and right into an ambush."

"An *ambush*?" Keturah squealed and clapped her hands, as if we discussed a surprise treat to be served at dinner, not armed conflict.

Tabitha inhaled and covered her mouth with her hand. "She was abducted," she whispered.

Raziela fixed her with a condescending stare. "No. She wasn't abducted. She planned the whole thing so she could flee back to Nabataea, to her father's open arms. We all know King Aretas has never been fond of his son-in-law Herod."

The implications of this news dumbfounded me. How could a woman risk angering her husband by such a reckless action? If Herod hadn't been seeking a divorce before, he might now.

Raz smiled at seeing our wide eyes and open mouths, no doubt the reaction she'd hoped to elicit. "Wait until I tell my husband. That senseless woman may just start a war." She strutted from the room with Keturah trailing behind like a faithful hound.

I stared in annoyance at the unfilled lamps left conveniently abandoned.

"Can you believe it?" Tabitha asked.

I shook my head and realized I still clutched the oil I'd carried from the cellar. I put it down with shaky hands and took a seat. "Who do you think told Raz the news? Do you think Olmer's made it back as far as Perea and sent her word from the south?"

"I'm sure Raz would have told you if she'd had any word from him." Tabitha rested the tips of her fingers on my forearm. "He's been away for months. You must miss him very much."

I hesitated before answering. Olmer's younger brother had died from a fever three years ago leaving Tabitha bereft with young children to raise on her own. I had no right to complain to her that even when he was physically near, my husband remained distant from me. Trying to lighten the mood, I smiled. "Well, wherever he is, at least I know Olmer isn't in Rome petitioning for a divorce."

She frowned. "I forgot to bring the funnel from the cellar," she muttered and fled from the room.

Poor Phasaelis, I thought as I arranged the wicks into a neat row. None of her children had survived their first decade of life. Now her husband cavorted with his half-brother's wife, Herodias. Phasaelis must have been desperate to escape to her father's kingdom where people loved her. What I wouldn't give to return to my father's arms if he still lived. But what kind of life would she have now? Regardless of Herod's infidelity, Phasaelis would bear the shame if he divorced her. And she'd be alone and scorned.

I shuddered and rubbed my arms at the frightening prospect. I had naively assumed once married, I would always be secure. But if even a princess could be disposed of . . .

It didn't bear thinking upon. Especially considering how Olmer and I had quarreled the last time he was home. Of course I suspected that, out of my hearing, Raz had stoked the flames of his discontent. My hand stilled, and I rebuked myself for being ungrateful and petty.

An abundance of wealth was at my disposal. Yes, my marriage might not have been as loving as my parents', but I was thankful to have a husband. Certainly I could tolerate Raz's cruel barbs if Olmer was pleased with me. I'd just have to try harder to be a good wife until I could provide him with a son.

I sighed. How many times had I made this resolution? And how many times, despite my best intentions, had I fallen back into my usual state of frustration, or worse, depressed resignation?

Well, self-pity wouldn't get the lamps filled any faster. I left the table to see what kept Tabitha.

CHAPTER 24

Despite the heat of the day, or more likely because of it, Raz assigned me the onerous task of replenishing the straw in her mattress. She banished me to the roof under a blazing sun to complete the task, rather than to the shaded area behind the manner, explaining it wouldn't be seemly for everyone in the yard to see her bedding. I was fairly sure by now the servants suspected even the great Raziela must sleep. Besides which, nearly everyone was away from the house, occupied in the fields and vineyard these days.

I grabbed a handful of chaff from the basket in front of me and pounded it mercilessly into the pocket made of tightly woven rope. Sweat ran down my back and tiny bits of straw clung to my forearms and neck, making me itchy and even more irritated with Raz. Standing to shake myself off, I spotted a cloud of dust on the horizon and ran to the parapet. Sure enough, a caravan approached. Olmer had returned.

My belly fluttered when I recognized him steering one of the wagons. Even from a distance, there was a surety about the way he carried his broad shoulders, a confident lift of his chin and tilt of his head as he held the reins. I imagined vanquishing warriors could not rival his posture as he traveled the final stretch of road, the spoils not of war but of successful negotiating in evidence behind him.

Suddenly, I recalled my own disheveled state. If I hurried, I might have time to wash and put on a clean mantle before he reached the door. I scampered downstairs and dashed toward our room when Raz called me.

"Hannah. Make yourself useful and find the steward."

I stared at her. "But Olmer is on the road home."

"Yes. And he'll need help taking inventory and transferring merchandise to the cellar. Why do you think I want you to fetch Iakovos?"

I could think of plenty of reasons. The main one being she didn't want me present in the welcoming party lest Olmer greet me first and somehow diminish her standing. And I was sure she hoped to catch her son's ear before I did so she could apprise him of my latest domestic failures.

"Well? Go on." She fluttered her hands at me. "He'll be here any minute."

I clenched my teeth and exhaled loudly through my nose. For a moment I thought of defying her, but I didn't want Olmer to return and find us just as he left us—bickering. So I changed direction and descended to the cellar.

As my eyes adjusted to the dim light, I knocked at the door to the steward's office. It was usually locked so I was surprised when the door gave way. "Iakovos? Hello?" I glanced over my shoulder, then risked stepping inside.

The room smelled of leather with hints of the scented oils stored on the lower shelves built along two walls. The upper ledges were packed with Raziela's precious scrolls. I gingerly brushed my finger around the end of a rolled parchment. Some of these writings belonged to her ancestors. Other scrolls she had purchased at great price—works of poetry, philosophy, and history meticulously copied by scribes living hundreds of miles away and years ago. My spoken Greek had greatly improved since living in Sepphoris, but written Greek still eluded me. Even so, I fought the desire to unroll one. But time was short today.

As I turned to go, the writing tablet on the steward's work table drew my eye. I recognized the crude diagram of our property carved in the wax. Squares marked the manor, servants' quarters and stable, the threshing floor and grain storehouses. But near the edge of the tablet someone had carved two other squares.

I tilted my head to get a different angle. Were they landmarks that don't yet exist? No one had mentioned any building projects to me. As I puzzled over the map, footsteps echoed from the hall, and I hastily retreated. Hakon, Olmer's elder brother, blocked my way before I cleared the threshold.

"What are you doing?" he asked, craning his neck to peer behind me.

"I'm looking for Iakovos. What else would I be doing?"

"Unless he's greatly shrunk in size, I don't think you'll find him on the table." Hakon chuckled at his own wit.

As with Raziela, I had found the best strategy to escape Hakon's criticism was to remain mute. Better to appear simpleminded than risk irritating him with a smart retort.

"And while you've been down here snooping about, your husband has returned with no wife to greet him." He shook his head in disapproval. "At least his family was there for the homecoming."

I pushed past Hakon in my frustration, determined to at least be clean when I greeted Olmer.

Halfway up the stairs, I realized what had bothered me about the drawing. The land south of the vineyard, where the two mystery squares had been carved, was well onto our neighbors' property. Iakovos must have gotten the scale wrong and meant to draw the buildings farther north. I would have to tell him. Iakovos wasn't my favorite person, but I wouldn't wish a scolding from my father-in-law Gal on anyone.

Once I reached the courtyard, the excitement of seeing my husband pushed all other thoughts from my mind. Olmer stood almost a head above the tenants and servants who gathered around him. I eyed the stairs leading to our room and made a dash for them before he saw me.

"Hannah, where have you been?" Raz called out. "Your husband has returned. And what is that filth you're covered with?"

I cringed as a dozen pairs of eyes fixed on me.

"I thought when you weren't here to greet Olmer that at least you were off making yourself presentable." She made a tut-tut noise with her tongue. "Anyone looking at you would think you were the one who's been on the road for days."

I caught the satisfied smirk on her lips as the onlookers laughed at her teasing.

"Hannah. It's good to see you, wife." Olmer approached me, and I forgot my mother-in-law's treachery.

I bowed my head in greeting. "And you." My words were true. It was good to see him. Despite all of our discord, his presence still caused a quickening of my heartbeat. I noted a few new flecks of silver nestled amid his black curls. He smiled, not with the teasing charm of boyhood, but with a commanding assurance that left me self-conscious. If anything, he'd become more handsome since we met. I swallowed and reminded myself that this was my husband, not a stranger.

"Come upstairs, help me wash," he said, hand extended in invitation.

"Don't be long. We have so much to discuss." Raziela took

hold of his forearm to balance on tiptoe and kiss his cheek before I could reach him.

I turned on my heel and climbed the stairs to keep from strangling her. But as I entered our room, I stopped short, amazed at the transformation it had undergone.

Olmer passed me and walked to the side table where a copper basin and water jug sat. He put the basin on the floor before glancing back over his shoulder. "You know, most wives would insist on doing this for their husbands."

"Oh. I'm sorry. Please sit. It's just . . . the room looks so different now."

He stopped untying the leather strap of his sandal and raised an eyebrow. "It looks the same to me."

"No, there were other cots in here this morning, and the children's belongings."

"What children?" He looked at me like I was addled.

I hesitated, loathe to complain so soon after his return. I poured water into the basin, then knelt to untie his other sandal. "Your mother moved Keturah's younger daughters into our room while you were away," I said, trying for nonchalance but unable to hide the irritation I felt. I peeked at him to gauge his reaction.

He dipped his feet into the bowl, mindless of the water sloshing over the sides, and shrugged.

"She didn't even consult me about the decision," I explained.

"I wish you'd stop being so critical of her. They're your nieces, after all. Besides, I'm sure she thought you'd enjoy some company during your lonely nights without me." He leered and wiggled his eyebrows.

I attempted a smile, but it hurt that he didn't understand. This latest insult, moving another woman's children into the room intended for my own, violated the only sanctuary I had in the house. I had protested, of course. But Raz had employed the one response she knew would silence me: "It's not as if you have children of your own who need the space." How could I have argued against such a truth?

"Hannah. Are you trying to drown my feet?" Olmer asked.

"No, of course not." I released my grip on his ankles and began drying his feet with my hem. How silly of me to be thinking about such things when I finally had my husband home again. I smiled up at him, but now he was the one who appeared serious. "Your trip was prosperous, wasn't it?"

"Yes, but I'm afraid not all of the news I bring home is good." He looked at me with the faintest hint of annoyance, which I could not understand. I waited for him to elaborate, but he shook his head. "There's time for discussion later. I would have some peace between us first."

I averted my eyes, overcome with shyness at the intensity of his gaze. I picked at some straw clinging to my sleeve.

"Come here," he said softly.

Before I could take a step, the door swung open with a crash. "Olmer, what's keeping you?" Raz demanded. "There are already five councilmen downstairs waiting to hear the whole story from you."

"Councilmen? How did they get here so fast?" I asked loudly, irritated by the interruption.

"Fast?" Raziela looked thoughtful. "I'm sure it took them the same amount of time it always does to travel here. Wait. Didn't I tell you? When word arrived last week to expect Olmer's return today, I sent a messenger inviting the council to join us for a celebration." She snickered. "Obviously I didn't or you'd have dressed for the occasion."

I clenched fistfuls of fabric at my sides and glared at her.

Olmer dropped his head in his hand on the pretense of

smoothing his hair back, but I detected his amusement. It was infuriating how he indulged her.

Raz rushed forward and practically dragged Olmer out the door. "Come on. Everyone is waiting for you. You'll have to start from the beginning and tell us the news."

"What news?" I called after them.

Raziela stuck her head back around the doorframe. "Herod got his divorce."

CHAPTER 25

A great number of the city's administrators had joined our tenants and servants to welcome Olmer home—some out of true admiration, others no doubt to benefit from a sumptuous meal. Now a dozen carousers lingered at the table, showing every intention of remaining until the morning watch.

Myrinne entered the salon carrying yet another jug of wine to add to the copious containers already scattered around the room. She offered an apologetic smile when I approached her.

"Do we have any more food left to serve?" I asked.

"I'll see what's happening in the kitchen. Why don't you carry this to our guests."

"Guests? More like scavengers."

As I turned around, I was embarrassed to hear Olmer finishing a lewd story about his recent travels to Corinth. "I wish our temple had worshippers as fervent and devoted as the 'Corinthian girls' at Aphrodite's temple."

From the hoots and whistles, I surmised that these "adorers" must be nothing more than prostitutes.

I marched up to the table across from Olmer. He had the decency to avert his eyes but continued to smile. Hakon, reclining, looked back over his shoulder to the councilman behind him and winked. The man loudly whispered a Greek phrase I didn't understand, but the others must have. They burst out laughing. Olmer shook his head to discourage them, even as he wiped tears from his eyes.

I banged the jug down on the table with enough force to shake their cups, and the chuckles subsided. But the second I stormed out of the hall, laughter erupted behind me.

It was nearly dawn before Olmer staggered into our room. He held the lamp over the bed and I glared at him, fuming inside. "You're still awake."

"Why did you let them mock me?"

Olmer pounded his chest and belched. "We were just enjoying ourselves. Why do you always assume everything is about you?"

I gasped, affronted, and jumped out of bed.

He just laughed. "Don't be angry, Hannah. To me, everything is about you." He set the lamp down. "Help me undress."

I kept my arms crossed and my expression fierce.

He dropped his head like a chastened dog then pulled a shiny item from the pouch tied to his belt.

And just like that my defenses were breached. "What's that? What do you have there?"

"Hmm? Oh, this?" He displayed a silver ring set with a garnet stone. "I wanted to give my lovely bride a gift, but if you're too angry to accept it . . ." He shrugged.

I reached forward, but he closed his fist around the ring, crossed the room, and thrust his hand out the square window. "I guess I'll just toss it away."

"Olmer. Don't play. Let me see it."

"Oh, you *do* want it?" he asked with mock surprise. He leaned farther out the window.

"Careful." I grabbed his tunic to pull him back and couldn't help but smile at his antics. "You're just drunk enough to drop it by mistake. Here, give it to me."

I reached up to close my fingers over his fist, and he turned around, putting me dangerously close to his lips. Soon any protests I had were silenced.

***

With just the immediate family gathered for the afternoon meal, Olmer spoke freely of his latest travels. I discreetly admired my husband. It was good to have him home. This time would be different, I was sure of it.

"Tension's growing at the border," he said. "Shipments are being held up. Some merchants were forced to abandon their wares altogether. I had to pay the Nabataeans three times the regular tariff to bring the spices into Judea. Soon we'll be fortunate to get home with just the clothes on our backs."

"Three times the usual tariff? Hmpf," my father-in-law grumbled. He took a slurp from his bowl, and his bulbous nose looked like an encroaching mud bank threatening to slide over his upper lip and drop into the stew below. Gal had deep-set dark eyes that made it difficult to distinguish his emotions, but I sensed his displeasure.

"It's not the first report I've heard, and I fear it won't be the last. We could lose access to the eastern land routes altogether." My father-in-law looked up from his now empty bowl and addressed his sons. "I have plans for more storehouses. Secure as much balsam and spices as possible. I want to have sufficient supply on hand if the goodwill of the Nabataeans dries up . . . especially if it comes to war with our neighbors."

I supposed Gal would be a formidable adversary in battle, commanding forces and calculating expendable lives for the greater good—or in his case, greater profits.

Olmer nodded.

Furrows of worry crossed Raziela's brow.

"Do you think it will come to war?" I asked.

Not surprisingly, my father-in-law ignored me. I could count on one hand the number of times he'd spoken directly to me.

We sat in silence, and I contemplated the implications of this news. Olmer frequently traveled with goods from the western ports of Caesarea and Akko on the Great Sea, south into Gaza and then east into Nabataea. From there, his route crossed the desert to the south of the Parthian territories until he arrived at port cities to the east where vessels brought in dried plants, animal skins, and spices from the kingdoms of India. If war began with Nabataea, the only way to the eastern ports would be by ship around the entire peninsula of Arabia. That would mean more expense and longer time away from home.

Olmer lowered his cup. "I spent the entire trip placating Nabataean merchants who think it's their duty to defend Princess Phasaelis's honor. I tried to assure them our ties will withstand Herod's divorce, but there's increasing hostility toward Antipas."

"It's always a woman's fault," Hakon said. "Since the beginning of time, women have caused men nothing but trouble."

Raz pursed her lips as her oldest son enlightened us all with his wisdom. It seemed none of his opinions, however ignorant, went unspoken.

Olmer continued, "I'm afraid the Nabataeans aren't the only ones causing trouble at the border in Perea. Yochanon, the one they call the Immerser, has been beating the hornet's nest with his public criticism of Herod's divorce. Every time rational minds prevail, this lunatic appears in the markets and synagogues with his followers, shouting about the whole sordid affair and decrying his message of repentance. He's inflaming the Nabateans and the Jews."

I feigned great interest in eating my lentils and remained silent. Every time Yochanon's name was mentioned, I felt somehow responsible for his actions. And his name came up more and more of late, as increasing numbers of men heeded his call to repent and be washed clean of past wrongs. Emmi had been close to Yochanon's mother before I was born, but truthfully, I couldn't remember meeting Yochanon more than a handful of times as a child. It was hard to reconcile the serious, reserved boy from my youth with the stories of this public figure.

Gal shook his head and muttered, "The shemittah year can't end soon enough for my liking. People have too much time to traipse about the hills listening to rabble-rousers."

I gasped. I'd never heard anyone wish it weren't a Sabbath year. It went against Elohim's very laws governing the times and cycles of the earth. Besides, I hardly considered Yochanon a rabble-rouser.

"What a loathsome man, so full of himself." Raziela banged her cup on the table for emphasis. "Does he think he's a great prophet to pour out such criticism? Why doesn't he go to the Sanhedrin with his complaints? If he's the Lord's mouthpiece, why hide in the desert like a wild beast?"

I gave Olmer a desperate glance hoping he'd change the subject and was surprised to see him scowling at me.

"Your relative's actions reflect poorly on us," he said. "He could cause us serious problems, Hannah."

"Everyone has the odd relative who causes embarrassment." I dismissed him with a wave of my spoon. "What about your grandfather's sister who shouts out vulgarities at inopportune times? No one would hold you accountable for her behavior."

Gal's cheek twitched. Tabitha clutched her hand to her chest. I had forgotten I wasn't supposed to know about that.

"I'm afraid it's more serious than an aunt's fits," Raz barked gruffly. "An eccentric old woman doesn't pose a threat to Herod."

Keturah scoffed at this. "A pious recluse is no threat to Antipas. Yochanon's rumored to eat bugs to survive." She smirked. "He can't even afford meat for his supper."

My father-in-law responded to Keturah's remark by addressing Hakon with a disapproving frown. "Bugs or not, he's gaining support. It doesn't matter if Yochanon intends to actually lead a revolt. Just the possibility may provoke royal paranoia. When have any of King Herod's sons waited for proof of guilt before condemning and meting out punishment? Olmer's right, this is worrisome."

"Few people even know Yochanon is related to me," I said. "No one will associate his actions with us."

Olmer ran his hand through his hair before cradling the top of his head in his hand. I recognized this gesture—something else bothered him.

"What is it, Olmer?" his mother asked.

He dropped his hand and his eyes pleaded with me, for what I didn't know. Understanding? Forgiveness? He picked up his cup and gulped down some wine before speaking. "When I was in Perea, I learned that Hannah's brother had arrived there before me." He spat out the word brother scornfully, so I knew without asking which brother he meant. Only one evoked such antipathy from my husband—Yeshua.

"What business did he have in Perea?" Gal asked.

"Yeshua's been baptized by Yochanon. Apparently, he's become a follower of Yochanon's extreme sect."

I didn't know if it was anxiety or hysteria, but I had to stifle a laugh. Olmer must have gotten the story all wrong. It was hard to conceive of any sect being more extreme than Yeshua in observing the laws of Torah and calling for repentance. Then I had a more sobering thought.

"You didn't confront Yeshua, did you?" I asked. Every time Olmer and Yeshua were in a room together, there was verbal sparring that ended with my husband's pride wounded. I couldn't help but think Yeshua enjoyed outwitting my spouse.

Olmer shook his head. "I looked for him, but he was gone. He couldn't have been more than a day or two ahead of me. But no one had seen or heard from him in any of the towns I passed. It's like he just disappeared somewhere in the wilderness."

Gal snorted. "More likely, he regrets meeting with Yochanon and wants to keep out of sight for a while."

I had no idea where my brother could be, but I knew he wasn't hiding. I didn't think Yeshua regretted anything in his life, nor did he care what people thought about him. But I kept this to myself.

"This is a bad time for your family to cause problems," Olmer said.

I bowed my head not out of remorse, but disappointment. Why didn't Olmer share these things with me in private instead of chastising me in front of Raz and the others?

"Now we have to secure new suppliers in case this whole thing goes poorly with the Nabataeans," he explained. "My family has worked very hard to get where we are. We can't afford even a whiff of impropriety associated with our name."

"What did I say, women are always causing problems," Hakon mumbled between bites of food.

I ignored him. But Olmer's not-so-subtle way of delineating my family from his disturbed me. Our families were joined together in covenant now, were they not? "Even if my brother did go to Yochanon as a sign of repentance—"

"Hannah, are you saying that Olmer fabricated some story?" Raziela asked with exaggerated alarm. "Olmer, do you hear this? Your wife doubts your word."

My mouth opened in outrage, and I looked around the table for support. Keturah covered her mouth, but not before I heard her snicker. Tabitha fiddled with a string on her dress. I suspected she was sympathetic to my plight but equally relieved not to be Raz's target this time. I had no allies here.

Squaring my shoulders, I tried to keep my voice from wavering. "I would never doubt Olmer's word. All I meant is there's no harm done by Yeshua immersing himself as a sign of repentance. Really, it's not much different than any other mikveh cleansing. And from what I've heard, Yeshua isn't alone. Yochanon has immersed hundreds, if not thousands of men."

"That's the problem," Olmer said. "If Yochanon were only a teacher in a small village, perhaps he'd go unnoticed by the government. But it appears he won't be satisfied until all of Judea capitulates to his demands. We need to find out what your brother's intentions are in joining with him. I fear nothing good can come of the relationship."

Raz nodded. "And nothing good will come of us being associated with him either." She stared pointedly at me. "We must distant ourselves from any connection to the man."

***

I wasn't accustomed to sharing the bed with my husband's bulk. My back ached from the contorted position I lay in but repositioning my weight meant risking awakening Olmer. So I listened to his heavy breathing and mulled over our earlier conversation.

"What does your brother hope to gain by following Yochanon?" Olmer had asked me once we were alone.

Guilt had frozen my tongue. I had wanted to tell him that Yeshua was raised to believe he was different. I had wanted to tell him that Yeshua's need for righteousness stemmed from his very essence, not political motivation or criticism of my in-laws. But the time for having such conversations with Olmer had long passed, so I had only shrugged like a simpleton in response.

The truth was I had never found the right opportunity to tell Olmer about Emmi's angelic visitation or Abba's dreams or the odd circumstances surrounding Yeshua's conception and birth. At first, I had feared Olmer would call off the engagement if I told such tales. Later I couldn't risk my fragile standing with my in-laws. As the years had passed, the facts faded into the realm of childhood fantasies, and I had naively thought I'd escaped my brother and his peculiar ways.

But it seemed it wasn't enough for Yeshua to eclipse me in childhood. Now he intruded on my marriage as well.

I wouldn't permit him to destroy what chance of happiness I had left.

CHAPTER 26

Late Fall of the Year 3788 (CE 27)

I peered at the door where new arrivals were greeted. On this third day of the wedding celebration, guests still trickled in from the farthest destinations, having just received news of the private family celebration held two days ago.

Aunt Lilit's grandson had grown into a handsome bridegroom. Her daughter Rivkah beamed as her husband placed an arm around their son's shoulders, giving him a playful shake. The day was gray, but it didn't seem to dampen the family's mirth. How different from my own wedding where, apart from the summer sun, there had been little warmth at all. I tossed my head to expel these melancholy thoughts. It was time for rejoicing, not remembering.

Raz cackled raucously behind me. I turned to see her fawning over her cousin Theokritos, who was reenacting a scene from some recently attended comedy. The odious man had been staying with us since the Feast of Tabernacles. Hopefully he'd complete his journey home to Miletus following this celebration, the Lord and weather permitting. It wouldn't be a minute too soon for my liking.

Since his arrival, Raziela had been more condescending

than ever, endlessly bemoaning the lack of fine conversation and culture in Sepphoris compared to their beloved Greek city. Theokritos had heartily sympathized with her plight while indulging his insatiable appetite for food and drink. If nothing else here satisfied him, the bounty of our storehouses clearly met his standards.

He repeatedly wiped sweat from his forehead and across his bald head to the folds of fat spilling over his collar as he recited lewd dialogue. I was disgusted that Raz and Hakon rewarded his bawdy performance with hearty laughs. Olmer smiled at the appropriate times, but I knew he was distracted keeping watch for Yeshua.

I scanned the room in case I had missed my brother's entrance. So far, I'd seen only my mother and Yosi. Maybe Yeshua wouldn't come after all, and we could enjoy the wedding in peace.

"Hannah!" Raziela's bellow interrupted my thoughts.

"Yes?"

"Make yourself useful and refill our cups."

"Of course." As I rose to my feet, my heart sank. Yeshua stood in the doorway, extending congratulations to the newlyweds. I sprang for the door, determined to reach my brother before Olmer noticed him. Hopefully I could dissuade him from engaging with Olmer at all.

"There he is," Olmer called from behind me. "Yeshua, come and join us."

I cringed as my brother immediately fixed his eyes on Olmer. Yeshua appraised my husband for a few seconds, his expression inscrutable. Then he addressed the strange entourage behind him—four men I didn't recognize—and walked our way.

A ripple of silence followed in his wake as he glided

through the crowd, conversations momentarily forgotten. He'd lost weight since I had last seen him—maybe he'd adopted Yochanon's austere diet of locusts. But he didn't appear ill. In fact, he exuded a radiance and strength I hadn't seen in him before. His stare unsettled me.

"Welcome Yeshua of Nazareth." Olmer's voice dripped with contempt as my brother sat on a cushion across the table from Theokritos. "This is a treat. Maybe Yeshua will entertain us with his recent adventures."

Theokritos looked intrigued. "Yeshua of Nazareth? The name is familiar to me. Perhaps we recently met in Jerusalem during the festival?"

"Oh, I'm sure you must be thinking of someone else," Raz said. "This is one of my sister-in-law Lilit's cousins. He's no one of import."

I looked at her with annoyance but said nothing to clarify her misleading introduction.

The household steward appeared with a bowl of water and towel to wash Yeshua's feet. Yeshua smiled kindly at the man who couldn't hide a satisfied grin. The steward bobbed repeatedly, backing away from my brother as if from a member of royalty.

I rolled my eyes.

But Theokritos observed this behavior and studied Yeshua with greater interest. "So, 'No One of Import,' are you a fan of the theater?" Theokritos shoveled more bread into his mouth and spewed crumbs while speaking. "I'm growing weary of having to perform entire productions so that my references are understood by this group."

"Yeshua spends more time in the synagogue than the theater," Olmer said. "I'm sure you'll find he's more ignorant of your plays than we are. If it wasn't written at least four hundred years ago, he's not interested."

And so it began.

"The classics." Theokritos reached for his kerchief again and wiped his brow. "I admire them myself. Let's see, who shall we discuss . . . Sophocles? Aristophanes? Ah, I know. Euripides. Who doesn't love a great tragedy?"

Yeshua regarded him calmly. "It's a tragedy that man turns to his own wisdom for enlightenment when the truth stands before him."

Raz glared at Yeshua, no doubt taking this as an affront to her cousin, but Theokritos smiled.

"Ah," he said, pointing a pudgy finger at my brother. "I see from your disapproving look that you must be one of those delightful Pharisees. The type who shuns wisdom found in writings other than our own, fearing contamination from outside thought rather than lauding its benefits. Let me ask you something . . ." Theokritos put down his cup and leaned forward. "Isn't it Adonai himself who created all things, including the human mind? Didn't the Lord give the ability to reason and to create, to experiment and come up with new ideas? One could argue it's a divine mission to inquire and search all available sources to gain understanding and knowledge."

"It is written, 'The fear of the Lord is the beginning of knowledge, but fools despise wisdom and discipline,'"[13] Yeshua replied.

Olmer sat taller in his seat, puffing his chest out.

Theokritos chuckled and raised his eyes as if he addressed a multitude behind us. "But how will we know to fear the Lord unless we know what it is *not* to fear the Lord? Only by expanding our knowledge, studying the writings of the pagan teachers, are we better able to confirm for ourselves what we know to be true. And what man will hear our truth if we judge his ways in ignorance? Without doubt the Lord calls us to study and understand the nations, for only in so doing are we able to fulfill our mandate to be a light for all nations." He concluded with a dramatic outstretching of both arms.

Raziela applauded.

I closed my eyes for a moment and thought longingly of distant lands myself.

Yeshua heaped roast lamb and salted fish onto a plate from the trays in front of him—so he was not following an insect diet, I noted with relief. He held up a piece of fish, turning his hand for all to examine it. "This fish comes from Magdala."

Conversations around us ceased as others watched with fascination.

"It should have rotted before reaching Cana and been tossed away. But it's still good because of one thing. Salt." He popped a morsel into his mouth and took his time chewing while those around him waited with expressions varying from perplexity to annoyance. He addressed two of his companions who'd come up behind him. "You are the salt of the earth. But if the salt loses its saltiness, how can it be made salty again? It's no longer good for anything, except to be thrown out and trampled by men."[14] He turned his gaze on me.

My heart pounded in my chest. Why was he looking at me? I wasn't the one going to pagan theaters and studying Greek scholars.

"Personally, I didn't find the fish to my liking," Hakon muttered.

Raz snapped at me, "Why are you standing there? Didn't I ask you to fetch some wine? Good, here comes the servant."

"I don't like being trampled and pressed in by men either, so I seek escape where it can be found. And I'll say this for the Romans," Theokritos said, changing topics, "they do a fine work of building bath houses. I had a wonderful soak before leaving Sepphoris. Highly recommend it."

One of the men who had entered with my brother maneuvered closer to our table. "You wouldn't catch me in those pagan pools," he said, looking to Yeshua like a pup seeking approval from its master.

Theokritos regarded the man. "The great Rabbi Hillel would certainly disagree with you, sir."

The man's mouth fell open and he looked flummoxed. That wasn't the bone he had hoped to receive.

"That's right," Raziela said. "Hillel was a frequent visitor and admirer of the bath houses." She cleared her throat and with hand upon heart paraphrased the great Rabbi's words. "Aren't the statues in the theater and circus always washed clean by their caretakers? If such care is taken with the works of man, surely it is a holy duty to keep scrupulously clean the handiwork of God."[15] It seemed Theokritos wasn't the only family member with a penchant for the stage.

Olmer had been quiet, but now he pounced on this new topic. "If a man as revered as Hillel indulged in such pleasures, we'd do well to imitate him. Have you had a chance to enjoy the baths, Yeshua?"

I scowled at Olmer. He knew Yeshua didn't have the luxury or desire to while away the hours in Sepphoris' public baths.

Yeshua blinked at my husband. "Which do you think is more important—the cleanliness of the outside of the temple, which is seen by men, or the cleanliness of the inside, which is seen only by the Lord?"

Olmer flushed. From the set of his jaw, an explosion was imminent.

I attempted to steer the conversation to more lighthearted fare. "My brother spoke with Hillel's students at the temple courts in Jerusalem as a boy. Remember, Yeshua? During the Feast of Unleavened Bread? It's a funny story. We nearly left the city without him."

My brother just smiled and refused to take the offered diversion.

"So then, you're a follower of Hillel?" Theokritos asked.

Yeshua sipped his wine, taking his time setting the cup down. "Hillel was correct in admonishing his followers to love their fellow men and leading them toward the Torah."

Olmer looked gleeful, which worried me. "But isn't it true that you disagree with Hillel, that you oppose the prosbul that he and other lawmakers helped to pass?"

"Oh?" Theokritos leaned in closer. "You oppose the law?"

I sighed. Not the prosbul again. The law had been the source of much debate recently. The shemittah year had just ended, when debts between individuals traditionally were forgiven according to the requirements of Torah. But the prosbul had allowed lenders like my father-in-law to transfer loans to the court before the shemittah. Because a debt administered through a public court didn't explicitly fall under the requirements of the Torah, which only addressed private debts, Gal had avoided the need to release borrowers from their obligations. Now Gal could have the loans transferred back to him from the court so he could collect them in the future.

"My understanding is that the prosbul greatly benefits the poor," Theokritos said. "Without it, if a businessman knows a Sabbath year is close, he's not likely to lend any money. No loan to a man in need means no seed purchased, no harvest, unpaid taxes, and homes and lands being seized." Theokritos raised an eyebrow at my brother. "So if you're opposed to the prosbul and helping the poor, you must support people going to debtors' prison."

"I oppose setting aside the unchangeable law of Elohim to satisfy men's desires. The poor would benefit more from men following the Lord's command to ensure mercy instead of loans." Yeshua ripped some bread from the loaf on the table and wiped his plate with it. "Wasn't Hillel's brother Shebna a merchant and businessman?"

"What does that have to do with anything?" Raz asked suspiciously.

"I wonder, of those who favored creating this law, how many were lenders and how many were borrowers." Yeshua said.

Olmer slammed down his cup. "I'm sure the Sanhedrin didn't have their own families' interests in mind when they passed the prosbul."

Yeshua glanced at Olmer. "And I'm sure they didn't have the Lord's interest in mind." He chewed the last piece of meat, then pushed the plate away. "It is written, 'The rich rule over the poor, and the borrower is slave to the lender.'"[16]

Olmer jumped to his feet, arms clutched to his side, and began shouting. "The prosbul was passed for the greater good of society! It doesn't just help the poor. Would you deprive creditors their right to be repaid?"

The whole crowd gawked at us now. I was mortified. This was exactly what I had hoped to avoid. "Olmer, *please*," I whispered. "Keep your voice down."

Yeshua remained unperturbed. "The toll collectors have their wages taken from them each Sabbath day when the roads are void of travelers. Do you propose, therefore, that we stop observing Shabbat?"

"Of course not," Olmer said.

"So you believe man is worthy of deciding which commandments to observe and which to discard? Do you think that man's clever circumvention of the law will hold up in the courts of heaven against Adonai's wisdom?"

"That's not what I am saying. Of course I honor the Torah. But much has changed since the time the law was written. Society benefits from wise men codifying their interpretation of the law. That way we preserve its intent but adapt it to be practical, to apply to the present day. Otherwise, our economy will falter. And if we become obsolete, no one will benefit from the Torah."

A fleeting look of sad resignation flitted across Yeshua's face. "It is written, 'How can you say, "We are wise; Adonai's Torah is with us," when in fact the lying pen of the scribes has turned it into falsehood?'[17] You seek to change the law so that you may boast of keeping it, but your hearts are far from the Lord. Is the Creator of the universe unable to return to you double for the amount lost by forgiving a loan?" He locked eyes with each person at the table in turn, now quite serious. "You trust in your own cleverness more than you trust in the goodness of the Lord. Your hearts have become proud, and you have forgotten that it is Adonai who provides and gave you the ability to make the wealth you so covet." He pushed himself up from the floor and faced his two companions. "I believe our friends are waiting for us."

With that, he was gone. Gone like an autumn gale that left piles of debris in its wake. And once again, I was left to pick up the mess.

"He's a strange character but most intriguing," Theokritos said. "So if he's not a follower of Hillel, I'm guessing he must be conservative . . . maybe a follower of Shammai?"

"Please excuse me," I mumbled and followed my brother.

CHAPTER 27

"Yeshua." I wove through the well-wishers outside the house, trying to catch up with him.

He spun around and smiled as if it were the first time he'd greeted me this evening. His quick dismissal of the argument momentarily threw me off, but I was determined.

Crossing my arms, I pelted him with angry questions. "What was that about? Who do you think you are to say such things?"

"Hannah, you should know by now." He paused and searched my eyes expectantly. "I am who I am."

I let out an unladylike sound and threw my hands up. "I don't understand you. Why is it you're so kind to complete strangers,"—I jerked my head toward the four men who accompanied him and were awkwardly pretending to not hear us—"but so rude to my in-laws? All you do is belittle them. Not everyone can recite Torah like you, but that doesn't mean they're bad people. Don't you care about their feelings? Do you know how fortunate we are to be connected to such prominent people? They could send you a lot of work. Don't you care about your business, about your future?"

He studied me before answering. "Why do you fear man more than the Lord?" he asked gently.

"Why do *you* speak harshly to men when you've hardly taken the time to know them?"

"I say only those things Abba tells me to say."

I huffed. "Don't you dare bring Abba into this—even in jest." But I realized from his expression he spoke in earnest. And he hadn't referred to my Abba. Distraught, I waggled my head at him. "I don't understand you." I turned on my heel and walked away.

I wanted to keep walking forever and put as much distance between us as possible, but footsteps followed me. I swung around, ready to rebuff any of Yeshua's conciliatory efforts, but instead saw my sister.

"Hannah, we've been looking for you. Come see how your nephews have grown. They're enormous." Shlomit hurried toward me, still as slight and bubbly as a child.

I didn't respond but looked beyond her to where Yeshua stood.

Her smile faltered and she smoothed a lock of hair off my forehead, tucking it back under my headdress. "You look flushed. Are you unwell?"

I dipped my head toward my shoulder to shake off her hand. "I'm fine."

She examined me, not the least bit offended by my churlish tone of voice. Then her gaze followed the direction of mine and saw Yeshua. "Family can be difficult sometimes," she said with kindness in her eyes. "I remember some of the early days of my marriage to Uri. The hazzan respects our family and loves his grandson enough not to argue. But some of Uri's other relatives made it clear they don't accept the truth about Yeshua."

"The truth?" I snorted.

She tilted her head in annoyance.

But I lacked the energy for another argument. "Who are those men with Yeshua?" They appeared transfixed by his words. When he turned to enter the house, they followed like baby chicks, a behavior endearing in birds but unbecoming for grown men.

"Oh. Two sets of brothers from Capernaum. They're fishermen."

"Fishermen?" Well that explained their drab clothes. Was that why my brother was talking about fish earlier?

"Yeshua is teaching them."

"About what? Carpentry?"

She grinned and shook her head. "No, no. Yeshua's given all his tools to Shim'on and Yosef."

"What? How's he planning on earning a living?"

A gust of wind billowed her tunic like a sail and she hugged herself. "Oooh, are you cold? It's getting chilly. Come sit by the fire with the children and we'll catch up."

I had nowhere better to go, so I followed her. The sky was at that awkward stage of dusk when the sun could not be seen, but a remnant of light lingered, not yet ready to give up on the past day. Amid the women gathered around the fire, I noticed Yosi's wife, Ayelet. My sister-in-law greeted me with a wave from under a pile of small children, all grabbing at her and chatting at once.

"Careful," Tabitha called out. Her youngest son was apparently making a game of roasting leaves on the end of a stick and stood perilously close to the flames. Keturah's two eldest girls sat a little way off from the women. I could tell from their whispering and pointing that they probably gossiped about the other guests. Truly, they were the fruit of their mother's womb.

The comfort of such a normal domestic scene eased my taut

mood. Soon I couldn't resist making silly faces at my youngest nephew, Shlomit's boy. He cooed in response, unbothered by the drool spilling down his chin. Shlomit shared the village happenings of the past months—who was betrothed, who was with child, who had died. I let the words wash over me while I nuzzled my nephew's neck and admired his tiny fingernails.

"Soon, Elan will be the only man of an age to marry who isn't spoken for," Shlomit said.

My head turned sharply of its own accord. I pretended to have an itch to hide my reaction to Elan's name. But Shlomit knew me too well.

"I don't think Elan will ever give his heart away again," she added softly.

"Elan? Who's that?" Tabitha asked. She looked back and forth between Shlomit and me. "Who holds his heart? That sounds like a good story. Oh. Isn't he the shepherd who worked for your family when I first met you, Hannah?"

Shlomit looked at me sharply. I flushed with embarrassment to have been caught having described him this way to Tabitha.

"Um, yes," I stammered. "But actually he's been like a part of the family ever since Yeshua found him."

"Found him? Like baby Moshe in a basket?" Tabitha smiled at the other women.

"Not quite as exciting as that. Though it was remarkable from what I hear," Shlomit said. "It all happened before I was born. Hannah was there. She tells the story better."

Tabitha's son ran back toward her, and she grabbed the stick from his hand before he could impale someone. "Hannah, why didn't you mention this before? Tell us the story." She spiked more leaves onto the end of the stick and handed it back to her boy, adding, "Walk with that. Don't run."

I looked around at the expectant faces of the women and stopped on Shlomit's. She nodded encouragement. After a deep breath, I began the story.

CHAPTER 28

"Growing up, we joked that Elan was one of Yeshua's many strays. My brother was always finding some mangy critter that needed his care. I think the only time my parents objected was when he brought home a baby fox, but that was only out of consideration for the chickens' comfort."

Appreciative murmurings came from the women around me who no doubt had experienced their own children bringing home snails, frogs and other unsavory creatures.

"Abba told us Elan's father, Heletz, was a shepherd. He appeared in Nazareth from the mountains to the north one day around the time of year the peaches and pears ripen. Heletz rarely came into the village. When he did, he muttered a steady stream of babble as he went about his business. I guess sheep aren't concerned with what a shepherd says as long as they hear his voice. But his mutterings didn't do much to help his reputation. Rumors were the man was fond of wine."

"Hannah," Shlomit scolded.

I shrugged her off. "Coarser folk even suggested he stole the herd and was on the run. But Abba said he probably led a nomad's life because his family couldn't spare the extra ten acres required for a flock of fifty or sixty animals to graze. Anyway, at least Elan's mother Genna was well received when she came into town to sell wool in exchange for barley.

"I'm told Elan inherited Genna's genial disposition as well as her freckles. Emmi immediately took to her, probably because both women were with child at the time. She'd sneak extra food into Genna's bags and invite her to linger by the hearth as the days grew shorter and the rains began. Emmi insisted that Genna should stay in our home when her time drew near. Genna thanked Emmi with an awkward hug across their two round bellies, and the women shared a laugh before Genna picked up her bundles and bade farewell. She headed back to her son and husband in the hills. Then tragedy struck."

I paused there just as Abba used to when he had told the story. I had everyone's attention now.

"My parents awoke to Heletz's frantic pounding at our door near dawn. After the evening meal, Genna had been struck with terrible back and belly pain but without the normal interruptions of labor pains. At first, the couple thought this delivery was just going to be different from Elan's birthing. Then Heletz felt the sticky dampness of her shift and watched in horror as dark blood soaked the bedding beneath her.

"Her face was so pale and contorted with anguish, Heletz couldn't bear to leave her alone. But he didn't know what to do for bleeding before a babe had even come. So he stoked the fire and put a waterskin within her reach then sprinted, desperate and stumbling, over the rocky path to the village in search of help. It only took a few minutes for Abba to rouse some of our neighbors, but by the time they neared Heletz's camp, it was quiet. Too quiet."

Sympathetic moans and a few gasps escaped from the women, and I awkwardly averted my eyes. Of those gathered, I alone hadn't experienced labor firsthand or the fear it undoubtedly brought.

Shlomit cleared her throat, and I continued.

"Heletz ran ahead of the others, crying out Genna's name. When Abba reached the fire he heard moaning, but it came from Heletz. The poor soul clutched the lifeless bodies of Genna and her unborn child. It took some persuading for him to release her so they could set about the task of washing the body. Abba headed back to the village to organize a proper burial procession. It was several hours before anyone even thought of the missing toddler, Elan. They found him huddled amid the flock."

"Is that when Elan came to live with you?" Tabitha asked, her voice grave.

I shook my head. "No. In the month after Genna's death, Heletz came to the village only once to trade wool for skins of wine. Elan was thinner and dirtier than a little boy should ever be. When Emmi saw how Elan's cut and swollen toes hanged over the soles of his sandals, she took the pair off my brother Ya'akov's feet and tied them onto Elan's so quickly the leather didn't cool. But my parents couldn't convince Heletz to let them care for the boy.

"Another week went by and a storm brought a biting wind and pelting, freezing rain. A rumble of thunder wakened Emmi in the middle of the night. She glanced around the room to ensure all were still sleeping soundly and realized one dark curly-haired head was missing—Yeshua was gone.

"She jostled Abba awake to search for him. To hear Abba tell the tale, at the exact moment he opened the door, a flash of lightning illuminated two figures standing in the clearing in front of our home." I smiled. "He might have added that part for dramatic enhancement."

Shlomit nodded. "Abba was the best storyteller I've heard to this day."

"However it happened," I said, "Yeshua stood there holding Elan by the hand, the pair of them mud-splattered and soaked through. My parents later ascertained that Heletz slipped and fell, dying from a blow to the head. Most people thought he was in a drunken stupor when it happened."

Shlomit scowled at me again.

"The poor man probably drank to forget his loss," Tabitha said. "Or to forget the guilt of leaving Genna in her last moments. Though what could he have done to save her? It's terrible."

"I don't know." I shrugged, shaking my head. "And I don't know what prompted Yeshua to go out in such a storm or how he came to find the child. It's amazing. I was only three years old at the time. But I vividly remember waking up that morning and seeing Elan playing with Yeshua. Only later, when Emmi gave birth to my real brother, could I be convinced Elan hadn't just emerged fully grown from my mother's womb that night." Smiling, I waited for the laughter to subside. "My parents took him in with no more thought than what they'd have given to Yeshua bringing home another wounded creature."

"This Elan is one of Yeshua's strays," Tabitha said.

The grin on my face faltered. Considering the fishermen who followed Yeshua around tonight, it seemed my brother's habit of collecting misfits continued. I hoped these latest strays quickly returned to the wild before more joined them.

"So Elan's been like a brother to you."

I appreciated the unspoken question behind Tabitha's words and nodded my assurance. "Yes, nothing more."

Tabitha looked satisfied, but I didn't dare meet Shlomit's eyes.

CHAPTER 29

Well past midnight, the musicians animated the festivities with a lively tune. More women joined us by the fire, clapping and smiling as the men danced in elaborate, frenzied rings. I searched for my husband, but my gaze fell instead on Yeshua. He'd always enjoyed dancing, and his smile was infectious as he circled past me now. It was difficult to hold onto my earlier anger.

If only Olmer and my in-laws could get to know this carefree side of him, I was sure they'd get along.

The steward tried to catch Aunt Lilit's attention as she sat conversing with Emmi. Knowing his hair would turn gray if he waited for a pause in her chatter, I tapped my aunt on the shoulder, and the man tipped his head in gratitude as he approached.

He covered his mouth to whisper into her ear, and she twisted violently to look him in the eye. He whispered something else, and alarm crossed her features. When she murmured a curt word, he bowed and made a hasty departure.

"Is anything wrong, dear?" Raziela's inquiry seemed to hold less concern than curiosity.

"What is it, Lilit?" Emmi asked kindly.

Lilit turned from one face to the other, tears welling in

her eyes as she bit her lower lip. "I suppose you'll know soon enough. Everyone will."

"Well, are you going to tell us or not?" Raz asked.

"Rivkah's husband, and of course Uzziah and I have done our part, rationing the wine all year. We thought we were ready. But there wasn't a vintage last year of course since it was a shemittah, and we weren't expecting so many to come . . . and then the wine in one amphora was found to have turned and we had to discard it, so now . . ."

We leaned closer, straining to understand her flustered ramblings.

She blurted out, "They're nearly finished pouring from the last wine jar. We'll be disgraced. *Ruined.*" She sobbed while the rest of us sat in shocked silence. For once she didn't exaggerate. This *was* disastrous news.

"Now Lilit, there's no need for tears." Raz spread her fingers to better appreciate the light glistening off the jewels in her rings—a habit of hers that annoyed me to no end. "I'm sure everyone will understand why the party will end early . . . *days* ahead of time."

The glow in her eyes and the smugness of her tone indicated Raz would be all too happy to help everyone understand. Firsthand experience had taught me that for Raz, one woman's tragedy was another woman's entertainment.

Emmi studied Raz. I could tell she'd interpreted the woman's true motive as well. "Lilit, I'm sure we can think of something. We could send our men back to Nazareth to bring the wine skins we have at our home. We could borrow some from our neighbors as well. We'll just tell all of our immediate family not to drink anything until the men return."

Raziela snorted. "It will take hours to make the trip there, load a cart, and return in the dark. Besides which, you're hardly capable of satiating a crowd this size from your meager stores."

My eyes widened in outrage on my mother's behalf. Raz was right, of course, but her rudeness was shocking. Especially when we all knew she was the one person who was in a position to help, and she hadn't made the offer.

Emmi slapped her hands down on the ground on either side of her, then jumped to her feet.

"What is it? Where are you going?" I asked.

"Lilit, don't worry," she said. "Just go and gather the servants, but keep this to yourself. Everything's going to be fine." She marched directly into the circling dancers and captured Yeshua's sleeve, pulling him from the human chain, which flailed a moment before the men linked arms again, sealing up the gap.

Lilit appeared befuddled but followed Emmi's instructions. Raz looked suspicious. I just shrugged my shoulders.

Emmi gesticulated wildly, perhaps trying to convince him to organize a caravan back to Nazareth despite the late hour. Then she and Yeshua followed the steward behind the house with the four fishermen in tow. I frowned at the sundry procession. Yeshua *should* do something to help after inviting so many guests of his own.

Raziela wasted no time following Lilit. "Please excuse me while I address some necessities."

I was certain it wasn't her bladder she needed to release, but her tongue. She had never forgiven Lilit for her role in bringing me into the family. Denouncing her in such a public forum might even the score in Raz's mind. As the men wove and spun before me, I intermittently spotted the groom laughing as he danced, oblivious to the impending social disaster. I prayed his new in-laws were kinder than mine.

Skirting the dancers, I made my way through the house to find Olmer. He was where I'd left him hours ago, lounging on a pile of cushions next to Theokritos. Several women had gathered around the table now, gazing appreciatively at Hakon and, to my annoyance, Olmer.

"Husband," I called with a challenging stare for the brazen, bare-headed female seated closest to Olmer.

Olmer's eyes lazily drifted away from his companion's face and rested on me.

I pushed aside my annoyance at this lackluster greeting. "Did Aunt Lilit speak with you about going to Nazareth?"

"What crime have I committed that anyone would speak to me about going to Nazareth?" he asked.

This earned a chuckle from Hakon and smug giggles from the women.

Olmer smiled. "Besides, why would I go anywhere when everything I desire is right here?" He swept his hand in a broad gesture to take in the celebration and had to halt himself from toppling over.

If all the men were this tipsy, no wonder the wine was dwindling.

I stepped closer so I didn't have to shout my words. "Someone has to make the trip. There's no more wine," I hissed into his ear.

He grabbed his belly and threw his head back, roaring with laughter.

Anger flushed my cheeks. "Did you hear what I said?"

He grinned from ear to ear. "No more wine? Hannah, are you blind? The steward just brought out a new batch. And you have to try it. I can't place its origins. Maybe Cyprus." He pounded his chest, emitting a hearty belch. "It's certainly finer than the swill from Gamla they've served up until now."

"No, no. It's definitely not from Cyprus." Theokritos held his cup under his chin and stared into its depths. "The Romans add lead to wines to make them sweet, but this is even sweeter and more delightful than any vintage I've ever had." He frowned in puzzlement. "Though I don't understand why they'd store it in stone water jars." With a shrug, he lifted his cup in salute to me before resuming the conversation with the women.

My mind whirled. They must have been drunk. How could there be a new batch of wine? Why wouldn't the steward know what supplies were on hand? The man should be fired if he was that incompetent.

That very moment the steward pranced past me, refilling cups with such glee that I began to wonder if the man was, perhaps, insane.

I set off to find my aunt to curtail any further lunacy from the man.

Raz intercepted my path, staring at me with hostility. "Something is strange here."

"I know. I was just going to tell Aunt Lilit. The steward's pouring wine, and it doesn't even look like he mixed it with water. At this rate, the party will be over within the next hour."

I tried to continue on my way, but she clutched my arm, her nails digging painfully into my flesh and her eyes full of accusation. "There's enough wine for this celebration to continue for weeks." She flung my arm away with a look of disgust and made her way toward her sons.

As I digested this news, Shlomit bounded toward me. She wore the same maniacal grin as the steward, and, I now realized, the majority of those present in the room. Had everyone gone mad?

"Hannah!" She waved at me. "There's been a miracle."

CHAPTER 30

"Yeshua's done a miracle. He turned water into *wine*." Shlomit abandoned all decorum and actually jumped up and down.

"What are you doing?" I put a restraining hand on her shoulder.

"I saw the servants draw water from the well—*water*—and fill pots, but when Yeshua told them to pour it out, it was wine."

"What? That's not possible." Scoffing at the idea, I shook my head. "There must have been wine left in the bottom of the pots that mixed with the water and turned it red."

Shlomit squealed with delight. "No, they were stone water pots, for ceremonial cleaning. There was no wine, no anything, in them until the servants filled them with water. But when they poured from the pots, there was wine. It's truly a miracle!"

The hair on my arms lifted and fear gripped my belly.

"Don't be dramatic. That's absurd. How much wine did you drink yourself?"

Rather than dampening her spirits, my question made her laugh harder. "I have to find Uri and tell him the news." She hustled away.

Yeshua couldn't have traveled even one way to Nazareth in the short time since I saw Emmi speak to him. So there must have been wine left here. There was no other explanation. I shoved my way through the guests to exit the house.

Outside an even more bizarre scene greeted me. The household servants freely mingled with the guests and everyone waved their arms and jumped about praising the Lord as if they were in the temple courtyard. In the light of the fire, their faces glowed with ecstasy. Even my usually sedate Uncle Uzziah swung Aunt Lilit around, and she giggled like a young bride herself. In the midst of this uproar, Emmi embraced Yeshua's waist, a look of pure adoration on her upturned face. He shared her smile and then, as if feeling my eyes on him, looked over her head, directly at me.

In that moment, the crowd fell away, and only my brother and I existed in the world. His eyes both challenged me and drew me in. His vision seemed to penetrate to my very core, leaving me strangely exposed. Suddenly, the words my parents spoke in my youth echoed in my head: "Your brother is special."

Could it be true after all? Was it possible? Just as quickly as the questions entered, I pushed them from my mind. Once I would have given credence to the idea, before I discovered believing in Yeshua only led to disappointment. I wouldn't be duped again.

Yeshua frowned slightly, and I looked away first.

"Hannah, what's going on?" Tabitha's query jolted me back to the present. "The servants are saying your brother has powers. Why would they say that? It's not true, is it?" She laughed nervously, but her expression was hungry—for confirmation or dismissal I wasn't sure.

Before I could answer, Raziela approached at a brisk clip.

"Girls, we're leaving."

"Leaving? What? Why?" I asked.

Raz didn't bother answering. As she marched away, she beckoned to Keturah, who fell in beside her with her own daughters reluctantly trailing behind. I had to trot to catch up to my mother-in-law.

"But it's still night."

She whirled to a stop and thrusted a finger at me, nearly poking me in the chest. "You listen to me. Our family won't be taken in by your brother's trickery. Does he think we'd accept this nonsense about a miracle? He planted his own followers in the crowd to stir up the feeble minds of those drunk enough to believe such nonsense." She crossed her arms over her chest. "I have no doubt the servants are in on it too. Maybe they hoped to bring honor to their employers and make this wedding the talk of the season. Well, I for one won't play along with Lilit's or Rivkah's schemes."

She pushed me aside and kept walking. Tabitha and I blinked at each other in astonishment. Dawn wouldn't break for hours. Not only was it dark, but I looked around and realized our men were not coming. Did I stay with my husband or follow Raz? Olmer wouldn't miss my company, and if he did he'd forgive me. But my mother-in-law kept a long record of offenses, so I decided to follow her. Besides, the scene around the fire unsettled me. I welcomed putting distance between Yeshua and me.

"Do you think it's a ruse?" Tabitha whispered.

"I did see Yeshua being friendly with the steward earlier. Maybe Raz is right, and they wanted the celebration to be memorable. It's just like Yeshua to help Aunt Lilit and Rivkah make the wedding a success."

"That does make sense." Tabitha's response held a trace of disappointment.

She seemed willing to put the matter behind her.

We silently navigated the path, our efforts concentrated on finding our footing in the dark. I was glad she didn't question me further, because I already felt guilty for misleading her. Unfortunately, I was not able to mislead myself. Yeshua had never been one for pranks, and as he had proved earlier, he certainly didn't care about improving anyone's social standing. But the alternative was unacceptable. There had to be another explanation.

Shlomit and Emmi were so quick to believe the unbelievable. How I envied their gullible minds. It must be wonderful to think my brother was the answer to our problems, the long-awaited one who would set our people free once and for all. But I couldn't ignore reality. He was just a man—a good man, even a holy man—but not a great king.

Part of me felt bad for doubting my brother, but in my defense, hadn't I waited for a sign from him for years? Was I now to believe that after three decades, he suddenly had the ability to perform miracles? That his first anointed work had come not on a battlefield but at a wedding feast? I snickered. He could have at least changed his friends' attire into something more respectable for the occasion. That would be no less absurd.

Being on the road at this hour felt strange. The only noise came from the crunching of earth beneath our feet or the occasional muffled complaint when someone stubbed a toe. We'd lost sight of the fires from town, and it seemed like we were the only people on earth.

A star streaked across the sky. I looked excitedly at Tabitha, but she focused on the ground in front of us.

As a child, I loved gazing at the stars. Of course, it had been Yeshua who inspired that in me.

Somehow everything always returned to Yeshua.

CHAPTER 31

Two days had passed since the men returned from the wedding in Cana with what seemed like half the party in tow. As yet another night of debauchery ensued, I fumed silently. More revelers crowded into the salon until Iakovos was compelled to set additional tables in the courtyard to accommodate the new arrivals. I'd yet to find an opportunity to question Olmer about what had transpired after I left Cana.

"So we can't convince you to stay?" Raziela asked Theokritos.

"No," he answered, "Soon the rains will set in and the winds are already unfavorable for a sea voyage west. Besides, I'm eager to be back to Miletus, enjoying more . . . cosmopolitan settings."

Good. I for one would not miss him or his self-aggrandizing.

"But how shall I manage after you've gone? With whom in Sepphoris shall I share an intellectual conversation?" Raz lamented.

Her words shocked me. A handful of Gal's fellow council members were among those at the table, but they appeared unfazed by the implied insult.

"I know." Raz snapped her fingers. "Bartal, you must visit us more often through the winter to make up for his absence. Otherwise I may die of boredom."

All eyes turned to the most honored guest, a member of the Jerusalem Sanhedrin. Bartal smiled and reclined with one arm on the table while swirling his cup with the other.

"I'm flattered by your gracious invitation," he said with his grating nasal voice. "But I'm sure there's sufficient entertainment in Galilee to keep one from such a fate. In fact, I heard there was quite a dramatic wedding celebration recently." He glanced around the room for confirmation.

All conversation stopped. For weeks there'd been an unspoken understanding that no one publicly mentioned the scandalous wedding between the tetrarch and Herodias. We'd chosen to pretend they'd always been married—not to legitimize their inappropriate union, but to preserve our own well-being.

"Hmm? No, I don't think so." Raz batted her eyelashes.

"What a shame. I hoped you could tell me about this man who makes wine appear out of the air." Bartal leaned back over his shoulder and grinned at the man behind him. "I'd like to hire him for my own grandson's wedding."

Some relieved laughs sounded around the table.

I grew tense, sure Raz was as perturbed at the mention of Yeshua as I was, but her smile didn't belie it.

"What a gift that would be, would it not? Sadly, I must report the entire thing was just a stunt meant to bolster an otherwise flagging party," she said.

"Ah. But just imagine, creating wine on a whim. What a more pleasant place the world would be." Bartal raised his cup as others voiced their assent.

Theokritos placed the back of his hand to his brow. "Alas, I fear we are doomed to toil in the vineyards. For it is impossible to create something out of nothing. Isn't that what Lucretius said in his teachings?" He paused and scratched his head. "The exact words escape me. Raz, you know the quote I want, from *'Of the Nature of Things'*?"

Recognition lit her features. "Oh, yes. Iakovos, fetch me the work, will you? It's one of the scrolls Olmer purchased last year from the bookseller on the Vicus Sandaliarius in Rome."

Cups were refilled and some excused themselves to find relief outside while the steward departed on this errand. Several of the wives twittered with nervous anticipation. Few Hebrew families in Judea had access to such luxurious and provocative items. I was surprised Raz would share such writings with her guests as I'd rarely heard anything read aloud from one of her precious scrolls even when the family was alone. I felt some excitement myself.

When the scroll was brought forth, Theokritos stood from the table with considerable effort and swayed tipsily before adjusting to being upright. He held the scroll in his left hand and unrolled the right side to scan the columns of text. The gathering grew silent.

"Ah, here we are. As you know, Lucretius has greatly expanded upon the teachings of Epicurus regarding the physical laws of nature. I trust you're all familiar with his writings?"

The averted eyes and blank stares indicated few were as well read as Theokritos, as he no doubt was aware. But no one admitted their ignorance or reluctance to read pagan philosophy.

No wonder our government acquiesced to the might of the Romans. These councilmen weren't even willing to speak truth at a dinner party if it meant jeopardizing their reputation.

"Let's see what the great scholar's theory says about a man from Nazareth claiming to create wine from nothing by divine power," Theokritos said with a smug grin. He cleared his throat and read. "'Nothing from nothing ever yet was born. Fear holds dominion over mortality only because, seeing in land and sky so much the cause whereof no wise they know, men think Divinities are working there. Meantime, when once we know from nothing still nothing can be created, we shall divine more clearly what we seek: those elements from which alone all things created are, and how accomplished by no tools of Gods.'[18] There you have it, my friends. There must be a natural explanation. It's impossible for wine to materialize out of air by divine will. The Nazarene is a fraud."

Theokritos rolled up the scroll and took a small bow.

Raziela's need to appear knowledgeable had clouded her caution. But to my astonishment, no censure came forth. In fact, people raised their bowls and banged on the table appreciatively. Did they deny the power of Elohim, the Creator of the universe? How could Theokritos read such blasphemy aloud, let alone to an audience?

I looked to Bartal. Surely a learned teacher on the highest court of the land would speak out against such nonsense. He must have believed in divine creation. But he busied himself sopping up meat juices with a hunk of bread, looking thoughtful, but showing no signs of contradicting the hostess or her cousin.

"It was not created from air," I whispered.

More than a dozen faces looked at me. I hadn't intended to share my thoughts aloud, but seeing their simpering faces mocking my brother made me bold. Now everyone waited for elaboration. I swallowed and averted my eyes.

"It was not created from air." My voice didn't reflect the same confidence. "The wine, I mean. It was created from water."

There was total silence in the room except for the pounding of my heart, which must have been audible to all.

Then Theokritos let out a whoop and slapped his knee, and

relieved laughter broke out.

"Ah, what a treasure you are. What a clever wife you have, Olmer."

"But I—"

"That's enough, Hannah," Olmer interrupted. "We're all in mortal fear of perishing from merriment as it is. Please don't deliver the fatal blow." He smiled and nudged the man behind him with his elbow.

"As you wish," I replied deferentially, but my insides churned with anger. How could my own husband abandon what he knew was right and true to impress a vile man like Theokritos and this Bartal fellow? Olmer couldn't believe everything in the world depended only on chance and physical laws, could he? Yet why would any of them expend cost and effort to obtain these writings just to refute them?

On important matters of religion, my in-laws had always seemed obedient. Granted, Raziela's prayers were only long and eloquent on holy days when company was present. And on more than one fast day, I'd had to endure Olmer's groans about his sacrifice, only to later discover half-eaten crusts of bread among our linens. I'd excused these small hypocrisies, believing, as Olmer suggested, that not every family was as fanatical as my own in adhering to every letter of Torah.

But this was different. I hadn't approved of Yeshua's harsh criticism of my in-laws, but perhaps his words were well-founded after all.

When the steward passed the scroll back to his wife, I seized the opportunity to flee from the table and follow behind her. I waited until she approached the cellar stairs before calling her name.

"Myrinne."

"Yes mistress?"

"Are all the scrolls full of such teachings?"

She cast a nervous glance around the courtyard. The steward's wife was a slight woman who never drew attention to herself, choosing instead to work behind the scenes to make her husband shine. But I knew that while her mouth remained closed, her eyes and ears were open. Nothing that occurred at the manor escaped her.

"I'm sure I don't know," she said. "As a woman, I find that I don't need to concern myself with such things."

Her tone conveyed a slight reproach, or perhaps a cautionary plea, but I persisted.

"Myrinne, I know you can read Greek. I've seen you helping Iakovos with the record keeping. You've never read the scrolls?"

"There's certainly sufficient work in the here and now to occupy a servant such as myself. I leave the debate of higher matters to those with the luxury of time and wealth needed to contemplate such things." She looked at me meaningfully. "Besides, who would want to know the opinion of an uneducated woman?"

My shoulders slumped in defeat. She was right, of course. What good would it do to expose my in-laws when these days, half the priesthood subscribed to the same secular practices? And who was I to criticize them? Hadn't I also allowed my need for approval to prevail over what I knew to be right? I'd been so busy trying to please Raz, to prove myself worthy of this family, that I hadn't even questioned what it was I wanted to be a part of.

Myrinne touched my arm lightly. "If you're feeling unwell, I'll be happy to make your excuses for you."

Truthfully, the thought of enduring hours more of the present company did make me ill.

"Yes, thank you. I think I'll retire now."

She nodded, visibly reassured that at least for the moment, I'd keep quiet.

CHAPTER 32

I picked at the blanket beneath me in the dark reviewing the earlier conversation in the hall. Of course now I was able to compose wonderful rebuttals and stirring speeches that would never be heard by the guests below.

Light illuminated the hallway outside our room, catching my eye. I hadn't thought to shut the door before, so I jumped up to close it in case one of the guests was exploring. Just as I reached the door, Olmer rounded the corner.

I shrieked.

"My, my. Running eagerly to the door to meet your husband this evening?"

He kissed me, hitting more of my chin than my lips. His breath smelled sour, and I reflexively held my hand up to stop a second attempt.

"No, Olmer. I thought you might be someone else."

"Someone else? Here I think my wife's in a rare amorous mood, but she's expecting someone else?"

"Don't be silly. Here, put down the lamp before you burn yourself."

He set it on the table, and I couldn't help but adjust its position so it was farther from the edge. He raised an eyebrow at me, but how did I explain the compulsion that drove me to keep everything in certain order lately? I stepped toward him and helped pull his tunic up over his head, then hung it on a peg near the door as he collapsed on the bed. He patted the mattress beside him in invitation.

"Olmer?"

"Yes?" He drew the word out with irritation.

"We haven't had a chance to talk. About what happened at the wedding feast."

He rolled his eyes. "Please tell me you're not bringing up your brother. I came upstairs to escape that nonsense."

"I just wondered . . . did anything else happen after we left Cana?"

"Like what? Did Yeshua change a servant into a tree or a rock into a ruby?"

I crossed my arms over my chest. "That's not what I meant."

"Come here."

I sat on the edge of the bed, and he propped himself up on his elbow. He rubbed circles on the small of my back with his free hand. I exhaled and let my shoulders relax.

"Nothing happened," he said. "Your brother raved all night about the kingdom being at hand. Then he and his . . . friends left soon after dawn."

"Kingdom? What kingdom?"

"I told you he wasn't making sense. But then again, none of these dreamers do."

"Dreamers? What do you mean?" I shifted my weight to see his face.

He dropped his hand with a sigh.

"Your Uncle Cleopas, your brother . . . they're no different from every other fanatic who's living in the past. Do you know how many rebellions my family has endured in the last century? Not one had lasting success. Every time someone gets it in his head to fight back, we all end up worse than before. But these Zealots don't care. They're degenerates with no standing and no property to lose. They're happy to endanger the rest of us, the law-abiding ones trying to preserve something for the future."

I looked away. An unbidden picture of my neighbor Tobias entered my mind. The last uprising in Sepphoris had led to his cousin's crucifixion. Later, Tobias himself was accused of aiding the rebels and was executed without trial. The potter may have been careless in managing his money, but he was a kind man with a young family. He had done nothing to deserve such cruel punishment, and he certainly hadn't been a degenerate.

"Holding on to what you know to be true isn't the same as living in the past," I argued.

"Why risk making things worse? The Romans allow us our expression of Torah and respect the role of Jewish law. They don't force us to engage in commerce or pay taxes on Shabbat. The temple will stand forever and so will we, if we accept reality. And the reality is that the Romans are here for now. Instead of provoking them, why not work with what they can give us and use it to our advantage? What harm is there in that?"

I didn't object, but thinking on the Romans' gross injustices, I was not entirely convinced.

He took advantage of my silence to press his point.

"What if we hadn't built aqueducts because we didn't want Greek influence? Would Jerusalem or Caesarea, or Sepphoris for that matter, flourish like they have without adequate water supply? What if we shunned the Romans' paved roads in favor of the rutted, muddy tracts of the past?" He leered at me before continuing in what was probably meant to be a seductive voice, saying, "Easier traveling means your husband returns to your bed sooner."

He sat up to kiss my cheek, but I was in no mood to have my concerns brushed aside to placate his needs.

"I'm not talking about things like aqueducts and roads. It's the more subtle compromises that are dangerous."

Olmer struck the mattress with frustration.

"I'll tell you what's dangerous—commenting on things beyond your understanding instead of focusing on your wifely duties."

I sprang from the bed, and Olmer let his torso fall back onto the mattress.

Perhaps regretting the affront, or more likely trying to steer us back to amorous endeavors, he softened his tone.

"Hannah, maybe I'm not explaining in a way you can understand."

I listened but remained standing, eyeing him warily.

"I've come to value peace and prosperity," he said, propping himself up on his elbows. "You would also if you'd witnessed what I did. I was a child when Judas and his rebels took advantage of King Herod's death to storm the palace. I remember they took to the streets, whooping and hollering like adolescents on a playing field. And yes, for a brief time the Jews took control of coins and weapons, but at what cost? When the Romans subdued the revolt, hundreds were taken away and sold into slavery. And they were the fortunate ones. Sepphoris was put to the torch, and innocent men lost their livelihood, their homes, and their loved ones in a matter of hours."

I looked down. Of course, this was history I knew. Abba and the boys' carpentry skills had helped rebuild the ruined parts of Sepphoris into the impressive modern city that it was today under Herod Antipas's rule.

"You're right, Olmer. I'm sorry." I reached my hands toward him. "I'm just thankful that the Lord protected you and your family, and that your home was spared the flames."

"Don't be naive. The Lord didn't intervene."

I gasped and for a moment my arms remained frozen awkwardly in front of me.

"Of course He did," I whispered.

Olmer sat up and his eyes shone with cold intensity. "The only reason we were spared is because my grandfather had the sense to take action. When he learned General Vanus was on the march, he used his connections to inform on the rebellious Jews and pay the Romans to spare our lands."

Outrage shook me.

"He used bribery and betrayed his *own people*? Why didn't I know this before?"

"They were already doomed by their own actions." He gave a dismissive wave. "If a little money was exchanged to secure our family's lot, what more harm was done? I'm not ashamed that my family has learned to flourish no matter what circumstances we face. Besides, don't you want our children to inherit the best possible position in life?"

"Not at someone else's expense. I'm sure those who rebelled just did what they thought best for their families too. They just wanted a life free from foreign influence. A life lived according to what Adonai requires of us."

Olmer stood. "Save your speeches. You needn't pretend to be righteous with me."

"I'm speaking from my heart. What do we gain in surviving if we lose the only thing worth fighting for? Torah and family are all that matters."

"That's amusing coming from you. I'll keep it in mind when I next travel."

"What does that mean?"

"Don't you enjoy having servants? Don't you enjoy the flavorful food on our table each night—the spices, the salt?" He looked down and grabbed the carved beads dangling from my neck. "And I notice you've taken to wearing the fragrant oils and kohl that I bring home from pagan lands. I won't buy them now that I know you don't care about such superficial things."

I puffed myself up with indignation. "Looking one's best has nothing to do with compromising beliefs."

"Oh, is that right?" He flung my necklace to the side.

I clutched it to my chest, fingering the beads to ensure they hadn't come loose from his rough treatment. His lips curled into a sneer.

"Luxuries come at a price. You can't have it both ways, Hannah. You accuse my family of selling out to the Romans, but you're quite willing to benefit from it." He eyed me a moment with a small pout on his lips. "Do you know that every time you see your family, you act differently toward me afterward? Despite all my efforts to share the riches of the whole world with you . . ." He shook his head. "I thought by now you would've outgrown your past. But in your heart, you've never left the village."

"Don't say such things. My heart is here, with you." I put my hands on his chest. "*You're* my family now, Olmer. I'm sorry if . . . Wait, where are you going?"

He stepped past me and pulled the tunic back over his shoulders.

"Downstairs, where I'm welcome. I'll need more wine to find your company agreeable."

He turned on his heel and left.

CHAPTER 33

I awoke several hours later shivering from the cold. The bed was empty beside me. It was time to get up and begin the day's chores, but I couldn't bring myself to leave the meager heat remaining under the blanket. Shame seeped into my bones, adding to my chill as I recalled the night's events. In the light of dawn, I regretted my behavior.

Why did I quarrel with my husband when all I really wanted was his affection? From now on, I'd keep silent. He deserved my respect, not an earful of opinions. No doubt I'd hear an earful myself from Raziela about speaking out in front of her guests. And if she found out I chased my husband from our bed . . .

Imagining the consequences propelled me to get up and apologize to Olmer before he mentioned it to her.

Downstairs, the only activity came from the hearth, where Myrinne supervised the grinding of flour for the day's bread. Three servants glanced at me and turned away quickly. Myrinne frowned at them before welcoming me.

"Hannah, would you mind bringing in the eggs? The men need a hearty meal before starting their journey to Miletus."

"The men?" I asked. "You mean Theokritos?"

"Yes. Theokritos and Olmer, of course."

Her eyes held sympathy, and my heart dropped. At least Myrinne had been thoughtful enough to convey the news in a way that didn't expose my ignorance to the other servants.

"You'll probably find Olmer at the stables overseeing the loading of provisions. I know they're anxious to be on the road soon."

"Of course." I managed a smile, but inside I was devastated.

She handed me a bowl for the egg collection, and I shuffled numbly through the door.

Why hadn't Olmer shared his plans with me? He must have known last night he intended to leave this morning. I stomped past the entrance to the stables, growing more irritated with each step. I wouldn't go chasing after my husband. Let him come to me and tell me himself that he was traveling.

I walked toward the chicken hutch and almost reached the entrance of the rectangular stone structure when I overheard men in conversation behind the building. It was none of my affair, but my feet ignored my conscience. I inched along the wall to identify who could be speaking in this strange location before it was fully light outside.

"That's going to be another ten shekels paid in advance."

"Ten shekels? I'm already paying you fifty."

My father-in-law's voice. The only time Gal displayed this much emotion was when he had to spend money.

I strained to make out some familiar quality to the other man's voice.

"Fifty is for the task, ten to guarantee my position isn't jeopardized. I've paid handsomely for this post. I want some reassurance you won't get nervous and change your mind. And just so there's no confusion, I mean Tyrian shekels."

Now I was intrigued. Sixty Tyrian shekels could buy a good pair of oxen or a dozen calves. Not significant money to my father-in-law, but for most men it was a small fortune. Yet from the other man's tone, it seemed he was willing to risk losing it if his conditions weren't met. So that eliminated any of the tenants or servants as the speaker who would be tempted to act without reservation to obtain such riches. But who else would Gal be meeting with? I risked peeking around the corner. The slight man speaking with Gal faced away from me, but the richness of his clothes confirmed my earlier assumptions.

"I'm not asking you to do anything outside your normal range of . . . enforcement." Gal sniffed and spit a glob of phlegm perilously close to the other man's feet.

"Give me the ten shekels, and I'll never say you asked me to do anything at all."

"Fine, just take care of it. But wait until the whole family is in Jerusalem. I don't want any complications."

The man nodded. As he turned to go, I caught a glimpse of his face.

My heart lurched to a stop. Alvon, the tax collector. His hair was now almost as white as his skin, making his actual appearance as ghoulish as the recollections of my nightmares.

I flung myself into the hutch, reliving the fear I had felt witnessing his ruthless collection tactics in Nazareth. Forcing myself to breathe, I remembered that as Olmer's wife, the perils of lack were no longer a concern.

But why would Gal speak to such a detestable man, let alone employ his services? My conversation with Olmer last night came to mind. Was Gal carrying on the family business of bribery? I dismissed the thought. Not because I thought my father-in-law above it but because he knew government officials with more influence. No one respected tax collectors.

I gathered a bowl of eggs with shaking hands and tried to make sense of the strange meeting. After several minutes, I emerged no closer to solving the mystery. A quick check behind the hutch showed the men had departed. I set off for the stables.

"Olmer!" I shouted, waving my arm as I rushed toward him. "I need to speak with you alone."

Olmer made a provocative face and winked at the stable boy standing beside him. The boy, who couldn't have been more than ten years of age, covered a smile and veered off in a different direction to give us privacy.

Olmer waited until the boy was out of hearing range. "What do you want?"

"I overheard your father speaking with that criminal, Alvon. The tax collector. He's an evil man. Why would Gal let him on the property?"

A puff of air exploded from Olmer's lips and he shook his head. "You're unbelievable, Hannah. That's what you wanted to talk to me about? How daft of me to think you wanted to apologize."

"What? No, I . . . That's not the only reason, of course," I stammered.

He turned away, striding toward the manor, and any resolve I had about not chasing after him went with him.

"Olmer, wait." I trotted after him like a dog begging for scraps. "Why didn't you mention you're going to Miletus? Will you return before Pesach?"

"No. I'll go directly to Jerusalem depending on the weather and the timing."

That meant he'd be gone for months. And, worse still, I wouldn't be going to Jerusalem for the feast. I couldn't hide my disappointment.

"I don't understand. Weren't you just in Miletus last year? Why are you returning so soon?"

"With the trouble about to boil over with the Nabateans, our eastern trade could be curtailed. We can't afford to suffer losses of that kind. My parents think it's time I go to Miletus to ensure we'll have . . . inseverable ties to the west, to the Greek shipping routes, in case we need to expand trade that direction."

"Can't the managers in Tyre and Patara oversee the trade from Asia and the Greek cities? Why do you have to go?"

"*Woman*. Enough with the questions."

I stepped back, startled by his brusqueness. We walked a moment without speaking, then I decided to salvage the situation. After all, this might be our last time alone for months.

"I certainly wish you every success, husband." I offered a feeble smile. "I'll miss you."

Instead of softening his countenance as I had hoped, my comment seemed to increase his annoyance.

Our exchange left me feeling confused and humiliated. Why couldn't I ever get things right with him?

CHAPTER 34

Pesach of the Year 3788 (CE 28)

"Hannah, did you check the roof and all the rooms upstairs?"

"Yes, Myrinne," I assured her for the third time.

The ordinarily calm and composed Myrinne paced around the courtyard like a general under siege. Every year she became obsessed with last-minute preparations before Pesach. Her quest? Eliminate every trace of enemy leaven.

I giggled at the thought of Myrinne wearing armor as she scoured the house for bread crumbs. She scowled at my levity, and I composed myself. I'd have to wait until after the feast to safely tease her.

"Where are those girls?" She asked. "They should be back by now. I need more pairs of eyes to be sure we've gotten everything."

"Don't worry, I'll search high and low. No leaven will escape me." I couldn't resist saluting.

She looked skeptical—of my abilities and my mental state. But I was the only help available so she headed off in the opposite direction without comment.

Olmer had sent word that he wouldn't have time to return

to Sepphoris after all. Everyone else had left for Jerusalem for the feast to meet him. Besides Myrinne and me, only Tabitha's youngest son and Keturah and her girls remained behind. And Keturah had announced this morning that due to her condition, she couldn't help us with chores. When I had protested, she delivered the usual argument:

"You just don't understand what it's like to be with child, Hannah."

She was in her fifth month of pregnancy and appeared healthy and robust to me, but how could I argue with the truth of that? Who was I to point out that spending hours walking the markets in town was a more strenuous activity than sweeping a couple of rooms? Besides, I preferred having more work if it was the price to pay for the peace her absence provided.

When I lifted the wooden door covering the stairs to the roof, a gust of wind caught it and banged it open. I began sweeping, but quickly realized the futility of the task on such a blustery day.

Walking to the low wall that served as a railing, I surveyed the fields. The winter rains had been sparse this year leaving the ground unseasonably dry. After the feast, we'd cut the barley. Only then could we assess the true effects of the drought on the harvest.

Thoughts of the feast brought Yeshua to mind. Rather than subsiding after the incident in Cana, talk about my brother had increased. Not a week went by without news trickling in of his provocative teachings or outlandish behavior. Hopefully, it had been exaggerated with the retelling from person to person. I couldn't fathom why he roamed the countryside instead of staying in Nazareth where he belonged.

Maybe Olmer had been right that Yochanon, the baptizer,

encouraged Yeshua somehow. Only after he'd been immersed did Yeshua become intent on proclaiming that the kingdom of the Lord was here. Hadn't it always been here? Weren't we the only people who worshiped the one true Lord?

I could only hope Yeshua stayed far from Olmer. To think they'd cross paths amid the thousands of pilgrims in Jerusalem was irrational, but the possibility still worried me. Olmer and I had parted on bad terms as it was. An encounter with Yeshua would make reconciling that much more difficult. If only I could somehow distance myself from my brother's actions.

A kestrel hovered beneath the sparse clouds high overhead. I rested my hands on the top of the broom handle and watched its flight. Its black-tipped tail feathers fanned out proudly as it glided in tightening circles before stalling in midair. I held my breath as it seemed to teeter on an invisible point in space. What must it have felt like to have such freedom, to take to the sky leaving every care behind?

The kestrel flapped its wings and flew behind a hill out of sight, leaving me oddly bereft by its absence. I picked up the broom again. Staring at the sky wouldn't remedy my marriage woes. And it certainly wouldn't get my errands done.

I turned from the north wall to head back downstairs and was baffled by the black funnel twisting in front of me on the horizon. I stared for a second and blinked my eyes. Then alarm registered.

"Fff -fire. Fire!" I dropped the broom and stumbled down the stairs, my voice increasing in volume.

"Fire! Help!" Jogging around the balcony shouting into the rooms on the second floor, I only managed to rouse my young nephew from his nap. I hurtled my body down two flights of stairs into the cellar storehouses and heard the scrape of jars moving across the tiled floor.

"Fire," I croaked, bending forward gulping air, my hands on my knees.

Myrinne's startled face appeared around a doorframe. "What? Where? The kitchen?" She picked up her hem, sprinting past me up the stairs.

I chased after her and pointed across the courtyard toward the door. In the minutes it took us to exit and run beyond the corner of the manor walls, the plume of smoke had widened. It undulated, dancing on gusts of wind.

"Is the vineyard on fire?" she asked, eyes wide.

"I don't know. Where is everyone?" I yelled in a panic, although knowing they were all on the road to Jerusalem.

We ran as far as the stables, where the stable boy struggled to harness a mule to a cart. I hesitated within a few cubits of them. The animal stamped back and forth like it would gladly trample the child rather than cooperate.

"Hannah, just start putting jars of water on the cart!" Myrinne shouted, rushing to aid the boy.

I skirted around their strange dance as they attempted to subdue the beast and dashed into the stables. It took surprising effort to keep the jugs from crashing to the ground once I managed to tip them over. Finally, I got one rolling in the direction of the cart. The acrid smell of smoke was strong now.

"Let me do that." The boy approached to take over my rolling.

"No, just get another one!" I shrieked.

For a moment he looked torn between decorum and practicality. Then he sprinted back into the barn. We loaded six jars on the cart and grabbed some blankets before whipping the reluctant mule away from the safety of the stable.

A path cut through the fields, passing alternating rows of grapevines and barley, grapevines and barley. The repetition made me feel like we were in a dream, moving as fast as we could but making no progress. Finally, we descended the hill and turned onto the dirt road that encircled our property. The mule balked and tossed its head in protest, bringing us to an abrupt stop. I couldn't fault it. The sight in front of us terrified me too.

Fire licked up the window shutters and consumed the roof of the neighbors' home. Behind the building was a backdrop of inferno. The wind whipped fire in a circular dance of destruction through the dry barley fields around the house. Flames swayed one way and then another, igniting new stalks that dipped and swayed like thousands of tiny torches. Some moments the wind blew hard enough that it appeared to knock down the flames, but when the gust stopped, the circle of fire had grown even bigger. The enormity of the blaze paralyzed me.

"Hannah! Here."

Myrinne threw a sopping wet blanket at me and ran toward a woman and a boy who futilely stamped at the flames on the perimeter. Iakovos and several men spread out along the outskirts of our property, beating any embers that drifted across the road, to stop the fire from jumping the gap and endangering our vineyard.

"What are they doing?" I shouted as I slapped at the grass, eyes stinging and mouth parched from the intense heat of the blaze. "Why aren't they pouring water on the house?"

But it was beyond saving. Some stones would withstand the flames, but everything inside was probably lost. A sickening creak from the direction of the house confirmed my thought. The roof collapsed with a crash onto breaking pottery and timbers below, sending an explosion of orange sparks into the sky. Then the piteous scream of a man registered above the din.

"Aharon!" The woman wailed and sprinted toward the house.

Part of the wreckage appeared to break free in a barely perceptible human form. The man's hair and clothes were ablaze as he staggered forward screeching. Men ran to smother him with wet blankets.

I gaped horrified at the scene.

"Hannah, get back. Get back!" Myrinne shouted.

I retreated across the road on quaking legs as the wind shifted again and fire engulfed the area where I had just stood. The men lifted the pile of blankets from the ground into the cart bed, and I heard the man whimper with the movement. He was alive. Whether this was a good thing or not was yet to be known. I turned away and saw the boy standing transfixed, watching it all.

"Hannah, come take the reins," Myrinne commanded.

The mule was more than eager to put distance between itself and the fire, so it didn't require any coaxing on my part to head back up the hill. I glanced back over my shoulder.

Myrinne had wrapped her arm around the woman as if she led a small child behind the cart. The wall of fire loomed behind them. I couldn't see where the immense wall of flames ended on the other side. What a miracle the vineyard and all of our property remained unscathed.

I counted the rows of grapevines we passed to keep from thinking about the man on the cart behind me. My counting faltered as the grapevines were interrupted by rows of barley making me aware for the first time of the absence of barley in the rows closest to our neighbor's property. Something unsettled me about this.

Olmer had once explained that the barley helped keep the soil from eroding and other weeds from growing in between the grapes. Usually the barley was harvested and cut back well before the grape harvest, allowing workers to move down the rows unimpeded. It was not permissible to harvest barley until the Feast of First Fruits, still days away. So if there was no barley present, then no barley had been planted this winter in the outer rows closest to the fire.

A dreadful suspicion overtook me. I wanted to think that divine intervention orchestrated this absence of dry grass amid the vines closest to the fire. But somehow I feared it was not the Lord's favor, but someone's premeditated caution.

The man groaned from the cart's jostling. His wife kept up a steady stream of assurances that were more pitiful than comforting. When we reached the stable, I tied up the mule and moved to the back of the cart.

Never had I seen anything so gruesome.

Myrinne and the woman had managed to pull the man up while his legs dangled over the edge. Only clumps of hair remained amid the bright red, oozing blisters on the right side of his head. It reminded me of a goat carcass after the skin was removed. The left side of his face was even more frightening. No eye could be distinguished from the black-and-white mottled flesh. I averted my eyes to his chest. But what I first took for a smoke-darkened leather garment was actually what remained of his skin. He fought to take in quick raspy gasps of air while his wife frantically uttered reassurances.

Bile rose in my throat and I turned my head to keep from retching.

"Help me bring him inside," Myrinne ordered sternly, but when I met her eyes, I saw she was afraid.

I struggled not to embarrass myself by being sick as my hands touched his back. We managed to pull him off the cart, but he resisted our efforts to push him to the ground and he ended up slumped against a wheel. His arms flailed about as he wheezed, trying to take in air. His distressed wife knelt at his side and reached for his hand, but stopped short seeing the blistered flesh there.

"Why did you go back in? Why?" she sobbed, settling for resting a hand on his unburned calf, which looked shockingly normal compared to the rest of him. The man's visible eye focused on her for an instant. I couldn't tell if the pain I saw there was entirely physical.

She turned to us. "We told them we'd pay. I said we'd have the money after the harvest. They didn't care. They had torches and . . . oh, Lord." She buried her face in the crook of her arm and cried.

"Who?" I asked. "Who did you tell? The tax collector?"

"There'll be time for that later," Myrinne snapped. "Go see if you can find someone to help. We'll stay here."

Where else would they go anyway? I nodded. "Should I make some willow tea for the pain?"

Myrinne shook her head almost imperceptibly.

I knew then that he wouldn't survive.

"Aharon. Aharon, please don't leave me," his wife pleaded.

I bit my lip, and tears rolled down my cheeks unchecked.

"Go on," Myrinne urged me gently.

I fled to the manor.

When I reached the open doors, Keturah stood just inside the courtyard.

"What is going on?" she asked with disgust. "Why do you look like that?"

"Oh, Keturah." I panted from the uphill run and paused for a breath. Grabbing her hands, I licked my parched lips to speak better. "Send the girls for help. There's a fire."

She ripped her hands free and stepped back. "Obviously, I

can see there is a fire. But we're safe here."

"No." I shook my head at her lack of understanding and pointed behind me. "Our neighbor, he's dying."

"Dying? Here? We can't have a dead person here. It's almost Pesach."

The callous words stunned me.

She shoved past me to shut the door—as if it were that simple to put the whole thing out of sight and out of mind.

I looked at her, repulsed.

"Never mind. I'll go for help myself."

Just as I pulled the door halfway open again, a woman's cry of distress pierced the silence from the direction of the stables.

There was nothing more to be done now.

***

Tragedy or not, the feast days arrived. Although we were nowhere near Jerusalem, we sat outside on the roof and faced south towards the temple to eat our Passover meal. But all I could focus on was the path of destruction in my view. Pictures of the dead man—Aharon, I corrected myself—were seared into my mind. I tried to guess the age of the boy I had seen among those trying to put out the fire. Now he was fatherless. My own past pain mingled with concern for the child.

Since the hasty burial, Myrinne and I hadn't mentioned a word about the fire. When I would catch her looking at me, she turned away. I did the same when she glanced my way. Both of us were probably afraid to meet the other's eyes for fear that our own suspicions would be mirrored there—suspicions that the cruel men responsible for the blaze might have given advance warning to someone under our own roof. So we celebrated somberly, counting the days until the others returned from Jerusalem.

CHAPTER 35

Any hopes of a joyous homecoming with Olmer were marred by my lingering doubts. After the blessing and breaking of the bread, I studied his and my in-laws reactions while Keturah recounted the horror of the fire as if she herself had been in imminent danger. Gal and Raz certainly voiced concern at the appropriate times and appeared as surprised as could be expected. Olmer seemed distracted, as if he only half listened.

Seeing them face-to-face, I now thought perhaps I'd been paranoid for suspecting they had known anything about it before. Aharon's wife never mentioned anyone by name, did she? And I had assumed the family owed a tax collector, but they could have owed money to anyone. Just because Alvon was notorious, didn't mean he was the only depraved man in the Galil. Besides, I had heard Gal tell Alvon to ensure the family wasn't home when he did whatever task he was hired for. Whoever started the fire did so with full knowledge that the family had been present.

"Hannah, are you even listening?" Olmer dropped his spoon with a clatter while challenging me with his eyes.

"I'm sorry. My mind must have wandered." I smiled and bit into my bread.

"Your kinsman is in prison."

The crust I swallowed went down like a rock as images of my loved ones came to mind. Yeshua? Uncle Cleopas? My cousin Shim'on?

My husband furrowed his brow and looked disgusted, perhaps realizing so many in my family could be considered seditionists that I couldn't immediately identify the kinsman in question.

"It's no surprise," Gal stated impassively and blew across the surface of his spoon. "We all knew Yochanon's tirades would have consequences."

Yochanon. I exhaled, unable to hide my relief. "What will they do with him?"

"Nothing more than he deserves," Raz said. "Though Antipas is wavering and will likely temper the punishment to assuage public opinion. He's wracked with indecision trying to balance Herodias's outrage against the man's popularity. Yochanon may succumb to old age before the tetrarch decides what to do with him." She snorted. "If it were up to me, all of Yochanon's followers would be punished as well. I can't fathom why the impudent curs weren't arrested." Raz stared at me several seconds before finishing. "Especially the one who ran amok through the temple courts."

"*No.* Really?" Keturah leaned in closer. "What happened?"

Gal looked to Raziela and lifted an eyebrow. Tabitha fiddled with a knife, eyes downcast. Hakon's eyes twinkled. Something was amiss, but I didn't know what it could be.

"Is it true?" I asked Olmer.

Olmer looked to Raziela before answering me. "I'm afraid so. The man shouted and brandished a whip. He flipped over the money exchangers' tables. It was mayhem—coins scattered everywhere, pigeons fluttering about, people hurling themselves out of the path of riled cattle. I've never seen such a spectacle. No doubt his accomplices pocketed money during the commotion."

"That's terrible. Was he arrested?"

"No," Hakon answered. "The soldiers held their posts as if they didn't see a thing, even when bloodshed seemed imminent."

Surprising. Pilate, the latest prefect in Judea, had scarcely been in office two years and had already demonstrated disdain for the sanctity of the temple and our feast days. He'd hardly shrink away from a confrontation, especially to squelch any perceived insurgence.

Hakon glanced at Raz. "The man even threatened to destroy the temple and raise it up again."

"What?" I laughed at the absurdity of the boast. "Destroy the temple?"

Keturah shared my smile, but the rest of them stared at me. I continued undeterred. "It's obvious the man is deranged and jeopardizing public safety. He should've been detained at the very least." I ripped another piece of bread and swabbed the juices from my bowl with vigor to emphasize my point.

Raziela's lips curled up, but lacked the warmth of a smile. "I'm glad to hear you share my opinion. Be sure to tell him such behavior won't be overlooked forever."

I looked up at her, puzzled.

She seemed to savor my confusion while Hakon bounced up and down on the bench like a child who knew the answer to a riddle and could barely contain himself.

"It was your *brother*," he blurted out.

"My brother?" I whispered. It didn't seem possible.

"Her brother?" Keturah echoed with eyes wide and head whipping back and forth between Raziela and me.

Raz ignored her and pierced Hakon with a look of annoyance. No doubt she had hoped to deliver this blow herself.

"Yes, your brother. Yeshua." She spat out his name like a curse. "He was carrying on like a madman. I expect you'll be eager to speak with him about this outrage."

"I . . . I don't understand," I stammered. My brother had never done anything like this. I'd only seen him angry a few times and always on account of an injustice, like the day he had confronted Silas the blacksmith. But even then, Yeshua had showed complete restraint. Why would he suddenly become violent and irrational? There had to be more to the story.

"What is there to understand?" Raz asked. "You'll speak with your family and find out when he returns home. Then you'll make it clear that his behavior is unacceptable. He can join Yochanon in jail for all I care, but he will not jeopardize all that my family has accomplished, do you understand that?"

I waited for Olmer to speak up. Instead of protesting his mother's orders, he calmly hunted for a piece of lamb among the vegetables in his broth. I grew angry that he was complicit in this little trap. No wonder she treated me with contempt when my own husband wouldn't even defend me.

"Olmer, you know what to do," my father-in-law mumbled as he chewed. We could have been discussing his grandchildren's drawings for all the concern Gal showed.

I took a deep breath to compose myself and picked up my spoon, but the shaking in my hand belied my indifference. I didn't know who had disappointed me more at this point, my brother the berserker or my husband the betrayer. Mulling over my options, I realized I had none, so I tried to contain my tears of rage until the servants cleared the table.

When Olmer stood up to go outside, I followed closely on his heels.

"You could have said something in my defense. You are my husband."

He gave a cursory glance around before he responded, no doubt to ensure no one witnessed my insolence.

"Do you think I need to be reminded of that?"

I sucked in my lower lip and took a shaky breath. The cold contempt behind his words made it impossible to hide my shock and hurt.

Olmer let out a laugh.

"Hannah, I'm only teasing. Come see the new mare we've bought." He took hold of my hand, which remained limp in his. He chuckled again. "I forgive you because I can see you've been woefully uninformed in my absence."

His emotional turnabout made me wary, but I couldn't help but be curious.

"My father is under a lot of pressure to make the business profitable."

"Profitable at the expense of my family?" I pulled my hand back and folded my arms over my chest. "What does his business have to do with Yeshua?"

"Father is doing his best to please both Rome and Antipas while still making a living. He used to have sway over Herod's politics when Sepphoris served as capital of the Galil. But ever since Antipas moved the capital to Tiberias, the high court here has little say about economic decisions. Herod's influenced by those deplorable councilmen in Tiberias."

I could only guess at the caliber of men who held power in Tiberias. No Torah-abiding Jew would ever enter the confines of that city. It was bad enough that Herod had named the city after Emperor Tiberius, a man whose mistreatment of the Jews in Rome was well known. When workers digging foundations for a proposed stadium had discovered an ancient graveyard, the city should have been abandoned altogether. Instead of repenting, Antipas had destroyed what was left of the cemetery and built right over it. He'd been bribing people to populate the unclean city ever since, offering free houses, promises of tax immunity, and even freedom to slaves in exchange for their residency. If Herod was taking the counsel of Tiberias's citizens, then we all had cause for concern.

"I did hear Herod's brother-in-law benefits from his position as overseer of the Tiberian market, often at the expense of the city's coffers," I admitted.

Olmer nodded. "Whether or not Agrippa's corrupt or just inept remains to be seen, but since his sister is married to Antipas, it's not likely he'll be replaced any time soon." He waited until a passing servant was well out of earshot before continuing. "And to complicate things further, Herod is going to mint his own coins in Tiberias."

"Oh no. Like his brother's? I still can't believe Philip engraved his own likeness on his coins."

"No, Herod's doing nothing that so blatantly disregards the Lord's commandments," he said with a wry smile.

"What is it then?"

"I've seen the design for the molds. On one side of the coin, within a wreath, the name '*Tiberias*' is inscribed. On the other side, Antipas put his name and the image of a reed. He probably selected the plant because Tiberias is on the lakeshore. But he's given men more ammunition with which to mock him. 'The Reed' has become his new moniker. He does sway back and forth depending which way the political wind blows."

"So the design's an embarrassment. I don't understand how that affects us."

"We'll have to use the new coin in our business dealings here to show loyalty to Herod. But for our foreign transactions, on top of all the other tariffs we pay, we'll have to change our currency before purchasing goods. No one in Nabatea will want a coin with Antipas written on it after he divorced and insulted their Princess Phasaelis. Not to mention there's great speculation about the exchange rates for the new coin. The whole thing is a costly headache that has my father testy."

My heart softened toward Olmer. I'd been insensitive to his position of needing to support Gal and an often unsupportable sovereign.

"I see. I didn't realize."

Olmer smiled at me.

Relief flooded by body. He wasn't angry with me after all, just burdened by business.

We walked a few more paces.

"So you agree we can't have your brother causing any mayhem."

I stopped short. There was always a condition attached to his affection.

"Hannah, my father must be above reproach in Herod's eyes. There can be no doubt of his loyalty if he's to maintain any type of stature among Herod's increasing number of counselors."

"Your family holds a position of great power," I argued. "You have contracts to provide balsam and spices to the palace, and your taxes fill Herod's chests. You're important people. Herod won't possibly hold you responsible for Yeshua's actions."

"It's because we're close to the tetrarch that we're more at risk. Any hint of rebellion, any taint of betrayal, and we could lose our heads. When pushed, Herod is his father's son. He will not hesitate to end any threat, real or not. And even if he does hesitate, his wife Herodias would prevail upon him to take action. The woman is more power hungry than he is." He ground out the words with contempt.

I stared at my feet, my emotions in turmoil.

He stepped in front of me and placed a hand on each of my shoulders, expectantly raising his eyebrows.

"Listen. This is not just my father's position we're talking about. Didn't I warn you before? Didn't I tell your brothers to rein in Yeshua before things got out of hand? Now there's real danger here to my family and to yours. We have to speak with him."

I opened my mouth to protest, but he touched a finger to my lips.

"You know your brother has never been fond of me. And before you defend him, let me say I know he wasn't pleased about our union from the beginning. And I understand why, as your brother, he was concerned. I can only hope to earn his trust one day. But for now, I think it best we both broach the subject with him."

He softened his voice. "The sooner he returns to his work, the sooner we can move forward. We can concentrate on enjoying each other again. You'd like that wouldn't you?"

Such reasonableness from Olmer was strange but refreshing. And I did want to put this in the past, more than anything. But I wished there were another way that didn't involve speaking with Yeshua.

"Stop eating your thumb, will you?" he barked. "I detest that habit of yours. I'm trying to have an intelligent conversation with you and you're behaving like a child."

"Sorry." I dropped my hand from my mouth.

"Please, Hannah." His eyes were warm and beseeching, his tone gentle again. "You know I don't need your approval, but I would like you to support me in this because you care about our future. You do care about us, don't you?"

He lightly traced a line from my temple along my jaw, then tilted my chin up with his fingertips.

I'd lost track of how much time had passed since he showed me such tenderness. Despite my reservations, I still craved his affection. I relented and nodded.

"You'll support me in this?"

"Yes."

He rewarded me with his most dazzling smile. I smiled back. Hope grew inside me for the first time in months. I reached out my hand to him.

"It's such a lovely day. Since we're already outdoors, shall we walk together as we used to?"

He snorted. "I've more important things to do than wander about like some lovesick pup."

I reeled my arm back in slowly hoping to minimize the awkward rejection.

"Hurry up if you want to see the mare. I've much to do in the next week if I'm to go to Damascus before returning to Jerusalem for Shavuot."

"You're leaving again already?" I couldn't hide the desperation in my voice.

He put his hands on his hips.

"Oh."

And the bud of hope within me wilted, choked by the growing weeds of doubt and disappointment. How gullible I was to think that he cared about our future, about my opinion. The only sincere words Olmer ever uttered were at the start of our relationship. He told me that in the end, he always got what he desired. And he was right.

CHAPTER 36

"We've waited months already," I said to Olmer as we ascended the winding trail to Nazareth. "I still don't see why we can't wait until after Shabbat to speak with Yeshua."

"We're done discussing this. Besides, who knows when he will take to roaming the countryside again? We can't miss this opportunity." He moved ahead of me.

Defeated, I fell silent.

Stone-bordered fields cascaded beneath us like overlapping hems of gold and green garments. The view brought a bittersweet sense of homecoming, as if I were stepping onto a well-known set to resume my childhood lines where I'd left off. Over a year had passed since I made the short trip home. I loved my family, but sometimes it was easier not to visit. Seeing evidence of the life I used to have tempted me to entertain regrets.

From this vantage point, I watched families harvesting wheat in several plots of land below us where the slope was less steep. My breath caught and I stood still for a moment, remembering the last time Abba had been with us for the wheat harvest.

That year the latter rains had lingered and winds from the west prevailed over drier eastern winds. There had been great uncertainty about the wheat crop, and as we counted the seven weeks following Pesach, prayers went up night and day that the harvest would be sufficient. At last Shavuot had arrived and with it the time to cut the wheat. I could picture the first morning of that harvest.

***

Billowing clouds glided lazily across a vibrant blue sky, and the morning sun pleasantly warmed my shoulders. Only the rhythmic thwack of scythes and the rustle of stalks hitting the ground cut the silence. I had stopped my task of bundling wheat to stretch and admire Abba's work ahead of me. He expertly swung the blade so the cut wheat sheaves fell into a neat row at his side as he moved down the field.

By comparison, Ya'akov cut like a wild man in the row next to us. He had a haphazard circular swing, his arms flailing at varying heights, which left wheat strewn every which way. Poor Elan following behind him was having a hard time arranging the stalks into loose bundles.

"Keep going, Hannah," Emmi encouraged from behind me. "We're almost finished this row."

She pulled two handfuls of stalks from the pile I had just gathered, then twisted them expertly around the middle of the remainder of the stalks, securely tying them into a bundle.

Yeshua mimicked her actions with the piles Elan gathered. But he didn't seem to be as good as Emmi at tying his bundles.

"Emmi. Yeshua's dropping too much wheat back on the ground," I said, pointing to my brother. We were supposed to leave something behind for the poor to glean later, but this was excessive. What if we didn't have enough for ourselves?

Emmi glanced up and smiled proudly at her eldest son. "His work is good. Just focus on your own."

I looked over Emmi's shoulder to catch Shim'on's eye. He brought up the rear, stacking the tied bundles into heaps, where they would sit in the sun to finish drying. I pointed at Yeshua's sloppy work, but Shim'on only shrugged. Was I the only one who cared about the family's future?

Across the field, Tobias raised his voice in song as he worked his own plot. Abba whistled in accompaniment. The harvest was turning out to be good after all, and I began to enjoy the work. Maybe Abba wouldn't have to be away as much on building projects, and Emmi would discard the frown lines she wore in times of careful rationing.

I don't know when the family tradition began, but when the sun set on our first day of harvesting, Emmi would rub oil into our palms, one at a time, from the youngest to the oldest. She always spoke a kind word as she eased the tension in our dry, sore hands and then deposited a kiss on our cheeks. That year, I thought myself too old for such a silly ritual. When my turn came, I scampered out of reach.

Emmi didn't comment but moved on to Yeshua. She started to massage his hands, but then she grew still, staring at his upturned palms in hers. After tenderly kissing the center of each palm, she brushed a tear from her eye. Yeshua cupped her cheek in his hand, and Emmi smiled and turned to Abba.

Instead of holding out his palms, Abba grabbed the jar of oil from her and set it down. He caught Emmi's hands in his before she could react, then kissed the back of each with a loud smacking noise, keeping his eyes on her face as she flushed prettily. My brothers and I snickered and twittered as kids will do, shocked to think of our parents having romantic feelings for each other. Abba waggled his eyebrows at us, and I grinned at his antics.

I had resolved at the time never to act so soppy when I

was a grown woman. Now I longed for the imprint of Emmi's soft lips on my cheek, and the optimism of childhood, when I never doubted Abba would be with me always. Why hadn't I seen that everything I could ever want had been right there before me?

I took a faltering breath and determined not to be so emotional. This was exactly why I stayed away from Nazareth. The past was best left in the past.

CHAPTER 37

Olmer halted just before entering the clearing outside my childhood home. I hurried to catch up, but he appeared in no apparent rush to step onto the property—as if his sandals might be contaminated, as if the taint of sedition could be caught on contact. Surveying the pens, the house, and then the work shed, he wrinkled his nose like he'd caught a foul odor but couldn't identify the offending source. He probably regretted volunteering to spend Shabbat amid such relative squalor. Well, any discomfort he'd endure was of his own doing.

"Now remember, we're not here to visit," he said.

I put my hands on my hips. "How could I forget? You never visit my family."

"You know that's unfair. I travel most of the year. When I'm in the Galil, I want to be at home, with you."

It was all I could do not to roll my eyes.

Olmer touched my forearm to stop me from entering the house.

"I know this isn't pleasant for you. But remember, it's for Yeshua's own good that he must be made to see reason. His actions have consequences for all of us. I won't let him jeopardize my family's standing."

"My family is your family. Yeshua is your brother by marriage now." I started to walk forward, but he tightened his grip on my arm and pulled me toward him.

"Listen. I hope he sees reason. I hope he enjoys a productive, peaceable life. But know this . . . I will not tolerate his current behavior whether he's my wife's brother or not. And I will not tolerate any disloyalty from you."

Before I responded, Yosi's son Binyamin ran out of the house.

Olmer seamlessly assumed a jovial manner.

"My, who is this frightening young man?" he quipped with a grin, tousling the boy's hair. "Maybe we're at the wrong house."

Four-year-old Binyamin gave him a cautious smile.

I fought the urge to shout a warning to my nephew not to succumb to this ruse.

Perhaps hearing our voices, one of my sisters-in-law exited the house. I felt a twinge of despair as Talia's belly led her out the door. She self-consciously placed a hand over the girth of her abdomen, and I caught the sympathy in her eyes before she shielded it behind a welcoming smile.

"Ayelet, come see who's here," she called over her shoulder.

"Talia, you look lovely," I said, genuinely happy for her. It had been ten years since she bore my brother Shim'on a son, and I knew she longed for another babe.

Ayelet popped her head out the door and nodded respectfully to Olmer. "We didn't know you were coming." She raised her eyebrows at me in silent question.

"It wasn't a planned trip," I lied, averting my eyes.

"Ayelet, don't be rude." Talia looked back to me. "This is your home. You're welcome whenever you like. Please come in, come in."

"Emmi?" Binyamin pulled on Ayelet's skirt while keeping a careful eye on Olmer. "Can I still play with my cousins?"

"Yes, but why don't you ask your Aunt Shlomit to bring the boys here? I'm sure they'll want to see their Aunt Hannah too."

Olmer and I entered the home with the women as the boy dashed off.

"What a wonderful surprise." My mother pushed herself up from the floor to embrace me and beamed at Olmer.

My husband made polite conversation about the children and the crops. I nodded and smiled to mask my unease. Our motive for being here seemed so transparent that I was ashamed to dupe them so easily. My eyes returned frequently to the door, anticipating Yeshua's arrival and the inevitable confrontation to come. I didn't have to wait long.

But it would seem that I was the one who had been duped. In the planning and rehearsing of imaginary conversations with Yeshua over the last weeks, I'd forgotten what it was actually like to be in his presence. As soon as he walked into the room, the atmosphere changed. And the rational arguments I had prepared with such confidence in Sepphoris now seemed flawed. All my in-laws' concerns seemed petty and inflated. How could he be threatening to anyone?

Yeshua hugged each family member in turn. He smiled at me over Ayelet's head. I couldn't remember why I'd been angry with him at the wedding and smiled back with sincere affection—until Olmer's foot nudged mine. Then I panicked. I didn't want to offend my brother, but I couldn't very well tumble into his arms like everything was fine, especially with Olmer strung as taut as a lyre string beside me.

"I've missed you, Hannah." Yeshua said.

As he attempted to hug me, I awkwardly put my arms around myself as if chilled. "It's good to see you," I mumbled.

His eyes held mine, and I detected a knowing resignation there. Or maybe it was my overactive guilty conscience. Still, I looked away, unable to bear the intensity of his gaze. Yeshua stepped forward and placed his hands on my shoulders and kissed the top of my head. Then he turned to Emmi.

I wished I could just forget the whole reason for our visit and run far away. Olmer bumped against my side as if reading my treasonous thoughts.

Before the other women could turn back to their work, Shlomit entered with a train of youngsters trailing behind.

"We saw you coming!" shouted her four- and six-year-old sons.

"We saw you," Binyamin echoed despite already greeting us. Then there was a great commotion as all the boys chattered at once, clearly enthralled with Yeshua.

Shlomit laughed as she tried in vain to hold them back while adjusting the toddler on her hip.

"Leave your uncle in peace. He hasn't even washed the dust from his feet and you're harassing him."

Yeshua chuckled. "It's all right. I'm good at caring for children. You pick them up like this, am I right?" He crossed his arms and grabbed Binyamin by the waist, turning the child upside down as he stood up again.

Binyamin squealed with delight while the other boys jumped up and down, shouting with arms outstretched, awaiting a turn to be manhandled.

"Be careful," Emmi cried, but the joy on her face negated any true warning.

Yeshua attempted to put the boy on the ground, but Binyamin thrust his arms around Yeshua's neck and refused to let go. My other nephews, not wanting to be left out, threw themselves on top of Yeshua.

"I have some work to do yet before sundown," he said. "Boys, come with me and be my helpers."

Yeshua winked at us over the fray and led my nephews outside, all of them talking at once.

I turned to offer help with the meal and found the four women staring besotted after Yeshua. Olmer and I would have to rely on my brothers if we were to have any support for our cause, as the women in the family appeared beyond hope.

Olmer glared at me, his nostrils flaring with each livid breath. Yeshua hadn't even acknowledged him in all the commotion.

I sighed. We'd been here less than an hour, and already things were not going as planned.

CHAPTER 38

"He knows he's acting irrationally," Olmer said. "That's why he's avoiding us."

I had entertained the same thoughts when Yeshua didn't return with my nephews last night. I'm not sure my brother had even slept at the house. But it shamed me to listen to Olmer harping on the topic. It was a relief to be on our way to the synagogue where he'd have to be quiet.

"Yeshua has many friends here. He probably passed the evening with the hazzan or another family in the village," Emmi said.

I nodded in agreement, detecting the hint of annoyance in her voice.

We walked a few more steps before Olmer revisited the subject. "I hope he visited someone wise enough to advise him to show restraint and diplomacy in his public interactions."

Emmi took a deep breath but remained silent.

"Of course," Olmer continued, "my only concern is for Yeshua's welfare."

She eyed him. "Your concern is evident."

He considered her a moment before tipping his head and leaving us to join the men gathered near the village mikveh.

Emmi fixed her stare on me, but I glanced away, pretending

not to notice.

Olmer stopped to speak with Silas and his son. The years had not been kind to the blacksmith. His skin had an ashen appearance, and he puffed his chest in and out as if the fresh morning air was somehow less agreeable than the thick forge smoke to which he'd grown accustomed. Silas met my gaze then, and I looked away as if I were a young child again, caught spying on his work.

Ordinarily, most villagers would have been inside the synagogue by now, vying for bench seats on the perimeter of the room. But today dozens of people still perched on the stairs and milled about in front of the building. Sparrows darted back and forth between the roof and a nearby jujube tree, their chirps and trills echoing the chatter below. Suddenly, conversations ceased, throats cleared, and feet shuffled. I looked behind me to see what had captured everyone's attention.

Yeshua approached the building with the hazzan, Uri, and Shlomit. The townspeople bent to and fro, craning their necks to get a better view of them. Any hope that word of my brother's recent activities had not reached Nazareth was dashed. Their faces looked hungry for answers to unasked questions: Did he really perform miracles like the prophets of old? Was he organizing an army of followers to start another rebellion? Had Yosef's son gone insane?

I let Yeshua enter the building ahead of me, slowing my pace to put as much distance between us as possible. To escape the staring eyes inside, I practically dove into the first open space I saw among the women seated on the floor.

Uri escorted his grandfather to a seat on the stone benches at the front of the room. With the old man settled, he arranged the day's Torah scrolls with shaking hands. I wasn't sure who had planned to read today, but Yeshua remained standing and walked to the raised platform at the front of the synagogue.

I tried to measure the hazzan's reaction to my brother approaching the seat of Moshe. Itamar appeared to be dozing off, oblivious to the tension in the room. But at his side Uri's leg bounced and his throat was covered with telltale blotches that betrayed his agitation. Yeshua stretched out his hand, palm extended. Uri's eyes darted between Yeshua and his grandfather, seemingly pleading for guidance. He looked reluctant as he handed Yeshua the scroll, as if it were a lethal sword rather than aged leather.

Yeshua unrolled the scroll, then faced the audience. But instead of reading, he remained quiet, his eyes traveling to neighbors, former playmates, and relatives. The length of the silence grew uncomfortable, but no one dared move. At last he lowered his head. His rich voice brought the words of the prophet Yesha'yahu to life.

"'The Spirit of Adonai is upon me; because he has anointed me to announce Good News to the poor; he has sent me to proclaim freedom for the imprisoned and renewed sight for the blind, to release those who have been crushed, to proclaim a year of the favor of Adonai.'"[19]

The whole room appeared enthralled. No toes tapped, no eyes wandered, no child fussed. The very air in the room felt weightier and more tangible as if it also drew near to absorb the sound of his voice. Even the particles of dust floating in the sunbeams from the windows overhead suspended their motion.

Yeshua scanned the faces of his listeners and rolled the scroll back up. Without turning, he handed it to Uri, whose mouth hung open, agog.

"Today, this Scripture is fulfilled in your hearing,"[20] Yeshua declared in a ringing voice.

His tone wasn't so much challenging as it was confident. He spoke the words with the surety one would expect from an official making a royal pronouncement.

A chill washed over me. Was he saying what I thought he was saying? Was Yeshua proclaiming himself the Anointed One? In public? *Was* he the Messiah?

Before I reined in these riotous thoughts, a deep voice murmured somewhere off to my left. People awoke from their collective stupor. They turned to one another in astonishment and wonder. Muttering came from behind me, and the crowd turned in unison to see who spoke.

Silas cleared his throat and repeated with greater volume, "Isn't this the son of Yosef?"

No one responded.

He stood up and addressed the room with a sneer. "Isn't he the carpenter's boy?"

This new idea took root, then grew. Soon, reality encroached on our thoughts once more. A palpable sense of disappointment spread, then a collective brushing off of our earlier amazement as if we had all fallen prey to an illusion created by a skilled performer and were now quick to deny being tricked.

"It is Yosef's son," a woman called.

"How dare he make such an absurd claim?" another asked.

"Who does he think he is to talk down to us?" Silas demanded. "Didn't he grow up among us here?"

"That's right. Isn't he just Miryam's son the carpenter? Look right there. Those are his sisters." Silas's son pointed an accusing finger in each of our directions. "He's just the brother of Ya'akov, Yosef, Y'hudah, and Shim'on."[21]

I flushed and shrank farther toward the floor to avoid the hostile stares. Well, at least Yeshua was being confronted with the truth. Wasn't that what Olmer and I had come here for? The best possible outcome had occurred, hadn't it? Yet, strangely, I couldn't help but feel betrayed by the town's attempts to humiliate Yeshua.

Of course Silas would voice his disapproval. He'd never been fond of my brother. But the outrage of the others surprised me. Weren't these the same people who week after week sought his opinion on Torah? The ones who had benefitted from his free labor and acts of kindness for years? Their disbelief embarrassed me even as they expressed my own doubts. But it was different coming from strangers. I was his sister.

Voices toward the front of the room rose in dissent. I couldn't distinguish the comments, but from the tone I knew they were unkind. If people mocked me like this, I'd be in tears. But Yeshua appeared calm and didn't shy away from meeting the eyes of those who scorned him. In spite of my growing convictions about his deluded state, I felt proud of him for this.

Yeshua held up his hand and projected his voice so that everyone in the building could hear.

"I tell you the truth. Only in his hometown . . . and in his own house . . . is a prophet without honor."[22]

Suddenly, the whole gathering erupted. I'd never heard anyone shout inside the synagogue, let alone hundreds of people. I could see the top of the hazzan's bald head and his upraised arms, but his pleas for peace, if anyone heard them, went unheeded.

My brother made his way toward the exit, but every few paces someone jostled him with a shove or push. He reached the door at last, but one man blocked his escape. As I listened to the man incite the crowd, it took a moment for my mind to recognize what my eyes conveyed. I moved forward to get a closer look, but an irate group of women accosted me. They couldn't reach Yeshua, so they spewed their vitriol at me.

I pulled my veil across my face and ducked between them, pushing through their ranks, all semblance of polite behavior abandoned in my need to get outside. By the time I passed through the door, the crowd of people had swept both the man and Yeshua away toward the edge of town. I ran to catch up with Olmer and Ya'akov, who trailed behind the crowd having a heated discussion themselves.

"Olmer. *Wait*. Was that Iakovos inside? What is the steward doing here?" My words held more accusation than I originally had intended as the repercussions dawned on me. It was inconceivable that the steward would have travelled here of his own accord, let alone violated the rules for walking such a distance on the day of rest. He must have arrived yesterday, meaning his presence here today had been planned in advance.

Olmer considered me in a detached manner. "Go to your mother's home," he said with the same frosty tone he employed for dismissing servants. Then he pushed through the back of the crowd, which parted to let him pass and then swallowed him up.

Ya'akov, who had overheard this exchange, held my gaze for a moment, but said nothing. What was there to say at a time like this?

Emmi raised her voice in Yeshua's defense, and I turned to see who had upset her so.

The blacksmith's wife stared back at me over Emmi's shoulder. It was all I could do to keep from slapping the look of malevolent satisfaction from her face. I never did like that woman.

"Please, tell Silas to leave him alone," Emmi pleaded. "Just let me talk with him." Getting no response, she spun around, looking for someone to take up her cause. She spotted Uri, though what good he'd do anyone, I couldn't imagine.

My brother-in-law appeared to have collapsed on the synagogue stairs, apparently overwhelmed by the events unfolding around him. His face was flushed and he held both hands to his head as if to quiet a maelstrom of thoughts whirling inside.

"Uri, do something," Emmi cried.

"*Uri!*" Shlomit barked. Looking appalled at her husband's lack of decorum, she yanked at the ends of the shawl around his neck, trying to physically lift her husband from the ground. "Uri, get up. Stop those men."

Shim'on rushed to Emmi's aide, murmuring assurances and guiding her in the direction opposite the crowd, leading her back toward our home. By now the voices of the mob receded in the distance, so I followed behind Emmi. But when I reached the clearing, I couldn't bring myself to enter the house.

I had too much nervous energy to be trapped indoors again. I worried for Yeshua's safety but had to admit that underlying my fear was a tinge of excitement to have witnessed such a thing. I needed time by myself to make sense of it all.

How could this have happened? How could Yeshua become so reviled in his own town? Just yesterday people had welcomed him into their homes. Then again, yesterday he hadn't been claiming to be the Messiah. And that passage he had read—did he really think the words described him? Abba had always taught us that true fasting meant releasing those unjustly bound, letting those oppressed go free, sharing food with the hungry, and clothing the naked. Was that why Yeshua got the idea that he needed to be the one to literally do it? Or had Abba been teaching us about his son all along? Or rather,

Adonai's son.

The thoughts buzzed inside my head like flies searching for an open window. Nothing made sense anymore, and I just wanted to escape. Immediately, the cave came to mind. I debated sharing my plans with my family but reasoned there was probably such a commotion in the house that I'd return before anyone noticed my absence. I dashed past the pen and up the hill through the gardens, feeling better with each step away from the village.

Pausing to study the rocks along the ridgeline, I found what I searched for, the almost imperceptible track downhill. A brief glance over my shoulder satisfied me that no one followed. I scrambled down, waving my arm in front of me as I ducked into the cave, hoping both to clear any spiderwebs and appear menacing should there be any animals in residence. I'd never noticed that the stone outcropping on the back wall of the cave looked like a figure. I squinted and let my eyes adjust to the dim light.

Then I realized it was a figure. I froze.

CHAPTER 39

"Elan?" I whispered, wondering if I'd conjured him from my recollections.

"What are you doing here?" By his tone, it seemed I'd lost the right to visit this place we had shared together as children.

"What are *you* doing here?" I retorted, but the effect of superiority was diminished by the undignified way I had to hunch over near the entranceway. I hadn't visited the cave since I was engaged to be married. In my memories, it was quite spacious, but actually the ceiling height only accommodated an adult farther inside where Elan stood now. Either I remained bent in half, or I'd have to get closer. I walked towards him, stopping as soon as I could fully straighten.

Although several hand spans separated us, this was the closest I'd been to him in years. In the first year of my marriage, I'd expectantly gone to Nazareth hoping to receive forgiveness or at least words of acceptance from Elan. But after the first several trips, I had to acknowledge it was no coincidence that he was never to be found when I visited.

He succeeded in avoiding me until the day of Shlomit and Uri's wedding celebration eight years ago when he was forced to be in my presence. But that day my hopes for reconciliation were dashed as soon as I greeted him. Elan had affected an exaggerated look of surprise as he took in the richness of my garb, my braided hair, and the paint on my face. He said he hadn't recognized me "now that I had transformed into a real lady." From the sarcastic delivery, I knew "real lady" wasn't intended as a compliment.

I self-consciously pulled the material on my head down to cover the jeweled leather band on my forehead. When we left Sepphoris yesterday, I thought myself modestly attired, but now I felt garishly overdressed. And I realized that, as with the cave, my mental remembrance of Elan was flawed. His beard was full now and darker than his sandy-colored hair. It didn't cover the familiar constellations of freckles high on his cheeks, but it did make his hazel eyes appear more striking. And when had he become so much taller than me?

Elan shifted uncomfortably under my scrutiny and cleared his throat.

"Is Yeshua safely home?"

"What? No, I don't think so."

He looked concerned. "I was following alongside when he left the synagogue. The townspeople were driving us closer and closer to the edge of the cliff. First I hoped they just wanted to corner him, to get a chance to question him. But there was still a danger they'd accidentally push him over the precipice by sheer momentum from the crowd behind. Then I heard men shouting their intent to throw him off. So I turned and planted my feet, hoping to shield him or at least slow them down." His eyes widened. "No one even acknowledged me. They shoved past me and kept going after Yeshua. But when I turned back around, he'd vanished."

Panic gripped me. "People don't vanish!" I took a deep breath and tried for a more measured tone. "Where did he go after that?"

Elan shook his head. "That's what I'm saying . . . I don't know."

My mind sketched a terrible picture, but Elan quickly reassured me. "No. I looked over the edge. He didn't fall."

My breath slipped out in a sigh. I'd forgotten how comforting it was to have someone know me well enough to answer unasked questions. I'd also forgotten how painful it was to know I had discounted the importance of that someone. It was my turn to look away from Elan's intense stare.

"Anyway," he said, "I came here. He used to pray here so I thought maybe he would appear."

"Appear? Don't you mean arrive? People don't just disappear and appear out of the air, Elan. He probably just covered his head to disguise himself and blended into the crowd."

He considered this, but I could tell he wasn't convinced.

"I'm telling you, Hannah. He's incredible. He's always been remarkable, but it's like he's finally come into his inheritance. People are saying the Lord has anointed him with gifts that have not been seen since the days of Elisha. Who knows what he can do?"

I scoffed at the idea and looked around the cave.

"I mean it. And it's not just once or twice that he's demonstrated this power. He heals all who come to him. Madmen regain their right minds at a word from him. Blind people see. You heard him today. How could he do the things he does if he isn't who he says he is?"

"Don't tell me you believe him, that he's, he's . . ." I couldn't even bring myself to utter the words out loud. "Why haven't I ever seen any of these so-called healings?"

"I don't know, but I have. Yesterday when I saw you arrive, I left for the widow Vana's house . . ." His eyes darted away and he flushed.

His making himself scarce on account of my arrival annoyed me, but it was awkward to address, so I nodded my head indicating that he should continue.

"I had to visit her anyway. I've been helping her with some of her chores. You know how her joints are stiff and it pains her to move most days."

Even when we were young, Vana had a twisted back and could scarcely lift her chin off her chest. Her knobby fingers held a cane back then, so she must be in a terrible state now.

"Well," he continued, "Yeshua came by. Vana was tickled that he had thought of her. She picked up her cane to get up from her stool to fetch water for him even though it clearly hurt her to stand. Yeshua's eyes held such compassion . . ." Elan creased his brow like he always did when he concentrated, and the familiar expression tugged at my heart.

"Go on."

"I can't explain it. She was already standing up, but he said, 'Stand up.' And just like that, she did. Another handspan and her spine was straight. She dropped her cane and laughed and laughed with tears streaming down her face and wouldn't let go of Yeshua's sleeve. I laughed too. It was amazing. Your brother just smiled and blessed her and went on his way, saying he had to do something else before nightfall. How do you explain that?"

I couldn't, but I wouldn't admit it. I tried to recall Vana's appearance today at the synagogue, but realized I hadn't seen her there.

"If she were well, why didn't she come to the synagogue to show everyone?"

"She set off right away to reach her relatives in Cana before Shabbat began, to share the news."

How convenient. Still, I knew Vana would never miss

attending synagogue. And only an able-bodied person could walk fast enough to reach Cana before sundown if she'd left Nazareth shortly after I last saw Yeshua yesterday. But if Yeshua really had this power, then why, after all the years that I lived with him, had I never seen him do a miracle?

"I'll grant that he's special. Maybe even a prophet. But Messiah?" I snickered. "If he keeps proclaiming such things, he's going to end up in prison like Yochanon. That's why we came to stop him."

The moment the words came out, I realized I'd divulged too much.

Elan's demeanor changed as he processed the implications.

"You came to stop him?" He looked aghast. "Did you know what would happen? Is that why your family's steward was here, to incite a riot? To make sure you stopped him one way or another?"

The mention of the steward took me aback. How did he know who Iakovos was? Suddenly the answer occurred to me, and my face flushed with heat remembering the awful day of their meeting.

Elan misinterpreted the reason for my shame and continued to lob questions at me.

"Were others in on it? Silas was, wasn't he? This whole thing was some kind of trap, wasn't it? I don't believe it."

"If you'll just be quiet, I'll explain." I inhaled slowly and willed an explanation to come to me, my mind frantically cobbling together a plausible defense.

"Go ahead," he challenged. "Explain."

"Olmer and I have been concerned for him."

Elan scowled at me.

Undeterred, I continued. "Yeshua's not acting rationally. It wasn't anyone's idea for him to read today except his own.

How could we have known he would say what he did? If there was any plan, it was meant to keep him *out* of danger."

Elan let out a noise that could have been outrage or disbelief.

"You have to believe me. I didn't know anything about the steward's being there. You saw the people, how quickly they turned violent. They would have done the same thing even if Iakovos hadn't perhaps . . . encouraged their disapproval."

"Disapproval? Hannah, they were hunting him down and had every intention of throwing him off a cliff. And if they had killed him, your own brother's blood would cry out against you."

I couldn't deny the truth of his words. Trapped in a guilty mess of my own making, I began to cry. Initially, it was to garner some sympathy for my cause. But once the first tear fell, it was as if the wall holding back years of emotions had been breached. All of the fear and hurt and loneliness refused to be contained any longer.

"I never wanted him to be hurt," I wailed. "I just want him to be *normal*. I want him to stop antagonizing my family. You don't know what it's like, how unkindly they treat me, how hard it is for me."

He looked flustered and more angry than surprised by this information, but didn't speak.

"I know it's my fault, Elan. I don't deny that. I should never have married Olmer. If only I'd listened to Yeshua. If only I had waited and married—"

"Stop." He held his hand out. "Just stop."

He lowered his hand, but our eyes remained locked. His lips were pressed tightly together. I'd never seen him so agitated and held perfectly still, afraid to move or say anything else to provoke him further. The enormity of what I'd just said stole my breath. It was what I'd been thinking for years, but never admitted to myself until now. I didn't regret saying it because it was true, but I did regret bringing Elan more pain.

He turned away from me and grabbed his hair with both hands. "I shouldn't even be talking here with you," he whispered.

I didn't know if he spoke to me or to himself.

Lowering my head, I wiped my face on the neckline of my tunic. Even his sandals seemed to mock me with their simplicity. My own were finely wrought of supple leather, a decorative pattern punched out along the strap, more expensive than anything he had ever owned. Elan and I were part of separate worlds now. The past was the past, and nothing would be gained by dwelling on it.

Elan exhaled loudly, his thoughts probably echoing mine.

But I still felt the need to justify my present actions.

"I know you love him, Elan. I do too."

His features softened, and I should have stopped there. Should've, but didn't.

"But Yeshua needs to consider how his actions affect other people's lives. He can't just think of himself."

Elan snorted. "Forgive me if I find that amusing coming from you."

Offended, I crossed my arms. "And what's that supposed to mean?"

Elan opened his mouth to respond, but the voice I heard came from behind me, from the entrance to the cave.

"What is going on here?"

I whirled around, startled, but saw it was only Ya'akov and relaxed. But he looked far from relaxed.

He glanced over his shoulder and then turned to us again.

"You shouldn't be here," he whispered furiously. "Your husband has been looking for you."

He directed the last comment to me but gave his look of disapproval to Elan.

Elan looked abashed, which annoyed me almost as much as Ya'akov's overbearing attitude. I cocked my head to the side and pursed my lips at Ya'akov, hoping to intimidate him.

Today he was resolute.

"Don't look at me like that, Hannah. This family already has one scandal to address, we don't need another. Come on. *Both* of you."

He was right. I stared at Elan, but he wouldn't acknowledge me.

Ya'akov pulled me by the elbow back into the harsh afternoon light.

CHAPTER 40

We found the rest of the family at the hazzan's property seated under a sycamine tree, its limbs heavy with dark red fruit. Despite the warmth of the day, someone had taken care to tuck a blanket snuggly across the hazzan's lap. He looked even older than he had this morning and impossibly frail.

My eyes traveled around the circle of those gathered, and I was startled to see Olmer glaring back at me. Walking up the path with Elan and Ya'akov had felt so natural that the sight of my husband jerked me cruelly back into my present life.

Emmi jumped up and scanned our faces. "Did you find him? Do you know where he is?"

"No, Emmi," Ya'akov said quietly. "Don't worry. I'm sure he's safe."

"But where could he *be*?" She held a hand to her forehead. "He wouldn't have walked far on the Sabbath, but not one person in the village has seen him. It's as if he disappeared."

I glanced at Elan and he raised his eyebrow. I answered with a barely perceptible shake of my head. As I sat next to Shlomit, Olmer measured Elan with deadly interest. I berated myself and determined not to look at Elan again.

Emmi paced and waved her arms wildly. "I can't believe these people. They've known Yeshua since he was a toddler.

How could they turn against him like this?"

I wondered again about the steward and what role he might have played. He seemed to have disappeared too.

"Now, Miryam. There's no need to fret," Itamar said. "Once the men go home and break bread with their families, I'm sure the women will talk sense into them. You'll see. They'll welcome Yeshua back in no time. It was just the shock of hearing such a statement . . ." He scratched his head, looking dazed himself.

"Maybe it's my fault." Emmi collapsed to the ground heavily. "If we'd been more forthright from the beginning, perhaps people would be more accepting of the truth by now. I should have tried harder to convince them—"

"Emmi, shall we eat soon? I'm sure we're all hungry," I interrupted. Mention of "the beginning" seemed like dangerous ground that I'd rather not cross with Olmer present.

Olmer wasn't so easily distracted. "Convince them about what?"

Shlomit spoke up. "Convince them Yeshua's the one we have waited for, the right arm of the Lord who will bring justice to our people."

Olmer's mouth opened in disbelief.

My sister looked pleased with herself until our gazes met. She returned my withering look, as if disgusted that I had allowed my husband to be so ignorant.

"What are you saying? Yeshua's the Anointed One?" Olmer seemed genuinely amazed at the news.

For a moment, optimism grew. Maybe I could explain everything, maybe he'd finally begin to understand me, to know what I've had to live with my whole life.

But then he threw his head back and laughed.

"You don't seriously believe this, do you?" he asked, looking from man to man.

My brothers shifted and squirmed. Elan stared back at him with open hostility. Uri appeared fascinated with a thread on his sleeve.

Olmer turned to Itamar.

"Sir, as the Torah keeper, tell me *you* don't share this opinion."

The hazzan stroked his beard several times before answering. "I don't think Yeshua spends his days eating curds and honey as the Messiah ought." He chuckled, but it quickly deteriorated into a cough. When he recovered his breath, he continued. "But he does speak with wisdom and authority. Haven't we seen in the writings that prophets were ridiculed until what they foretold came to pass? Then again, for every true prophet there were tens of false ones who were rightly ridiculed. Well, time will tell if he's a true prophet of the Lord."

"He's *not* just another prophet," Shlomit blurted out. "Yochanon is a prophet. Yeshua is more than that. Tell him, Uri."

Uri flushed and looked at his grandfather.

Shlomit nudged her husband with her elbow.

He cleared his throat and looked at the ground as he spoke.

"Yeshua was born in Bethlehem. And it's written that even though Bethlehem is small among the clans of Y'hudah, out of it will come forth the future ruler of Isra'el, whose origins are far in the past, back in ancient times."[23]

"And based on that, you think Yeshua will deliver us?" Olmer shook his head. "Do you know how many babes are born in Bethlehem each year? And Yeshua's not much older than thirty years. How can he have origins far in the past?"

I glanced around, hoping no one would bring up the story of Emmi's miraculous conception. Then again, they probably assumed Olmer had heard the tale from me already—not an unlikely assumption given I'd had plenty of time to tell him. Despite myself, I looked at Elan. Displeasure hardened his face as he returned my stare. I got the sense he knew I'd never told Olmer.

Elan directed his focus to my husband. "I've seen Yeshua's wonders for myself. You can't deny people flock to him. He's a leader, just like his ancestor King David before him."

Olmer batted his hand in dismissal. "Attracting fishermen and farmers with food and showy tricks hardly constitutes leading an army. The Messiah will return self-rule to Israel, he'll bring lasting peace. Yeshua doesn't know the first thing about military strategy. His followers don't have armor or weapons or a stronghold from which to fight. Oh. I forgot,"— his tone now decidedly mocking, oblivious to the growing resentment around him—"he'll make gold miraculously appear to pay for it all. Listen, it's one thing to cause mischief here and there, but to take territory? They'd be decimated in hours if they went head to head with Rome's mercenaries. It would be a massacre."

Emmi gasped.

I gave Olmer a wide-eyed look of disapproval, silently urging him to desist.

He seemed to recall his audience then and softened his tone.

"All I'm saying is that greater men have tried and failed. Remember Antigonus? He had a legitimate claim to the throne *and* the wealth of the Persian kingdom backing his war against Rome. And what did it get him? Executed."

Olmer whipped his head toward me like he'd just uncovered a great plot. "You don't think Yeshua is seeking foreign support, do you? From Parthia or the Nabateans?"

"No, of course not," I said sharply.

He looked relieved. "Good. No, even if you wanted to defeat the Romans now, it would take resources beyond Yeshua's, believe me."

Ya'akov had quietly listened until now, but he didn't let these words pass. "What do you mean, 'even if you wanted to'? Don't you want to see the land free from Rome?"

Olmer gave a derisive snort. "Of course I do—in an ideal world. But this isn't an ideal world. Be practical."

I might not have agreed with them, but it angered me to see him patronize my family.

"Practical? Or complicit? We'll all be judged guilty for Rome's crimes if we do nothing to stop them."

"Quiet," he snapped. "I don't tolerate such dangerous talk from my workers and I certainly won't tolerate it from you."

Heat rushed to my cheeks and I looked away, but not before seeing Elan stare at Olmer with unveiled hatred. Then he stood and walked away. Olmer watched his retreating figure before turning his head to meet my eyes. His expression was inscrutable.

Emmi fussed with the hazzan's blanket. "I think you're right, Itamar. We all need to eat. Once we satisfy our bellies, cooler minds will prevail. Are you sure you're warm enough, Itamar? Would you like something to drink?"

Itamar patted her hand. "Everything's fine."

But was it? Would it ever be again?

We sat in tense silence. No one could excuse themselves with chores on Shabbat. So we feigned interest in the children's idle chatter and waited for the sun to set.

CHAPTER 41

Over the years our house had grown to accommodate Shim'on's and Yosi's expanding families—Y'hudah alone left to live in Gamla, the town of his wife's family. The small storage room above the stables where Olmer and I rested tonight was part of the original structure, virtually unchanged from my childhood. We reclined between tools, sacks of barley grain, and skins of new wine. This was Elan's abode when he wasn't out with the flock, but he must have left. That thought had me torn between relief and regret.

Even though Olmer and I were man and wife, lying here with him amid vivid reminders of the past felt odd. He didn't fit into this world of my childhood. I studied my husband, wondering how he slept soundly with the snorts and shuffling of the animals below. I closed my eyes and willed my thoughts to be silent, but sleep eluded me.

Maybe it was me, not Olmer, who was out of place here. In Sepphoris, I was criticized for being unsophisticated and following antiquated religious traditions. In Nazareth, my own family was reserved around me. They were too kind to criticize, but I suspected they thought I'd been contaminated by wealth and pagan influences. I straddled two worlds and didn't feel at home in either.

Suddenly, unbidden questions entered my mind. Was this how Yeshua felt, like he straddled two worlds? What if it was all true and he was the Anointed One? What must it be like for him?

Did Yeshua have a longing to know the heavenly realm of Adonai? Or was heaven more real to him than earth? And was he a divine being because of his patriarch? If that were true, it must pain him to be trapped here, susceptible to mortal failings and living amid a people unable to comprehend his reality. He'd probably laugh at me, but I almost felt sympathy for him having to tolerate our far-too-human family.

I shook my head at such musing. I was beginning to think we were all deluded. How could he really be the son of Elohim? But if Abba wasn't his father, who was? Abba had been a righteous man—he wouldn't have tolerated any indiscretion on Emmi's part before marriage. Maybe the story was crafted to cover their own youthful dalliance before the wedding ceremony, and with so many retellings, they had convinced themselves it was true? Still, it was hard to believe either of them capable of such deceit. Then again, it was easier to believe human failing than divine intervention.

I searched for a comfortable position but only grew more aware my bladder was full. The more I concentrated on it, the more I realized I wouldn't fall asleep until I got up again. I crawled over Olmer's bulky form, pushing my legs out into the open air behind me, my feet flailing until they found purchase on a ladder rung.

When I exited the stable, I nearly tripped over Yeshua sleeping, wrapped in his cloak. My head whipped around to check that Olmer had not stirred. Why would Yeshua return here? Had he no fear?

Yeshua moaned, then breathed heavily again. He must have

been dreaming.

I remembered how as a boy he would sometimes come awake from deep sleep with a start and a cry. He'd have a distant look of wonder or intense thought on his face. My other brothers and I had liked sharing our dreams in the morning, laughing at the absurdity of our nighttime adventures. But Yeshua had never spoken of his dreams. I'd assumed at the time it was because he didn't remember them. Now I wondered if it was because his dreams were full of fantastical places more real to him than this world.

I peered at his face. The corner of his mouth was wet with drool, his features slack and nondescript in sleep. He looked so vulnerable that my heart grew tender toward him.

He *was* special . . .but just a man.

***

As the sky lightened, Olmer and I bid awkward goodbyes and set off for Sepphoris. There was no sign of Yeshua, and I wondered if I had dreamt seeing him last night. Regardless, I didn't volunteer the information to my husband. In fact, we didn't even speak until we were almost back to the manor.

"If you really care about your brother's safety, you'll stop him," Olmer said without prelude.

"Stop him? You know I have no sway over what my brother does or doesn't do."

He pointed his finger in my face. "If you care about his life, you'll try."

A chill went up my spine, and I looked at him trying to ascertain the unspoken message. "Do you know something you're not telling me? Does someone wish him ill? I know you've never gotten along with my brother, but if you know he's in danger, you have to tell me."

"Your brother creates danger for himself. Look what's become of Yochanon. Do you think Yeshua will be spared a similar fate? How long do you think he can travel the countryside speaking about ushering in a new kingdom without the Romans noticing?"

I tried to absorb this information and keep pace with Olmer's long strides at the same time.

"What can I do? He's a man and will do what he thinks is best. Besides, I've never known him to be wrong about anything." I hesitated, thinking of the recent criticisms my brother had expressed about Olmer and his family's actions. I chose my next words carefully.

"You just haven't been able to see Yeshua's true nature. How patient and wise and caring he can be. If you'd just make an effort to understand him, you'd see he's not just trying to cause trouble."

Olmer stopped short and glared down at me. "I don't understand why you behave this way, as if I'm to blame for being concerned. I'm not the enemy."

My heart sank.

He shook his head and began walking again.

"Olmer. Olmer, wait." I lunged for his arm to stop him, but he whirled around to face me before I reached him.

"My mother warned me not to marry you. But I insisted that you would fit in with our family, that you weren't like other villagers, that you could be educated. But she was right. You'll always be common. I guess how you start a marriage predicts how it will end."

"What exactly are you saying?" I asked, my earlier guilt replaced with cold fury.

He leaned close and pointed a finger at my face. "Where were you yesterday?"

"You know where I was," I replied, too angry to be shaken by his interrogation.

He eyed me up and down and paced around me like a wolf searching for weakness in the herd. "Were you alone with that man after leaving the synagogue?"

"What man? Iakovos? Do you mean before or after he riled the townspeople to drive my brother off a cliff?" If I had hoped my husband would wince or flush with guilt, I was disappointed.

"You know the man of whom I speak. The shepherd."

"His name is Elan. And he's part of my family, and yours by marriage. If anyone should determine someone's where-abouts, it's me. You're the one who spends more time in the company of strangers than in the presence of your wife. Just who has been offering you hospitality on all your frequent travels?"

There, I'd said it, what had grieved me of late.

Olmer threw his hands up and shook his head. He appeared hurt and offended.

Instantly I was ashamed again for accusing him like some jealous hag. I dropped my defenses against my better judgment.

"I'm sorry. I didn't mean that. I've just missed you. It's hard when you're away."

"Can't you see that everything I do is for your benefit? All of the traveling. All of the hours away. Even this trip to Nazareth. And all I want is the respect due me from my wife and her kin."

"Olmer, I'm sorry. We do respect you."

"No, you don't. Your brothers don't listen to me. Yeshua wouldn't even speak with me despite all my efforts to treat him as my equal. I hope he comes to his senses soon. It would be tragic if harm came to someone in your family. You'll all wish you'd listened to me then."

Any sympathy I felt for him disappeared, and I stared at him with unconcealed disgust.

He turned his back and walked away.

Only much later did I realize he'd never directly answered my question about knowing of plots against Yeshua.

CHAPTER 42

My eyes strained to focus on the tiny stitches of embroidery I sewed on a smock for my nephew. Keturah, at last, had birthed a healthy son for Hakon three weeks ago. The boy was adorable and a delightful distraction, but I wondered how long it would be before his personality matched that of his parents.

Keturah was insufferable now. She paraded around the house like a newly coronated princess, her status secure as both the wife of the heir and now mother of the second-in-line to inherit. I resolved not to hold it against my nephew, and tied off the final stitch around the neckline of the smock.

After briefly admiring my work, I decided to reward myself with a walk outside to stretch my legs and ease the cramps in my belly that had begun once again. I dreaded having to disappoint my own husband with the news, or lack thereof, when he returned home.

Entering the courtyard, I was surprised to see how many people still waited to speak with Gal. Today was a business day at the manor—a day for tenants to bring payments, workers to receive wages, and my father-in-law to render judgment on matters that fell outside these two categories. But some councilmen and a representative from the tetrarch had arrived earlier this morning to meet with Gal and Hakon. They must not have been finished conferring with him, because Raziela, the queen herself, hovered outside the door feigning an uncharacteristic interest in dusting.

I shook my head at her.

"I wouldn't go far, if I were you," she whispered.

I ignored her as I passed by, deciding to exit through the back of the manor to avoid the press of people at the front entrance. At the foot of the cellar stairs, I nearly collided with Tabitha.

"Oh, good. Tell me what you think of this." She held out a bowl filled with the dried insects needed to produce a scarlet dye. "Should I use red cloth for the boys' cloaks? Keturah thinks it's unnecessary, but of course she would. She thinks only her own children are worthy of admiration, but I want my boys to stand out as well."

"Mmm . . ." I pondered the question.

She tipped a few of the scaly creatures into her palm and tossed them about.

"These were pulled from the trees last summer. Do you think the color will be as vibrant? I suppose I'll have to boil them to find out. We really need to start weaving to make sure all the cloaks are finished before the feast . . . Hannah, are you listening?"

"Sorry. I was wondering where Olmer must be by now."

"At least you know he didn't travel to Miletus again," she stated a bit too emphatically before turning into one of the storage rooms off the hall.

I followed her into the shelf-lined room. "What do you mean? What difference does it make where he travels if he's not at home?"

She deflected my questions with a laugh. "Oh, I'm just being foolish." She dumped the insects back into the jar they'd come from and clapped her hands to remove any dust. "Ships seem so dangerous, don't they? I just meant at least he's not relying on the winds and the seas to travel this time because he's traveling east into Perea. Maybe yellow would be better than red?"

I raised my eyebrow at her. Never had she voiced concerns about sea travel.

"Would you mind finding Myrinne and asking what she thinks?" she asked sweetly. "I want to see what other dyes we have."

I frowned to let her know I suspected there was something more, then headed upstairs. Walking the perimeter of the courtyard took me to the kitchen door without bearing the stares of the strangers lined up outside the banquet room. But before I entered, I recognized a familiar pair.

The woman stood side by side with a gaunt young man. He ignored her, but the matching grave expressions they wore indicated they were together. He must have been her son, although I didn't see much resemblance. Perhaps he favored his father.

No sooner did I think this than realization dawned—she was our neighbor, the wife of the man who had been killed in the fire. My heart filled with compassion as I examined the young man again, searching for a hint of what Aharon, his father, might have looked like before he was so cruelly disfigured.

Unbidden, my feet carried me toward them.

The woman lifted her head, perhaps sensing my gaze. She stared at me, her face expressionless.

I immediately regretted coming this way. Now I'd have to speak with her.

"How have you been?" I winced inwardly. How *could* she

be with her husband and home gone and the responsibility of feeding her family solely on her shoulders?

"You remember my son, Gershem?"

The boy's eyes darted my direction. Closer up, I better appreciated his youth as well as the discoloration of fading bruises around his left eye and cheek.

My brow must have creased in concern, because his mother answered my unasked question. "That's the work of that devil. He beat my boy."

"Who did? Who would do this?" I asked, dreading the answer.

"Emmi . . ." the boy cautioned.

"It's no secret. The reason for our visit will be plain to all soon enough."

Gershem twisted his lips to the side but didn't protest further.

"He's ashamed that I have made him come today, calling on the generosity of a neighbor again," she explained. "I've told him, there's no shame in making sure the young ones are fed and clothed. There's no shame in trying to keep him out of debtor's prison." Her voice trembled on the last words, and tears sprang to her eyes.

I stared at my feet and allowed her to compose herself.

"Excuse me, miss. Things have been difficult since . . . well, you know. The barley that we lost was the first planting we'd made following the shemittah year. The remainder of the stored grain that was meant to carry us through until the harvest was destroyed as well. We borrowed what we could from relatives, but they're not much better off than we are. Helping us only hastens their decline into desperation." She halted to take a shaky breath.

I ignored the rules of decorum and placed my hand on her

forearm, giving what I hoped was a reassuring squeeze.

"I'm so sorry . . . but I still don't understand. Who hit your son?"

"That tax collector came back." She turned her head over her shoulder and looked as if she would have spat on the ground but remembered her surroundings and thought better of it. "He's demanding payment of last year's taxes. He well knows we couldn't pay the taxes *before* he set the fire, let alone after. Gershem asked for more time and the brute struck him. Said he didn't want excuses, only coin."

My heart beat faster. "The tax collector. Do you know his name?"

The doors of the banquet room swung open, nearly striking Raz in her attempt to look nonchalant. As Iakovos ushered the men out, his eyebrows rose in surprise when he saw me standing in the queue, but he summoned the woman and her son forward without comment. I followed them in with Raz right on my heels.

Gal sat behind the table, looking implacable. To his right, Hakon stared at me with his mouth open.

I lowered my eyes but remained where I was, listening while Gershem explained their circumstances. Finally, in a halting voice he requested a loan and offered his own labor as collateral.

Gal said nothing.

"They need our help," I said. "You'll give them the funds needed until they can recover, won't you?"

"Goodness, Hannah," Raziela said with forced lightness. "Why don't you leave financial matters to the men, hmm?"

I pursed my lips and focused on my father-in-law.

He appeared to ponder all of this for a moment before addressing the boy.

"You've been honest with me. Let me be honest with you about what informs my decision. The truth is, I'm not presently in a position to hire additional workers. Why, I'm struggling to keep my laborers fed and clothed as it is. It wouldn't be right to divide up what meager resources we have among even more people, would it? I can't take a share away from those to whom I'm already committed, can I?"

The boy shook his head. What else could he do? But the opulence before his eyes testified that this was far from the honest conversation Gal touted it as being.

"Even if I had additional land to work, which I don't, and hired you as a laborer," Gal said with an exaggerated shrug, "you still wouldn't be able to pay the taxes you already owe and this year's taxes . . . let alone provide for your family. You yourself have said that you have not a single seed to plant. And if you're working my fields, who would work yours? No, I don't think a loan is the most charitable option under the circumstances."

The boy's cheeks flushed and he glared at his mother. Now I appreciated why he had been loath to ask for help. Gal's words disgusted me. No wonder Yeshua thought my in-laws were hypocrites. They argued in favor of the prosbul and purported to stand for the poor, but their mercy only extended as far as there was personal gain to be had.

"In fact, the more I think on it, the best solution is for you to sell me your land," Gal said.

Gershem gasped.

"Now, wait, hear me out. Sell me the land and you'll have coin to pay your taxes and then some to help your kinsmen. Sow and work their fields with them. Then, once your siblings are grown and you have the savings and labor to handle the land, you can buy it back from me." He finished the statement with a rare smile as if it were all so simple.

The woman muffled a sob. Despite having his inheritance slip away from him, Gershem held his head high. He put an arm around her shoulders.

"At least this way we'll be free of Alvon."

My head whipped around, eyes protruding. "Alvon? He's the one who set fire to your home? The tax collector who beat you? I knew—"

"Hannah," Raziela scolded. "Where are your manners? What does it matter who it was?" She approached them with exaggerated pity on her face. "One tax collector is the same as the next—horrible men, all of them. I'm sure these dear people don't want to relive such frightful memories."

Raz steered them toward the door. "Iakovos will prepare a contract. You go to the kitchens and tell Myrinne she's to make a decent meal for you while you wait."

The woman started to speak, but Raz cut her off. "No need to thank me. It's the neighborly thing to do. Go on." She practically closed the door on them.

I turned my attention back to the men at the table, not concealing my repulsion. Of course Gal had orchestrated the tax collector's actions. The drawings for buildings on the neighbor's property hadn't been a mistake. Gal had intended to buy the land from the beginning. This meant the absence of grasses in the vineyard near the neighbor's fields hadn't been an oversight either. Gal had taken care to eliminate the risk of his vines inadvertently catching fire when the neighbors' land was set ablaze. And, I belatedly realized, Gal hadn't instructed Alvon to do the act when the family was absent. *Ours* was the family that Gal meant to be absent during the fire to avoid any hint of culpability. He hadn't cared about anyone else's safety at all. And a man had died because of it.

Hakon shifted nervously in the face of my contempt and averted his eyes. Gal met my stare with a cold, challenging one of his own.

A cauldron of fury boiled in my belly, and my face flushed from the need to vent the tirade within. I clenched my teeth to keep from screaming at this injustice as I stomped toward the door.

"Come back here," Gal bellowed. All my bravado deserted me in an instant.

Raziela smirked. "I told you not to go far. Remember?" she whispered.

My knees wobbled as I retraced my steps. *I don't need be intimidated,* I assured myself. *This is my father-in-law. And I'm not on trial. He's the one in the wrong, not me.* But my fear grew as Gal waited an uncomfortable amount of time before speaking.

"Herod requests Yeshua's presence at court."

"What?" My mind reeled. Of all the things he could've said, I hadn't anticipated this. "Why would Herod want to meet Yeshua? I know he's a gifted rabbi, but Herod must have access to the greatest teachers of the law. Yeshua is a carpenter with only a dozen followers at most."

"Ha!" Hakon exclaimed. "Why would Herod want to meet Yeshua? Everywhere Yeshua goes he draws an audience of thousands. And his motives are clear. He's not come to bring peace but a sword—he said it himself. Brother fighting brother, children having their parents put to death. He's threatening to restart civil war in our land."

Would Yeshua really say such things? Surely Hakon was mistaken.

"When you get word of your brother's whereabouts, you'll report it to me," Gal ordered.

"But we can't comply with the tetrarch's request."

"You insolent girl!" he shouted with a loud smack of his hand on the table that caused me to flinch. Taking a deep breath, he composed himself. "I'll not tolerate your defiance. You'll do as I say."

I bowed my head in submission, hiding the tears welling in my eyes.

"Of course."

Gal signaled the steward to open the door. I had been dismissed.

***

I took deliberate, measured steps past those remaining in the courtyard. How many of their lives had Gal manipulated to suit his purposes? "Do not covet your neighbor's property."[24] That was what the Torah told us. Who was Gal to think his desires outweighed the Lord's commands? How did he dare presume his welfare superseded that of his neighbors? I thought of the dreams Aharon's family must have had for the future, the inheritance that they had been building for generations to come, all dashed with the toss of a torch.

What would the family do now? Who would set this right?

Suddenly I pictured Yeshua, turning over tables and disrupting the business in the temple courts. This was how he must have felt, fueled by indignation at men who defiled the house of the Lord with their greed. Men who sought to profit off pilgrims who, out of their meager resources, did what was honorable and right in the sight of the Lord. How did any man dare impede their worship by demanding payment before they were allowed to make their sacrifice? It was incomprehensible.

A crowd blocked the main courtyard entrance so I returned to the cellar stairs. Once downstairs, I picked up my pace. I wanted nothing more than to distance myself from the despicable people I called family. Bursting through the back doors, I squinted from the glare of the sun.

"There you are," Tabitha said. With a long wooden pole, she prodded the cloth floating in a pot of dye. "Where have you been? I thought you were coming right back." She paused to wipe her brow and stared at me. "What is it, what's wrong?"

I considered the question, not knowing where to begin. She laid the pole on the ground and crossed the distance between us.

"Did something happen?"

"Yes. Well, not now, but yes."

"Here, sit down. Tell me what's going on."

I eyed the distant hills, not ready to give up on fleeing, but where would I go? She beckoned me to follow her to the narrow band of shade near the wall.

I put my back against the stone and slid to the ground with a thump.

"Gal was responsible for the tax collector burning down the neighbor's home last year. He paid that man sixty shekels to start the fire. A man died for sixty shekels."

Instead of the anger I expected, fear showed on Tabitha's face.

"You didn't confront him, did you?"

"Not in words, but—"

"Oh, Hannah. You must be very careful. Don't mention this to anyone, especially your family in Nazareth."

"My family?" I shook my head in bafflement. "What do they have to do with it?"

"You said there's already discord between Olmer and your brother. I'd hate for there to be further cause for animosity. For your sake."

"I hope you're not implying that Olmer knew of Gal's scheming? My husband may have his faults, but that doesn't mean he's complicit in this. You don't seem very surprised by Gal's actions yourself, now that I think about it."

"Are *you*? You know Gal wanted to build new storehouses. You saw how quickly he volunteered help to raze the ruins of the house and make the ground level."

"I thought he wanted to help the family rebuild." Even I recognized what a ridiculous statement I'd made. When had Gal done anything charitable? But I was loath to admit I'd willfully ignored the truth. "Why didn't you say something to me before if you knew about this?"

"I decided long ago to keep out of matters that don't concern me. I have the boys' welfare to think of, not just my own."

I didn't hide my disappointment. "You're their mother. You must teach them wrong from right. How's it in their best interest to grow up thinking self-serving greed and hypocrisy are acceptable?"

She shushed me and glanced around nervously. "What choice do I have? Tell me. I am a widow. I don't have any other family to take me in. At least you have your own kin if . . ."

"If what?"

"If, the Lord forbid, anything should happen."

I didn't know if she meant happen to Olmer or happen to *me*. I turned away from her to think, cupping my hand to shield my eyes from the sun. She was right, of course. We had no other choice but to make the best of our circumstances. Until Olmer returned, I'd be at the mercy of his parents.

"Gal wants me to tell him when Yeshua returns to the Galil. Herod wants to speak with my brother."

She nodded. "Yeshua's reputation is growing. Many are saying he is Eliyahu raised from the dead."

I smirked at her gullibility. "What?"

"*I'm* not saying it. But there is something special about Yeshua, isn't there?" She tilted her head and lifted her eyebrows. "The way the wine suddenly appeared at the wedding . . . and when I first met you, I remember your sister Shlomit speaking about an angel."

She searched my face.

I tried not to let my expression waver and began to push myself up to a standing position.

"Shouldn't you be stirring that pot?"

"Please, Hannah, tell me about the angel messenger. When did it appear? What did it say?"

The story pushed against my closed lips, wanting me to lend it my voice. I'd hesitated too long to deny it now anyway. And it *would* be comforting to gain an ally in the house . . . or at least a sympathetic ear to help me make sense of these events.

Tabitha leaned closer, her eyes alight. "You can trust me."

"If I tell you, you must promise not to speak of this to anyone."

She inhaled deeply and clasped her hands in front of her chest. Her face beamed like that of a child about to receive a sweet.

"I *mean* it. I haven't even told these things to Olmer."

She pulled her head back in surprise but gravely nodded her understanding.

I sat back down and tucked my knees up under my dress, hugging them for support.

"My mother says she was visited by an angel before she and Abba completed their wedding ceremony. The angel told her that she would be overshadowed by the power of the Most High and then . . . she would be with child, the Son of Ha

'Elyon. And then she gave birth to Yeshua."[25]

Her eyes grew large but not mocking, so I continued.

"The Lord's messenger told her Yeshua would reign over the house of Ya'akov one day. That's why he grew up thinking he is the Anointed One." I stared at my lap.

"You don't think he is?"

"I don't know what to think anymore." I traced circles in the dirt at my side. "Sometimes I begin to believe it's possible, but then he does things that aren't logical or rational. And why doesn't he have the support of the Sanhedrin and the Torah teachers? Shouldn't they be venerating him, not cursing him? And now Herod requests his presence. What can that mean?"

Her mouth opened, but the cellar door banged against the wall.

Keturah popped her head out, and upon seeing us she held the door with her foot and folded her arms on her chest looking annoyed.

"There you are, lazing away the day. I should have guessed. Idan's crying and making a fuss. He woke the baby."

Tabitha sprang to her feet. "Is he all right?"

"There's nothing wrong with him. He fell and scraped his knee. I'm the one who should be crying. I should be resting, not having to chase you down." The door closed again.

I grabbed Tabitha by her wrist. "Remember, you can't tell anyone," I hissed.

She slapped at my hand, eager to be off to console her youngest son. "I won't mention it to Olmer. I promise."

I released her, satisfied with her answer but still troubled. Confiding in her hadn't brought me the solace I had sought.

CHAPTER 43

Early Winter of the Year 3789 (Late CE 28)

Yeshua somehow had evaded Herod's request for months. Just when I thought the matter had been forgotten, Raz demanded I go to Nazareth to learn Yeshua's whereabouts. She rushed me out the door three days after the Feast of Dedication, insisting I not return until I had delivered Herod's message to Yeshua. By the time Iakovos deposited me safely at my family's door, I felt less like an emissary of the court and more like a traitor.

I didn't discover Yeshua, but my aunt and uncle had visited Nazareth for the celebration. Thankful for a reprieve, I decided my message could keep until after their departure. We passed a pleasant hour reclining around the dying embers of the cooking fire enjoying its warmth on the winter evening.

I watched my niece, Shim'on and Talia's newborn, and grinned. Aunt Miryam blew on her round little tummy and she cooed and kicked her legs back and forth before my aunt swaddled her again.

"Cleopas, look how precious she is," Aunt Miryam said with marvel.

"Don't be getting ideas. I'm too old for babies."

"Oh, you." Aunt Miryam giggled.

He had spoken in jest, but now I noted the deeper crinkles at the corners of my uncle's eyes when he smiled, the absence of a tooth at the side of his grin. His thick curls remained but now were more silver than sable. I wondered if this was how Abba would appear if he were alive. In my memories he never aged. Pressing my lips together, I exhaled through my nose.

"Oh, come now," Uncle Cleopas said. "Why the sad face? I'm not *that* old." He threw his arm around my shoulders and squeezed until he coaxed a smile from me. Then he kissed the top of my head before releasing me.

"Uri said he spotted a fox trying to get into the dovecote last night." Ya'akov said.

"When it comes here, I'll be ready for it." Shim'on clapped his hands together and startled the baby.

"Shim'on," Emmi admonished.

Uncle Cleopas glanced surreptitiously at my aunt. Seeing she was distracted with comforting the little one, he commented, "Speaking of foxes . . ."

My aunt whipped her head up and fixed my uncle with a stern look. "No politics. We agreed."

"What is it, Uncle?" Ya'akov asked.

"Well, since you ask." Uncle Cleopas looked sheepishly at my aunt. "Yeshua publicly decried Herod for being a fox."

"What?" I was scandalized. Everyone knew Herod could be devious and wasn't above gaining at another's expense. But to disparage him openly? How could Yeshua be so reckless?

Instead of being appalled, my uncle was beaming. "Yeshua has him marked for sure. Herod and that woman he calls his wife can scheme all they want, but they'll never be the true rulers over the House of Ya'akov."

"Please, Cleopas. Can't we have one night free of such

talk?" Aunt Miryam lifted my niece to her shoulder, patting the squirming infant's back.

He ignored her. "From the way Yeshua's speaking, it won't be long before he makes his rise to power. I heard him tell the crowds that those who aren't for him are against him. It's time to take a stand. We can't pretend any longer that anything short of armed revolt will bring change. The arm of the Lord has been revealed. Yeshua will purge the whole horde of idol worshippers from the land, and we'll rule ourselves once more."

I shook my head, vexed by his ranting. "Don't even utter such things aloud. Do you have any idea the trouble this kind of talk is causing? It's no wonder Gal sent me here."

All eyes fixed on me and I froze, realizing I'd said too much. Even the baby grew quiet as if expecting elaboration.

I shrugged to downplay my coming explanation. "Herod's men approached Gal. The tetrarch seeks an audience with Yeshua." I frowned, realizing I'd gotten it backward. The lesser man usually sought an audience with the ruler, not the other way around. But no one corrected me.

Shim'on recovered first. "Someone should warn Yeshua."

"Warn him? It's an honor to be invited to the palace. And it's no wonder the tetrarch is curious about Yeshua if he's heard only half the ridiculous accounts I have."

"Oh, you're right, Hannah. No doubt an entire entourage of soldiers will escort Yeshua on a tour of the palace—starting with the prison."

Emmi looked alarmed, and Ya'akov reached over to take her hand.

"He's right. Herod has no respect for Torah or its prophets," he said. "He's imprisoned Yochanon. What makes you think he wouldn't imprison Yeshua?"

I crossed my arms defensively. We'd reverted back to our usual roles. Yeshua could do no wrong, and I wasn't taken seriously. I didn't disagree with my brother's motives, but he was the one bringing trouble on himself.

"I'm afraid there is some credence to the threats against Yeshua's safety." Uncle Cleopas spoke softly. "It's no secret that Herod's supporters have tried to stop him."

Emmi gasped. "What? Why didn't you tell me?"

"Now don't fret, Miryam. I told you, Yeshua's not intimidated by Herod. The Lord won't allow any harm to come to Yeshua. Besides, he's yet to fulfill the prophecies written about him."

She nodded but was visibly distressed. "I think I'll just take the baby to Talia. She must be hungry."

She scooped up the baby so abruptly, my niece wailed in protest.

Aunt Miryam frowned at my uncle and he shrugged and mouthed, "It's not my fault."

My aunt followed Emmi into the house.

Uncle Cleopas leaned forward conspiratorially. "Men don't readily yield their power. The more signs and miracles that Yeshua demonstrates, the more the people turn to him and away from the established leaders. The more Yeshua's power grows, the more persecution he'll face from those desperate to hold their positions. And Yeshua's power is growing. That's why we must be ready to take action and fight. The time's coming for Yeshua to take his rightful place as Israel's leader."

"This is absurd." I threw my hands up in exasperation. "I can't believe you're entertaining rebellion, let alone voicing it aloud. Yeshua doesn't know the first thing about military operations."

"He doesn't have to. He just needs to have the right men at

his side. We heard in Gamla that one of his closest men is a Zealot called Shim'on. I'm certain that man has connections."

"Gamla? What business did you have there?" Ya'akov asked.

I looked at my uncle also. Gamla was a haven for rebels who were as cruel in their tactics as the Romans. When the last census was ordered, they had set fire to the homes of those who complied with the order. These were not desirable companions.

Uncle Cleopas hesitated and cleared his throat. He peered over his shoulder to make sure Emmi and Aunt Miryam were still out of hearing. "Your cousin Shim'on and I had a meeting with some supporters of Yeshua's cause."

"What cause is that? Suicide by rebellion?" Shim'on snorted.

Uncle Cleopas ignored him. "And I think Yeshua's getting financial backing. He's enlisted a tax collector, Mattiyahu, to his cause and has been dining with others."

"A tax collector?" I exclaimed.

My uncle held up a hand to quiet me.

I lowered my voice but not my urgency. "How *could* he?"

"There must be some explanation," Ya'akov said. "We should ask Yeshua before accusing him based on gossip."

"Tax collectors are violent and despicable traitors to their own people," I argued. "What explanation can he possibly have?"

"Hannah's right. This is too much, even for Yeshua," Shim'on said. "We need to stop him before he gets involved in something that can't be stopped."

"Do you think you can stop the word of the Lord from coming to pass? I'm telling you, Yeshua is the Messiah." Uncle Cleopas looked at each of us in turn. "Of course there will be difficulties and decisions made that we may not understand, but we must trust him, support him."

I turned away in disgust. Why should any of us trust Yeshua? What had he ever done to demonstrate that he was trustworthy? All he did was create havoc in my life.

"Your brother will be king of Isra'el, mark my words," he said.

At that moment the fire flickered wildly, almost extinguished by a brisk gust of wind. I heard a noise behind me and jumped, clutching my chest. Seeing it was only the others returning, I scolded myself for allowing my uncle's words to unnerve me.

"Why the grim faces? Did someone die?" Yosi teased. He looked worried when no one laughed.

"Did someone?" he whispered.

"Of course not," Shim'on snapped. "Not yet anyway."

CHAPTER 44

The clouds hung low, sprinkling us with occasional drizzle. *I should be sitting in front of the loom, dry and warm, not slogging through mud in search of my brother,* I thought as we skirted the base of Mount Arbel and made our way north along the shoreline of the lake.

Ya'akov had hardly spoken a word for hours. His furrowed brow confirmed that he was disturbed, no doubt anticipating the confrontation to come. Yeshua had always been something of a hero to him, so I knew this wouldn't be easy for Ya'akov. Emmi also looked glum. She insisted she was just weary, but my uncle's talk had clearly disturbed her. Shim'on alone seemed perfectly content despite our mission and the weather. He'd been whistling the same chipper tune since daybreak.

Finally, Emmi voiced aloud what I was sure we were all thinking. "Shim'on, love, could you please stop or at least come up with another song?"

"Oh, was I whistling?" he asked with mock innocence.

I huffed and plodded on.

As the winds picked up, we approached the outskirts of Capernaum. I don't know what I expected to find when we arrived. My uncle nearly had me convinced that Yeshua had transformed into the mighty general of armed combatants.

But if my brother planned a rebellion, he couldn't have chosen a less covert place to do so. The town straddled one of the most traveled international routes and was home for a garrison of Roman troops. I doubted anything that happened here went unnoticed.

No soldiers were in evidence now. Three filthy children played a game, tossing pebbles onto a grid drawn in the mud. A mangy dog scampered about sniffing for scraps, and finding none, let out a pitiful whine. People had set up makeshift tents out of clothes draped over sticks and crutches. In fact, many seemed infirm. A decrepit woman with milky eyes huddled in a doorway for shelter. A man with a shriveled hand watched us pass. I pulled my cloak securely around me and avoided looking at their sorry faces.

The rain began in earnest now. We followed the hum of voices and found a mass of humanity surrounding a building north of the synagogue. Men and women alike elbowed, jostled, and even hopped up and down in an uncouth manner, craning necks to get a better view of the house. I could understand such actions from the poor, but richly attired men and even some Torah teachers joined the fray.

Ya'akov addressed a man at the back of the crowd. "Sir, we're visitors from Nazareth trying to locate our brother Yeshua. Perhaps you know of him or could direct us to him?"

"Yeshua is your brother?" The man laughed. "Sure, he is. And he's my uncle. Forget it. You're not getting ahead of us. My wife and I have traveled from Salamis to see him."

"Salamis?" I repeated. People had traveled all the way from the island of Cyprus to see Yeshua?

Ya'akov seemed more flummoxed that he hadn't been taken at his word than by the distance they'd come. "No, you misunderstand. He *is* my brother. We have to see him."

"Listen, you have to wait like everyone else." The man turned his back on us.

Ya'akov and I stared at each other incredulously.

"Miryam? Is that you? It *is* you. Miryam, over here."

I heard the voice, but it took a moment to locate its owner—a woman who was ample in width but quite short in stature. As she pushed through a line of women in front of us, they quickly fought to fill the gap she'd left a cubit closer to the house's entrance. Emmi reached for the woman's hand.

"Neriah. How good to see you. How is your family?"

"Well. Yours?"

"See for yourself. Here they are." Emmi turned and made introductions.

"Hannah, I've heard wonderful words about you." Neriah smiled, revealing deep dimples. "But I didn't realize how beautiful you would be."

I nodded politely. I knew Emmi had visited the city after the wedding in Cana, but I found it unsettling to think I'd been a topic of discussion among strangers.

Neriah beckoned us to follow her as she wove through the crowd along the side of the house. I slipped in a puddle, and Ya'akov steadied me. Cold mud oozed inbetween my toes and sandal, and I flicked my foot in disgust, trying to shake it loose.

Neriah waved her arms overhead in an unseemly manner.

"Andrew!" she called. "Andrew, down here."

A man's face and shoulders became visible in one of the windows. He scanned the crowd, and recognition lit his features when he spotted Neriah.

"It's the rabbi's family come from Nazareth!" she shouted. Then by way of explanation, she added to us over her shoulder, "My husband."

The man nodded at her and disappeared, his head instantly

replaced by another man's at the window. The house must have been as crowded as the street outside. Neriah ruthlessly asserted herself and people parted, gawking curiously at us as we passed by. She secured a spot under the window, and Emmi and I joined her directly beneath the opening. We couldn't see inside, but emotions clearly ran high within. Terrible accusations and outraged demands flew through the air. Then I detected Yeshua's voice.

"A wicked and adulterous generation asks for a sign? No! None will be given to it but the sign of the prophet Yonah. For just as Yonah was three days and three nights in the belly of the sea-monster, so will the Son of Man be three days and three nights in the depths of the earth."[26]

What is he talking about? He really has gone mad. One minute he spoke of Yonah, the next he talked gibberish about spirits living in houses. He paused only to heap further insults on his listeners. Angry murmurs came from the audience, and I couldn't say I blamed them.

I raised my eyebrows at Emmi, and she puckered her lips. She couldn't make sense of Yeshua's words either. I couldn't help but feel smug. At last she heard for herself that the things he said were outrageous.

The man called Andrew must have made his way to Yeshua because I heard him interrupt tentatively, "Rabbi, your family has come. They are outside, wanting to speak to you."

At least our visit would put an end to this madness. Yeshua would have to stop antagonizing people and come outside before any more damage could be done.

"Who is my mother?" Yeshua answered in a loud voice. "And who are my brothers?"[27]

I whipped my head around to look at Emmi, my eyes wide with outrage.

"Did you *hear* that?"

Emmi shushed me.

"*Look.* Here are my mother and my brothers," Yeshua pronounced. I couldn't see to whom he referred, but it was certainly not us. "Whoever does what my Father in heaven wants, that person is my brother and sister and mother."[28]

I grunted, stamping my foot and spraying droplets of mud on those around me. "This is too much. Who does he think he is? We walked all the way from Nazareth in this foul weather and he can't even come outside to greet us? Now do you see why we had to come?"

"What does he mean about Abba?" Ya'akov asked. "Wouldn't Abba want him to speak with us?"

Emmi appeared confused and wounded. But even in the face of such a snub, she didn't criticize.

Neriah looked uncomfortable to witness us questioning our mother. She stepped in to soothe us.

"Many people claim to know Yeshua in order to get an audience with him. I'm sure he doesn't realize it's truly you. Just wait until he's finished teaching and comes out. Everything will get sorted, you'll see."

Emmi nodded feebly.

My anger toward Yeshua swelled all over again, seeing her so dejected. I intended to let him know just what I thought of this snubbing. If anyone should disown a family member, it was us, not him. "Just wait until he comes out, all right," I muttered.

"Please. You must be tired from your journey." Neriah nodded as if answering her own question. "Come with me and let's get you something to eat." She put her hand on Emmi's forearm and steered her away.

As we followed, shouting came from the entrance to the house.

"This man is a heretic! He's overcome by the influence of Beelzebub. Go to your homes and do not be deceived by this demonic teaching."

I could just see the head coverings of a cluster of men shoving their way through the crowd. When they came into view, I saw they were teachers of the Law. One man noticed Ya'akov gaping at him and lifted an accusing finger.

"This is the devil's work, and all who follow him will pay the consequences!" he shouted.

The color drained from Ya'akov's face.

"Come on." Shim'on tugged his sleeve. "Don't listen to them."

But how could we not? Weren't we to respect and heed these men's words?

A few people skulked away. Others cast their eyes downward, looking abashed. Now it seemed best that Yeshua hadn't acknowledged us as relatives. I was ashamed and shaken enough as it was.

Neriah led us past the synagogue, where a group of women shamelessly mingled with men outside. I couldn't help but gawk. Could they be prostitutes?

To my horror, Neriah waved and called out a greeting to them. One of the men glanced over his shoulder, and my breath caught when I recognized him.

"*Elan*," I reprimanded softly.

CHAPTER 45

Elan's face lit up. He rushed to hug Emmi and addressed me with an eager grin.

"I'm surprised to see you here, Hannah. I'm glad you've finally come to hear Yeshua teach."

"I came to talk to him, not listen," I retorted. "And what are you thinking, associating with those . . . women?" I spat the word out, disdain dripping from my tongue.

His delight turned to confusion, then annoyance.

"Hannah, you're not in any position to tell me whom I should and shouldn't be speaking with."

"But they're vulgar. Look how they brazenly parade themselves in broad daylight."

"They're not vulgar. They're Yeshua's friends," he said as if *that* lent them credibility.

"Where are their husbands? Where is their shame?" I asked, but Elan didn't balk at my disapproving scowl as he once would have. I turned away first.

Ya'akov blushed furiously as any decent man would when faced with further damning evidence of a brother's fall from respectability. Shim'on looked amused, craning his neck to get a better glance over Emmi's head at the women in question.

Neriah cleared her throat. "I know some of those women. I

can attest they are good people."

Now Ya'akov's eyes popped open in surprise. "You know them?"

Emmi shot daggers at Ya'akov with her eyes. "Ya'akov, please don't be rude. I'm so sorry, Neriah."

Neriah smiled but looked disappointed. "I understand."

She squeezed through the doorway of a house close to the water's edge. At first I thought she'd left us, but then she popped her head outside again, beckoning us to join her.

I had reservations about entering a strange woman's home, but Emmi didn't hesitate. The practicality of shelter from the rain won out over my scruples.

Inside, the rough black stone walls seemed to swallow the feeble light that dared to enter through slits high in the walls. We crammed together taking seats on the floor below the haze of smoke filling the room. An older woman, introduced as Neriah's mother, assessed us and added more water to a pot of beans she stirred over a rectangular stone fire pit at the back of the room. Emmi produced some of our own supplies to add to the meal—though not the raisin cakes she'd brought for Yeshua. Neriah filled a bowl with water, and we washed as best we could. Our damp and soiled clothing was beyond help at the moment.

While Neriah helped her mother, Elan recounted the events of the past weeks to Emmi and my brothers without meeting my gaze once.

"Just before you arrived, Yeshua touched a man who was deaf and mute his whole life. And the man could hear! His first words were shouts of praise. It was awesome to witness, I tell you. I get shivers just thinking about it."

"Hmph. Odd how these events always seem to occur right before we arrive or right after we leave," I remarked. "Doesn't it strike you as convenient that we're never around to witness these *healings* for ourselves?"

"What are you saying, Hannah? You don't believe me?" Elan's stare challenged me.

"I'm sure that's not what she means," Emmi assured him with a squeeze of his hand.

"That's exactly what I mean," I said. "I don't believe you. I don't believe any of this. Why wouldn't Yeshua let us into the house today? Why is it we're never there to see these astounding things? Hmm? I'll tell you why. Because we'd expose these acts as foolishness. People see what they want to see, nothing more."

"Exactly, and you've already made up your mind not to believe what is evident to others," Elan said. "Maybe he didn't invite you inside today because your lack of faith would have ruined other people's opportunity to receive what he freely gives away."

"Oh, and what's that? His self-righteous criticism? That's the only thing I've seen him give away freely."

A gasp came from behind me and I turned to see Neriah and her mother staring in wide-eyed shock at my words. My behavior mortified me. I didn't even know why I was so upset with Elan. It wasn't his fault we were here. I busied myself playing with the folds of my cloak, scraping off the drying flecks of dirt.

Ya'akov shook his head at me. "You never did like it when Elan paid more attention to Yeshua than to you."

My mouth fell open.

Splotchy red patches erupted on Elan's neck and cheeks.

"Go on, Elan," Emmi encouraged with a pat on his arm. "Tell us more. What else has Yeshua done?"

He cleared his throat. "The other day, Yeshua was teaching

in a different house. You couldn't turn around, the space was so crowded. All of a sudden, debris started falling from the roof. Some people pushed their way out the door, fearful that the whole structure was falling apart. I was pinned against a wall and couldn't have moved if I wanted to. Then a man dangled through the opening! It was remarkable. Apparently, out of desperation, some friends lowered the man right through the roof of the house to get him close to Yeshua."

I snickered.

Elan locked eyes with me. "He was paralyzed," he said as if that explained such inappropriate behavior.

"What happened?" Shim'on said.

"Yeshua did the most extraordinary thing. He forgave the man of his sins."

"What?" Ya'akov cried out in shock. "He can't do that! He's not a priest. Only a priest can make atonement for the sins of the people. What about the sacrifice? The Lord requires a blood sacrifice for sin. The Torah says so. We're not even Levites!" Ya'akov looked at each of us for confirmation, as if everything he knew as an unshakable truth was suddenly up for debate. Elan may as well have said the sun didn't rise in the east.

"Is Yeshua discounting the law?" Shim'on asked Elan. "Does he think a man can now be cleansed just by his saying he's cleansed?"

How appalling. If the man had done something to bring about his condition, maybe Yeshua had hoped to comfort him. But it was still inexcusable. Heretical even. Maybe those men today had been right.

Elan looked somber. "Yeshua says he's come to fulfill and complete the law, not destroy it. In fact, he's calling us to be even more holy than what the law requires. He said unless we're more righteous than the Torah teachers, we won't gain entrance to the heavenly kingdom."[29]

If Elan meant to reassure us, his words had the opposite effect.

"He said *what*?" Shim'on said.

"How can any of us hope to be saved if that's the case?" Ya'akov whined.

"I don't know. I don't understand it either. But listen, will you? Let me finish. The people there thought it was blasphemy too. But when they challenged Yeshua, he asked, 'Which is easier, to forgive a man or heal him?'[30] and no sooner did he utter the words than this crippled man jumped up before our eyes."

"What?" I couldn't believe it.

Emmi covered her open mouth with her hand, her eyes wide in amazement. Neriah and her mother smiled and nodded at Elan. They had all taken leave of their senses.

Elan grinned. "You heard me. One minute the man's lying on the ground. The next his scrawny limbs took on strength and flesh and, I'm telling you, the man sprang to his feet and walked away. How could such a sign follow one who does not have the authority to say such things?"

"But that's not possible," I insisted. "How could such a thing be?"

Emmi clasped her hands in front of her and smiled. "The angel told me, 'Nothing will be impossible with God.'"[31]

Chills surged through my body and the hairs on my arms stood on end.

"But we're not talking about God, we're talking about Yeshua." My voice came out as a whisper as if my rebellious tongue was less certain than my mind of this fact. The image of water pots filled with wine at the wedding entered my thoughts unbidden, and fear took hold of me.

"I don't believe it," I declared more emphatically.

"Whether or not you believe it has no bearing on the fact that it occurred," Elan gently asserted.

Awkward silence ensued as we considered the enormity of his words.

Shim'on lifted one side of his mouth in a nervous smile. "No wonder those Pharisees were angry with Yeshua. Now another person is able to run away from their boring teaching."

No one laughed.

"This past Shabbat, the Master read from the writing of the prophet Yirmeyahu." Neriah focused her eyes up at the ceiling, then recited, "'No longer will they teach their neighbor, or say to one another, "Know the Lord," because they will all know me, from the least of them to the greatest . . . For I will forgive their wickedness and will remember their sins no more.'"[32]

Shim'on sniffed and rubbed a hand across his mouth. "How can we all know the Lord? Only Moshe went up the mountain to receive the Torah, not the people. And even he couldn't meet the Lord face-to-face."

I thought on this. It seemed frightening to me. I didn't want to meet the Lord face-to-face. Who could look upon Adonai and live? It was better to have a consecrated holy man to go into the temple on my behalf. Let him risk *his* life.

Neriah shrugged, apparently unconcerned with my brother's logic. "All I know is that when Yeshua speaks, I desire to know the Lord for myself in a new way. And I feel that I do when I'm near him."

She crossed the room and, taking the ladle from her mother, filled a small bowl with deft motions. Setting it down, she looked to us again and her eyebrows rose in question.

"Maybe these are those days of which the prophet spoke?

I'm going to see if the rabbi and my husband have eaten."

Elan jumped up. "I'll come with you."

"Please take him these cakes." Emmi rooted through her bag.

I rolled my eyes. She thought the man had enough power to forgive sins and make the lame walk, but he couldn't survive without her cooking.

Elan frowned at me, and I lifted the corner of my mouth to sneer in return. Why was he in such a hurry to leave anyway? To meet those women who were outside earlier? The thought irritated me, and I refused to acknowledge him as he said his goodbyes.

Shim'on was the first to speak up after they had gone. "I don't understand any of this."

Emmi looked defiant while Ya'akov held his head in his hands so I couldn't see his face.

"I can understand that our ancestors believed in miracles, but that was hundreds of years ago," Shim'on argued. "No one in modern times has ever witnessed a miracle."

Ya'akov looked up, clearly affronted by this observation as if Shim'on had just called our predecessors simpleminded. "Do you doubt the written word? Don't you believe it's possible? Just because we haven't seen any miracles doesn't mean the miracles weren't real. You sound like Hannah and her Sadducee family."

I put my hands on my hips, but Shim'on spoke before I managed a retort.

"I'm not saying the miracles weren't real or didn't serve a purpose at that time. But hundreds of years have passed since then." Shim'on tossed his hands in the air. "People don't just call down hail from the heavens to fight their enemies anymore." He shook his head, his expression sad. "Maybe Hannah's right.

None of us have seen Yeshua do anything miraculous. We would be the first to know if he had special powers, wouldn't we? We grew up with him."

I felt a mixture of pride, in having my argument acknowledged, and sadness, at being the speaker of such pessimistic words. Ya'akov looked conflicted now.

"What about the wine?" Emmi interjected. "You were all at the wedding when he did that."

No one responded.

She huffed.

"I for one am not going to listen to any more of this talk." Wrapping her cloak around her shoulders, she looked over her shoulder on the way to the door, but no one tried to stop her.

A small voice came from the back of the room as the door closed. "Your brother healed me."

We all looked up. It was the first time Neriah's mother had spoken. I had forgotten she was even there.

"I scalded my arm and had a terrible burn," she said. "He touched me and made me well. Everyone that comes to him is made well." Then she returned to her stew as if she spoke of nothing more than the morning's catch of fish or the price of oil.

No one mustered a response.

The patter on the roof increased as the rain picked up again. Resentment simmered in my belly, and I embraced it and stewed in my bitterness. How could this woman who knew nothing of my brother say that everyone who came to him was healed?

The accounts of miracles were idle storytelling or propaganda, as I suspected. She'd been swept up in the hysteria. Elan too. It was the only explanation.

Because the alternative didn't bear thinking about.

CHAPTER 46

The house was still dark when I awoke.

Emmi slept by my side, no doubt exhausted after our harrowing experiences yesterday. We never had succeeded in speaking with Yeshua. While he addressed the crowd before evening, we had tried once more to approach him, but thousands were clamoring for his attention by that point. In fact, so many had sought to touch him that he had nearly been trampled by his own adorers. Eventually, some of his fishermen friends put out a boat where Yeshua could teach, safe from the press of the mob. And it had helped the hearing, if not the understanding, of his words.

I shook my head at the recollection. He had mostly rambled on about farming. I just didn't understand why people would come such distances to hear a man talk about sowing seed—especially a man who owned no land. Then when the rain had set in again, Emmi conceded that we would have to wait until nightfall to speak with him. But neither Yeshua nor Neriah's husband had returned to shore before we slept. Well, he couldn't avoid us forever.

The shutters remained closed, and the air was thick with the stale smell of slumbering bodies. I wriggled out from under the blanket I shared with Emmi and tiptoed around my brothers, then stepped into the gray light of dawn for some fresh air.

The morning coolness chilled me. Within minutes, a biting wind left my cheeks cold to the touch and my eyes watering. A silver blanket of clouds hovered close to the earth, but at least the rain had stopped. Peaks of hundreds of tiny waves rushed diagonally across the lake to lap rhythmically against the gravelly shore, the water still choppy from last night's storm. In the harbor, many boats bobbed at anchor. Apparently, no one had been brave or foolhardy enough to set out to fish in such foul weather.

"Hannah."

I didn't need to turn my head. I knew the voice. I bent down to pick up a flat stone and examined it, ignoring his presence.

"I'm sorry we had words yesterday," Elan said. "I don't want to argue with you."

I didn't want to argue either, but I also couldn't accept his ideas about Yeshua. I flung the rock, and it sank with a splash.

"Do you remember when Abba tried to skip stones?" he asked.

I did, and couldn't help but smile. Abba used to insist we just didn't have adequate vision to see how quickly his rocks skimmed the water. But we all had known he threw terribly.

Elan stepped forward to stand at my side. The wind blew his hair forward over his eyes, and he smoothed it back as he stared out over the water.

"Yeshua and his students left in the boat after sunset. I don't think they'll return."

"They were out on the lake in that squall last night?" I knew he had avoided us, but the risk he had taken to escape our presence surprised me. We had traveled all this way for nothing, then. I should have been more perturbed but, truthfully, I didn't even want to speak with Yeshua now.

"Elan. Tell me honestly. Do you believe he can heal the sick?"

He didn't seem surprised by my question, but he paused before responding.

"You heard what he said in Nazareth. You know the prophecies spoken over him as a baby. I told you I've witnessed the results of this power he has. And yesterday alone, dozens were healed after hearing him teach. I don't understand why you *don't* believe in his abilities."

I couldn't deny that by the end of the day, the people around my brother had seemed transformed. Gone were the crutches and coughing among the crowd—I had only seen and heard praise. But maybe the sick had left early to find a place to rest.

"I'd like to. I would. But . . . it doesn't make sense." I sniffed and took a faltering breath, hoping to dampen the confused hurt I felt deep inside.

"What is it? What troubles you?"

Several obvious and sarcastic replies came to mind. But this was Elan asking, the one person who had always understood me, so I shared the truth.

"Why now? If it's true, why did it take so many years for him to act?"

"His followers say the Spirit of the Lord came on him when he was baptized by Yochanon. Some even report the voice of the Almighty was heard that day, acknowledging Yeshua as his son. That's when power entered Yeshua. Haven't you noticed that since around that time, Yeshua carries himself differently? It's like he wears a mantle of anointing." He shrugged.

I resented his simple explanation—it wasn't the answer I had hoped for. Really, I didn't want an answer. I just wanted someone to stand with me for once, to comfort me instead of defending Yeshua.

Elan seemed unmoved by my surly expression. "You know how, as children, we asked when Yeshua would show himself to be the Anointed One? You remember what your parents always told us?"

I did, but I also refused to abandon my brooding to answer him.

"'It's not his time yet,' they'd say, remember? Well, maybe now it is. Maybe this is the appointed time."

"But why did it take so long?" My chin trembled and my eyes grew moist. "Why didn't he demonstrate his power until now—almost twenty years too late? Why did Abba have to die? Can you explain that? *Why*?"

I wiped my dripping nose with my sleeve, knowing I looked as pitiful as I felt.

Elan stood still, seemingly unaffected by this display. His unresponsiveness upset me even more.

I raised my voice over the blowing wind.

"If Yeshua cared about Abba he would have healed him. But Yeshua cares more about these strangers than about his own family. What did any of these people ever do to deserve such treatment? Some of the people here are goyim. And they're getting miracles? It's not fair."

Elan looked at me incredulously.

"Who are you to question the mercy of the Lord?" He flung his hands through the air. "What harm does it do you if someone receives healing from Yeshua? If a blind woman sees her family members for the first time? If a lame man is able to work and support himself? How dare you begrudge another of good health when you yourself are so blessed!"

His vehemence startled me. I'd never considered it that way before.

His gaze softened, and he turned to face the water again. When he spoke again, his tone was firm but not unkind.

"How can you think Yeshua didn't care about Abba? Do you think he doesn't know what it is to suffer, to grieve? He loved Abba. We all did." He looked up and took a deep breath. "You were not left orphaned and alone when Abba died. Look how many people care for you, Hannah. You're ready to blame Yeshua for everything wrong in your life, for things he didn't even do, yet you won't accept the good he keeps offering you." He shook his head, staring at me. "Yeshua's not the cause of your problems. He could be the answer if you'd let him. But you won't. You'd rather reject the people who really . . ."—he swallowed and looked away—"who really love you."

Elan glanced sideways at me, no doubt awaiting a response, but I was speechless. I didn't know whether to be hurt, angry, or reassured by this speech. Had I been looking at things the wrong way all these years? I wasn't sure.

He frowned and whipped his shawl up over his head, either to block the gusts of wind or to block me from his sight. He spoke again, but his voice was muffled and I strained to make out his words.

"I meant what I said yesterday . . . when I said I was glad you came," he said. "It *is* good to see you."

I squeezed my lips together. If I let one word escape my mouth, I feared a flood of others held back these many years would breach the gap and spill into the open. Hugging my cloak tighter around me, I stared straight ahead.

"Hey!" Shim'on called out. "There you are."

His strides slowed when he saw my tear-streaked face. He glanced at Elan, whose face was covered from view, then lifted his eyebrow in question to me.

I shook my head at him.

Shim'on cleared his throat and shifted his weight back and forth. "Have you been out on one of those?" he asked Elan, gesturing to the boats in the harbor.

"No." Elan paused. "I'd rather herd sheep than fish."

Shim'on laughed, and Elan turned to offer him a smile.

"My boys are getting good at shearing now," Shim'on boasted.

Elan nodded. "They are. Justus doesn't quite have Ezra's dexterity yet. I caught him laying his whole body across a sheep to hold it still. Then, when he finally got the sheep in place, he realized he didn't have an arm free to sheer it. You should have seen his face." He pushed his shawl back down around his neck. "But he's determined. His technique will get better as he grows."

Shim'on nodded. "Ezra will come of age this month. It seems just yesterday, we were his age ourselves."

We shared a companionable silence as the city awakened around us. I followed the flight of a gull hovering over the beach in search of some remnant of yesterday's catch.

"Uncle Cleopas told us men are plotting against Yeshua," Shim'on said to Elan. "Have you heard anything like that?"

Elan's expression turned grim.

"I don't understand why anyone would want to harm him, but yes. I'm afraid I've heard the reports. Still, Yeshua's heard the rumors. And he doesn't seem disturbed. I guess he believes the Lord's word and the prophecies that say he will be victorious, so he doesn't worry." He shrugged.

But what if the prophecies weren't about him? What would happen then?

"Hannah's father-in-law and husband want Yeshua to meet with Herod."

Elan fixed me with an intense stare. I clenched my jaw at

my brother's obtuseness. Honestly, sometimes Shim'on acted like he was still a five-year-old boy telling tales on me.

"Please be careful," Elan said.

"Me? Yeshua's the one who needs to be careful. Not me."

"I don't trust your relatives. They seem capable of anything."

I frowned. He didn't know how much truth he'd conveyed with these words.

"I mean it." He must have misinterpreted my expression. "I'm sure Herod isn't the only one who wouldn't be sorry to hear Yeshua went missing . . . permanently." He gave me a pointed look, and cold fingers crawled up my spine.

Shim'on glanced back and forth between the two of us. "Are you saying it's a trap? That's why Gal wants Yeshua to meet with Herod?"

"Yes, tell us. What exactly are you trying to say?" I laughed with empty humor. "I think you're letting wounded pride get in the way of your judgment."

"I think you know what I'm saying." Elan looked at me earnestly. "I'd recommend keeping your mouth closed and your ears open."

I snorted. "Don't be silly."

But my voice lacked conviction. I couldn't help but picture the fire, our neighbor gasping for air. I shook my head to dislodge the image. Olmer would never let anything bad happen to me or my family . . . would he?

"Listen," I said, "all I'm suggesting is that maybe if Yeshua presented himself before Herod, all these misunderstandings would be resolved. If Yeshua would just promise to come home, we could all return to our normal lives—"

"Hannah, do you even hear what you're saying?" Elan raised his arms, shaking his head. "It's too late. Things can never return to normal. People can't just come back home. We can't turn back time, no matter how much we want to. Believe me, I know." He crossed his arms and looked away.

Shim'on gaped at Elan.

I felt bewildered myself. Were we still talking about Yeshua? Or our own relationship? *Past* relationship.

Elan kicked at a rock, then suddenly turned around.

"Please let the boys know I appreciate their help with the flock. I'll be back by the full moon."

Shim'on nodded. "You're not returning with us, then?"

"No."

He wheeled around and marched past Neriah's home and the synagogue.

I watched his retreat until he turned a corner out of view. Biting my lower lip was the only thing that kept me from calling him back, from asking him to say he wasn't disappointed in me and that everything would be normal someday.

When I turned around, Shim'on fixed me with an accusing look.

"What?" I asked. "It's not *my* fault."

I made a childish face at him.

With a disgusted look, he walked away.

CHAPTER 47

"I'm so excited to commemorate Herod's birthday." Aunt Lilit let out a girlish squeal.

"Two weeks late," I murmured.

"Uzziah wouldn't say so, but I know he was as disappointed as the other councilmen not to get an invitation to the official celebration at Machaerus. That's why I thought it a clever idea to celebrate a second time here in Sepphoris. It's still going to be spectacular regardless of the date."

"Discounting the fact that the guest of honor won't be attending."

She put her hands on her hips. "Well, not for lack of trying on my part. I'm sure Herod was flattered and would gladly have accepted my invitation if it weren't for that pompous woman he married."

I took the other end of the embroidered tablecloth that she held and helped spread it over the table between us. "I'm sorry, you're right. It was a clever idea. Raz was irked that she and Gal were snubbed by Herodias as well."

"Speaking of Raziela. She's the only one who hasn't responded to my invitation."

She smoothed the wrinkles out of the cloth and looked at me, her eyes questioning.

I didn't have the heart to repeat Raziela's exact words to my aunt—that she'd rather be dragged naked through the hippodrome than endure an evening of Lilit's hospitality.

"I'm sure Raz will make every effort to be here," I lied.

My aunt mustered a smile. I suspected she knew the truth. But knowing the truth and hearing it spoken aloud were two different things. Sometimes I thought polite pretenses were all that held this family together.

"I'm surprised Emmi hasn't arrived yet. She usually arrives early everywhere."

I placed a jug with purple lupines and irises in the center of the table and admired my work. A pause during conversation with my aunt was unusual, so I looked up. Lilit busied herself with buffing the metal serving spoons.

"Aunt Lilit? You did invite her, didn't you?" I asked.

She puckered her mouth and lifted her shoulders feigning innocence. "I forgot? Oh, now don't look at me that way. You know your mother is welcome anytime."

"Anytime you don't have other guests." I slapped the serving platters onto the table with a thud. "This is about Yeshua, isn't it?"

"I adore your brother, really I do. It's just that he's so . . . unpredictable. He's always been a bit odd. I'm sure that's from his father's side of the family, not ours. But lately his actions are beyond disconcerting. As hostess, I must ensure people enjoy themselves. I can't have my other guests feeling uncomfortable, can I?"

I couldn't fault her for saying that he was odd, but I was puzzled. "Aunt Lilit, do you really believe that? About Yeshua's traits coming from Abba? I mean, do you believe that Abba sired him?"

She laughed heartily. "Don't tell me you're bringing up that nonsense. I thought you had more intelligence than that. You and I both know how babies are born." She looked alarmed. "Oh, I'm sorry."

I pretended not to notice her gaffe. "So you don't think that Yeshua is the Lord's son?"

"Who ever heard of such a thing? Besides, just ask yourself, out of *all* the women in the world, why choose your mother? Miryam is lovely and kind, I mean no offense. We're related, after all. But if the Lord wanted his son to dwell among us, would he really condemn him to living in Nazareth? There's not even a proper market there, let alone a theater."

"I know. It sounds ridiculous. But still. There's something different about him, something good. Everywhere he goes, people are changed. They say he works signs and miracles that have not been seen since the days of Eliyahu. Tell me. What really happened at the wedding with the wine? *Was* it a miracle? Could Yeshua be the Anointed One?"

Aunt Lilit waved her hands in dismissal. "Do we really need to discuss such things? Goodness, we're not Torah teachers. Leave such matters to the rabbis."

"But some of the rabbis are furious with Yeshua. It's so confusing. I don't understand why they fault him for loving the Torah and helping people. And Herod wants to meet Yeshua, but Uncle Cleopas and others say Herod plots against Yeshua. I just don't know who is right or what to believe anymore."

"That uncle of yours has always been one to credit conspiracies. But even if half of what he says is true, worrying about it has done nothing but put gray hairs on your head and wrinkles on your face."

My hand reflexively checked my cheek. "What?"

"Hannah, you're a stunning woman, but beauty won't last forever. You need to keep yourself attractive—at least until you get with child. You want to please your husband, don't you?"

I was flabbergasted. How had we gotten on this topic?

She answered her own question. "Of course you do. Now I wasn't going to say anything about your being away. I know you're concerned about your brother, and how could you not be? But if you want my advice, you'd best make sure you're never far from the bedroom when Olmer's at home." She nodded toward my belly. "You're not getting any younger, you know. You can't afford to miss another opportunity like last time."

I looked down at my stomach and back up at her. "What are you talking about?"

"Do you think we should put the cups out ahead of time? Or maybe greet everyone at the door with wine?"

"Aunt Lilit. What opportunity?"

"Hmm? When Olmer was last home."

"Last summer? I know we had some words, but—"

"No, when he was here after the Feast of Dedication. You know. Before he left for Miletus?" Her inflection and her eyebrows rose as she spoke the last sentence.

My mouth opened, but no words came forth. How could he have returned to Sepphoris without my knowing it? Then understanding dawned. Raz. She must have had word that he'd return after celebrating the holiday and made sure I'd miss him by sending me chasing after Yeshua. I slumped onto the bench.

"Oh dear," Lilit said.

"Why would Olmer leave Sepphoris without waiting to see me? I was gone only a few weeks. What could be so important that couldn't wait?"

Lilit shrugged.

What could this mean? Was he still angry about what

happened in Nazareth? *This is all Yeshua's fault.* As soon as the thought came, I recalled Elan's accusation that I always blamed things on Yeshua. Maybe I did, but it *was* his fault.

"Excuse me." One of Lilit's servants stood in the doorway wearing a grim expression. "Your sister-in-law has just arrived."

"Raziela? Here?" Aunt Lilit turned to me with round eyes and clasped her hands together.

I stood up.

"You see, Hannah? With enough time, problems have a way of sorting themselves out. I knew she'd accept my invitation." She grinned. "This is going to be the best party we've had in years."

Unbelievable.

Then Raz sauntered in wearing a smug expression.

"I'm so sorry to interrupt your work, Lilit." She perused the table display. "Up to your usual standards, I see. Such a shame." Raz pouted.

"A shame?" Lilit repeated.

"You haven't heard?" Raz covered her mouth. "Goodness, I hate to be the one to have to tell you bad news . . . Perhaps it's best you both sit down."

I crossed my arms and glared at her. "What is it this time? We picked the wrong color flowers?"

Raziela locked eyes with me. "It's your relative, Yochanon. He's dead."

"What?" I stared in bewilderment.

"I hadn't heard he was ill," Lilit said as if she had final authority over such things.

"He wasn't. Until Herod severed Yochanon's head from his body and placed it on a serving tray for Herodias," Raz said.

My heart pounded. The smell of the cut blooms suddenly

nauseated me, and I swallowed the hot bile that rose in my throat.

For a moment Raz seemed genuinely remorseful. "I knew he'd overstepped his bounds by criticizing Herod's marriage. Didn't I say that? Didn't I say he'd be silenced?" She waved her hand at me. "There's a limit to what a ruler will tolerate."

"How awful." Lilit reached across the table to straighten a crooked spoon.

"Given the timing of events, I knew you wouldn't want to remind people you have ties to the man. Or his followers."

"Hmm? No, of course not," Aunt Lilit answered as she rearranged the flowers.

"So"—Raz paused to offer an insincere smile—"I took the liberty of sending Iakovos to tell all your guests you've canceled the party."

Cutlery flew in all directions with a loud crash as Lilit swooned across the table at this tragic news.

***

Usually the rhythm of weaving soothed me, but I was distracted tonight, haunted by the senseless cruelty of Yochanon's death. The poor man. When had he realized the guards opening his cell led him not to freedom, but to death? I replayed the scene in my mind and with macabre curiosity wondered how long he had remained conscious after the blade sliced his neck. Shivering, I tried to dispel the gruesome imaginations.

A worse thought pressed in. If Herod killed one prophet, what would keep him from slaying another? I could no longer pretend his intent toward my brother was any less malevolent.

Reports of violence against perceived dissenters increased every day. Like the three prefects who had preceded him, Pilate sought to advance his own interests for the duration of his post in Judea—hoping to move up the political ranks and extract what little coin remained from his subjects to line his own pockets. But his habit of arbitrarily using fatal military force set him apart as a man to be feared as well as despised.

When had everything become so dangerous? I wished I could go back to the days of peace and safety. But even as I thought this, I remembered Tobias the potter. Even growing up in the relative seclusion of Nazareth, we couldn't escape the world's brutality unscathed. All I wanted to do was keep out of the fray, but trouble seemed to find me, refusing to be ignored.

"Hannah. Mind what you're doing."

I jumped, startled from my dark thoughts. "I'm sorry. Did you say something?"

"You're using the wrong color," Tabitha said.

I looked at the loom. Sure enough I'd shuttled the wrong spool through the warp threads, ruining the pattern. I began painstakingly undoing my work.

"What's bothering you? Is it Theokritos? I can't believe that detestable man is back. Did you see how many trunks he brought? I don't think he's planning to leave for months."

My hands stilled, and I stared at her as if seeing her there for the first time.

She lifted her eyebrows in question.

"Why didn't you tell me Olmer had returned in my absence?"

Her mouth froze for a moment as if unsure whether to confess or deny the truth. "Lilit told you?"

"Yes."

"I'm sorry. By the time you returned, he'd been on the road several days. I thought it would only upset you to know you'd missed him."

"I feel like such a fool. When I returned, I expected a scolding or some retaliation from Raz for failing to speak with Yeshua. But she said she appreciated my effort." I shook my head. "I actually thought she was being reasonable for once. Can you imagine? Raz, reasonable?"

I laughed a little too long, the kind of laughter that tends to dissolve into tears.

Tabitha's eyes showed concern.

I took a deep breath.

"Olmer must have been angry when he found me absent." I hoped she'd contradict me.

She picked up her spindle again and wordlessly worked the wool into thread.

"He already thinks I put my family above him," I said. "I should've trusted his judgment. It turns out he was right all along in warning Yeshua to keep quiet."

"Tell him what you told me. Then Olmer would understand why Yeshua acts as he does."

"I can't. It's too late now."

"You don't know that. It's worth a try."

"He'd never believe me. Besides, no matter what prophetic words Emmi and Uncle Cleopas like to reference, it's impossible to take on Rome. Yeshua's foolhardy in speaking out against the rulers, no matter how just his cause. I worry about him, but I can't get caught up in his fantasies." I munched on the side of my thumb. "And don't you talk to Olmer either."

She held up her hands. "I won't, I told you."

"I can't risk angering my husband any further."

CHAPTER 48

Fall of the Year 3789 (CE 29)

The market bustled today. Everyone rushed to make preparations before the sounding of the shofar any day now signifying the arrival of Yom Teruah, the Feast of Trumpets. Men from each household had to be ready to immediately depart for Jerusalem at the horn's blast. I suspected Olmer's ship had landed and that he was on the road to Jerusalem already. My in-laws and I planned to meet him there for the great fast of Yom Kippur and the harvest festival of Sukkot.

I captured the vendor's attention and exchanged coins for my purchase, a sharp-edged dagger made from obsidian imported from the territories beyond Egypt. A unique and practical gift for Olmer. I was determined my husband and I would have a good reunion this time, no matter what the cost.

Scanning the nearby crowd for Aunt Lilit and Keturah, I navigated past several booths to rejoin them. Then the way ahead cleared unexpectedly. Before I had time to consider my good fortune, the reason for the opening became clear. A unit of eight Roman soldiers and their pack mule came right at me. A contubernium was a frequent-enough sight near the market, but I averted my eyes and ducked into the booth of a leather worker, deciding to wait until the soldiers moved on before stepping back into the street.

"Unnerving dogs, aren't they?"

I met the gaze of the shop owner but didn't answer.

"My cousin knew some of the men from Galilee they butchered last month."

"My condolences."

I had heard of the incident, another minor skirmish that had escalated to outright slaughter. It was a wonder all of Sepphoris wasn't hiding in the stall with me to avoid the Roman infantrymen.

"Is there something you like? A new belt for your loved one perhaps? Ah! A scabbard for your weapon."

She handed me a finely embellished sheath with ornate cutouts.

"What? Oh, no thank you." I smiled at the woman and returned the scabbard to the pile, but she wouldn't be put off so easily.

"A satchel perhaps? New sandals? Say, I recognize your face."

I laughed at her gambit to push her wares.

"You're the wife of Gal's youngest son, aren't you?"

Taken aback, I hesitated before answering, danger still fresh in my thoughts. She took my silence as assent and called to another vendor across the street.

"Ephres. *Ephres!* Come here. It's Yeshua of Nazareth's sister."

My eyes grew round in surprise. How did she know that? Did everyone? As interested faces turned my direction, I started to back away.

"Wait!" she shouted. "Is your brother here? Is Yeshua of Nazareth here?" She exited the stall to get closer.

I fled, shoving those who blocked my path as my brother's name was bandied about.

"Where? Where is Yeshua of Nazareth?"

"The miracle worker is here in the market?"

I blindly pushed forward, searching for Aunt Lilit or Keturah. A mule neighed close behind me, and my stomach sank. The soldiers must have returned to see what the commotion was about.

"Let me through, let me by," I cried in panic, knocking a woman off balance. I hesitated before leaning over her to see if she'd been hurt.

"Help!" she cried. "She's trying to stab me!"

"What? No." I waved my arms in denial, belatedly remembering I clutched Olmer's gift.

The woman screamed.

Great commotion surrounded us as some tried to flee while others pressed forward, curiosity outweighing personal safety. I detected the clapping of the mule's hooves striking stone and cringed at the authoritative shout behind me.

"What's going on here? Who's responsible for this uproar?"

I thrashed at the people nearest me, frantic in my need to escape the soldiers. A hand gripped my arm and I desperately tried to pry it loose.

"Hannah, it's me."

I turned at Aunt Lilit's harsh whisper. She yanked me behind a large cistern of collected rainwater. Keturah pressed her body between the wall and the cistern, shaking and pale.

"Hannah, *please*." She whimpered. "Get down."

I half stooped and half crawled behind the cistern, still clutching the dagger to my chest. Aunt Lilit led us out the other side into a narrow opening that served as a channel for waste water to run off between buildings. We squeezed through a series of alleyways and tunnels, waiting until the sounds of the market grew distant before stopping to catch our breath.

"That was something, wasn't it?" I gave a wavering smile as my whole body began to tremble.

"Raz is not going to be happy about this. I dropped a perfectly good comb in the fray." Keturah pursed her lips and flicked at the damp hem of her garment.

I looked to Aunt Lilit for support, hoping she'd make light of our escapade. Maybe we wouldn't have to mention it to Raz at all.

Lilit folded her arms across her chest. "I'm going home. Alone."

CHAPTER 49

"I can't believe it. I'm not allowed to travel to Jerusalem to meet Olmer," I lamented to the steward's wife as she worked behind the manor the following morning. "Raz says I'm to stay here until he returns home. That won't be until weeks after Sukkot. I'm a prisoner."

Myrinne wiped her brow with her sleeve and nervously assessed the bruised grape bunch in my hands.

"I can take care of the rest of these if you like."

"Hmm? Oh, sorry." I sheepishly popped the grapes with torn skins into my mouth. I was supposed to help by pulling the stems and leaves off the grapes before washing them, not ripping them apart. Focusing on the task at hand, I stepped further down the table to collect a new bunch from the pile.

"You should have heard Raziela." I mimicked her dramatic tone, "'Keturah was almost trampled by the mob. Hakon's unweaned son was almost left motherless. Hannah, you are too dangerous to be out among the public.' Ha."

Myrinne looked both horrified and amused. Finally, she smiled at my impression despite her best efforts to remain the ever loyal and austere servant.

"She acts as if I were deliberately brandishing weapons and inciting riots." I yanked at the stems. "I don't believe for a second that she really cared about our safety. She practically gloated over the incident."

"I'm sure it wasn't because you were in danger. She probably was pleased you offered her the excuse she needed to keep you away from Jerusalem." Myrinne's smile suddenly faltered and she looked alarmed. She quickly stepped away to sort through another basket of grapes.

"What do you mean? She already intended to keep me from going to Jerusalem?" Now that I considered it, Raz had been unusually happy at the prospect of my captivity. Normally she tried to be rid of me.

"Would you mind putting these grapes in the sun to dry while I see how things fare at the wine press?"

"Wait. There's something else going on here, isn't there? I can tell from your face."

Myrinne did look distraught. Her hands trembled. She cast a furtive glance around, but no one could hear us. My concern grew.

"Please. Why does Raz want to keep me here under her watch?"

She gulped and took a steadying breath. "A week ago I overheard Hakon and Raziela speaking with some men. They discussed a plan to have someone taken in Jerusalem during Sukkot."

"Taken? Who? Where? What will they do with him?"

"Shhh." She glanced over her shoulder. "Iakovos had taken coin from the coffers that morning, but then he didn't leave the manor. That night when I checked, the money hadn't been returned. So he must have given it to those men as payment. I don't know anything else, I promise. When I realized what I was hearing, I was frightened and fled to the cellar."

"Did you ask Iakovos about it?"

"No, it's none of my affair. I don't interfere with my husband's duties."

"But they paid someone to . . . Wait, it's Yeshua. You think he's who they intend to capture, don't you?"

She evaded my eyes and busied herself spreading grapes on the table. I clamped a hand on her shoulder and jerked her around to face me.

"Myrinne, we have to do something. We have to warn him. You must send a messenger. I can't leave, but you can."

"I'm sorry, but I can't. I can't," she insisted, shaking her head longer than necessary.

I released my grip and felt ashamed for my temper. Myrinne wasn't the one I wanted to shake, after all.

"You know my husband," she whispered, her eyes filled with an urgent plea. "How could I send a messenger without his knowledge? I shouldn't have even said anything. Besides, we don't even know if Yeshua is the one they want. It could be anyone."

But her words lacked conviction. I slumped forward and held my head in my hands. "What am I going to do?"

She bit her lower lip and shook her head. "I'm sorry. Your brother is a kind man. I've heard of the things he does, how he cares for people regardless of their station. He doesn't deserve to be punished for doing good."

"Punished?" Punished like our Yochanon was punished? Panic gripped me. "No. I can't let that happen. I must do something."

"Quiet," she implored, tipping her head to indicate we were no longer alone.

We resumed sorting through the grapes, and Myrinne nodded to the stable boy crossing the clearing behind the manor. After a minute, she spoke in a low voice.

"I don't presume to instruct you what to do. But think, Hannah. How will it help your brother to place yourself in danger? You don't want more trouble. Wait until your husband returns. He'll tell you what to do."

"By then it will be too late."

In response, she flapped her hand to disperse the tiny flies hovering over the fruit, but I saw the concern in her eyes. "Even if you were able to send a message to Yeshua—and I'm not saying you should—do you even know where to send it? He's as elusive as the wind."

I had to admit she was right. "No. I don't."

Myrinne's shoulders lowered. "So then, it's settled. It will be fine, you'll see. Maybe I misheard. There's probably an innocent explanation for the whole thing." She pressed her lips into a grim attempt at a smile and resumed her work.

Maybe, but I was not willing to risk my brother's life. I might not know where Yeshua was, but someone in Nazareth would. I had to find a way to stop him from going to Jerusalem for Sukkot.

CHAPTER 50

An hour before dawn, I rose. The girls slept, so lighting a lamp was too risky. My fingertips skimmed the wall, searching for the peg holding my cloak. I considered waking Tabitha to tell her why I was leaving in case Olmer returned in my absence, but dismissed the idea just as quickly. He wasn't due back for weeks, and I didn't want Tabitha to suffer any repercussions for my actions. Though, strictly speaking, Raz only forbade me to go to Jerusalem—not Nazareth. But I didn't think semantics would save me when she found out I'd gone.

I couldn't worry now. Reaching under my cot, I retrieved the pouch of belongings I'd stashed and slipped through the door. Halfway down the stairs, a noise stopped me with one foot suspended in air. The servants were already at work at the hearth.

This was madness. What was I thinking? I should turn around right now.

I placed my foot on the next tread with agonizing care and listened again, every fiber of my body alert. *I can do this. I have to do this.* After scampering across the courtyard, I tugged one of the doors open wide enough to step through. Safely on the outside, I let out my breath.

"Going somewhere?"

I jumped, my heart thudding against my chest. Theokritos's bulky figure emerged from the darkness. He stepped in front of me, and I pressed myself against the door.

"Someone as lovely as you shouldn't be alone in the dark," he said, placing his palms on either side of my head. He leaned forward until his fat belly brushed against the bag I wielded in front of me like a weapon. His smell overwhelmed me—a sickly, sweaty scent mingled with wine and a cloying note of what could only be . . . perfume? That explained why he was skulking about at such a late hour. Raziela indulged most of her cousin's desires, but even she did not condone his cavorting.

"Perhaps you don't intend to remain alone, hmm?" he asked. "You've been without your husband's company for a long time." He traced a line down my cheek with his finger, and I recoiled. "Perhaps you've come looking for a late-night tryst?"

I pushed against him, then tried ducking under his arm. He laughed at my futile efforts to escape. Though I tried to reassure myself that he was bluffing, fear grew inside me.

"Get away from me. I'm going home. I just want to see my family."

In a mocking voice he echoed, "I just want to see my family."

In sheer desperation, I kicked him hard in the shin. That distracted him for a second, and I ran. But Theokritos was surprisingly spry for his size and caught me by my headdress before I got far. He took a few breaths before speaking.

"I'm afraid I can't let you leave just yet. I believe my cousin ordered you to remain here. Let's just make sure this little trip is authorized, shall we?"

He released me and gestured back to the doors. I weighed the possibility of running again, but with one yell he would wake the whole household. I straightened my skirts and squared my shoulders before marching back inside. He snickered but followed closely behind me until assuring I went upstairs.

I flopped on my bed in the gloom, listening to my nieces breathing and awaiting my fate. Within the hour, I heard a rap on the door. The girls stirred as I opened it. The lamp the steward held cast sinister shadows on his face as we locked eyes.

"Raziela requests your presence in the salon."

***

"What would my son think of your running off in the night?" Raz asked, blinking her eyes at me from her seat at the table. "Out in the hills, all alone . . . except for the shepherds, of course. You're fond of shepherds, aren't you?"

I kept my voice neutral when I answered. "I'm going to Nazareth to visit my family."

"Why, dear, we're your family now. You seem to have forgotten that. Well, I'm just so grateful it was Theo who found you. I hate to think what vile things might have happened if it had been anyone less reputable. This is exactly why I told you to stay at the manor. You act without thinking of consequences, so I'm compelled to look after your safety."

"Are you going to let me go or not? You can't keep me here forever."

She coolly appraised me, then picked under a fingernail. "Why on earth would you think I want to keep you here forever? Nothing could be further from the truth. I'm simply saying you may want to reconsider leaving at this particular time."

"Ha. You may want to reconsider keeping me here like a prisoner. I don't think you want word to spread that Gal conspired with tax collectors and caused an innocent man to die."

She didn't faint or beg for mercy. Instead she just stared at me with a quizzical look. "And who might that be?"

"You know who—our neighbor Aharon."

"Ah, yes. What a tragic accident. But I'm afraid he has only himself to blame for running into a burning building."

"We both know that fire was no accident. And I'm sure if the council members knew, Gal would be shunned." My hands tremored, but it felt good to finally confront her, to finally be the one in control.

Raz forced a smile to her lips. "Oh, Hannah. Your ingenuousness never ceases to astound me . . . but it has long since ceased to amuse me." She stood and approached me with more menace than any four-legged predator. "I could forgive the fact that you entranced my son and ruined any chance for a decent match. I could even forgive the fact that you've failed to perform your one wifely duty. But the fact that you would falsely accuse us, after every kindness and luxury we've lavished upon you . . . that is unforgivable. I won't tolerate a threat to my family."

"Neither shall I. So you of all people can appreciate why I must go to Nazareth." As soon as the words escaped my lips, I suspected I'd divulged too much.

Just stay calm. I have the upper hand after all. There was no way she could have known I discovered her scheme to ambush Yeshua.

I started for the door, but her hand clamped onto my arm. I froze but refused to meet her eyes. She wrenched my arm until I had to lean toward her to stop the pain.

"When you get to Nazareth, don't forget to give your mother a farewell for me," she whispered in my ear.

I couldn't help but give her a questioning look. "Farewell? You mean give her greetings?"

"No. I mean, say farewell."

I should have broken free from her grip and run as fast and far as I could, but terror shackled my feet. What horrible scheme had she hatched now?

She released my arm and held her hand out, rolling her fingers to admire her glistening rings. I detested her so much in that moment, it was all I could do not to strike her.

"Funny," Raz said. "Most people haven't surmised that Yeshua believes he's the son of the Almighty. Of course, in making such a claim, he's admitting that he's not the son of his poor earthly father. I admit it's a rather clever twist on the age-old story of cuckolding—Yeshua hides the shame of being a bastard under the guise of holiness. Oh, don't look so alarmed. I give him credit for finding a way to turn a weakness into an asset."

My thoughts raced. How long had she been savoring the delivery of that strike? Had she waited all these years to inflict the greatest damage? No, I couldn't believe she had known about this from the beginning. She would have stopped Olmer from marrying me. So she must have learned it recently. And then, like a punch in the gut, the answer hit me. Tabitha had told her.

Raz pouted. "Oh my, you look ill. Did you think you could keep such a salacious secret from me forever? That I wouldn't find out your lovely mother was . . . too lovely for her own good? Getting with child before marriage. Your poor father. I hear he couldn't bring himself to lie with the shameless woman until the evidence of her infidelity was expelled from her body."

"I'm not sure I know what you mean," I managed to say.

"Hmm. I think you do. There's no law limiting the amount of time for bringing an accusation of adultery—did you know that? And adultery is a crime punishable by death. I'm *sure* you know that. Don't you?"

I swallowed and my eyes darted around while my mind screamed for an answer to silence her. The only defense against adultery would be for my mother to profess Yeshua was the son of Adonai. Such a blasphemous statement would also bring death.

"You have my permission to go to Nazareth to speak with your family as you so eagerly desire. Just remember . . . if you say too much, I may find the need to speak about some things myself."

Raziela glided serenely past me and out the door.

While she let me leave, we both knew who'd won.

CHAPTER 51

I waited to be sure Raz had left the courtyard, then sprinted up the stairs to retrieve my bag. Trying to calm my breathing, I assessed the implications of what she'd said—or rather left unsaid. I threw open the door to my room, ready to confront my nieces, but they'd gone.

Suddenly, a head popped out from under the sleeping cot. I screamed despite recognizing it was only my nephew.

Idan squealed with delight at receiving this better-than-hoped-for reaction. He put a finger to his lips and ducked back under the bed. I was so distraught I didn't understand what was happening until I heard Tabitha speaking in a sing-song voice.

"Idan's not in here . . . Where is Idan? I wonder where he is. Could he be in here?"

As she rounded the corner and glimpsed the furious glare on my face, her smile vanished. We stared at one another as we listened to the stifled giggles coming from under the bed.

"Aren't you going to ask me what's wrong?" I challenged.

"Hannah. Hannah, I'm sorry." She held her hands in front of her to ward off my anger.

"Emmi, here I am." Idan stuck his head out but seemed disappointed by the less-than-enthusiastic response we gave him.

"Yes, dear. Emmi and Auntie Nah need to have an adult talk. Go find your brother, and I'll be down shortly."

"But, Emmi," he whined.

I nodded and patted Idan's head.

"Listen to your Emmi. Go on." Upon hearing the patter of his feet receding down the hall, I spoke again.

"I knew it. I knew you were fishing for information. *How could you?* What I shared with you was shared in confidence."

"I wanted to help. I thought if I explained to Raziela—"

"What? Explained what exactly?" I shrieked. "That my brother is a . . . that he was conceived out of the marriage bed? How could that possibly help?"

"Please listen. I wanted to convince Raz that he isn't just some troublemaker—that he's special, that he was born with a calling on his life."

"You know what I think? I think you wanted to convince Raz that you're special. Ever since Keturah gave birth to a son, you and the boys have fallen in stature in Raziela's estimation. You probably thought spying could get you back into her good graces."

"I won't deny that things have changed. I do have less standing now. And it does frighten me. But I swear to you, that is *not* why I told her."

"What happened to keeping out of matters that don't concern you?" I shook my head and picked up my belongings.

Her eyes darted back and forth between me and the bag. "Where are you going? What are you planning to do?"

I pushed past her. "I don't know. But even if I did, do you think I would tell you?"

"Please wait."

I ignored her.

"Wait!" She grabbed my cloak and a hunk of hair by mistake, causing me to wince. When I wheeled around, her mouth opened in shock.

"I'm sorry, I didn't mean to hurt you." She backed away as if expecting me to reciprocate. "But there's something you should know before you do something rash."

I rubbed my head and glared at her. She sat on the edge of the bed and took a deep breath.

"Theokritos and I are to be wed."

What? My first reaction was to comfort her, but then I suspected it was a ploy to gain my sympathy.

"Congratulations. Up until today, I wouldn't have thought you suited for someone so contemptible, but now I think you'll be quite happy together."

Her eyes filled with tears, but I refused to care.

"I'm not telling you because I want you to feel sorry for me," she said. "I'm telling you so that you remember that you and I are alike. We're both at the mercy of this family."

I shook my head. "Tabitha, I'm sorry that your husband died. I'm even sorry that you have to marry that man. But you and I are nothing alike."

"Have you ever wondered why Olmer travels so frequently to Miletus of late?" she asked.

I scowled. "What does that have to do with anything?"

She ran her palm over a wrinkle on the blanket. "You remember that Raz had originally intended Olmer to marry into a rich family in Miletus? Before your engagement?"

I didn't think it was possible to feel any worse after the morning I'd had, but somehow my spirits sank lower.

"So? That was years ago. The girl she had in mind must be . . ." I did a quick calculation in my mind. "She's twenty-one years of age by now. I'm sure she's long since been married."

"Yes, she's married. But Keturah let slip that the woman

has a younger sister whose marriage has yet to be arranged. There was something about her demeanor when she told me. I thought you should know."

"Know what exactly?" I demanded.

"I just don't think it would be wise to upset things now, given that . . ." Her eyes pleaded with me to understand.

"Go on, say it. Given that I'm barren? Given that my husband may be in the market for a more fertile wife? I never thought you'd use idle gossip to turn me against my own husband—just to keep from looking bad yourself. You disgust me."

This time I made it through the door despite her protestations. I stomped downstairs and across the courtyard but stopped at the exit. Myrinne. Hopefully she hadn't told Iakovos I knew about Raz's plans for Yeshua. I turned down the stairs to the cellar to search her out.

There was no one in sight. On impulse, I childishly snatched the most portable item around and stuffed it into my bag, then ran up the stairs and outside. I scurried down the hill, past curious stares from the stable boy and a few vineyard workers at seeing me leaving alone, but no one tried to stop me. A momentary triumph energized me as I put the manor behind me, but the euphoria of my petty revenge was fleeting. My fears returned, keeping me company on the walk home.

CHAPTER 52

A both familiar and surreally calm sight greeted me in Nazareth after the morning's earlier drama. Emmi sat on a stool in the garden next to a tarp covered with hundreds of shucked almonds. A delicate smile rested on her lips as she tossed almond shells aside, dropping the edible kernels into a jar. Some of my younger nephews and nieces played with wooden blocks at her feet.

I stood still, unwilling to intrude on the serenity of the scene.

My heart squeezed with longing. How I'd missed the pleasant hours spent on simple tasks in her company. Finally, I called out my greeting.

Emmi's face lit up.

"Hannah. How wonderful to see you."

I held up my hand to keep her from standing. "I brought you a gift."

I presented her with my contraband jar from the cellar. "It's made of the dark clay from Kefar Hananya. Myrinne says it's especially good for keeping olive oil."

"Oh," she remarked with a polite but puzzled look. "Thank you."

My nephew ran to embrace my leg, and I smiled and

stroked his wispy hair. Crouching down, I inhaled the sweet smell of his young neck and couldn't resist kissing his cheek. He squealed and wiped his face before running back to play with his brother.

"We weren't expecting you. Do you come with news?" Her eyebrows raised expectantly.

I knew my mother well enough to know what particular piece of news she hoped to hear—an impending birth announcement.

"You know if I had news I would've told you right away. Besides, I haven't seen Olmer for over a year." I didn't mean to snap at her, but I was still shaken from earlier events in Sepphoris. I had enough to worry about without being reminded of my inadequacies. Maybe it wasn't a good idea to come here after all.

"I'm sorry. I thought maybe he had returned. We don't get much news from you anymore." Emmi measured my reaction carefully. She probably suspected I withheld something, but she didn't push for clarification. "No matter. There's still plenty of time for starting a family. And it's lovely to have time alone to enjoy as a couple."

I bit back a retort about my husband's frequent and increasingly deliberate absences because I knew Emmi still missed Abba dearly. And so did I. Suddenly I burst into tears.

"What is it, sweetheart?" She stood to embrace me, and nuts rained from her skirt.

The children stopped their play and stared. Binyamin pouted. "Don't cry, Aunt Hannah."

"I'm sorry. I'm just so sad."

I continued to sob but with less vehemence now, mopping my face with my sleeve. I didn't know if it was being home or Emmi's obliviousness to the devious plotting against her and those she loved that upset me more.

She seemed shorter than I remembered, more fragile, now that she stood so close. How could I tell her what it was like to live in the manor? What Raziela had threatened? How scared I was? Unburdening my cares would only place more worry on her.

"Goodness, look at me. My eyes are leaking." I attempted a feeble laugh and sniffed.

Binyamin looked unsure of me but returned to playing. I stepped away from Emmi and began picking up the dropped almonds. She took a seat again without taking her eyes from my face.

"Olmer is away more and more," I explained. "When he is home, we argue."

"All marriages have times of adjustment. You'll see. Things will get better."

"I've been married more than half my life. Shouldn't we be adjusted by now?"

Emmi flinched at my tone.

"I'm sorry, it's not just Olmer. My relationship with Raziela has gotten worse too."

Emmi made a sympathetic noise.

I dabbed under my nose with the edge of my headdress and took a bracing breath. Staring at her, I told myself to keep quiet, but the need for absolution was too strong.

"Emmi, I may have done a bad thing."

"What do you mean?"

"I told Tabitha about Yeshua, about everything—the angel, the prophecy . . . and about Abba not being his father. I didn't mean to cause trouble. I told her not to tell anyone, but now Raz knows. Soon Olmer will know. I don't know how he'll react."

She pulled a few more nuts free from their shells while I nervously bit my thumb, waiting for her to speak.

"It's never a bad thing to speak the truth," she said.

"But all these years, you've kept it in the family. You were trying to hide it, weren't you?"

"Hide it?" She smiled at the idea. "Hannah, I am *blessed* to have been chosen to be Yeshua's mother. The Lord has done great things for me. Why would I hide such a thing?"

"But I've never heard you talk of it outside the family."

"Over the years, I've found that the Lord has revealed it to some, to those who would believe, without my even having to speak a word. And those who won't believe the truth . . ." She shrugged. "They cannot be convinced by my account."

I paused to consider this. It shamed me to know I fell somewhere in between these two categories.

"But what should we do? What if Raziela tells other people? What if they think you're lying?"

She seemed unfazed by my worrying. "I know the truth. It doesn't matter what others say."

I wasn't convinced. She didn't realize the bounds of Raziela's malicious nature.

Sitting at her feet, I let her pat my arm in assurance. The calluses on her hand scratched where she touched my forearm. Hers were the hands of a lifetime of physical labor, a life I had managed to escape by marrying into wealth. I examined her face, the deep lines etched in her forehead, the heaviness of her eyelids spilling onto her lashes. The years of physical labor had taken their toll. But of our two lives, hers was the one to be envied. She appeared to speak the truth when she said she wasn't afraid. I wished I shared her courage.

"Maybe if Yeshua would stop drawing attention to himself, we could put things right again."

Emmi pulled her hand back into her lap.

"I know things are confusing at times, Hannah. We may not understand everything Yeshua says or does. But how can we? He is obeying what the Lord would have him do. Ours isn't to understand everything, but to trust and have faith."

"Now you sound like Elan."

"Is that a bad thing?"

"No," I grudgingly admitted.

"Besides, can you honestly tell me that Yeshua is the cause for your problems with Olmer? I seem to remember that you were not content with the match even from the beginning. How many times did you tell me that you wished things were different, that you wanted something to change? Well, now you have what you desired. Things are changing."

She surprised me less by the truth of her assertions and more by her detached delivery. Sometimes I underestimated my mother. Part of me was defensive, but she was right. There had been another choice, but I had chosen Olmer.

I helped her shuck the almonds and listened to the children's banter and the leaves rustling overhead.

"Is he here?"

"Yeshua?"

"Elan."

Emmi gave me a look as if questioning why a married woman would want to know such a thing, then softened.

"He went to hear your brother teach."

"Again? Who is tending the flocks?"

She hesitated. "Elan sold most of the animals. Your older nephews are caring for the others in his absence. They've worked out an arrangement."

"*Sold* most of them?" My voice rose in indignation. "But that's his livelihood, his only inheritance from his father. Is that how Yeshua is funding this movement of his? By coercing gullible fools into selling their property?"

I'd seen the state of some of the beggars and undesirables who followed Yeshua. I had assumed they'd always been that way, but maybe they'd lost all they had in their eagerness to chase a dreamer.

Emmi looked ready to rebuke me when we heard the snap of a branch. I looked up just as two figures emerged from behind the nearby tree trunk as they crested the hill.

"Yeshua!" Emmi jumped to her feet like a little girl.

Beside him, Elan stared at me with his right eyebrow raised, and I blushed. No doubt he'd overheard my comments.

Yeshua presented a package from the sack slung over his shoulder. "These are for you."

From the twine-wrapped leaves covering the gift, I could tell it contained the pickled fish from Magdala that Emmi adored. She could also. Looking nearly giddy with delight, she hugged him.

"Oh, you're so thoughtful." She clutched the package to her breast.

The dumb fish cost only a fraction of what was paid for the container I brought. Even as I thought it, part of me knew it was petty to blame Yeshua for showing me up, especially as my gift was arguably stolen. But I was still annoyed and embarrassed to have been caught speaking my earlier words.

"What brings you to Nazareth, Hannah?" Elan kept his tone casual, but his eyes searched my face with concern.

I touched a hand to my cheek and realized my eyes must be red and puffy from crying.

"Your face is always a welcome sight, regardless of your reasons for being here," Yeshua said. "I'm glad to see you." He stepped forward and brushed my cheek with his thumb tracing the track of my recent tears before placing his hand on my shoulder.

"And I'm glad to see you." With surprise, I realized how much I meant it. I almost cried again when I saw the love in his eyes.

He squeezed my shoulder, and the warmth of his touch carried a weight to it that seemed to push all the tension from my shoulders down through my body and out my feet. I felt heavy and lethargic and strange . . . but in a good way. Was this what it felt like to be at peace?

"Let us wash the dust from our travels. Then Elan will regale you both with his latest adventures."

I nodded, my lips upturned irrationally as if time had fallen away and I was a carefree girl again. Emmi was here, Elan was here, and my brother was back. Betrayal and threats of violence seemed like inconsequential ideas from a fictitious land.

Yeshua smiled at me, and all I could think was I didn't ever want him to remove his hand from my shoulder.

"Emmi, have you been hiding all these visitors from us?" Shlomit called with glee. She strode forward to scoop up her sons in greeting.

Yeshua dropped his hand as he turned his attention to Shlomit. The moment had passed, but the calm remained.

I decided to enjoy this short respite from my worries and my mission in coming here. There would be plenty of time later to figure out together what to do.

CHAPTER 53

"Didn't you hear me?" Y'hudah banged the tabletop between us. "He has to take Jerusalem. And you're either for him or against him. You have to choose a side, Hannah. No wonder Yeshua said that anyone who follows him must hate his family. I'm beginning to see that not all family members are as loyal as they should be."

Any earlier peace abandoned me, and my mouth fell open at this hurtful remark. It'd been over a year since I last saw my brother Y'hudah. Despite my earlier delight in finding him in Nazareth, I now feared he kept company with the same crowd that Uncle Cleopas favored in Gamla—dangerous men who would bring about our destruction with their loose tongues.

"All I suggested is that Yeshua might want to lay low for a while, to avoid angering the leaders further. How dare you be so glib? You're speaking about starting another civil war."

Ya'akov turned to Emmi as she stood to clear the bowls. "Did Yeshua really say that about hating his family? Why is he angry with us?"

"I'm sure that's not what he meant." Emmi looked weary that yet another evening meal had been spoiled by argument.

"He did say it," Y'hudah insisted, unabashed despite her correction. "And when someone else said, 'Bless the one who nursed you,' Yeshua said it would be better to bless the one who obeys God."[33]

Now we all watched for Emmi's response.

"We just need to ask Yeshua about these things. I cannot believe that he meant them for our harm." She banged the bowls together as she stacked them. By her expression, she was hurt, but apparently not enough to abandon her blind adoration of Yeshua.

"You're always so quick to defend him." I put my hands on my hips.

"Yes, Hannah, I do defend him. He's the One who will bring our salvation."

I groaned and threw my head back.

"You weren't there from the beginning," she continued. "You didn't see the angel. You didn't hear Yochanon's father Z'kharyah confirm it. Or hear the prophecy spoken over Yeshua at the temple when we presented him as an infant."

"Spoken by that old man wandering the temple courts? He wasn't a priest or even a rabbi." Ya'akov's words crawled to a halt at Emmi's scowl.

"No, he wasn't." Emmi's voice trembled with indignation. "But not all revelation comes through rabbis."

Ya'akov's mouth opened to protest, but she ignored him.

"He was a righteous man," she said, "and his words were from the Lord. As soon as he saw your brother, he knew he was Adonai's yeshu'ah. The man told me Yeshua would cause many in this land to fall and many to rise . . . that he'd become a sign whom people would speak against. That's certainly come to pass." Emmi's brow creased. "The old man prophesied a sword will pierce my own heart too. He said, 'All this will happen in order to reveal many people's inmost thoughts.'"[34]

Silence prevailed for an uncomfortable length of time. I

didn't think any of us wanted to share our inmost thoughts at that point. I listened to Ayelet and Talia trying to get the little ones to sleep in the next room.

What did the man's words mean, that a sword would pierce Emmi's heart? She grieved when people criticized Yeshua. Was that what he meant? Or was it something more sinister? Was the man predicting armed conflict? Could Yeshua and Emmi both die by the sword? That was too terrible to consider.

"Emmi, you have to convince Yeshua to stay here. You're the only one who can keep him from danger."

My comment garnered everyone's attention. I had to tread carefully. As much as I wanted to warn them of the trap looming in Jerusalem at this very moment, I couldn't, not without implicating my in-laws. Raz had made it clear that I needed to keep silent in order for her to keep silent about Emmi.

I cleared my throat. "He's angered too many members of the Sanhedrin, let alone the prefect. I've heard men plot against him."

"That's why he has to go to Jerusalem. Can't you see?" Y'hudah paced back and forth now. "It's time for him to take back the kingdom. We know he'll be victorious. It's time he set us free from the Romans."

"Be quiet, you fool!" Yosi shouted. "Don't you think if he could, he would have done it by now? I won't have any more of your incendiary remarks under my roof."

Y'hudah's eyebrows shot up. "Your roof? Since when did this become your property? Yeshua's the oldest. It's his house."

"Then he should live in it," Yosi said.

"And do the work," Shim'on added. "What has Yeshua contributed over the last years? He's abandoned his carpentry work. He hasn't been here for the harvests. If it were up to him, we'd all be beggars."

The door opened and Yeshua entered. He expressed no surprise or concern at our awkward silence.

"Here he is now . . . the savior of the world. What exactly are your future plans, brother?" Shim'on asked. "Are you leaving with us for Jerusalem in the morning or not?"

"We've heard men are plotting against you." Emmi crossed the room to touch Yeshua's arm. "Is it safe for you to go to the feast? Maybe you should stay in Nazareth."

"Tell them, Yeshua. Tell them why you have to go to Judea." Y'hudah charged forward, pointing at those of us left at the table.

Yeshua turned from Emmi to study me. I tried to appear detached but held my breath as I awaited his response.

"I will not be going with you to Jerusalem for the feast," Yeshua said.

I let out my breath, relieved to be absolved of further action.

"What? You have to." Y'hudah whined and slapped his thighs in frustration. "The time for hiding is over. The people are ready. You need to take up your responsibilities."

"I do have to undergo a baptism," Yeshua said seriously, "but it is not yet time."

The rest of us exchanged puzzled glances. It wasn't much in the way of an explanation.

"Yochanon baptized you already. What do you mean you have to undergo another baptism?" Ya'akov asked.

Shim'on grunted. "It seems to me, getting baptized by that man is what started all this trouble."

"Is there another one of Yochanon's followers who is baptizing now?" Emmi asked. "Is that what you mean?"

We all waited for enlightenment, but none was forthcoming. My earlier relief gave way to annoyance when Yeshua refused to answer.

"Why must you always speak in riddles and parables?" I asked Yeshua. "Surely you can share your plans with us. You shouldn't keep secrets from your own family."

He lifted one eyebrow, and I blushed guiltily.

"I told you. He talks in riddles to avoid the truth," Yosi said. "Anyone who wants to be a public figure, a leader, doesn't hide out in the Galil—he goes to Judea. But you don't act like one who is eager to rule. You alienate anyone wealthy enough to provide the backing you need. You've practically shunned the Torah teachers. How can anyone who wants to be a leader act alone, in secret?"

"He's right," Shim'on agreed. "Why do we only hear rumors and whispers of these great things you do? I've never seen you do anything extraordinary. If you can do miracles, then go to Jerusalem. Show these miracles to the Sanhedrin. Prove that you're our leader."

Yosi snickered. "He's only capable of leading trash. You've seen his followers—lepers, prostitutes, tax collectors . . . gentiles."

Yeshua took a seat at the table.

"It is written, 'For your sake I suffer insults, shame covers my face. I am estranged from my brothers, an alien to my mother's children, because zeal for your house is eating me up, and on me are falling the insults of those insulting you.'"[35]

Shim'on's face turned the color of poppies. "You must see why your brothers would be estranged from your cause if you're not even willing to show yourself in public. How do you expect us to believe you're Adonai's Anointed One? If you are who you say you are, why not gather an army now and ride into Jerusalem? Then we'd support you."

Y'hudah sat up taller, anxious for Yeshua's answer. He was far too eager for battle.

Ya'akov looked at Yeshua with questioning eyes. "You have to admit that you are acting a bit . . . unusual." He tried for a more diplomatic tone. "Why wouldn't you want to go to the temple and demonstrate this power to everyone?"

"Yes." Yosi smirked. "Act on your words. Go to the Sanhedrin and declare yourself."

Yeshua just smiled. "The right time for me has not yet come. Any time is right for you. The world can't hate you, but it hates me because I testify that what it does is evil. You go to the feast."[36]

Yosi and Shim'on scowled as if they suspected they'd been insulted but couldn't quite say how.

"So . . . you're not going to Jerusalem?" Y'hudah collapsed onto the edge of Emmi and Abba's bed across the room. He held his head in his hands. "How will I explain to those who are counting on you?"

Yeshua held my gaze as he answered. "I am not going up to this feast because the right time for me has not yet come."

"You all heard your brother." Emmi placed her hands on Yeshua's shoulders. "Let me get you some stew. You must be hungry. Hannah, clean a bowl for Yeshua."

The discussion, it appeared, was over.

CHAPTER 54

It was nearly sundown of the day following my brothers' departure to Jerusalem with the other pilgrims. I found myself alone inside the house with the youngest children, who were quietly occupied for the moment in the next room. Maybe too quietly, but I decided not to check on them just yet. A pile of worn clothing cascaded off the table, but my hand rested idly in my lap. I lacked the patience for darning today.

Yeshua's words echoed in my mind. *The right time has not yet come for me to go to Jerusalem.*[37] How could it not be the right time if it was a feast? Or did he mean that he would declare himself the Messiah on a future date? His secrecy concerned me.

The door creaked, and I looked up.

"I've come to say farewell," Yeshua said.

"Farewell?" I laughed without humor. "Don't you get tired of roaming far and wide? Where are you off to now?"

"Where Abba sends me."

I ignored this cryptic but familiar response. As long as he wasn't going to Jerusalem, I didn't care where he went.

Yeshua sat next to me and picked up a tunic. He turned the garment inside out and carefully aligned the edges of the seam that had been pulled apart. Then covering a yawn with the back of his wrist and catching me observing him, he grinned almost bashfully.

Tenderness welled up inside of me. I didn't see him as a dissenter or a lunatic or a miracle worker. I saw only the boy I grew up with, my brother.

"I'm going to the feast."

"What?" I slapped my hand on my knee, sending any kind thoughts scurrying. "No. You told everyone you weren't going. They've already left. It's almost evening. You can't go."

Yeshua measured my response curiously.

I picked up my mending and stabbed my finger with the needle. Wincing, I flung the cloth aside, sucked on my finger, and met his gaze.

"Listen. Please don't ask me how I know this, but you can't go to Jerusalem. There are men waiting there. Men who seek to do you harm, possibly to kill you."

He didn't appear the least bit affected by this revelation. In fact, he seemed mildly pleased and smiled as he placed his hand on my shoulder.

I stared at him in disbelief and brushed his hand away.

"Did you not understand a word I just said? I worry about you. We all do. *Please*. Go to Capernaum if you must, but just stay in the Galil."

"Hannah, don't let your heart be troubled. You'll face trials and even persecution, but don't be afraid. Trust in Adonai. Trust also in me.[38] Seek treasures that can't be destroyed or stripped away. Don't be afraid to lose your life, for by losing it you will live forever."[39]

I frowned. Not for the first time, I questioned my brother's state of mind.

"What are you saying? That there will be an attack on Sepphoris? That our property will be destroyed? How do you expect me to trust you when you're risking all of our lives?" I shook my head. "I understand your desire to put things right. Really, I do. But I can't sanction a revolt. You can't expect me to go against my husband's wishes . . . even if you are in the right. I'm not like you. I am afraid. I don't want to be part of any fighting, and I certainly don't want to die." I grabbed his sleeve and pled with him, "Emmi is so worried for your safety. We all are. Please. You need to stay in Nazareth. Settle down, take a wife. You don't have to do this."

He remained quiet, which I interpreted as an encouraging sign that he mulled over my words, so I pressed on.

"You could take up the business again with Shim'on and Y'hudah. You love building and your carpentry work. You said it yourself—those who take up the sword die by the sword. You don't want to risk death, do you? Don't you want to be happy? Don't you want to live a long, contented life?"

"Stop."

The word rang out making the silence that followed more profound.

Sadness filled me. How could he not heed such sound advice? I released his sleeve and my hand fell limp at my side.

"The Son of Man must be lifted up that all who believe in him will have life.[40] A time is coming when you'll need to decide for yourself whom you'll serve. Believe in the one who sent me and believe in me."[41]

He placed the torn tunic on the table and stood, untying the pouch tied to his belt. After retrieving a small bundle of cloth, he reached for my hand, but I jerked it back.

"I found this. I expect you'll be happy to have it one day. Be well, Hannah."

He leaned forward and lightly brushed my forehead with a kiss, then dropped the object into my lap. I gave him a puzzled look, but he'd already exited and pulled the door closed behind him. This mysterious exchange shocked me so much that I stared after him for a minute before unwrapping the strip of cloth to reveal its contents.

There before me was my doll, the one he and Elan had made for me when I was a child. Where had he found it? And how was it possible it survived and looked so well preserved after all these years?

Then I knew the answer . . . it couldn't have survived outside. He must have retrieved it soon after I recklessly pitched it off the hillside and had kept it safe for me all this time. My heart swelled. I might not understand my brother, but I knew he really loved me. A strange chill ran through my body. What did he mean that I'd be happy to have it one day? Why would I need a doll unless . . .

The bench scraped across the floor, and I rushed to the door. In the clearing, Emmi sat on the ground grinding lentils and Yeshua stood speaking to her. I started to close the door, not wanting to intrude on their conversation. But then I watched Emmi vehemently shake her head and mash the pestle into the bowl with exaggerated force. Yeshua stooped down and put his hand on her arm to still it. Curious, I peeked out the opening and strained to catch their voices. Whatever he was saying agitated her more. She continued to shake her head without meeting his gaze.

Suddenly her face contorted and tears cascaded down her cheeks. I covered my mouth with my hand as Yeshua guided her to her feet. He held her in his arms, his chin easily clearing the top of her head. Watching such a tender scene was disconcerting, but I couldn't look away.

After a minute, she stopped crying and stepped back from his embrace. He picked up the hem of his shawl and wiped away her tears. She clutched the fabric to her cheek with the tassels intertwined in her fingers and took a few ragged breaths. Yeshua looked forlorn as he stared up at the sky over her head, his eyes both beseeching and resolute. The expression put me in remembrance of Abba. Whenever Abba had faced a necessary but unpleasant task, he would look heavenward, praying for strength to do what had to be done.

What could they be discussing to cause them both such distress?

Yeshua ducked his head and with two fingers gently tilted Emmi's chin up. He studied her intently as she murmured something. I recognized the resolute look in her eye, and Yeshua must have too, because finally he nodded. He produced a weak smile and kissed the top of her head like he had mine, then turned and gave a small wave in my direction.

Embarrassed to be caught spying on them, I fumbled to appear busy. But he'd already set off without a backward glance.

I should have allowed her some time to collect herself, but curiosity won out over decency. When Emmi noticed me approach, she searched the ground for the dropped pestle as if she had only been distracted from her task for a second.

"Emmi, what is it? What did Yeshua say to you?"

She blinked at me like she'd already forgotten my presence.

"Oh." She cleared her throat and appeared to consider her choice of words. "Yeshua is concerned about me meeting him in Jerusalem and thought to spare me any . . . unpleasantness. He suggested that I should stay at home."

I was confused. "But you aren't going to Jerusalem, are you?"

"Not this time. I plan on going for the Feast of Unleavened Bread. Ya'akov told me he'd escort me."

"Wait. Yeshua's not going to Jerusalem now, is he? After

what I just told him?" My irritation returned. "And what do you mean he's concerned about you going? Concerned about what? He's not thinking of doing anything foolhardy, is he? Is that when the revolt is planned? Pesach? Does he realize what kind of position this puts me in with Olmer? I'll have to tell him."

Her head whipped toward me, and she looked so fierce, I shrank back in surprise.

"Oh, Hannah. Just once, can't you think about someone other than yourself?"

Her words were not spoken in anger but with genuine wonder. She might as well have asked me if I thought I'd be able to fly someday.

How could she think that I, of all people, was selfish? I wasn't the one putting everyone's lives in jeopardy. I was here to help.

I held my tongue only because she was visibly distraught again. Taking the pestle from her hand, I started to grind the lentils as a gesture of reconciliation. We were quiet for a moment.

"So are you going to go? Will you meet him in Jerusalem during Pesach?" I asked.

"Of course. I'm his mother."

I didn't understand this logic, but her curt reply discouraged further inquiries, so I let it go for the moment. I belatedly realized I had forgotten to say farewell to Yeshua.

CHAPTER 55

I walked to the hazzan's home—Uri's home, now, I reminded myself—to get my sister's opinion about all this. The doors and shutters were open, and Shlomit's children shrieked and hollered out front, chasing each other in some game of tag. I couldn't remember ever playing with such abandon, but I supposed we had once. I stuck my head across the threshold.

"I mean it. Stay outside until I'm finished." Shlomit didn't look up from sweeping.

I giggled. Shlomit turned and laughed.

"Isn't it amazing such little creatures can carry so much dirt into a house?" Then her smile transformed into the familiar look of sympathy.

How I wished people would realize I wasn't constantly thinking about my lack of children—until they acted so awkward. Well, most days anyway.

"Did you speak with Yeshua?"

"Yes, he was here early this morning."

"Can you believe it? He's going to Jerusalem."

Shlomit paused her cleaning, and I sat while she leaned the broom against the wall.

"Now, tell me what's got you so upset. Why shouldn't he

go to the feast? He's never missed being at the temple on a holy day."

"I know, but things are different now. There are men who seek to do him harm in Jerusalem. He's going to get himself killed."

She considered this, then spoke quietly.

"I also worry sometimes. But then I remember that Yeshua is the Son of the Almighty. Do you really believe anything could happen to him that is outside the Lord's will for his life? We just have to trust that Yeshua knows what is best."

"But he's just a man. He's flesh and blood like the rest of us. You were just a baby when he got kicked by a horse. He had a bruise on his thigh for days after that. He's not immortal, Shlomit. Yochanon was a man of God. Look what they did to him."

Shlomit frowned. It pleased me despite myself to see concern tamper her usual blind optimism.

"Hannah, he told me to trust him. So that is what I'm going to do."

"But what if he doesn't know what he is doing? I know you think he can do anything, but let's be realistic. He can't."

"Can't he?"

A knock on the doorframe behind me caused me to whirl about.

A woman stood in the entrance. "Oh, excuse me. Shlomit, I just want to return your pot to you. Thank you again for the dates."

I stared at the woman. Her voice sounded familiar, but I couldn't place her face.

"Please, come inside," Shlomit said.

She held up a hand. "No, no. I won't keep you."

"Well, come for dinner sometime this week, Vana. I get

lonely for adult conversation when Uri is away."

Vana?

"I will. Thank you." She nodded to Shlomit, then turned to me. "Good to see you again, Hannah." She winked and marched off with a speed that astounded me.

I turned to Shlomit in disbelief. This Vana was the same decrepit woman from my childhood? She looked so vibrant and . . . upright. That's what struck me as odd. She wasn't hunched over, so I could actually see her face. And her hands—her fingers were as slim and straight as my own.

"How did . . . Did you see her? It's incredible."

The corner of Shlomit's mouth curled up. "What were you saying? Something about Yeshua not being able to do all things?"

"Elan told me that Yeshua had healed her, but I never thought . . . I didn't realize . . ." Words escaped me.

"I know." She couldn't repress her excitement any longer. "It is incredible. Now do you trust him?"

"Abba!" Cries of delight from the boys outside spared me from answering.

Shlomit and I exchanged a perplexed look. She started for the door as Uri rushed inside, his boys swarming around his legs.

"Where's Yeshua?" he demanded, breathing heavily.

"Uri, what is it?" she asked. "What are you doing here?"

He passed by us and searched the adjacent room, then returned. "Have you seen him? Where is he?"

"You're scaring me," I said. "He's not here. He left just an hour ago or so. What happened? Why are you back so soon?"

Uri collapsed onto a bench, gulping for air. He held up his hand to stay our questions.

Shlomit steered the boys back outdoors.

"But Emmi—"

"Abba will come see you in a minute," she insisted. "Scoot. Go on, scoot." She poured a cup of wine for him. "Here. Drink this and tell us what's going on."

Uri took two generous gulps of wine before answering.

"We made camp at sunset where we always do. We'd fallen asleep. Then, in the middle of the night, these men began kicking us awake."

"Men? What men? Pilgrims?"

"No, no. Big men armed with daggers. It was dark, but they looked like the foreign mercenary type, you know, that join the Roman army."

"Oh no." Terror contorted Shlomit's face despite the evidence standing in front of her that Uri had survived. "What happened? Did they hurt you?"

"Just bruises. But they interrogated your brothers and me, looking for Yeshua. They didn't believe he wasn't among us. They must have planned to ambush him on the road. They searched all around, but as more men awoke, it became clear they were greatly outnumbered, so they fled. Ya'akov and I waited until first light, then came back here as fast as we could to warn him."

"Yeshua just left for Jerusalem," I said, terrified he was heading right into a trap. "He's on the road now. Do you think they came back this way ahead of you?"

"No, they headed the opposite way. I guess they thought he was with an earlier group of travelers."

"Oh, thank goodness. But didn't you pass him on the road, then?" Shlomit asked.

Uri shook his head.

"This is exactly why I told him not to go." I swallowed back tears, frightened and relieved and traumatized at the same time. "This is my fault."

"You couldn't have known, Hannah." Shlomit shook her head. "You can't blame yourself. The important thing is they *didn't* take him. Everyone is safe."

She leaned down to place her arms around Uri's shoulders and he touched his cheek to hers.

I turned my head away, embarrassed at the tender display and guilty at her presumption of my innocence. I had known there was a real threat. I had just thought it would come in Jerusalem, not a day's journey from Nazareth. Yeshua couldn't have known those men would visit the campsite either. Yet somehow it seemed that he must have known. Why else would he have refused to leave with our brothers and shunned the safety of traveling with the hundreds of other pilgrims? If he had intended on going to the feast all along, why wait before leaving unless he somehow knew the danger? But how could he know?

I shivered. Could Yeshua really hear from the Lord? "Believe in me," he had said. I was beginning to do just that. I remembered then what else he had told me.

"Shlomit, Yeshua returned the doll to me." I put my hand on her arm.

She looked up at me. "What?"

"Before he left, he handed me the doll I used to own and said I would be happy to have it someday. Why would he say that? Why else would I want a doll unless . . ."

"Oh, Hannah." Shlomit lunged forward and embraced me joyfully.

"Do you think it's possible? After all these years?" I couldn't help but grin.

Shlomit pulled back and laughed. "Of course it's possible. Look at Emmi's relative Elisheva who had Yochanon so late in life. Don't you see? What Emmi has told us all these years is really true."

Uri finished her thought. "Nothing is impossible with God."

"But I've doubted Emmi's word. I haven't believed in Yeshua. I didn't even ask him. Why would the Lord allow me to have a child now?"

"Because he is good, Hannah," my sister said. "He is good."

I nodded and smiled in wonder and agreement.

***

I sat by the firepit in front of the house waiting for barley bread to bake, having decided to stay in Nazareth through the week following Sukkot to be sure Olmer had returned to Sepphoris before I faced my in-laws and that vile Theokritos again. Despite the conflict awaiting me at home, I felt lighter than I had in years, full of hope. Ironically, it was now Emmi who seemed to need my encouraging.

Yeshua had told me before to trust him when I was a young woman. The first time he had said it, I chose not to and ended up where I was now. But this time, I would. I would trust him. I didn't know how he would do it, but if Yeshua could really do the impossible, why couldn't he defeat our oppressors? I assumed he must be planning some type of offensive in the spring, given his warning to my mother.

Of course, I didn't welcome bloodshed, but maybe once he demonstrated his power in Jerusalem, the whole thing would end swiftly. At last, salvation would come to our people. Yeshua would be king, and he'd reward me for trusting him. Everything I'd ever wanted would be mine. Then my in-laws would have to respect and value me.

A finger of doubt tickled my newfound optimism. Yeshua had also said I would face trials, persecution. I pushed the thought aside as I poked the coals, hoping to speed the cooking.

I pulled the doll from my satchel and held it in my lap, rubbing my finger over the smooth faceless head carved of olive wood. Yeshua had said I would want this one day. I meditated on his words and bit my lip trying to suppress the growing joy inside me. Had he really meant I'd have a child of my own? I hugged the doll to myself and grinned before dropping it back into the bag and pulling the drawstring snug.

As I leaned forward to check on the bread, I stopped short. My husband stood in front of the stables.

"Olmer. You startled me."

I sprang to my feet to welcome him, but his features were so hard they could have been carved of dolomite. My heart sank before I got three steps.

"What are you doing behaving like a fool and playing with toys?" He squinted at me. "If anyone saw you, they would think you were daft . . . or mooning over a new lover."

"*Husband*. I was merely thinking about something Yeshua told me. I have news to share with you." I smiled tentatively and approached him again.

"Yeshua." Olmer spat toward my feet. "Yeshua, the mighty king of the Jews? The miraculous son of Elohim himself? Oh yes, I've heard all the news. Imagine my surprise to hear such an absurd tale—not from his sister, my very own wife, but from my *mother*. After all these years . . ." He shook his head at me. "Is this why your siblings and that crazy uncle of yours think Yeshua is so special? Because of his *divine* patronage?"

"Olmer." I spoke his name like a command, a hand in front of me trying to ward off his cold fury.

"Why am I just now finding out about your mother's infidelity? How could you shame me this way? Didn't you think it punishment enough to shame me with your barren womb?"

I was brought up short by this familiar but painful attack. Reality hit me like cold water in the face. How could I have hoped to get with child after all these years? Was I so gullible? Something inside me hardened.

"How could you know if I was barren or not, when you were barely home long enough to fulfill your duties?" I shrieked.

He raised his fist and I recoiled in fear, but he stayed still as if frozen by an invisible force. My mouth was dry and my knees trembled, but I held my ground. Finally, he dropped his arm.

"Do not speak to me in that tone of voice ever again," he said, rebuking with deadly calm. We stared each other down.

How had it come to this? Just moments ago I had contemplated our future, our happiness. He just didn't understand about Yeshua yet.

"Olmer, wait. Let me explain . . ."

"Oh, now you want to explain?" He stormed back and forth, fingers clutching his hair. I took a deep breath and willed my voice to be steady.

"Olmer, I wanted to tell you after we first met, really I did. But I was worried that you would reject me, that you would think it strange."

"Strange?" He wheeled around. "Why would I think it strange? Why, if Caesar Augustus thought he was the physical embodiment of a deity and called himself a son of a god, why shouldn't a carpenter from Nazareth? There's nothing strange about that." He chortled cruelly and, with his hair standing on end, he looked like a maniac.

"But listen, what if it's the other way around? What if the emperors are the pretenders, and Yeshua is the *true* son of God? What if he is the Messiah? It took me a long time to accept it too. But I think he's the one to save our people."

"You can't be serious." He laughed. When I said nothing, his expression turned incredulous and then outraged. "This is it, Hannah. This is really the last insult I can take. My mother was right about you all along."

What? Why would he—"Don't say that. What do you mean?"

"If your brother thinks he can invent some . . . title for himself to gain political power, he is mistaken. He cannot just liken himself to Caesar and expect to lead a nation without having the ruling class behind him. We will not allow another rebellion. We can't jeopardize what freedoms we have. And as long as you remain my wife, you will not mention such a foolhardy proposition again, do you understand me?"

I stared at him with my jaw thrust forward, breathing heavily. I caught myself before I chewed my thumb in nervous frustration. Instead I twisted the ring on my finger and looked down at the blood-hued garnet, remembering the night he had given it to me.

Olmer and I were far beyond our quick reconciliations of the past. I would no longer be swayed by sweet words or sparkling baubles. And he no longer offered them.

Realizing he awaited an answer, I gave a curt nod.

Ayelet came out of the house and smiled at Olmer. He turned his back on her, and she looked at me with her brow creased in question. I glanced away.

"Get your things," he commanded.

CHAPTER 56

When we returned to Sepphoris, we performed like actors who'd forgotten the lines of our play. No one mentioned my confrontation with Raz or the failed plans to ambush Yeshua on his way to the Feast of Tabernacles. It seemed we were all content to dismiss coercion and assassination attempts as trivial matters. In fact, I would have thought everyone at the manor had become mute if not for the snatches of whispered discussions that quickly halted upon my entering a room.

But beneath the quietness, I sensed great danger. Raziela continued to watch my every move. She gave the distinct impression of a cat that was so sure its prey wouldn't escape, it took time to enjoy the anticipation of the kill. The words of the prophet Micah came to my mind frequently, about daughters rising against mothers-in-law and mothers-in-law against daughters. I began to understand how an enemy could come from within one's own household.

I harbored my own secrets. I wanted to tell Olmer of Yeshua's cryptic warning to my mother about troubling times to come in Jerusalem, but I held my tongue. If I told Olmer about an imminent uprising, it would only solidify my husband's desire to stop Yeshua. And, sadly, I wasn't certain he wouldn't welcome Yeshua's demise if it came to armed conflict, and I wouldn't risk my brother's life again. I startled easily, expecting at any moment that Olmer might uncover Yeshua's intentions and accuse me of sedition.

But those fears were for naught. Olmer avoided me as one would a leper. It wasn't just words he withheld. For the first time, he rebuffed me when I had cleansed myself after my courses. In fact, he no longer shared my bed at all. While I couldn't say I longed for his touch, his cold rejection left me uncertain and depressed. For years, I had questioned his fidelity. Now I suspected he did have a mistress. Or worse still—as Tabitha had suggested—an arrangement for a potential wife in Miletus. The irony that I had thought Yeshua actually meant I would get with child was not lost on me. It certainly wasn't how events were unfolding.

As the day of our departure to celebrate the feast approached, my doubts and anxiety grew. I knew my brother had to become ruler. It was the only way my husband would believe in him, the only way there would be peace in my marriage. But I was torn between wishing Yeshua success and hoping he'd abandon this suicidal quest for power. He had told me to trust him, but I wondered if Yeshua had actually considered what a precarious position he'd put me in—put all of us in.

We stood to lose everything if he failed. Was it really worth it? Could I trust him with making decisions about my very life? Would he be there to protect me if and when fighting broke out? *Fighting?* More like massacre. The Romans were cruel and violent victors. I wouldn't wish their punishment on anyone—least of all myself. I couldn't remember my brother ever handling a sword, let alone brandishing it in battle. If Yeshua were Messiah, then all would end well. But if he wasn't . . .

My head hurt from circling around and around the same questions, finding no answer on which to stop. I didn't know what would happen, but I sensed that whatever it was, it would happen in Jerusalem.

PART 4

JERUSALEM

Pesach of the Year 3790 (Spring CE 30)

CHAPTER 57

We arrived to Jerusalem as the sun set at the start of the tenth day of Nissan. One of the Sanhedrin members, Bartal, had opened his home to us, so we were among the fortunate to have a real roof over our heads while we celebrated Pesach. I wasn't sure if the invitation had been extended spontaneously or with some cajoling, as I had overheard Raziela "reminding" Bartal's wife of the lucrative return on investment Gal achieved for her husband in the past two years. Regardless, it was a privilege to stay with such honored—and rich—hosts. And if I hadn't known that at first, I would have after hearing my mother-in-law mention it to everyone we encountered in the upper market.

While she haggled with a vendor over the cost of pepper, I stepped out from under one of the colonnades enclosing the market area and glanced at the skyline above me. No matter how many times I'd visited Jerusalem, the majesty of the architecture still demanded my admiration. Three distinct towers rose above the nearby roofs. My favorite, the smallest tower called Mariamne, was named after the wife King Herod murdered. Even the beauty of the city's stonework carried a taint of brutality these days.

A rude shove ended my reverie.

"Stop acting like a simpleton," my mother-in-law whispered. "Do you want people to think you're some village idiot?"

I didn't respond. I'd learned long ago that when Raz asked a question, she desired submissive assent, not an answer.

She shook her head in disgust.

"Really, Hannah, I'll be so glad when—" She abruptly coughed and pounded on her chest with enthusiasm, but there was a cruel gleam in her eye.

I squinted at her. Pride won out over curiosity, and I swallowed the question "When what?" before it passed through my lips.

She looked disappointed that I hadn't taken the bait. "Don't just stand there. Take this."

Raz draped a strap over my head, and I adjusted the other two sacks I carried. I couldn't fathom why a woman who owned a stable of donkeys and mules favored me as her beast of burden.

When Raz directed her focus on the unsuspecting seller at the next stall, I looked at Tabitha. She turned away to examine the citrus fruit on display.

Her reticent behavior puzzled me. I had made a point of forgiving my sister-in-law months ago. I had always known Yeshua's birth story would come out eventually, and Tabitha shouldn't be held accountable for how Raz used the information. Yet despite appearing genuinely relieved when I had voiced this to her, Tabitha still seemed uncomfortable around me.

"No. It's simply not possible," Raz said. "Don't be absurd."

I looked up to see whom she addressed.

"It's true." The woman fruit vendor looked unperturbed by Raz's glare. "I've seen the man here in the city with my own eyes."

"Then he was never really dead to begin with. I don't believe it."

"I mean you no disrespect, ma'am, but he was in the tomb four days."

Raziela stood as still as a statue but emitted an almost palpable rage. Keturah stared at me, pale and with her pupils dilated in horror.

"What are you talking about? Who was in a tomb?" I asked. Keturah took a step back, but the woman seemed happy to have a more receptive audience.

"A man called El'azar," she responded. "He was dead as dead can be until Yeshua of Nazareth told him to come out of his tomb. The man walked right out. Well, he was still bound up in grave clothes, but he was healthier than ever. Don't just take my word for it. There were over twelve witnesses who will tell you the same thing. People are saying this Yeshua is Eliyahu come again."

I opened my mouth, but before I could voice a coherent thought, Raz barked at the woman.

"He is certainly *not* Eliyahu. Any learned person knows there is no resurrection from the dead."

The murmurs of those standing closest to us subsided and heads turned our way. Raz's opinion about resurrection might have held sway with her Sadducee friends in Sepphoris, but here among the masses, the Pharisees' beliefs predominated.

Raz discreetly handed the woman some coins and moved on.

"This has gotten out of hand. I'll see this nonsense comes to an end even if I have to do it myself," she muttered, all thought of shopping apparently forgotten as she herded us forward. "I need to find Gal. Take these things back to the house. Go on, what are you waiting for? Go, go." She flapped her hands at the wrist to get us moving, as if directing wayward chickens.

I glanced over my shoulder at the vendor. The woman crossed her arms and nodded at me as if to confirm her story. Could this be true? I wanted to ask her a thousand questions, but Tabitha pushed me into the stream of shoppers.

We made our way through the streets back toward the Temple Mount, and Raziela and Keturah left us to find their husbands. The inspection of the lambs that would be sacrificed in four days' time was taking place. No doubt that was where the men were. Tabitha and I continued into the lower city. I felt lighter for their absence despite carrying all their packages.

"Did you hear what that woman said?" I shook my head in marvel. "A man emerged from a tomb, alive."

"Wait, where are you going?" Tabitha asked. "We should return to the house."

"I want to find my family. I want to find out what happened. Emmi will know."

She shook her head emphatically. "I don't think that's a good idea. Raz told us to go back to Bartal's home."

"And we will. Don't you want to know what happened? Yeshua raised a man from the dead, and you're worried about Raziela?"

"If you had any sense, you'd be worried about her too."

I put my hands on my hips. "Well, I'm going to find them."

Tabitha sighed and I knew then she'd follow me, albeit reluctantly. Now we were just faced with the somewhat daunting task of locating one family among the thousands of tents assembled on the opposite wall of the Kidron Valley. We had always set up camp in the same vicinity each year when I came with my parents. Staring up at the Mount of Olives, I paused to get my bearings.

Tabitha had stopped again and was staring wide-eyed to my right. I followed the direction of her gaze to the tombs carved into the hillside.

"Come on. There's nothing to be scared of. It's not as if he raised *all* the dead." I yanked her sleeve and we continued to climb. We passed the altar where the red heifer was sacrificed near the intersection of the bridge leading back to the eastern gate of the temple.

"It shouldn't be much farther."

The traffic of people in front of us slowed to a halt. A cohesive sound carried on the breeze above the usual sounds of the city, and I tried to see up the road, but a thick wall of people had amassed in front of us. Over their heads, I occasionally glimpsed arms undulating like a choppy sea as they waved palm branches to and fro. I didn't know why anyone would be making a wave offering today, or here of all places. The shouting grew in volume as it was carried down the hill toward us.

"What's all the commotion?" I called out. "Who's coming?"

An elderly woman with deeply grooved wrinkles turned around and greeted me with a huge, nearly toothless grin.

"It's Yeshua of Nazareth," she hollered before charging forward spryly, belying her apparent age.

Tabitha and I blinked at one another in disbelief.

Was he coming to claim his crown? Were these worshippers part of his plan? If so, they hardly looked like a unified fighting company.

Then, as if on command, I saw Yeshua round a turn in the path leading down the mountain. As astounded as I was, the scene still struck me as comical. My brother rode on a colt—not even a full-grown donkey, let alone a stallion befitting royalty or, in his case, a rebel leader. The entourage that traipsed behind him was even more pathetic—his usual fishermen friends, tax collectors, and a few women of questionable character bringing up the rear. It was a far cry from the army of rebels Uncle Cleopas hoped for and Gal feared. If Yeshua intended to intimidate the Roman soldiers who no doubt observed this parade from the fortress towers, it was a pitiful attempt indeed.

Yet the energy of the crowd couldn't be denied. As I observed Yeshua's bearing—poised, regal, resolute, and unhurried—the clouds parted overhead, allowing a beam of sunlight to bathe his path in golden light. It had a spellbinding effect, perfectly timed. For a second my eyes played a trick on me, and I envisioned him garbed in fine spun silk riding a beautiful white steed.

The cries of his followers swelled.

"Blessed is he who comes in the name of the Lord! Blessed is the coming kingdom!"

My heart beat faster and a chill traveled through my body. Then we were forced back by the crowd as Yeshua made his way past us. As preposterous as it all was, I found myself fighting the urge to join the throngs blatantly adoring him. I envied the joy of those who'd forsaken all reason and waved their arms in abandonment.

"Hannah, come away." Tabitha's fingers dug into the soft flesh on the inside of my arm and she jerked me backwards. This probably hadn't been her first attempt to garner my attention.

"It's amazing." I was dumbfounded, and not just a little proud. I craned my neck to look over my shoulder, but Yeshua was lost from view.

Tabitha clutched my arm as we pushed past the trailing admirers. She looked distraught, and I couldn't decide if she held on for support or was afraid I might escape to join

Yeshua's followers. Finally, I smacked at her hand.

"Hannah, please," she pleaded. "I want to go back. Now. I'm scared."

"Scared? It's just my brother."

But as I assured her, an inkling of uncertainty followed. Did Yeshua really wield the power to raise the dead back to life? The implications were enormous. I wondered if this man from Bethany was among those who followed Yeshua toward the temple even now. I hadn't seen anyone notable among the crowd. Then again, I didn't know what someone raised from the dead looked like.

The words of the prophet sprang to mind. I pictured a vast pile of bones taking on tendons and flesh and skin and breathing again. What if Yeshua intended to do battle using supernatural powers? If Yeshua had the power to raise the dead to life, he could raise up an army that would never be defeated. I shuddered as grisly images of marching skeletons filled my head.

I patted Tabitha's hand to reassure myself as much as her, and we turned back to the city.

CHAPTER 58

Two nights before Pesach, I awoke well past midnight with a full bladder. Our hosts had an inner room of the house designated as the latrine, necessitating a trip out of the room we were in. I felt around for my cloak and discovered Tabitha slept on it. Not wanting to disturb her, I wrapped a blanket around my shoulders. It would have to do.

Passing the main salon, I heard the men at the table still enjoying a boisterous discussion. Bartal had invited the many prominent visitors to the city as well as several distinguished teachers of the law to join with him. From the noise, I guessed several more hours would pass before they stumbled to their beds.

On my return, I made it only a quarter of the way across the courtyard when the volume of the voices increased as the door opened. I panicked at the state of my undress and ducked into the nearest doorway, hugging the wall as men exited the room.

The familiar voices caused me to cringe. Gal and Olmer as well as our host and a fourth man whose name I had forgotten but knew was a trustee of the temple treasury. I held my breath as they stopped a few paces away and conferred in hushed tones. As I wondered how long I'd have to stand in this position, the trustee raised his voice.

"The man publicly accused me of being a hypocrite," the man said. "*Me*, one of the *amarkelim*. No one has done as much as I have in support of the priesthood. I've dedicated my life to the service of the temple."

"Of course you have," Gal responded. "Anyone of import knows he speaks lies. His baseless accusations are meant to appease his followers. We all know his rants are without merit. He even accused me of being one who devours widows' homes."

I stifled a gasp. Hopefully Olmer didn't think I'd said anything to Yeshua about the fire or our neighbor's wife. It seemed my brother's frankness was matched only by his uncanny perception. The harsh criticisms Yeshua had levied against the priesthood these past days were shocking if not baseless. It seemed he was more intent on provoking his own people than confronting the Romans. Weren't they the enemy?

"What's being done to stifle this problem?" the man asked.

"We've had some prospects," Bartal answered. "If you push hard enough, all men have a price. Someone will turn. But we must be very careful about this. He's got the support of the people. We don't want angry mobs flocking to the cause of a martyr."

"A crowd can be turned easily enough with a few well-positioned, vocal protestors," Olmer remarked.

I remembered an earlier demonstration of this in Nazareth all too well. A surge of anger coursed through me and it was all I could do not to confront my husband. How could I have ever found him attractive? Of course, a neutral observer would still find him handsome. But to me, his conniving and manipulation marred his countenance like pockmarks. Why wouldn't they leave Yeshua be?

"Timing is crucial," Gal said. "Ordinarily I'd suggest patience, waiting for the numbers to decrease once everyone returns home. But his followers are growing every day. Sooner rather than later may be advisable before this movement can no longer be contained."

"My father's right. Today he was back to his tricks of rampaging through the temple courts." The antipathy in my husband's voice stunned me.

"He wouldn't let anyone through if they carried merchandise of any kind. He said he had the authority to do these things. How deluded is he to think of himself as the enforcer of the law? What does he know of the law or the way the market system works? He hasn't even worked in his own trade for years. But hundreds of ignorant pilgrims cheered him on, delighted and approving of his recklessness."

"His audacity is dangerous," Bartal said. "He veils his criticism in parables. Today he threatened that the owner of a vineyard will come to kill the tenants who murder his heir and give away his property.[42] I don't know what he meant, but his intent toward us is definitely hostile."

After a moment of silence, Gal replied, "We can work the crowd to our advantage. I'd be more concerned about dissent coming from your own after what I heard in that room back there."

"There are some who have been swayed by the man's teaching, some who even credit his claims to be the son of the Most High, but they are weak willed," Bartal said. "I can handle them. Once Yeshua's cause appears hopeless, they won't have the courage to challenge us. Not if it means damaging their own standing."

Footsteps approached. It must have been the household steward who interrupted them. "Pardon, sir. There is a messenger from Kayafa. He insists on speaking to you directly."

I risked a peek around the corner. Bartal motioned his assent, and a man dressed in garb indicating he was a member of the high priest's guard entered. He nodded his head to the men and approached Bartal. Their heads bent close so I couldn't hear what was said, then the guard tipped his head again and departed with haste.

"Gentlemen, we may have just received the news we hoped for. One within Yeshua's inner circle is willing to testify against him." Bartal snickered. "I told you, everyone has a price. Come. Let us share a cup together to drink to our good fortune."

What could this mean? Who would betray Yeshua? I waited until the footsteps receded, then slowly leaned forward to glance toward the dining room. I could see part of Gal's face through the half-open door, but I didn't think he would notice if I quickly darted past. I took a fortifying breath and dashed forward only to be stopped short by a hand over my mouth. I froze.

"Where do you think you're going?"

I realized it was Olmer and let out my breath, but my heart pounded wildly.

"I . . . I'm just returning to bed," I stammered.

"I'll see that you arrive safely." He wrenched my elbow and his fingers dug deep into my flesh, sending a painful tingling down my arm. I had to jog to keep from being dragged by his quick strides. When we reached the door, he swung me around to face him.

"I don't know what you heard or what you think you heard back there. But you'll mention this to no one, and you will not leave this house again until I tell you to, understood?"

My mouth opened slightly to speak, and he shook me so fiercely the back of my head banged against the door. I winced, and tears sprang to my eyes as much from the pain as the sinister glint in his eyes. He'd enjoyed hurting me.

"You may have disobeyed my mother without consequences, but I assure you, you'll pay dearly if you disobey me," he snarled.

I nodded.

He stared at me for a moment before releasing me and walking with measured steps back to the banquet room.

Gasping for air, I struggled to steady my emotions as I shut the door behind me with trembling hands.

I should try to leave, to warn Yeshua, but I'd never seen my husband so incensed. Olmer was not rational about matters concerning my brother. Was this the decision Yeshua had spoken of? That I must decide between him and my husband?

Well, I couldn't. I just couldn't. I wished I were as brave and bold as Yeshua, but I was scared. I curled up on my mat and surrendered to the shivering that racked my body.

CHAPTER 59

I couldn't wait to leave Bartal's house. At last, the evening of the fourteenth had arrived and Pesach was upon us. Hopefully no one would contemplate doing anything disruptive during the feast. The sheep would be presented in the morning and slaughtered in the afternoon. Tomorrow at this time we'd break our fast and dine on lamb, remembering what the Lord had done for us. Then, in a week's time, the festivities would be over and we'd return home. I just wanted our lives to go back to normal.

"Where do you think the men went?"

"I don't know, Hannah. Please stop asking."

"I'm worried about my brother. You don't think anything bad will happen to him, do you?"

She slapped her hands down onto the salon table.

I held mine up in surrender. "Sorry, sorry."

Tabitha had been short-tempered with me all evening. Not that I could blame her. My sequestration had somehow resulted in her being excluded from public activities as well these last two days. We were both irritable.

Standing from the table, I paced around the room. Our hostess had excused herself earlier on the basis of ensuring that everything was in place for tomorrow. The pits where the lambs would roast had been dug days ago, and the leaven removed from the home and piled outside where it would be burned in the morning. Nothing remained for us to do, so I suspected she just sought an escape from us, her awkward guests.

Raziela hadn't been present since morning—she had joined some of her relatives from Miletus. And Olmer and the other men had wasted no time in departing as soon as the sun set, on the pretense of some unfinished business. It didn't bode well that they'd not returned by this late hour.

"Hannah, will you please sit down? You're making me dizzy."

I walked back around the table but halted when I heard a loud banging coming from the door to the street. Tabitha and I exchanged a startled look. Most of Bartal's servants had left to be with their own families for the feast. Perhaps Raz had returned? I wasn't eager to let her enter but knew it was inevitable, so I passed into the courtyard.

Iakovos had reached the door before me but held it open only a crack.

"I need to speak with Olmer," the visitor said.

My pulse quickened. Elan? It certainly sounded like him. But how could that be?

"Sorry, he's not in." Iakovos's tone of voice indicated he was anything but sorry.

"Then I wish to speak with his wife."

It *was* Elan. How had he found us? And why was he here? I stepped toward the door, but Tabitha staid me with a touch on the arm.

"That, as you know, would be completely inappropriate," Iakovos said. "Come back in the morning if you seek Olmer."

"This can't wait until morning!" Elan said loudly enough

for me and anyone in the household and probably the neighbors to hear as well. "I need to speak with Hannah. She needs to know. Yeshua's been arrested!"

Tabitha and I stood just a stone's throw away from him on the other side of the door, but I couldn't move or speak. *Arrested? Yeshua?*

Iakovos battled to push the door closed without success. In his frustration he shouted at Elan, "Sir, I insist you leave at once or I will sound the alarm! If he is innocent, nothing will come of it. If he is guilty, this family wants nothing to do with such a man. In either case, only time will tell. *Good night.*"

Iakovos managed to shut the door, but Elan resumed pounding on the other side. The steward fixed me with a challenging scowl as he leaned his weight against the door and turned an intricate key in the wooden lock.

I clasped my hands in supplication. "Please, Iakovos, you must find Olmer. Yeshua is innocent. If they convene the Sanhedrin, the elders will want to hear his family's testimony. They'll need my brothers to testify. Olmer has to let me go to them."

"Groveling is not behavior suited to a lady of good standing," he said, admonishing me with clear contempt, tucking the bronze key away in the folds of his garment.

Tabitha pulled me back into the dining room. Eventually the knocking stopped.

"Arrested? Can they do that?" I asked. "What will they do to him?"

Tabitha had no answers, but at least she didn't complain about my pacing any longer.

I should have spoken up for Yeshua sooner. Maybe if I had tried harder to convince Olmer, or even if I had interrupted Bartal, it would not have come to this. I replayed the men's conversation in my mind, thinking of all the things I could have said in Yeshua's defense but hadn't. I had failed as a sister just as I had failed at being a wife.

"If he is innocent—"

"Of course he's innocent," I snapped. "My brother's the most righteous man ever to live."

Despite my tone, Tabitha continued in a kind voice. "Then there's reason to hope. The Sanhedrin is the highest court of the land, full of men of wisdom and integrity. They'll judge the facts and declare him innocent. This whole matter will be dismissed, you'll see."

She meant to console me, but her words had the opposite effect. Wasn't that the whole reason for his arrest in the first place—because the leaders in the highest positions of power were corrupt? I felt broken inside. How could this have happened? Why would anyone speak falsely against my brother?

"What a fool I've been to believe our elders fear the Lord. Bartal said it himself. Their hearts are tarnished and they're more fearful of losing their standing than they are of condemning an innocent man. What cowards, waiting until Pesach to commit their vile act. It makes me sick." I dared Tabitha to respond to my accusations, but she averted her eyes. "Who can we turn to for justice if those who are supposed to uphold the highest standards are filthy? Who can we trust?"

"Trust in me," my brother had said. But how could I trust in him now? How could he rule if he was in jail? Well, I had gotten what I deserved, exactly what I had wished to avoid—the disappointment that came when you put your hope and trust in Yeshua. He'd never be king. He'd be fortunate to even be a carpenter at this point.

"I'm so sorry, Hannah."

The finality of her tone pierced my heart.

***

Shortly after the morning watch ended, Raziela returned to the house.

I sprung up and rushed to meet her in the courtyard.

"They've taken Yeshua and I don't know what they will do to him. You have to let me out of here to find out what's happening."

Raziela assessed me coolly but didn't seem surprised by my news.

"Please, don't take out your hostility toward me on my brother. If no one in this family will do what's right, at least send word to Olmer to find my brothers to argue on Yeshua's behalf before the court."

"And why would Olmer want to do such a thing? Any arrest is Yeshua's own doing. It's time for the world to see him as the man he really is—a blasphemer."

I wasn't too distraught to note the irony of Raz being an authority on what sins are considered blasphemous. But I held my tongue. "Please," I urged.

"He openly claimed to be the Messiah. What defense can be made against such an admission? He's condemned by his own words. We cannot tolerate such an offense against the Lord. Anyway, it's no longer the decision of the chief priests. They've decided to take him to the Roman prefect."

I hadn't thought the situation could get worse. But it had. I could only pray he'd find mercy.

CHAPTER 60

I dreamt of a bird of prey circling in the sky overhead. But it was enormous, or I had shrunk. I sought cover amid towering grasses. But each time I concealed myself, the wind exposed me. The raptor swooped ever closer. I ran from hiding place to hiding place, terrified. I wanted to scream but didn't have enough air to expel a cry for help, the words thick and heavy in my throat.

Then I stood on a great expanse of rock with no shelter in sight. Over my shoulder, I saw the satisfied glint in the descending hunter's eyes. I prostrated myself, awaiting the tear of its talons through my flesh at any moment. A great shriek rang out, followed by the flapping of mighty wings. Suddenly the bird clutched Yeshua by his arms and carried him away, up and up into the sky.

I hadn't even known my brother was with me. I watched, horrified, as the raptor released him and his body writhed in the air, crashing onto the surface of the sea and plunging beneath. Then I was underwater, too, holding my breath, searching the gloomy depths for Yeshua. I coughed and sputtered and choked. Faint sunlight glimmered above, but no matter how hard I struggled, I couldn't break the surface.

I awoke, breathing heavily, confused by the water on my

face and unfamiliar surroundings.

"Make yourself presentable," Raziela barked, an empty pitcher in her hand.

I rubbed my eyes and touched the soaking-wet cloth at my collar, too shaken by the dream to muster any outrage that she'd apparently doused me as if I were the town drunkard. The events of the night returned like a punch to the gut. I must have drifted off for a short while. Judging from the light, it looked to be about the fifth hour. I surveyed the makeshift bedroom. There was no indication that Olmer had slept here.

"Where's my husband?"

Raz chuckled.

I stared at her, trying to perceive what ill lay behind her glee.

"*Olmer* has just returned from meeting with the Sanhedrin." She emphasized his name as if we spoke of two different people.

"The Sanhedrin?" My mind reeled with the news. Had Olmer changed his mind about Yeshua? "Did he get there in time to help my brother?"

"You fool. He didn't go to argue for that detestable pretender."

The blatant hatred in her voice shook me. Then she left before I could ask her why Olmer went to the court, if not to aid Yeshua.

Men's voices approached the door, and I jumped from the floor and quickly covered my head, not bothering to change my wet clothes.

The courtyard was empty. Everyone was assembled in the main room. All eyes turned to me as I entered except Bartal's, which looked longingly at the doorway behind me. No doubt he would rather be in his bed after being out all night. His wife scrutinized me.

I tried to subtly rub any remaining signs of sleep from my eyes and self-consciously pulled my headdress over my damp shift.

"Do you have news from the Sanhedrin?" I asked Olmer. "Have they freed Yeshua?"

I reached out to clasp his arm in desperation, but he pulled it back. His fingers untied the twine that held a small satchel to his belt, and he dropped the pouch in my still outstretched hand.

"What is this?" But now I felt the heft of metal coins shifting inside the leather pouch. My insides turned to ice. "I don't understand."

"There are fifty shekels of silver in the bag," he stated with formality.

The cold apathy in his eyes cut through my defenses. Then the tiny crack of realization split open deep inside me, expanding outward, threatening to shatter my whole being. I thrashed my head from side to side.

"No."

Raziela stepped forward, her lips smashed together as if holding back a satisfied smile. "Be thankful for my son's generosity. It's more than we ever got for your bride price and certainly more than you've earned as a wife."

Gal cleared his throat which seemed to signal Iakovos. The steward calmly handed Olmer a roll of parchment, which he in turn extended to me. I knew what it was without reading it—the *sefer keritut*, the required bill of divorce.

I crossed my arms and continued to shake my head like a petulant child. Perhaps if I didn't touch the parchment, this whole thing would stop.

"Take it." Olmer sounded annoyed now, and he tossed the

roll at my feet. Then he uttered the words that officially severed our marriage and ended my life. "You are not my wife, nor am I your husband."

"No." I began to weep. "No, you don't mean that. Please . . ."

I dropped the silver and threw myself down to kneel at his feet, grasping his calves in my arms.

My father-in-law sighed as if this were just one of many business transactions on his agenda today, and it had already taken longer than planned. Bartal's wife made a "tsk" sound as if I were a naughty child. Keturah and Hakon watched like entertained spectators, but I didn't care. I clung to Olmer's feet. Tears mingled with the mucus coursing down my face—a pathetic sight I was sure, but I'd suffer any humiliation to earn back my former status.

"Is this because I haven't been able to have a son?" I whimpered. "Please, I will bear you a son, many sons, just give me another chance."

Olmer lifted one foot and then the other, kicking ineffectually as I swayed back and forth, refusing to release him.

Raziela stepped in and grabbed a fistful of my scarf and hair, wrenching my head back.

"Get up, you loathsome girl. Go to your father's house. You're no longer welcome here."

My father's house? How could I do that? I didn't have a father.

Suddenly I was as bereft as I'd been when Abba died all those years ago. No, worse. All my fears of being alone, unwanted, and invisible had come to pass. I wailed inconsolably, wretchedly, uncaring even of the searing pain as Raziela yanked hairs from my head.

"Hannah, stop!" Tabitha cried out in pity or disgust.

I let go.

Raz threw my head forward, releasing me.

Still weeping softly, I looked up at Olmer. For a second I stared fascinated as his cheek twitched involuntarily under his left eye, but in seconds he appeared perfectly composed again.

"I have been more than patient with you, Hannah. Any other man would have divorced you long ago."

"Olmer."

He turned away.

"Olmer, I'm sorry," I bawled. "Please, don't leave. Ol-ol-mer."

He walked out the door. Gal and Bartal made a hasty retreat behind him.

Raz bored the tip of her sandal into my thigh. "Do not attempt to speak with my son or anyone in this family. Not only will I take the money back, but I'll see to it that you're stoned for adultery."

"What?" Surprise broke through my tears.

"Did you think I wouldn't find out about your little shepherd friend's visit last night?" she asked, a smug look on her face.

"But I didn't so much as speak with him. He gave a message to Iakovos at the door."

"That's your version of the story. The steward told me he came upon the two of you together. It certainly wouldn't be the first time you cornered a man for your purposes."

My own body betrayed me, and I blushed despite myself. I turned to Iakovos. He could have been a tree, as still and sure as he stood there ignoring my incredulous stare.

"So. Whose version do you suppose people will believe?" she asked, eyebrows lifted.

"But . . . but Tabitha was with me." I turned to her. "You saw what happened, didn't you?"

"Tabitha and I were asleep when it happened," Keturah

announced as if she'd been waiting for her line to come up in this drama.

"Tabitha?" My eyes pleaded with her.

One emotion after the other crossed Tabitha's face: outrage, fear, resignation. She blinked back tears.

"I think you'd best just leave now, Hannah," she whispered.

I felt strangely separated from myself, as if I really were watching a horrible stage performance. All that was left to do was exit. I shuffled through the door, and the coolness of the stones reminded me my feet were bare.

"My clothes," I muttered.

One of the female servants brought forth a bundle wrapped with my wool mantle and topped with my sandals. Iakovos pulled open the door to the street. They had really thought of everything.

I wandered outside, still oddly detached from myself. The bright sunlight seemed to mock me with its cheerfulness, and I squinted. Taking a few faltering steps with no destination in mind, I stubbed my toe and looked down at my feet somewhat puzzled. Then I dropped my mantle on the ground by the wall of the house, sitting heavily upon it.

Two women passing by glanced sideways at me, shocked to see what they must have assumed was a beggar here in such a wealthy neighborhood. I almost laughed.

As I laced up my sandals, the door to Bartal's home opened again.

I jumped up hopefully, but it was only Tabitha.

She held out the pouch of coins to me. When I stared at it, she thrust it against my abdomen.

"Don't be proud. You may need it. I'm sorry." And she scurried back inside. I heard the key turn in the lock.

Proud? I'd never been more ashamed in my life.

CHAPTER 61

I set off downhill, aimlessly putting distance between myself and the house. A profound fatigue overcame me, and soon I couldn't even manage the effort of walking. I tucked myself in the space between someone's stoop and a large stone pot that flanked it, putting the coins in my lap and drawing my knees up to my chest.

I needed to find my family. But I was so tired. I decided to rest my head on my knees for a few moments and wrapped the mantle about myself so that it covered my face, cocooning me from the world.

***

"Hey, girl. I said, 'How much?'"

Gruff shaking jarred me awake. It seemed I'd only closed my eyelids a moment ago—I certainly didn't feel rested. Yet the sky had grown dark. How long had I slept?

"Are you going to answer me?"

I stared dumbfounded at the man whose face hovered in front of me. His breath smelled rancid, and when he opened his mouth to speak again, his teeth were gray with rot, held in place only by the remains of his last meal. I instinctively clutched the pouch of coins to my chest, realizing with horror that he must have mistaken me for a prostitute.

"Hey, what do you have there?" he asked in an almost reverent tone, his greed apparently outweighing his lust when he heard the chink of coins.

"Get away from me," I shrieked, batting at his inquisitive hands. "Leave me be."

He grabbed my wrist. "Come on, woman. Show me what you're holding."

"Don't touch me!" I yelled.

The door above me swung open and a massive broom flailed back and forth. My attacker covered his head with his hands. He looked longingly at the pouch again, but self-preservation won out. He sprinted off.

"You too," the man above me instructed. "Go. This is a respectable home. We'll not tolerate your sort here."

I tried to stand while clutching the coins and protecting my head all at once, so I lurched about ungracefully. A hit landed on my shoulder, making me wince and bringing tears to my eyes.

"Please stop," I cried. "I'm going."

The man hesitated as he looked me up and down, likely noting my ring and the finery of my admittedly disheveled clothes.

"I'm sorry, miss. With all the strange happenings . . . Well, I thought that you—"

"It's all right," I interrupted, not wanting to hear the words spoken aloud. "It's my fault. I shouldn't be out alone, especially after sunset."

The man stared at me, eyes wide. "But don't you know? It's only just the eighth hour, not even two full hours past noon, and it grows darker by the minute. Get inside with your family and stay there if you know what's good for you. It's like the angel of death is going to pass over again."

"What?"

He looked quickly to the right and left, then slammed the door.

A chill shot up my spine. How could it only be the eighth hour when the sun no longer shone in the sky? What did this mean?

I no longer saw my assailant but decided to head the opposite direction. When I came out on a main street, many people walked about as if it were still day. But not a few cast furtive gazes to the heavens as they went on their way.

Panic seized me. I perceived an almost palpable heaviness to the air, as if darkness had taken on a physical presence that buffeted me from without as well as within. I wanted to run, but where? I considered returning to Bartal's home to beg Olmer to take me in, at least for the night. But Raz would never permit me to enter. I kept moving.

My family would be camped on the Mount of Olives. But if it was only the eighth hour, my brothers might yet be at the temple. At least Yeshua would certainly be somewhere in the temple courts. I staggered. *Yeshua.* How could I have forgotten about him?

I half walked and half trotted in the general direction to the temple complex. Someone there would know what the prefect had decided to do with Yeshua, where they were keeping him until his fate was decided. As I thought this, the sky grew as dark as night. I knew in that moment they had not found him innocent. This was what they had intended all along, to bring him to the authorities to silence him.

As I stumbled up the stairs of the entrance, I considered praying, but what would be an appropriate prayer to recite in the circumstances? Besides, I was as guilty as my in-laws.

I might as well have helped arrest him. I certainly had done nothing to aid him.

Emerging into the court of the gentiles, I paused and looked to the highest part of the temple itself, which housed the Holy of Holies. I bowed my head and uttered the only thing suitable that came to mind. "Lord, have mercy."

The unmistakable tang of blood grew stronger as I entered the women's court. A few bleats could be heard coming from the northern side of the altar where the lambs were brought forth for the slaughter, probably by the last division of appointed men by now.

Despite the strange sky, the crowd here was dense. I could just make out the reciting of praise as the lambs were killed—less robust and certain than the usual declarations. I didn't have to see them to picture the double line of priests standing in the inner court holding bowls of silver in one row, gold in the other. Probably more than one pair of hands were shaking and eyes were looking up into the inexplicable black sky as the priests exchanged full bowls of blood for empty ones down their rows until the final priest sprinkled the blood on the altar.

Taking a deep breath for courage, I searched for a sympathetic person I might stop to enquire about Yeshua. Two women stood ahead, and the shorter of the two turned to face me. I don't know which of us was more astounded.

"Aunt Lilit! Rivkah! Oh, thank goodness."

Rivkah turned at the sound of her name, and Aunt Lilit put her hand on Rivkah's forearm. Even in the flickering torch light, I read the panic on their faces.

"Hannah. I didn't think I'd see you in public," Rivkah stammered. "I mean, shouldn't you be with your mother?"

I grunted in disbelief. "Don't you mean with my husband?"

She couldn't conceal her guilt.

"I see you already know about Olmer's betrayal. Raz wasted no time in sharing the news."

"Now, Hannah, you can't take it out on us," Aunt Lilit said. "We didn't have anything to do with the decision. Of course it's upsetting for you, dear. But you knew it was never a good match even from the beginning."

"You were the one who pushed us together!" I exclaimed.

"Shhh. Now that's entirely untrue. Besides, how could I have known that you—well, that you'd be unable to perform your wifely duties."

Her words stung like salt on my raw hurt. Tears slid down my cheeks unabated.

"Let's just go," Rivkah said.

"No, don't leave me," I begged. Betrayed as I felt, the thought of being alone again terrified me. "I don't know what's happening. I don't know where to go."

"Lilit," a baritone voice commanded from behind me.

I glanced over my shoulder to find her husband, Uzziah, glowering at me.

"Get away, Hannah." Lilit harshly whispered. "Do you want us all to be divorced?"

"But you're my relatives. You *have* to help me."

"Really, we're only distant cousins. We can't risk being seen with you any longer, you understand, what with the divorce and your brother's madness. It's all so scandalous." She rushed to Uzziah's side.

"How can you say that? You know us. You know Yeshua'd never do anything wrong. Maybe if you say something—"

"Rivkah, come away this instant," Uzziah barked.

"But you all praised him." I turned to Rivkah, hoping someone would see reason. "You praised him when he turned water into wine and saved your son's wedding celebration. How can you turn against him when he needs you?"

Rivkah shook her head at me and her face softened. "What difference does it make now anyway?"

"What? What do you mean?"

She put her hand out as if to touch my arm but must have thought better of it. "They took him to be crucified this morning."

"*Crucified?*" My guts lurched in protest and my mind struggled to make sense of the words. "No, you must be mistaken. That happens to criminals, to the cursed. Yeshua's never done anything to incur a curse. He's never done anything wrong."

"I'm sorry." Then, as if that concluded everything, she followed after her parents.

Around me a quiet anticipation fell over the crowd. From the direction of the altar, a priest bellowed the awaited decree as the last Pesach lamb was sacrificed.

"*Nagmar!*" he cried.

It is finished.

CHAPTER 62

No sooner did the priest utter the words than a groan echoed through the court. Instead of fading away, the rumbling grew in intensity. The earth heaved angrily beneath me, causing the nearby columns to appear to sway. Had shock altered my senses? Then someone screamed as stone crashed to the tiles nearby. I don't know if I was more afraid or relieved that the world actually did tilt back and forth.

Panicked bodies lurched and careened around me. Above the din, I detected an even more ominous ripping sound that increased to a terrifying pitch. It sounded like the heavens above were being rent in two. People charged in all directions, shoving viciously at anyone blocking their escape. Some unfortunate soul moaned, trampled underfoot in the melee. I crouched and shielded my head. The collapse of the temple itself seemed imminent.

Suddenly the ground stilled. Now the lack of motion left me dizzy, and I placed my palms down to steady myself. Only a few torches remained lit. Amid the darkness, great commotion came from nearby. The inner court. Where moments ago priests had passed bowls of sacrificed blood, they now exchanged astounded shouts.

"Look! The veil is torn in half."

"The partition is rent!"

My knees trembled. What could it mean that the veil had been slashed open? Were the sacrifices rejected? What could save us from death now that we'd been exposed before the Holy of Holies?

Renewed mayhem surrounded me as the remaining pilgrims sought to distance themselves from the temple. I spun in circles, clutching the bag of coins to my chest, bereft of direction. Where on earth would we find refuge if this was the wrath of the Lord?

Suddenly, I heard in my mind my brother's words from our last conversation. *Do not be afraid.* Yeshua. I need to go to Yeshua.

I ran down the stairs past the *soreg* with renewed urgency, blindly pushing through the crowd. There were so many things I needed to say to him, so many apologies yet unspoken. I tried to recall what I knew of crucifixion. It was a ghastly, prolonged torture meant to punish slowly. So I had every hope, if not for my brother's sake but for mine, that he was still conscious. I needed to beg his forgiveness before it was too late.

Dashing toward the stairs leading to the southern exit onto the street, I met a standstill as hundreds of people ahead of me tried to funnel out the gates. I flailed my arms in frustration and then maneuvered back. The crowd was thinner along the wall near the eastern gate, so I skirted along it, flinching as pieces of plaster and rock loosened by the quake continued to fall around me.

Finally outside, my body acted with purpose. I charged ahead until a youth blocked my way.

"No, miss. It's not safe," he warned. "The bridge may collapse."

"Move," I said.

He held up his hand. "I don't think you understand—"

"Move!" I screamed.

He gaped at my reaction. I took advantage of his shock to slide past him. Stones were missing from the side walls of the bridge across the valley, but I stepped onto it with desperate determination. Lifting the hem of my skirt, I charged forward, focusing on the mount in front of me.

***

If not for my women kin standing at the crossroads, I wouldn't have recognized the wretched form at their feet. I came to a halt, unable to move forward, unable to accept that it was over. I was too late.

My brother was dead.

I took some ragged breaths and swallowed the bile rising in my throat. I hesitantly glanced at his body again. His mouth gaped open, as if singing an unheard song. One patch of pale skin below his clavicle stood out against the tanner skin of his throat. Above that, his face scarcely resembled a human. Purple and black mounds of swollen flesh protruded beneath his brow like the eyelids of baby birds fallen too soon from the nest. Barbs seemed to grow from his tangled mass of blood-stained hair. A wreath of *thorns*? Who would make such a monstrosity?

My eyes traveled lower. Someone had draped a beautifully constructed cloak across his body. Irrationally, I noted the orderly stitches and regretted that no one would be able to wash the stains from this luxurious garment.

A man bent over Yeshua's feet. I studied him with emotional detachment. He wore distinguished-looking linen garments, so it must have been his cloak that covered my brother's nakedness. He cast an apologetic look at my mother.

It took a moment for me to understand what he was doing. He struggled with the spike holding Yeshua's feet to the tree. The horror of the scene struck me again. I suspected the man felt reticent to inflict further damage by shattering Yeshua's bones. But what did it matter now? His attempt at gentleness only prolonged the suffering for the onlookers.

I turned away and noted no such care was taken with the other victims. Bones snapped as soldiers ripped limbs free from the wood of their crosses. Carrion birds circled overhead. When a bolder one landed nearby, a soldier kicked at it and shooed the cawing bird away.

The wind carried a familiar, rich scent that mixed with the fetid stench of emptied bowels—the wafting aroma of roasting lamb as thousands of families finished preparations for this most unusual Seder.

My mouth began to salivate unpleasantly. I scanned around for a private place, but only had time to register the raw anguish on Emmi's face before doubling over as involuntary spasms gripped my gut. I hadn't eaten for nearly a day, so I vomited only bile. My nostrils burned and I coughed a few times trying to expel the bitter taste from my throat.

They succeeded in freeing Yeshua from the timber. Emmi and Shlomit dabbed at his face, but flecks of dried blood tenaciously clung to his cheeks refusing to be smeared away. Emmi focused on scraping a spot with her fingernail, as if removing this one blemish might set everything in order again. This caused Yeshua's head to jiggle, and Shlomit reflexively held out her hands to still the rocking. She recoiled suddenly, staring at her upturned hand, as if trying to comprehend the ragged, worm-like piece of scalp now lying in her palm. Fresh tears flowed from her eyes as she appeared helpless to know what to do with it.

Aunt Miryam stepped forward and touched Emmi's back.

"Leave him for now. Yosef of Arimathea has arranged to take the body for burial. We'll bring water to the tomb. That will help with the cleaning."

Men were turning Yeshua, placing him on a makeshift bier, carrying him away. As I approached my family, I caught my sister's eye. My mouth opened, wanting to voice some words of apology or comfort. Shlomit looked initially surprised to see me, then stern, and I imagined my presence now served as a reminder of my earlier absence. She led Emmi away without comment, following the procession of mourners.

Aunt Miryam draped an arm over my shoulders. We watched soldiers drag the other two deceased to a pit for criminals. Their bodies left trailing dark stains in the dirt below the wooden posts.

"At least Yeshua was carried away," I said.

Then I laughed uncontrollably at the absurdity of my comment. His face had been beaten past recognition, his skull pierced by thorns. His back testified to the flogging he endured, muscles filleted open from the force of the whipping. He had suffered the most cruel punishment the Romans could inflict, and I was glad that his lifeless body had been carried, not dragged, to his final resting place?

My aunt regarded me as if I were possessed. My cackling sounded a bit deranged even to my own ears, like the brays of a wounded donkey. Soon my laughter transformed to choking sobs leaving me starved for air. I wondered if it was possible to actually die from grief.

"Shhh," Aunt Miryam soothed me like a child. "Come away. It's not good to be here." When I made no effort to move, she tried again. "It's almost sundown."

We both lifted our faces to the eerie light of the sky, neither day nor night.

"We'll need to cleanse ourselves. Come."

The appeal of bathing, something familiar and tangible that I could cling to amid the waves of grief and fear, motivated me to follow her. Besides, I had nowhere else to go.

CHAPTER 63

Aunt Miryam and I sat amid the sea of humanity gathered in view of the temple on the hillside for the Pesach meal. I doubted I'd be able to ever eat again. Then a portion of lamb was passed to me and my hunger betrayed me. I chewed the savory meat, noting I couldn't even fast well for my brother. Salt from my tears mingled with the food. Aunt Miryam patted my knee.

"Don't worry. If the Lord can bring us out of Egypt, He can bring us through this. After the meal, Cleopas will walk you back into the city. I'm sure your husband will be worried about you."

I bit my lip and stared at her.

"Oh," she said, rightly interpreting the forlorn look. "Then why don't you rest."

Wrapping myself in my cloak, I leaned against a wall of the tent and closed my eyes, wanting nothing more than to escape into unconsciousness. Something poked into my leg. I propped myself up, searching the ground for the offending object. Then reclining again, I tried to relax.

Sleep eluded me despite my exhaustion. The horrors inflicted on Yeshua played out in my mind like waking nightmares.

**

I came awake with a start. Rubbing the sleep from my eyes, I stared into the darkness.

"Why would he do that?" my uncle asked.

"Shhh," my aunt warned. "You'll wake everyone."

"Why would he let them take him without a fight? We deserved a fight at least. Where is our salvation now? How will we be redeemed if our dayspring's blood has been shed?"

I waited for a reply, but no sound came except cousin Shim'on's loud breathing nearby. Holding my head up with my hand, I strained to hear my aunt's soft voice.

"I don't know. We just have to trust that the Lord—"

"He was slaughtered, Miryam. *Slaughtered* . . . and I hid." His voice cracked on the last words. "I hid like a frightened child." He let out great wracking sobs.

I discreetly pulled my cloak over my ears and squeezed my eyes shut, tears wetting my hair.

**

The High Holy Day of the Feast of Unleavened Bread ended, but as our misfortune would have it, sunset on the sixteenth of Nissan brought the regular weekly Sabbath day. We were confined another day with nothing to do but ruminate—a cruel exercise.

Each consumed with personal grief, we moved little and spoke less. Finally, evening began the first day of the week, lifting the Shabbat restrictions. It was the seventeenth of Nissan. In the morning, all of Jerusalem would celebrate the Feast of First Fruits. Everyone, that was, except us.

Emmi and other women had gathered in the home of Yosef of Arimathea to make preparations for properly entombing my brother's body. When it was obvious neither my aunt nor I would be able to sleep anyway, we decided to walk to the house before daybreak. I wasn't sure what type of reception we'd receive within when we arrived at the finely appointed home, but I couldn't help but notice its proximity to Bartal's house, so I kept my head lowered as I knocked on the door.

Fortunately, Shlomit quickly rushed up behind the servant who answered the door and, without overly much explanation, ushered us inside an open courtyard.

More than a dozen female faces I didn't recognize packed the space. The smell of sandalwood and myrrh filled the air. Uri shuffled back and forth, looking anxious and unsure what to do amid so many women. He nodded his head to acknowledge me. I managed what was intended as a smile, but my face didn't fully cooperate.

"Oh, Hannah. I'm so sorry," Shlomit said. "We just heard the news."

She threw her arms around me.

I patted her back as if I were the one extending comfort.

"I don't want to talk about it now." Or ever.

I located Emmi. The flickering light from the torch above her revealed a face looking visibly aged since I last saw her. Avoiding her gaze directly, I sat at her side. Shlomit introduced me to the matron of the home, and I thanked the woman for having invited me to join them, as if we were here for a party. I grimaced and tried to explain myself better, but nothing emerging from my lips seemed appropriate under the circumstances. Emmi extended her hand to me like a rope thrown to a drowning man. I stopped rambling and took hold of it. She squeezed my hand in hers.

Insistent rapping at the door interrupted the reunion. I started for the entrance, anxious for the possibility of it being

Olmer. Perhaps he had seen me arrive? Emmi restrained me, and the look in her eyes reminded me of the very real danger we faced.

What a fool I was. Did I think he'd show up to take me home as if the divorce had been a big mistake? We were relatives of an executed criminal. He'd never take me back. And if someone as good as my brother had been executed, no one was safe.

We scarcely breathed as we listened to the hushed voices at the door. Then the servant opened the door fully, looking relieved, and one of my brother's followers entered. It was the man named Yochanon, one of the fishermen.

Yochanon's eyes scanned the room, briefly catching my own but resting on Emmi. He removed a pair of worn sandals from the satchel he wore strapped over his shoulder, then squatted before Emmi and offered them to her looking abashed.

"This was all he had with him. One of our companions had picked them up in the garden before . . ." He swallowed. "I thought you may want something of his to keep."

She clutched the worn leather to her chest, inhaling deeply either to still her emotions or recall his scent—I couldn't tell. Her chin quivered and tears filled her eyes.

"You were with him when they arrested him?" I asked with a sniff.

Yochanon nodded.

"Did he say *anything* in his defense?"

The man appeared stricken.

Uri spoke up. "I heard him say, 'Why have you forsaken me?'[43] When he hanged on the cross, I mean."

I looked up sharply, thinking he criticized my absence from these happenings, but there was no reproach in his eyes.

"Like David said in the psalm," Uri added in explanation.

I chuckled once. How typical that even moments before his death, Yeshua would still be quoting Scripture.

"That's all?"

"No, his last words were 'It is finished.'"[44]

A chill ran up my spine as I pictured the high priest saying these very words right before the earth lurched and the veil shielding the Holy of Holies was torn.

"You're sure? 'It is finished,' like the high priest declares on Pesach?"

Yochanon must have found his tongue again. "Yes." He nodded vigorously and his eyes shone as he thought on this. "Exactly like that. He told us before he died that he was going someplace we could not follow. He even predicted the Son of Man would be handed over. When the temple guard came to arrest him, he said that darkness was having its hour.[45] I believe he knew in advance what would happen."

"If he knew, then why would he let it happen? Why even come to Jerusalem if he knew he'd be killed?" I asked. "I just don't understand if he is . . . was . . . the Anointed One, the Messiah, how could he be killed?"

No one answered.

It didn't seem rational that my brother would become a martyr for a political cause. What would be gained? Momentary notoriety? A brief lifting of the people's morale? Did he die to keep his friends safe so they wouldn't be killed in a futile rebellion? I couldn't believe he'd just give up. Quitting wasn't in Yeshua's nature. He had never shied away from righting a wrong.

I worked the side of my thumb between my teeth. Yeshua always said he obeyed what Adonai commanded. Could the Lord have asked such a thing of his own son? If Yeshua had known he would die, what had it been like those final hours, waking to know he would not lie down to sleep again? It was too grim to even consider.

Suddenly, I feared I'd go mad sitting here with these strangers saying nothing. I wanted to get away from all of this pain.

"Emmi, let's go home. Back to Nazareth."

"Hannah, I can't leave now." She waved her hands to encompass the room. "We're all going to your brother's tomb as soon as it's light enough. I need to know that Yeshua's . . . taken care of."

"What more can be done?"

Emmi just stared at me as if I were daft. Uri cleared his throat.

"I spoke with Ya'akov before coming here. I know he's eager to be away too."

Emmi seemed disappointed. She probably expected me to accompany her at daybreak, but I couldn't. I couldn't see Yeshua looking like that again. Feeling like someone squeezed my chest, I panted, determined not to cry in front of these people.

Hadn't I known something terrible would happen? This was exactly why I hadn't wanted to get my hopes up. How foolish I'd been to think Yeshua would solve everything. If I had just minded my own husband, maybe he'd still be with me. My uncle was right. What had Yeshua been expecting? Had he really thought to defeat an entire Roman garrison? He had been deluded. And so were all of these followers of his. I had to get out of here.

Yochanon spoke in a soft voice. "Perhaps you should leave with your brother. I'll look after your mother. Don't be anxious for her." He smiled with such kindness in his eyes that I couldn't resent his intruding.

I nodded and sniffed, standing to my feet.

Shlomit stood to hug me. I felt ashamed for making a spectacle and tried to deflect her, but when she enfolded me in her arms, I grasped her waist tightly, and her scent was so familiar and comforting. The pain in my chest subsided, leaving me calmer if not at peace.

"Come," Uri said. "I'll take you to Ya'akov."

CHAPTER 64

The sun rose to greet us as Ya'akov and I departed the city. We lacked the safety of traveling in numbers since the pilgrims were all at the temple celebrating the Feast of First Fruits, but the empty roads also meant no crowds to slow our progress. And except for an anxious moment passing some Roman soldiers, we made good time for the first three days on the road. Although there was no need to race back to Nazareth. Allowing our relatives there to enjoy a few more days before learning of Yeshua's death would actually be a kindness.

I considered who would be burdened with my presence. Of all my brothers, I was closest to Ya'akov and Shim'on. Of course, Shim'on already had his own family to tend. Ya'akov had no other mouths to feed, but he also traveled depending on where he could find building work. Neither of them should have to care for a divorced woman.

How could I have been so blind to miss all the signs of impending disaster? Hadn't Tabitha practically forecast Olmer's intentions to take another wife? I wanted to believe he would consider a bride in Miletus only to gain strategic business alliances. But knowing Olmer, if he were really planning such a despicable action as another marriage, the woman must possess not only youth to bear him many sons but also beauty.

Why else would he have tarried so long on all his journeys there? The thought sickened me with jealousy and shame.

The perfection of our surroundings only depressed me further. Not a hint of a cloud interrupted the intense azure sky. Birds darted boldly among the tassels of ripe barley rippling under the sun. The world seemed to joyfully embrace the task of living in cruel disregard for my pain.

Didn't the Lord care that I was cast off, discarded, disgraced? And what about Yeshua? Why didn't Elohim's creation grieve with me over his loss? How could Hashem leave me alone after stripping away all I cared about?

A gnat flew into my eye and I halted my steps, squinting and trying to rub the offensive creature from my lashes. I laughed without humor. Could I be any more pathetic? If Yeshua had been here, he probably would have recited some wisdom on the futility of self-pity. And I would have resented it. How wonderful it would have been to be able to unfairly resent him again. I managed to extract the bug and idly rolled its remains between my fingers. How could someone's absence cause such heaviness of heart?

Up ahead, workers entered the fields. Now that the first fruits had been presented, they wasted no time in gathering the harvest. A sad crowd of gaunt-faced women waited patiently on the road. Whatever the workers left behind would be theirs to glean. I studied the women. How sobering to know only my brothers' charity would keep me from joining these scavengers.

I recalled then Yeshua's apparent clumsiness in gathering sheaves during the harvests in our youth. He had always left so many seeds behind. How could I have missed the truth of his goodness for so many years? If only I had listened to Yeshua in my youth, how much heartache I would have avoided. But

I hadn't. And in return for all my tantrums and angry words, he had showed me nothing but love.

Ahead of me, Ya'akov's shoulders began to shake. He pinched the bridge of his nose with his fingers and sobbed quietly.

"Oh, Ya'akov," I whispered, but I had no comfort to offer him.

CHAPTER 65

We rested under a copse of trees near the road. The skin filled with water grew lighter as we passed it wordlessly between us. Ya'akov and I should get moving again, but apathy had joined my tired muscles in keeping me rooted to the ground. I idly plucked off the heads of some wildflowers and watched their blooms wilt in my hand.

"Hannah."

"Hmm," I managed, not even looking up.

"*Hannah.*" Ya'akov's voice was insistent.

"What?"

"Someone's coming."

I shielded my eyes with my hand and scanned the road.

There was a figure less than a half a mile back the way we'd come, alone, jogging at a fast clip in our direction.

Fear gripped me, and I wrapped my cloak over my purse. The coins were all I had left in the world.

"What do you think he wants?"

"I don't know," Ya'akov uttered as he gathered our supplies.

I looked back down the road again. Whoever it was, he had definitely seen us and appeared intent on . . .

"Ya'akov, look."

I took a hesitant step forward and stopped. It couldn't be.

But it was.

"It's Elan." Ya'akov dropped our packs.

Elan frantically waved his arms in the air, shouting, "He's alive! He's alive!"

I remained motionless, trying to comprehend this bizarre greeting and his maniacal appearance: head uncovered, sweating and flushed, gasping, and beaming from ear to ear. When he reached us, he bent forward at the waist, hands on his thighs, heaving great gulps of air.

"Elan, where are you going? Have you followed us? What are you saying?" Ya'akov's perturbed voice demanded answers.

Elan laughed. He cleared his throat a few times to compose himself, but as he looked back and forth between the two of us, he couldn't stop grinning.

"He's alive."

My insides quivered.

"Is that all you can say?" Ya'akov asked with alarm. "Get hold of your senses."

Elan laughed again. "The women went to the tomb at daybreak, the same time you left the city. But it was empty. The tomb was empty. Angels spoke to them, and one of the women said she saw Yeshua."

No. He wouldn't. "Why would you say such a thing? How could you?" I glared at him. "I won't listen to this. You're being cruel. Was my mother there? Did she put you up to this? Why is it angels are always appearing to her and not to the rest of us?"

"Hannah, it's true. Yeshua said he would have to be handed over but would rise again on the third day. I heard him teach such things myself, but I hadn't understood at the time. But now it has happened, just like he said."

"Oh, just like people said Yeshua was Yochanon raised from

the dead?" Ya'akov balled his fists as if he'd hit Elan sooner than listen to any more absurd tales.

But Elan wasn't fazed by our scorn. "There's more. Your brother appeared to Cleopas and your cousin Shim'on as they traveled. Yeshua spoke of the prophecies of old and revealed what they meant."

He slumped to the ground, apparently satisfied now that he'd delivered this astounding blow.

Ya'akov and I exchanged baffled stares.

"Why did he appear to Uncle Cleopas and not us? We're his siblings," I said, irrationally hurt and belatedly realizing I'd given credence to his words.

"Well? What exactly did he reveal?" Ya'akov asked, always one who sought comfort in facts.

"What had been hidden in the writings of the prophets! That he is the Branch from David's line. He is the Redeemer that Yesha'yahu said would come to Tziyon.[46] He is I AM. The Lord Himself provided the sacrifice as he did for Avraham. Yeshua was—*is!*—a worthy lamb for sacrifice. It's why he went willingly to his death. The Lord put the guilt of us all on him when he hanged on the tree. And now he lives. Our savior lives."

"But that's not possible. Yeshua's dead. I saw it with my own eyes." I shook my head in denial and to dislodge the frightful memory of his corpse. Yet, at the same time, I wanted so desperately for Elan to be right. "Did you see him yourself? With your own eyes?"

Elan held my questioning gaze with kindness. "Hannah, the truth doesn't have to be seen to be believed."

My soul responded within me as if testifying to the soundness of his statement. In my mind, I was transported to the hills of our youth where Elan once again pointed to some discovery that I couldn't yet see. But I knew he was trustworthy, and if I believed the truth of his words, I would soon see it for myself.

I wanted to see it. I wanted to share his hope. But I wouldn't survive any more disappointment.

Then I heard Yeshua's words again. *Trust in me.* My heart pounded and my body thrummed with life. I looked to Ya'akov. His eyes shone and he cautiously smiled.

Maybe I'd gotten it wrong before in thinking that Yeshua had wanted me to choose between him and my husband. Maybe *this* was the moment to trust him, the moment a decision had to be made. After all that had happened, all I had witnessed, after all the pain, could I still trust him? Could I believe he was the Anointed One?

Yes.

An enormous smile erupted on my face as my spirit soared within me. My mirth must have been contagious. Elan laughed, and the three of us linked arms, dancing in a gleeful circle. The sorrow and tension from a thousand days lifted from me. I'd grown so accustomed to carrying the weight that now I felt unnaturally buoyant, as if my feet would rise off the ground if not for the others anchoring me to earth.

After a few minutes we broke apart, panting but still smiling.

"Come on. Let's go back to the city," Ya'akov urged.

Elan nodded and they began picking up our things once more. Suddenly the enormity of the truth caused my knees to buckle, and I knelt on the ground. All the years I had scorned my parents' tales of angelic visits, I had lived side by side with the Son of the Almighty One. Terror clutched my heart for all the angry and critical words I'd spoken to my brother, all my ungrateful, proud attitudes.

Elan glanced down at me.

"I don't know if I can go back," I said. "I mean, how could I ever stand before Yeshua now knowing what I know? He'll be angry with me. What if he rejects me because I didn't believe in him before?" I gnawed the skin on the end of my thumb.

Ya'akov regarded me somberly.

Elan stepped closer and pulled my thumb from my mouth. I averted my eyes, devastated by the tenderness on his features. How could he even bear to look at me after all that had happened, after all the shameful mistakes I'd made?

"I've already been rejected once," I whispered, awaiting his reaction to this news.

Elan raised his hand again as if to stroke my cheek but stopped short of touching me, his hand frozen in the air. He gazed at me intently, as if trying to convey something without words. Finally, his hand fell to his side.

"I don't understand it all. But I know Yeshua is not like other men. He will never reject you. He *loves* you." He busied himself with checking the strings tying his waterskin, then cast a quick glance at Ya'akov. "We all do," he murmured before turning abruptly and marching down the road.

My head whipped around to see if Ya'akov had heard him.

He shrugged and grinned before following Elan.

I took a deep breath and let the exquisite truth of Elan's words wash away all the doubts, all the striving, all the hurt. My brother lived. And I was loved.

I hurried after them, buoyed by the promise of even more glorious truths yet to be discovered.

ENDNOTES

Author's Note: Some of the Bible verses referenced below were paraphrased and/or removed from the original biblical context and used in a fictional setting.

1. 1 Kings 18:36 (CJB)
2. Deut. 15:10 (NIV)
3. Deut. 21:23 (CJB)
4. Gen. 15:5 (NIV)
5. 1 Sam. 15:22 (TLV)
6. Judg. 8:5 (CJB)
7. Ps. 145:8 (CJB)
8. Luke 2:48-49 (TLV)
9. Prov. 31:8–9 (NIV)
10. Prov. 19:1 (CJB)
11. Zech. 7:9-10 (NIV)
12. Isa. 57:2 (NIV)
13. Prov. 1:7 (NIV)
14. Matt. 5:13 (NIV)
15. Rapaport, Samuel. "Tales and Maxims from the Midrash." New York: E.P. Dutton, 1907. p. 128. https://archive.org/details/talesmaximsfromm00rapa/page/128 (accessed on or about December 13, 2016).
16. Prov. 22:7 (NIV)
17. Jer. 8:8 (CJB)
18. Lucretius Carus, Titus. "Of the Nature of Things." Translated by William Ellery Leonard. New York: E.P. Dutton, 1916. p.8. https://archive.org/details/naturethingsame00leongoog/page/n32 (accessed on or about August 30, 2016).

19. Luke 4:18–19 (CJB)
20. Luke 4:21 (NIV)
21. Mark 6:3 (CJB)
22. Mark 6:4 (NIV)
23. Micah 5:2 (NIV)
24. Exod. 20:17 (NIV)
25. Luke 1:32 (CJB)
26. Matt. 12:39–40 (CJB)
27. Matt. 12:48 (CJB)
28. Matt. 12:49-50 (CJB)
29. Matt. 5:20 (NIV)
30. Luke 5:23 (NIV)
31. Luke 1:37 (TLV)
32. Heb. 8:11–12; Jer. 31:34 (NIV)
33. Luke 11:27-28 (NIV)
34. Luke 2:34–35 (CJB)
35. Ps. 69:8(7)–10(9) (CJB)
36. John 7:6–8 (NIV)
37. John 7:8 (NIV)
38. John 14:1 (TLV)
39. Matt. 16:25 (NIV)
40. John 3:14-15 (NIV)
41. John 12:44 (NIV)
42. Luke 20:14-16 (NIV)
43. Ps. 22:1 (NIV)
44. John 19:30 (NIV)
45. Luke 22:53 (NIV)
46. Isa. 59:20 (CJB)